romantic fiction

romantic fiction

Melanie La'Brooy

BERKLEY BOOKS, NEW YORK

THE BERKLEY PUBLISHING GROUP
Published by the Penguin Group
Penguin Group (USA) Inc.
375 Hudson Street, New York, New York 10014, USA
Penguin Group (Canada), 10 Alcorn Avenue, Toronto, Ontario M4V 3B2, Canada
(a division of Pearson Penguin Canada Inc.)
Penguin Books Ltd., 80 Strand, London WC2R 0RL, England
Penguin Group Ireland, 25 St. Stephen's Green, Dublin 2, Ireland (a division of Penguin Books Ltd.)
Penguin Group (Australia), 250 Camberwell Road, Camberwell, Victoria 3124, Australia
(a division of Pearson Australia Group Pty. Ltd.)
Penguin Books India Pvt. Ltd., 11 Community Centre, Panchsheel Park, New Delhi—110 017, India
Penguin Group (NZ), Cnr. Airborne and Rosedale Roads, Albany, Auckland 1310, New Zealand
(a division of Pearson New Zealand Ltd.)
Penguin Books (South Africa) (Pty.) Ltd., 24 Sturdee Avenue, Rosebank, Johannesburg 2196,
South Africa

Penguin Books Ltd., Registered Offices, 80 Strand, London WC2R 0RL, England

This book is an original publication of The Berkley Publishing Group.

This is a work of fiction. Names, characters, places, and incidents either are the product of the author's imagination or are used fictitiously, and any resemblance to actual persons, living or dead, business establishments, events, or locales is entirely coincidental.

PRINTING HISTORY
Berkley trade paperback edition / July 2005

Library of Congress Cataloging-in-Publication Data

La'Brooy, Melanie, 1973–
    Romantic fiction / Melanie La'Brooy.—Berkley trade pbk. ed.
        p. cm.
    ISBN 0-425-20264-X
    1. Roommates—Fiction. 2. Friendship—Fiction. I. Title.

PR9619.4.L37R66 2005
823'.92—dc22

2005041138

PRINTED IN THE UNITED STATES OF AMERICA

10 9 8 7 6 5 4 3 2 1

For
Mum & Dad
who always said
yes
when I asked for a book

ACKNOWLEDGMENTS

To: Tom Keats
From: Melanie La'Brooy
Re: Bouquets

Gigantic sunflowers are to be sent to Tara (Tiara) Wynne of Curtis Brown in Sydney and Faye (JoJo) Bender in New York, for being the best damn agents since 99.

Tall poppies are to be delivered to my editor Christine Zika and to all at Penguin with immense gratitude for their support and efforts.

My parents Marie & Keith and my sister Janine are to receive dozens of red roses, for knowing that I'm a cactus but loving me anyway.

A framed piece of turf from the Melbourne Cricket Ground or something else suitably blokey is to be sent to the writer boys Leigh Whannell and Tony Wilson. The attached note is to read: Thank you for dinners, drinks, and phone calls that always lifted my spirits during the hard, lonely bits of being a writer and for not throwing me out of the gang when I asked if we could talk about Jane Austen first editions.

Please organize bright, exotic tropical flowers that can be worn in the hair and baths filled with frangipani and rose petals for the following intelligent, sassy, funny, glamorous girls who make me laugh and inspire me: Sarah Rogers (with special gratitude for making me godmother to Spoodle Jack); the party girls Jayne Tuttle, Estelle Andrewartha, and Vanessa Sheedy (for frocking up, rocking out, and generally causing a riot); Danielle Calder, Camilla Creswick, Alicia Dumais, Diana Hodgson, Jane Martino, Lara Merrett, Georgina Pemberton, Karen Stremski, and Lara Wiseman.

And finally, an entire garden filled with pink flowers of every possible kind is to be laid out with an abundance of love and gratitude to Charlie Daalder for: listening patiently to my many long and slightly hysterical telephone diatribes and never once pretending that we had accidentally been disconnected; having dinner delivered to my flat when I was busy writing and about to eat cheese on toast for the sixth night straight; becoming my hero by joining Australian Volunteers International and working as a volunteer lawyer in Papua New Guinea. And for loving me—not despite, but *because* I'm the sort of girl who names her car, becomes hysterically emotional after re-reading *Madame Bovary*, and wears far too much pink.

(The novels) were about love, lovers, loving, martyred maidens swooning in secluded lodges, postilions slain every other mile, horses ridden to death on every page, dark forests, aching hearts, promising, sobbing, kisses and tears, little boats by moonlight, nightingales in the grove, gentlemen brave as lions, tender as lambs, virtuous as a dream, always well dressed and weeping pints.

And Emma sought to find out exactly what was meant in real life by the words felicity, passion and rapture, which had seemed so fine on the pages of the books.

Gustave Flaubert, Madame Bovary

1.

the bet

Striding into the inner-city bar, which was already crowded with mid-week after work drinkers, Meg looked around for Lucy and Chloe. They weren't hard to spot, she reflected, even though they were seated at a tiny table in the corner and were hunched over a sheet of paper, which they appeared to be discussing animatedly. Lucy was wearing bright pink as usual and was sipping a luridly colored cocktail, which tended to make her stand out amongst the black-clad, beer-swilling Melbourne crowd. Chloe, on the other hand, was not wearing her usually sweet expression but instead looked rather frazzled. With her usual organized foresight, Meg stopped at the bar to order a drink and then leisurely strolled over to join her friends.

Chloe was clearly distressed and greeted Meg distractedly. Lucy moved her chair so Meg could squeeze in at their table and explained the cause of Chloe's anxiety.

"She's had a bad day at work. She's been given a dreadful girl that she can't do anything with," Lucy muttered briefly. Meg raised an eyebrow and gestured for the piece of paper, which turned out to be a badly-written résumé. While she scanned it Chloe continued to take large gulps of her vodka and rail incoherently at her fate.

Chloe worked for a human resources company that hired people for the corporate sector. She was terrible at it. She had an incredibly soft heart and an innate optimism and belief in people that constantly blinded her to their faults and shortcomings.

Meg raised one eyebrow. "She's listed on her CV that she's fluent in several languages. She studied French at school and she speaks English. Is it just me, or is it weird to list your native language as an accomplishment?"

Lucy peered over Meg's shoulder at the résumé. "Being ambidextrous isn't exactly an accomplishment either. It's more a fact of nature."

"I didn't know what to do," Chloe said helplessly. "It's the worst résumé that I've ever seen."

"So what did you do?" asked Meg, returning the résumé to Chloe.

Chloe gulped. "I hired her." She stared dismally into her drink while Meg and Lucy eyed her in disbelief.

"You *hired* her?" Meg said incredulously, snatching back the résumé and looking over it again in case she had missed something. "Chloe, she can't even spell. Her own name."

"Well, it's not like it's permanent," Chloe said defensively. "She's going to be my intern."

"That's not such a bad idea, Clo," Meg said with grudging respect. "I wouldn't mind a lackey to make coffee and do my photocopying and filing and pick up my dry cleaning."

"You're a solicitor in a major law firm, Meg. You have three assistants."

"Yes, but they're all law clerks. If I tried to get them to pick up my dry cleaning they'd sue me."

Lucy ignored this interruption. "Well I think it's very kind of you to give the poor girl a chance, Clo. Maybe all she needs is some office experience. She must have been very grateful."

Chloe appeared to find the contents of her glass fascinating once again.

Meg sighed. "Okay, Clo. What haven't you told us?"

Chloe looked up defensively. "Nothing. I mean—she wasn't grateful. Which of course she wouldn't be. Because I sort of had to hire her, and she knew it."

"Why on earth would you *have* to hire her?"

Chloe visibly shrank. "Her father is one of my company's biggest clients," she muttered.

"Are you telling me she blackmailed you into hiring her?"

"No. My boss blackmailed me into hiring her," said Chloe bitterly. "When I told her I couldn't place Ariel anywhere because it wouldn't be fair to our clients to send them someone so inexperienced and . . . well, she seemed to think I would be overjoyed to have an assistant."

"It might work out," Lucy said encouragingly.

"And what, Chloe?" asked Meg shrewdly.

Chloe looked at her in confusion. "What do you mean?"

"You said Ariel was inexperienced *and*. What were you about to say?"

Chloe looked guilty. "I wasn't going to say anything. That is, she was probably just nervous which was why she was so . . ."

"So . . . ?" prompted Lucy, who knew that Chloe could rarely bring herself to say a bad word about anyone. Apparently Chloe had worked on overcoming this tendency because she now answered flatly, "Horrible."

Meg looked at Chloe with fascination. "What exactly did this girl do to you?"

"I don't know!" Chloe said in frustration. "All I know is that I felt like I was back at high school and I was the new girl trying to impress the coolest girl in my class. She was just completely unimpressed by me or the fact that she was in a job interview."

"Well you're not at high school, and Ariel is your intern," said Lucy firmly, recognizing the signs of Chloe moving into muddled hysteria. "Just remember that you're her boss and she's there to learn some skills."

"And if she gives you any trouble send her to me," Meg drawled. Lucy and Chloe exchanged a grin. Meg's acerbic reputation was legendary.

"How's work, Meg?" asked Chloe, wanting to change the subject.

"Fine but too busy with a property dispute that's dragging on. I've had to do masses of overtime, which means that I haven't had a chance to see Blake of course. This is the first time that I've been out for a drink in ages."

"How are things with Blake?" Lucy ventured cautiously. Lucy didn't particularly like Blake, and Meg knew it, so it always made her feel slightly hypocritical to ask after him.

Meg gave a brief, sardonic smile. "You don't have to be polite about him anymore, Luce. We broke up."

"You broke up with Blake? When?" asked Chloe in surprise.

Meg shrugged. "Three days ago."

"You broke up with Blake *three* days ago and you're only telling us now?" Lucy said, completely aghast. "But Meg, why didn't you call? Are you okay?"

"I'm perfectly fine, Lucy," Meg said calmly. "And I knew that I'd be seeing you two tonight so there was no need to call."

"No *need?* You break up with your boyfriend and you don't even tell your best friends?"

Meg couldn't help laughing at the bewildered expression on Lucy's face. "Blake and I had only been seeing each other for two months. It's a shame, but my heart's not exactly broken. Oh Luce—I wish you could see your face. You have no idea what I'm talking about, have you?"

Lucy looked defensive. "Of course I do. Sort of. Well, actually no, not really. I don't understand how you can date men that you're not in love with in the first place, but if you do then I suppose that it makes sense that you're not that upset when it ends."

"You do know that for the vast majority of the world, falling in love comes *after* dating, don't you, Luce?"

Lucy sniffed. "Yes and quite frankly I've never understood it. It makes so much more sense to fall in love immediately. When you don't really know someone you can fantasize that they're intelligent and funny and share your political beliefs and taste in books and music and films. They can be perfect," she finished with a sigh.

Meg took a sip of her drink and looked at Lucy in amusement. "There's just one fatal flaw with your love at first sight approach."

Lucy waved one hand in the air dismissively, unwittingly knocking over a tray of glasses carried by a harassed waiter who was trying with difficulty to negotiate the crowded bar. "If you're about to lecture me on the whole 'no one will ever live up to my romantic fantasies' and 'real relationships aren't like that' then please don't bother. I've heard it all before and I refuse to believe it. I think that far too often people just get what they settle for. I believe in true love, and I'm happy to hold out for my knight in shining armor."

"Knights are a bit in short supply these days. Unless you want to date one of those computer technicians who dress up in medieval costume and hold jousting competitions on the weekends?" Meg suggested helpfully.

"There is absolutely no need to be so literal or sarcastic," Lucy said with dignity. "As my fairy godmother, who had better be listening, knows, the armor is negotiable. And anyway, to get back to the original topic, which was you and Blake, I just think there should be a strong attraction to begin with. You know, Megs, I never really understood your relationship with Blake."

"Meaning what?"

"Well he isn't exactly the liveliest bloke that you've ever met, is he?"

"If you mean he's never organized a dinner for ten people, including six girls, at a 'Tits & Schnitz' night at some dodgy restaurant then no, Blake isn't exactly the life and soul of the party."

"Tom only did that once," Lucy said defensively. "And the schnitzel was very good."

"Lucy, my date that night was a vegetarian sexual harassment lawyer."

"Well Tom couldn't know that. You'd only been going out with him for two weeks."

"Yes, and that particular relationship only lasted two weeks and three hours, thanks to Tom."

"Does anyone want another drink?" Chloe intervened, ever anxious to keep the peace.

Lucy caught Meg's wrist and turned it over to look at her watch. "Not for me, I've got to go. I'm late as usual."

"Are you meeting Taylor?" asked Chloe, finishing her drink.

"I'm having dinner with Tom," said Lucy, hunting around madly underneath the table for her belongings. "And before you ask, we're having dinner at Cicciolina's. The only breasts on display will be chicken."

Chloe and Meg exchanged a knowing look.

"What is it this week?" asked Meg wearily. "Best friends? Lovers? Or is it almost time for 'I Hate Tom Week' again?"

"We are simply having dinner together," Lucy said, with as much dignity as she could muster while crouched under the table still trying to find her keys, which had fallen out of her bag.

"The usual bet?" Meg asked Chloe, who, after a slight reluctant pause, assented with a nod.

"What was that?" Lucy asked, emerging flushed and disheveled but with all her belongings intact.

"It's nothing to do with you," said Meg. "It's just that I bet Chloe a bottle of wine that you'll end up sleeping with Tom tonight."

"That has everything to do with me!" Lucy said, outraged. "I can't believe that you two bet on my sex life."

"But we always do it," Meg said, which did nothing further to endear her to Lucy.

"I bet that you won't have sex, Luce," said Chloe earnestly.

Lucy frowned at her while she tried to work out whether this made Chloe better or worse than Meg. "I am *not* going to sleep with Tom tonight."

"It's more than likely you will, Luce," Meg disagreed knowingly. "Judging on past performances and the timing of tonight I'd put the odds at two to one."

"Stop talking about me like I'm a greyhound!"

"Not a greyhound," Chloe said soothingly. "A beautiful thorough-bred racehorse."

Meg shook her head. "Lucy can't be a racehorse. Tom will be riding her and he's too tall to be a jockey."

"If you've *quite* finished," Lucy said icily, "may I remind you that I'm seeing Taylor?"

"What's he got to do with it?"

"We've been seeing each other for three weeks!"

"But Luce, you've never once, not once, managed to stay faithful to anyone but Tom," said Meg reasonably. "You always end up going back to him. It's only a matter of time, and I think it will be tonight."

"Why is it more than likely I'll sleep with Tom tonight?" asked Lucy fretfully, now worried that Meg knew something that she didn't and wondering if she had time to race home and shave her legs.

"It's been six weeks since you last slept together as friends and about four months since you two tried to have a relationship for the—what number attempt was it, Chloe?"

"Seventh I think," said Chloe.

"Sounds right. So that makes it the seventh try in two years. Which means it's more than likely you'll sleep with Tom tonight." Seeing that Lucy was looking at her mutinously, she added, "It's like predicting the weather, Luce. Only you and Tom are rather more—predictable."

"I'm surprised you don't have graphs and pie charts," Lucy said irritably.

"We could put together something on PowerPoint," Chloe mused.

"I'm not sure I want visuals of Tom and Lucy—"

"You're both hilarious," said Lucy, getting up as Chloe and Meg dissolved into laughter. "I'll speak to you tomorrow, at which time you will discover that I have *not* slept with Tom."

"Don't forget to be safe," Meg called to her retreating back. Without turning around, Lucy stuck up her middle finger. Meg grinned and then turned back to Chloe. "I'll buy you a drink, Clo," she said generously. "It's only fair considering you'll owe me a bottle of wine tomorrow."

2.
dating food

As Tom left behind the warm summer's night on Acland Street and was ushered to a table at Cicciolina's, he wondered why he was bothering to search the restaurant for Lucy. She suffered from pathological lateness, and despite being ten minutes late, he was obviously the first to arrive. A pretty waitress promptly appeared at the table and handed him a wine list. Waiting patiently as he scanned it, her cheerful countenance expressed alarm when he asked her a question regarding one of the wines.

"It's my first night," the waitress confessed naively.

"Oh. What's your name?"

The waitress, not at all impervious to the charm of Tom's smile, flushed slightly. "Miranda."

"Pleased to meet you, Miranda. I'm Tom. I'll order a bottle of shiraz—actually scrap that—Lucy hates red wine. Make it a bottle of the pinot grigio."

Miranda looked uncertainly at the empty chair opposite him. "Did you want to wait for your companion to arrive before ordering?"

"Yes, I think so. Although, based on past experience with Lucy, she may show up anytime between now and midnight. In fact, perhaps I'd better give you my card now so that if I end up getting drunk alone you can put me in a taxi and give the driver my address."

A look of confusion passed over Miranda's face. "So you might end up dining alone? Should I remove the other set of cutlery?"

No sense of humor, Tom realized regretfully. And what was infinitely more unforgivable, she had absolutely no idea that he was trying to flirt with her. "No, I'm expecting a friend," he said cheerfully, promptly abandoning his flirtatious tone.

Miranda smiled gratefully and departed and a few minutes later managed to do a creditable job of opening the wine. Tom spent the next ten minutes looking at the assorted artworks that were crammed onto every possible space on the walls before the door of the restaurant was flung open with rather more force than was necessary and Lucy erupted into the room, all breathless energy and apologies.

"I'm so sorry," she gasped, while she was still about five feet away from the table.

"Aliens abducted you?" Tom asked sympathetically, standing up and kissing her flushed cheek.

Lucy collapsed into her chair. "I don't think so," she said cautiously. "Didn't I use that one already?"

"Probably. But we see each other at least twice a week so it's hard to keep track of your excuses."

"Don't you want to know the real reason that I'm late?"

"But it's probably not very interesting," Tom protested, pouring her a glass of wine. "It's bound to have something to do with traffic or the fact that you don't wear a watch and can't parallel park. I'd much rather you kept making things up."

"Oh fine," Lucy said impatiently. She concentrated for a moment and then her brow cleared. "I found the meaning of life and I had to return it to its rightful owner."

"And who is its rightful owner?"

"Deborah Lee Furness of course. She's married to Hugh Jackman, and he's the meaning of life as far as I'm concerned. Am I forgiven?" Lucy regarded him hopefully.

"I suppose so. Here." Tom tossed a bunch of flowers across the table. "I brought you these."

She caught them and peered cautiously at the wilted bunch of daffodils, encased in cheap cellophane with a ladybird pattern on it. Then she sniffed them. "Tom?"

"Yes?"

"These daffodils smell like gasoline."

"That's because I bought them at a gas station," he said proudly. "They're much worse than usual, aren't they?"

"Mmmm. You really have outdone yourself this time. Meg and Chloe say hello by the way."

"How are the other Charlie's Angels?"

"They're fine. Sort of. Chloe has some horribly intimidating intern and Meg has broken up with Blake, but apart from that they're fine."

"Don't worry about Meg and the pompous Blake. His expiry date was always looming. Meg's boyfriends never last for long."

"You can talk," Lucy said, stung by his criticism of Meg. "At least Meg's boyfriends *have* expiry dates. Your girlfriends just go straight to the refrigerated area. The poor things only have a shelf life of a few days in the right conditions at best."

"So according to you, Meg dates dry goods, whereas I'm more of a dairy man?"

"Exactly."

"Well I hate to tell you this, Lucy, but that makes you an imported groceries kind of a girl. You always go for the complicated, hard-to-procure items and end up wishing that you'd had a cheese sandwich instead."

"Oh I see. And you're the cheese sandwich I suppose?"

"I didn't say that, but it's interesting that you immediately leapt to that conclusion," Tom said, trying, and failing, to look modest.

Lucy laughed. "It's always about you, isn't it, Tom? Can we order first and argue later? I'm starving."

Tom obediently turned his attention to the menu and then peered up at the specials board.

"What do you reckon girello is?" Tom asked, still trying to decipher the chalk handwriting.

"No idea, but it's pickled and served with cabbage so I wouldn't recommend it," said Lucy, after a brief glance at the board.

"What do you think it is?"

Lucy considered carefully for a moment. "Eel," she decided.

"Why eel?"

"Why not?"

"But what is it about the word *girello* that made you think of eel?" he persisted.

"Can't we talk about what sort of day we had at work like normal people?"

"How was your day, dear?"

"Average apart from finding out that my best friends bet on my sex life. How was yours?"

"I saved several small children from a burning building and was nominated for a humanitarian award. Why do you think girello is eel?"

"Because it's pickled. Eels are always pickled. What do *you* think girello is?"

Tom looked thoughtful. "Bison," he finally pronounced.

"Of course it is. And exactly what part of the bison is the girello?"

"It's not a *part* of the bison, Lucinda," Tom said sternly. "It's a *breed* of bison."

"Sorry," she said meekly. "My tribe only ever ate wildebeest."

"Well that's patently obvious. My God, I can't believe that they're serving bison with cabbage. It's unheard of. What iniquitous den of nouvelle cuisine have you brought me to?"

"You have a very large vocabulary, haven't you?" Lucy said, impressed by his use of *iniquitous*.

"Yes. It's directly proportional to the length of my penis. Or is it my nose? I can never remember which is which."

"Well, I wouldn't recommend blowing your nose in public then. You might get arrested." She thought for a moment and then added dreamily, "Taylor has an *enormous* vocabulary."

Tom shot her a poisonous look. "I wondered how long it would be before you dragged the archaeologist into the conversation. Hasn't he run off overseas to rob tombs or dig up Fred Flintstone's bones yet? I'd be happy to supply him with a list of war zones that need excavating if he needs a push."

"You're just jealous because copywriters don't get Indiana Jones as their patron saint. And he's not leaving for another month yet." The smitten look crept back into Lucy's eyes. "Do you know that he used the word *quorum* the other day? I'd never heard anyone use the word *quorum* in context before."

"It'd be a damn sight more amazing if you'd ever heard anyone use it *out* of context before. I mean, what do you expect? Where's the quorum? Has anyone seen the quorum?"

"Shut up."

"Hey Darren, chuck us the quorum."

"Shut *up*, Tom."

"Well you must admit I have a point."

Before Lucy, who had absolutely no intention of admitting any such thing, could dispute this further, Miranda arrived to take their order. "I'll have the seafood linguine please," Lucy said politely.

"I think that I'm going to have the same, but could you just tell me what the girello is?" Tom asked.

"It's corn beef."

"Ah. Not bison then?" Tom asked regretfully.

"Excuse me?"

"Shut up, Tom. It's nothing," Lucy said, smiling sweetly at the confused girl.

"Do you realize that you spend an inordinate amount of your life telling me to shut up, Lucinda?" Tom asked conversationally.

"Well I wouldn't have to keep repeating myself if you'd listen to me," she said through gritted teeth.

"I do listen to you, I just don't always immediately do what you tell me to, unlike poor frickin' Taylor."

"Since when have you felt sorry for Taylor? You hate Taylor!"

"It's a male solidarity thing that comes to the fore when a dominating female has one of our brethren in her clutches."

"Solidarity?" Lucy snorted. "A moment ago you wanted to send him to a war zone."

Miranda was eyeing them uneasily. "Would you like me to come back, Tom?" she asked warily.

Lucy looked at her in surprise. "Do you two know each other?"

"No. But I needed someone to talk to while I was waiting for you," Tom said innocently. Lucy shot him a look through narrowed eyes and then turned to Miranda and smiled warmly at her. "There's no need for you to come back. We'll both have the linguine."

To the obvious relief of Miranda, Tom nodded assent, handed over the menu, and then gave the waitress a smile that made her visibly melt, much to Lucy's disgust.

"She's very pretty. Did you ask her out?" Lucy asked in a politely disinterested tone once Miranda had disappeared.

"I was thinking about it, but I have a foreboding feeling that Miranda's idea of funny would involve a sweet little dog performing tricks."

"Sounds like a perfect match to me, Rover. I'll even provide the hula hoop for you to jump through."

"Luce, you know that green doesn't suit you. So stop being jealous and tell me how the apartment-hunting is going."

Lucy grimaced. "Don't ask. I just can't bear it. Looking at rental properties ranks just under clearing out a deceased relative's wardrobe as the most depressing job in the world as far as I'm concerned."

"They can't all be that bad."

Lucy eyed him with disfavor. "That would be the sound of someone who owns his own place speaking," she said sourly. "Why don't you come apartment-hunting with me and I can demonstrate The Doorbell Principle in person?"

"What's The Doorbell Principle?"

"I named it after that apartment in North Fitzroy that I lived in. Do you remember the one that had the doorbell that played 'It's a Small World after All' twenty times if a visitor so much as touched the buzzer and didn't have any volume control to boot?"

Tom gave an elaborate shudder. "I remember. Isn't that why we broke up the first time?"

Lucy shook her head. "No, that was the second time we broke up. The first time was because you met that girl who you thought was the love of your life for about a week and a half."

Tom looked nostalgic. "That's right. But then *we* had to break up because she was a psychologist and she said that being with me made her feel like she was working all the time."

"Anyway," Lucy said frowning at him and reverting back to the original topic, "that's The Doorbell Principle. No matter how nice or clean or well-located a rental property is, it will always have one deliberately installed element designed to destroy the mental health of the renter just to remind them of their lowly place in the world."

"Sure you're not being slightly paranoid about this?"

Lucy shook her head vehemently. "I've looked at ten places so far, and they're all horrible *and* expensive. And real estate agents *hate* renters. I don't think I can afford to live by myself anyway. I'm not exactly on a lavish budget with my job at the gallery, and although I have to pay rent, I'm still keen on eating occasionally too."

"How soon do you have to be out of the place that you're in now?"

"Three weeks' time. That's when Alice is moving out, and I can't afford the rent by myself. But Chloe said that I can stay with her for a bit if I haven't found anything by then. She's just moved into that place that she's house-sitting so that she can save some money and there are two spare rooms."

"You could stay with me," Tom suggested.

"Very funny."

"I mean it. You'd have to sleep in my bed of course. And you'd have to perform light sexual duties and remember to leave the toilet seat up, but it would be much more fun for you than staying with Chloe."

"Does it bother you that I'd rather sleep in a cardboard box on the street than accept your offer?" Lucy asked acidly.

Tom shook his head vigorously. "No. Because I know that you're just in denial," he said kindly.

Lucy stiffled a giggle. "Will you stop being such an idiot? I'm off-limits, remember?"

Tom subsided as their meals arrived, and for the remainder of the evening they managed to chat amicably about books and acquaintances and for the twenty-eighth time tried to work out what had happened in *Mulholland Drive* after the car crash scene.

When their bill was presented Lucy looked at Tom with a wrinkled brow. "I can't remember which way we're doing it anymore," she confessed. "Are we paying half each or taking it in turns to treat each other?"

"What's the difference?" asked Tom, attempting to refill Lucy's wine glass.

She shook her head. "No more for me please. I'm driving. There's no difference really," she thought aloud. "I think we take it in turns to treat each other when we're going out, and we pay half each when we're just friends."

Tom poured the rest of the wine into his glass. "In that case I'll get the bill," he said, putting his credit card on the tray and handing it to a passing waiter.

He smiled at Lucy. "Now you're beholden to me. You have to come home with me."

Lucy tried to look stern. "Tom, I'm not going home with you."

Tom sat back in his chair and regarded her over the top of his wine glass. "I don't think you're looking at all well. You really shouldn't be alone."

"In that case, I should probably go home. To bed. By myself," Lucy said discouragingly.

Tom shook his head. "You're not *that* ill," he said reprovingly. "Don't be such a hypochondriac."

"Tom, I am *not* going home with you."

"Why not?" Tom persisted as he signed the bill, leaving a generous tip for Miranda, and they stood up to leave.

"Because you just want to sleep with me. Again. And it would be lots of fun because it always is with us, but we'd end up doing it again and again until we found ourselves having another argument in three weeks' time. And then we wouldn't speak to each other for a few weeks until one of us gives in because we're actually missing each other terribly, and then we'll try to be friends for a while until you try to sleep with me again. We've been doing this for almost two years now, and it makes me tired just thinking about it."

"That's a very good point, you know," Tom said, holding the restaurant door open for her as they stepped out into Acland Street and headed to where Lucy's car was parked down a nearby side street.

"Really?" Lucy asked, trying not to be upset that he was giving in so easily.

"Yes. Why is it always me who tries to sleep with you? Why don't you ever bring up the subject?"

"Because I'm trying very hard to have a certain level of self-respect and dignity."

"That sounds very worthy. Boring, but worthy."

"Thank you."

"Extremely dull and boring, but undoubtedly sensible."

"Much appreciated."

There was a small pause in which they listened to a late-night street performer, who was torturing both a set of bongo drums and all passersby within earshot.

"So a quickie is completely out of the question then?"

"Thomas!"

"Well it just seems ridiculous. I want to. I know you want to. So why go through all of this? Why can't it just be about two people who like being together and who want each other?"

"Because you want a casual relationship because you like sleeping with me. Whereas I like sleeping with you, talking to you, the way that you make me laugh, and waking up next to you. Do you see the problem?"

"Yes. I shouldn't be so damn attractive."

"You're not," she said witheringly. "I happen to have exceptionally low standards."

"It is ironic, isn't it?" he asked, striding along, his mind working on the problem. "You can't have a casual relationship with me because I'm actually too much of a Sensitive New Age Guy."

Lucy choked. "Excuse me? How does wanting to have a casual sexual relationship and being unable to commit to someone classify you as a SNAG?"

"It's true. We have a fantastic sexual relationship and do all of those couple things like holding hands in the movies and reading the paper in the park. I cook you dinner and treat you well and what do I get for it? Nothing. Ending of the sexual relationship because you want more. It's bitter irony, that's what it is. In fact," Tom said, warming to his theme, "you should sleep with me just for the sympathy factor."

"I'm sorry—you've lost me. I should sleep with you because I'm sorry for you because . . . ?"

"Because I have an identity crisis. I'm both a commitment-phobic sexual predator and a SNAG. And being caught between both is having a damaging impact on my sex life. I blame the feminists."

"You've never read a word of feminist theory in your life."

"Yes I know, but that's part of my macho side. I'm just positive that the feminists are to blame for my problems. Until they came along we all knew where we stood. Men with their clubs in hand and women redecorating the cave."

"That's a wonderful attitude, Tom," Lucy said encouragingly. "Stick with it and you can look forward to many more lonely nights with your club in your hand I'm sure. And anyway," she added, "in case you've forgotten, I'm seeing someone."

Tom shot her a wicked glance. "In case *I've* forgotten?" he murmured. "Seems to me *you* forgot the Tomb Raider there, Luce. Shouldn't he be the first reason why you won't come home with me rather than the last?"

"It's so patently obvious I didn't think I had to mention it," Lucy said loftily, trying not to bite her lip from anxiety over the fact that she had quite forgotten Taylor until now.

Tom opened his mouth to say something belittling about Taylor, but deciding to change tack he said, "Why can't you have both of us?"

"What on earth are you talking about?"

"Go out with Taylor if you must, although it's completely nauseating for all of us to have to watch. But you could just keep me on the side for . . . you know."

"I don't know. I think I know what you're suggesting, but I can't actually believe that you're suggesting it."

"I don't mind if you just use me for conversation and sex."

"Even if *you* seem to have lost all self-respect, Tom, I don't intend to lose mine by cheating on Taylor."

"It was just a thought. It seemed to solve both of our problems. You get me in private and Taylor as a boyfriend in public, and I get to have my evil way with you. Seems perfect really."

Lucy stopped dead and glared at him in disgust. "Only you could possibly think that a completely dysfunctional relationship like that could work or would be perfect. You're not just emotionally crippled,

Tom, you're like the Black Knight in *Monty Python and the Holy Grail* who had both of his arms and legs chopped off and kept lying there yelling for the other knight to fight him. You don't even realize how tragic your condition is."

"Damn, that was a bit deep, Luce," replied Tom equably, apparently unmoved by this stricture. "But if you start singing the lumberjack song or doing the dead parrot sketch I'm going to leave you here alone. Only first-year engineering students should quote Monty Python."

All of a sudden Lucy felt completely exhausted and unable to argue anymore. "You're absolutely right, Tom. It's all very easy in your world, isn't it? Funnily enough, I prefer my world with Taylor in it and, even stranger, it's not half as complicated with Taylor as it is with you. Thank you for walking me to my car. Next time we do this we must remember to leave straight after dessert so that we don't have this stupid argument for the fiftieth time."

Pleased with this dignified exit speech, Lucy opened her car door. She was therefore immensely annoyed to see Tom opening the passenger door and making himself comfortable in the front seat.

He gave her an angelic smile. "You promised to drive me home, Ginger," he reminded her.

Lucy shot him an evil look but turned the key in the engine. "Fine. But I've told you not to call me that anymore."

"Why not? It suits you."

"Because that nickname belongs to a different time when we were in a relationship and you loved me."

"I still love you," Tom said, trying unsuccessfully to sound wounded.

"Yes but—" Lucy stopped in frustration. "Look, it doesn't matter to you, but it matters to me. That name was special to me and I don't want you to use it out of context."

Tom considered this for a moment. "Are we back on the quorum conversation again?"

"It would kill you to take anything seriously for even a second, wouldn't it?"

They drove in silence until they pulled up in front of Tom's art deco apartment building on a tree-lined street in Prahran. Lucy pointedly left the engine running, which didn't deter Tom in the slightest.

"Why don't you come in for a bit?" he said persuasively, putting an arm around her shoulders.

"No," Lucy said, more firmly than she felt and insistently fixing her gaze straight ahead.

"I think you should come in," Tom said, placing a soft kiss behind her ear.

"I can't," she said, wretchedly aware that her resolve was starting to waver. With a valiant effort she managed to lie. "I'm staying at Taylor's tonight."

Tom pulled back and eyed her appreciatively. "That's my girl. Good backup plan. If you stay at his house tonight he'll know you just had dinner with a platonic friend, and at the same time it safeguards you from falling into my evil clutches."

"Stop having such a good opinion of yourself," Lucy said angrily, furious that he'd seen straight through her. "Not everything that I do is based around you, you conceited twat."

Unperturbed by this appellation, Tom leaned over and kissed her on the cheek. Trying not to be disappointed that he was giving in so easily, she watched as Tom unfolded himself from the car. As an afterthought she said politely, "Thank you for dinner."

Tom bent down and grinned wickedly. "You're welcome." He paused for maximum effect and then added, "Ginger."

3.

real estate

"Did I win?" Meg's voice was so gleefully loud that Lucy had to hold her cell phone slightly away from her ear.

"Yes, you won. Now leave me alone and break the news to Chloe. I've told the gallery I'm going to be in an hour late today because I'm apartment-hunting."

"So how come you slept with him?" Meg persisted.

"Haven't the faintest idea," Lucy sighed. "All I know is that he made me laugh and called me Ginger, and then the ratbag smiled at me. Next thing I knew we were breaking the land speed record to get to his bedroom. Anyway, why on earth are you asking me? I thought you had statistics and forecasts worked out that explained why Tom and I sleep together. I was kind of hoping *you* could explain it to *me*."

"Wouldn't have a clue," said Meg cheerfully. "I'm very fond of Tom but can't see the attraction myself. Have you broken the news to Taylor yet?"

"Not yet," said Lucy, trying unsuccessfully to sound choked up.

"Are you going to?"

"Of course I am. Look, Megs, I have to go—I've only got an hour and I want to look at two places. Tell Clo I'm sorry I lost her the bet."

"Don't feel too sorry for her. She's lost the past eight times. She should know better. Good luck with the apartment-hunting."

Lucy stopped outside the real estate agency and started to wistfully read the descriptions posted next to photographs of properties for sale or lease. She knew that she was starting to lose her mind because it was beginning to not sound unreasonable to pay five hundred dollars a week. At least then she knew that she'd be getting polished floorboards, a dishwasher, and no visible holes in the ceiling, floor, or walls. She peered through the window and eyed the girl behind the counter. As though feeling her gaze, the girl's head snapped up and she eyed Lucy suspiciously. Lucy promptly withdrew to the safety of a very large advertisement and, taking a deep breath, pushed the door open and barged in with considerably more bravado than she was feeling.

"Hello," she said cheerfully. At this point an ornate cuckoo clock on the wall behind the receptionist started to chime and go berserk, announcing to the world with somewhat over-hyped fanfare that it was nine o'clock.

The girl, whose nameplate read "Sybil," eyed her sulkily. "We just opened," she said moodily.

"Oh." *What the hell did that mean? So you're open. Do some work.*

Then with an effort at professionalism the girl said irritably, "What do you want?"

"I want the keys to look at some properties please."

Sybil's effort at politeness immediately vanished. "Oh. Right. Renter then are you?"

Actually no, Sybil. I'm a property mogul.

"That's right. I'm a renter." Lucy tried to inject pride into her voice.

"Which properties do you want to look at?" Sybil demanded sullenly. Before Lucy could answer the telephone rang and Sybil answered it. Instead of putting the call on hold and dealing with Lucy first, she continued to talk. There were no chairs to sit down on so Lucy stood there for ten minutes, growing increasingly frustrated as she listened to the unfolding saga of someone called Ben's complaints about a bathroom fan that refused to work properly.

Sybil finally hung up only to pause to light up a cigarette. She blew some smoke insolently towards Lucy as though daring her to say anything.

"I'd like the keys for the apartment in Marsden Road and the one in Carmichael Street," Lucy said as politely as she could through gritted teeth.

"You have to leave a fifty-dollar deposit," Sybil snarled.

"I know," Lucy said, equally grimly handing over a fifty-dollar bill.

Sybil looked at her with something akin to pleasure. "It's fifty dollars for each set of keys," she said sweetly.

Lucy stared at her in disbelief. "You're kidding."

"I don't kid."

"But I only have fifty dollars on me."

"You can take one set of keys," Sybil said generously.

"I *know* I can take one set of keys," Lucy said dangerously. "My point is I want *two* sets. I only have an hour, and Marsden Road and Carmichael Street are right next to one another."

Sybil sighed in mock sorrow and then took another drag on her cigarette. "Sorry, but those are the rules. You wouldn't want me to lose my job, would you?"

Yes, thought Lucy. *I'd like that a lot. I'd like for you to be begging on the street so I could tell you that I could only give you one half of a ten-dollar bill.*

Lucy took a deep breath to calm herself, but it didn't help much because she ended up choking on the smoke from Sybil's smoldering cigarette. She decided to be friendly and helpful towards Sybil as that would probably be more effective than pushing Sybil's head into the cuckoo clock, which was the other, considerably more attractive, alternative.

"Carspace has an *s*," Lucy said helpfully, looking over Sybil's shoulder at the computer screen.

"What?"

"*Carspace*. It's spelled with an *s*. You spelled it with three *a*'s. You might get tortoises trying to move in," Lucy joked feebly.

Sybil looked at her blankly as though she were speaking Pitjant-jatjara.

"A *carapace* is the shell of a—never mind," Lucy muttered, inwardly thinking *I hate you, I hate the fact that my future happiness and peace of mind depends on an illiterate refugee from a Macy's makeup counter*. Lucy watched Sybil for a few minutes, wondering if she stood there for half an hour whether Sybil would do anything. Probably not. "May I please have the keys that I've requested?" Lucy said as acidly as she could manage when she had waited for another two minutes.

"Huh?" Sybil glanced up briefly from her computer screen in annoyance. "Sure. Which properties?"

"Carmichael Street. And Marsden Road," Lucy enunciated very clearly and precisely. But then couldn't help adding, "S-O-U-G-H-T."

"What?"

"*Sought-after* location. It's spelled S-O-U-G-H-T. Not S-O-R-T."

"Who cares? It sounds the same."

"Yes, but you're writing an advertisement. People are going to *read* it."

Sybil looked at her with a combination of malice and sympathy. "I need to see your license. And I'll need a hundred-dollar deposit."

Lucy spent a few moments hoping that Sybil's head would catch on fire. Realizing that hope alone was not enough she spent a further few moments trying telepathically to *make* Sybil's head catch on fire while she foraged in her purse for her license.

She handed it over to Sybil, who took a long drag of her cigarette and then left it gently smoldering on the counter. Sybil accepted the items and then calmly asked Lucy which set of keys she would prefer to take.

"Carmichael Street," Lucy repeated robotically, wondering why she was still bothering. Even if the apartment was half-decent there was no way that Sybil would let her application get through now.

Sybil turned on her heel and went into an adjoining room to get the keys. The telephone rang and she heard Sybil answer it and commence another long and involved discussion. Lucy waited, growing increasingly frustrated as she realized that she now had only forty minutes to make it to Carmichael Street and back.

Lucy was distracted from her mounting anger by the unpleasant smell of burning plastic. She looked down and saw that Sybil's cigarette was burning through the plastic counter. She was half tempted to leave it there, but the smell was so unpleasant she picked it up and looked for something to stub it out in. There didn't appear to be an ashtray anywhere, which was unsurprising considering that it was illegal to smoke in a workplace. Lucy was just wondering what the hell she should do with it when she saw a brisk, efficient woman approaching the front door. Oh God. If she was a real estate agent and she caught Lucy with a cigarette indoors she'd never approve her application. Cursing Sybil, Lucy hastily thrust the cigarette into the recess of the cuckoo clock, and waved her hands around wildly to disperse the burning smell just as the woman walked through the door.

Lucy's suspicions were confirmed when the woman smiled at her and paused by the desk. "Hello there," said the agent. "Are you being looked after?"

"Yes, thank you," said Lucy weakly. And then, feeling as though she had earned a reward for getting Sybil out of trouble she added, "I wanted to look at two apartments this morning but I didn't realize that you had to leave a fifty-dollar deposit for each set of keys. I don't suppose you'd make an exception? It's just that I'm extremely short of time, and they're right next to one another."

"I don't think that's too much of a problem. Just speak to Sybil and tell her I said it was fine. Where is Sybil by the way?"

"She's getting me some keys."

The agent smiled at her again and then passed through the office. She stopped, wrinkled her nose, sniffed, and then turned to Lucy. "Do you smell something?"

"Like what?"

"Something burning maybe?"

Lucy emitted such a delicate sniff she would have had trouble detecting if her own head was on fire. "Don't think so."

"Oh. Okay. Well good luck with the apartment-hunting." The agent passed through to the rear offices just as Sybil returned.

"Here are the keys. You have to get them back to us within half an hour," Sybil said unpleasantly.

"I only have half an hour left now," Lucy said, equally unpleasantly. She was about to ask for the second set of keys when the clock on the wall started suddenly to scream.

"CUCKOO! CUCKOO!"

"That's weird," said Sybil, checking her watch.

"Okay, well I'll see you later then," said Lucy, grabbing the keys and deciding to make a fast exit.

"CUCKOO!" The bird shot out again at high speed and the little Alpine couple started to dance frantically around their home, which was now undeniably emitting smoke. Sybil, however, was concerned with a matter of greater importance.

"Where's my ciggie?" she snapped, looking directly at Lucy.

"In the cuckoo clock," Lucy said politely. "Which, I think, is on fire. You really should be nicer to people, you know. I'm only an arsonist but you'll be in serious trouble if you ever piss off a serial killer, Sybil. Bye."

And before Sybil could retaliate, Lucy fled.

Twenty minutes later, having done one hasty lap around a dark and dingy apartment with a pervasive smell that was somewhere between nine-day-old dead cat and ripe baby's diaper, Lucy frantically dialed Tom's number at work. As soon as she heard his voice, she blurted out,

"I need a favor. I need you to return some keys for me." Before he could ply her with questions she went on hurriedly, "They belong to a real estate agent. They're keys to a rental property. I need you to drop the keys back and pick up my deposit."

"Why can't you do it?"

"Because I set the receptionist's clock on fire."

There was a silence and then Tom asked, "What does the receptionist look like?"

"What does that have to do with anything?"

"Is she pretty?"

"Don't you want to know why I set the clock on fire?" asked Lucy, irritated that Tom wasn't interested in her role in the story.

"I'm sure you had your reasons. Is she blonde or brunette?"

"Redhead," said Lucy through gritted teeth. "Now will you please come and meet me so I can get my deposit back and go to work?" Before he could say anything she said warningly, "And don't even *think* about asking me if she's a natural redhead. Find out for yourself for all I care, just please, please come and help me."

"Has it occurred to you that I might be in the middle of something important?"

"No," said Lucy honestly. "You work in advertising. I haven't the faintest idea of what it is that you do at work apart from the fact that you go out to lunch with clients all the time and spend extraordinary amounts of time downloading pornographic e-mails from your football buddies. *Please* can you hurry?"

"You are such a drama queen, Ginger," Tom sighed. "All right, I'll come to your rescue. Where are you?"

4.

insignificant others

At roughly the same time that Lucy was setting fire to Sybil's clock, Chloe was pausing, prior to opening the door to her office, in order to take a deep breath.

She is twenty-one years old. She is my intern. It doesn't matter who her father is or that she's wearing an outfit that cost more than my car. Remembering Lucy's advice from the previous night she mentally intoned, *I am her boss and she is here to learn new skills.* Miserably aware that she was failing to convince herself, Chloe straightened her back, took a deep breath, and called upon her last resort.

I am Marcia Brady in the episode where she has stage-fright. Mike Brady has just taught me the secret to overcoming it and having confidence. I'll imagine that Ariel is wearing nothing but her underwear.

Still a trifle unconvinced that this strategy was going to work, Chloe added the clincher: *I will pretend to be Meg.*

Trying to banish the certain knowledge that there wasn't the faintest possibility that Meg would ever handle an insubordinate staff member by giving herself a lackluster pep talk while hiding in her own office, and conclude by pretending to be a member of the Brady Bunch, Chloe turned the handle on the door, and walked with what she hoped was determination and purpose to Ariel's desk.

"Ariel?" she asked tentatively.

Ariel didn't so much as raise her expensively cropped head. "Just a sec. I'm sending an e-mail."

From where Chloe was standing she could see that it was a personal e-mail. Ariel obviously felt that she was perfectly within her rights to keep her boss waiting while she sent personal e-mails, and her breathtaking self-assurance was so assertive that somehow Chloe felt she had the right as well. Invoking the ancient wisdom of the Brady Bunch, Chloe concentrated on imagining that Ariel was wearing nothing but her bra and knickers. That somehow felt a bit creepy and wrong and like she was breaking the Sexual Harassment Act so she made sure that the imaginary bra and knickers were a sturdy, functional set in a sensible shade of navy.

With the e-mail sent Ariel swiveled around in her chair to face Chloe and arched one eyebrow inquiringly.

"Ariel, I want to have a little talk," Chloe said, hating the phrase as soon as it was out of her mouth. It was such a lame, *elderly* thing to say. *Your father and I need to have a little talk.*

A corner of Ariel's mouth quirked up and Chloe knew that she thought it was a daggy thing to say too. "Sure. Do you want me to come into your office?"

"I, uh, no. Out here is fine." Chloe immediately regretted this as she felt at a disadvantage, standing in front of Ariel, who was leaning back in her chair. She felt as though Ariel was *her* boss and she was about to be reprimanded.

"I was just wondering what your long-term goals are. Professionally I mean."

This time both sides of Ariel's mouth quirked up. "My long-term professional goals?" she said slowly, somehow managing to make the question sound absurd. "I'm not really sure I have any right now, Chloe. I'm twenty-one. I want to travel some more—maybe go backpacking around India for a few months at the end of the year with my boyfriend."

"I backpacked through South America when I was twenty," said Chloe, glad to have found some common ground.

"Yeah? Well you should go to India sometime. But you have to be careful traveling around by yourself nowadays. It's not as safe as it was twenty years ago."

"I'm not *forty!*" Chloe sputtered in indignation, before she could stop herself.

"I didn't think you were," said Ariel, now evidently highly amused. "It was just a generalization."

Chloe had now also had time to register that Ariel had coolly assumed that she would be traveling alone. As it happened, Chloe was single, but Ariel's presumption unreasonably irritated her. Unfortunately she hadn't the faintest idea how to bring this point up in a dignified fashion without sounding petty and engaging in an inappropriate conversation about her personal life with an employee.

"Well, if you don't have any long-term goals, what would you like to achieve during your time here at Christabel Consulting?" Chloe groaned inwardly as soon as the words left her mouth. She sounded like a dork.

Ariel appeared to give the question her careful consideration. "Well, I'd like to be able to utilize my language skills."

"I see. Unfortunately we don't really have much need for French speakers in our Melbourne office, Ariel," Chloe said. There was a pause, and Chloe found herself begging *Please, please, God, don't let her point out that she speaks English.*

The phone rang at this point and with a show of efficiency, Ariel promptly answered it. "Hey Kenny babe—yeah it's me. What's up?" Ariel listened intently for a moment and then placed the call on hold. "Is it alright if I leave half an hour early tonight?" she asked Chloe. "My boyfriend is playing a gig at the Prince and he wants me to be there for the soundcheck and everything."

"Fine." Out of curiosity Chloe added, "What's the name of your boyfriend's band?"

"The Drones," Ariel said casually, pressing the hold button on the telephone.

"The Drones?" Chloe shrieked. "OH MY GOD—you're going out with Kenny from the Drones?"

Ariel glanced at her but placed a finger over her lips, requesting silence, and chastened, Chloe subsided. "Sorry, Kenny, I couldn't hear. My boss was screaming. Yeah, that's fine. I'll see you then." She replaced the receiver and turned, but Chloe, completely defeated by this demonstration of Ariel's coolness, had already dazedly made her way back into her office. Dimly aware that she had gone from being Marcia Brady conquering her stage-fright problem to Marcia in the episode where Davy Jones made a guest appearance, Chloe sat limply at her desk, belatedly realizing that she had achieved precisely nothing.

Pushing open the door to her house in Elwood that evening, Meg felt the sense of sanctuary that she always felt upon arriving home. The peace and uncluttered stillness of her home always had the power to calm her after another long day at work, and she sighed as she switched on the lights and air conditioner. Shedding her suit, she changed into a T-shirt and a pair of cargo pants and then made her way to the kitchen. She put a piece of fresh salmon under the grill and began to prepare a small salad. Occupied by the pleasingly mundane task, her thoughts drifted to Blake.

Although Lucy had instantly condemned him as boring, Meg and Lucy's taste in men was wildly divergent. Meg liked Tom, but she certainly wouldn't have put up with the sort of cavalier treatment that he regularly meted out to Lucy for more than ten minutes, let alone two years. Meg had liked Blake's air of quiet conservatism, and his lack of demonstrativeness had exactly suited her idea of propriety.

As she checked on her salmon, her cell phone rang. The display showed that the call was from a private number and she was tempted to leave it, but realizing that it would just mean she had to return the call later on, she pressed the answer key.

"Meg? It's Blake."

"Oh. Hi," Meg said cautiously, instantly regretting her decision to answer the call.

"How are you?"

"Fine, thanks. Blake, why are you calling?" Meg asked, not unkindly, but never one to waste time with unnecessary courtesies.

Blake gave a slightly forced laugh. "Oh you know. I thought you might be missing me."

Meg forced a slight twinge of regret to the back of her mind and took a deep breath. "Blake, I still have your jacket and that book you lent me, so we should make a time to meet up so that I can give them back. But after that I don't think we should see or call each other anymore."

"Right. So that's it then? It's all over? On to your next victim?" There was a note of bitterness in Blake's voice that Meg was all too familiar with from the ending of numerous past relationships.

"Go ahead and hate me if you need to," Meg said evenly, wondering why every man she dated always ended up feeling pathetically sorry for himself and needing to cast her in the role of a man-eater. "But it would be much easier on both of us if we just admitted that relationships don't always work out and ours simply didn't. There's really no need to make a drama out of it. You'll honestly be better off without me."

"And you'll be fine without me, Meg. You don't need anyone, least of all me. You're the original loner."

"That's completely untrue. I do like my time to myself, but I don't think that's so unreasonable."

"Time to yourself?" Blake snorted. "Meg, you make solitary confinement look like Times Square on New Year's Eve."

"Rubbish."

"Is that right? Do you want me to prove it to you?"

"How?" she asked suspiciously.

"Just answer the following questions honestly. What's your favorite book?"

"The Power of One," Meg said, before she could stop herself.

"Favorite card game?"

Glad that Blake couldn't see her, Meg grinned reluctantly. "Solitaire."

"Point already proven I think, but here's my final question—what's your favorite movie? Excluding anything with Johnny Depp in it," he added hastily.

"Star Wars."

"Hmmm." Meg could tell that Blake was turning her answer over in his mind. "Favorite character in *Star Wars?*"

"Han Solo," said Meg resignedly.

"Thought so. Not only is his last name eminently apt, from memory he later spent quite a bit of time trapped in cryogen."

Meg sighed. Why did it always have to end like this? "Goodbye, Blake," she said, a note of finality in her voice. "I honestly wish you well, and I hope you find the sort of person that you're looking for."

She pressed the button to end the call just as the smoke alarm in the kitchen went off. Racing towards the stove, she pulled out the smoking remains of her salmon. *Damn men,* she thought irritably, as she set about scraping off the burnt bits and trying to salvage her dinner. There were times when she would gladly have fed them all to Jabba the Hutt.

Chewing the nail on her pinky finger from nervousness, Lucy swallowed hard as she held the telephone to her ear and listened to it ring.

When it switched to voice mail she couldn't help heaving a sigh of relief.

"Taylor?" she started hesitantly, hating what she was about to say. "This is Lucy. I, er, um, hope you're well." Taking a deep breath, she launched in. "Look, I'm sorry to do this over the phone, but I know how busy you are getting ready for your trip, and well, you're great but I was kind of with someone else last night so I don't really think we should see each other anymore." She thought for a moment and then added, "Unless of course you don't mind that I was with someone else, but if you don't mind then I'm not sure that that's really a good basis for a relationship either. And, well, I'm sorry again and please call me if you want to because I feel terrible about this, but we never said we were seeing each other exclusively but I sort of assumed that we were and I think you probably did too because of how jealous I got over you liking the girl in the Victoria's Secret commercial." Realizing that she had wandered very far from the original intention of her call, Lucy hastily wound it up. "Anyway, I'm very sorry again, and I just know that you'll find someone lovely who deserves you and I hope that you find lots of dinosaur bones when you go to Libya. Oh—that reminds me. I heard a joke the other day about a cross-dressing dinosaur called Trannysaurus but I can't really remember how it goes. But you've probably heard it anyway. Okay then, bye."

Practically sweating, Lucy hung up the phone and tried to quell the knowledge that her overriding emotion was one of relief. One day, she knew, her prince would come. And in the meantime, she supposed with a sigh, there was always Tom.

5.

single white female

While Lucy's romantic life was conforming to an established pattern (break up with new boyfriend and fall back on Tom), her approach to solving her housing dilemma continued to fluctuate wildly. She had abandoned the idea of renting an apartment on her own, due to it being too expensive. Deciding to stay on in the apartment that she was currently in, she had begun a new mission to find a replacement roommate. Seemingly resigned to the idea, she had told Tom of her intention to place an advertisement in the newspaper, and that had been the last that he had heard until a somewhat incoherent telephone call early on Wednesday morning. Walking into the beer garden of the Windsor Castle, where they had arranged to meet that night, he spotted Lucy immediately.

It wasn't hard. She was sitting opposite Chloe, with tears rolling down her face. Her cell phone lay untouched on the large wooden table in front of her, its shrill ring growing increasingly louder as it practically jumped in a demand to be answered.

The ring was so irritatingly loud that, as he slid onto the bench beside Lucy, Tom's first instinct was to answer the phone, if only to shut it up.

Like a claw, Lucy's hand shot out and grabbed his wrist. "*Don't!*" she gasped hoarsely, her face twisted into a mask of terror.

Tom and Chloe both eyed her with considerable alarm. Thankfully, the phone finally switched to her message bank and lay silent. Tom shot Chloe a look that said, "Do you know what this is about?" and Chloe simply shrugged and shook her head in response and handed Lucy another tissue.

A waiter appeared, and with no hesitation Tom ordered a pot of chamomile tea and a triple gin and tonic. The waiter looked a bit surprised by this combination, but then, catching sight of Lucy, who was wearing an expression that was a combination of Early Christian martyr and Jack Nicholson in *The Shining,* he nodded understandingly and was soon to be seen pouring a very generous measure of gin into an extremely small glass.

Heroically sacrificing his shirt, Tom put an arm around Lucy, who continued to weep as she surreptitiously wiped her running nose on his shoulder. As her sobs started to abate, Chloe opened her mouth to ask Lucy what was wrong, but Tom shook his head to forestall her and mouthed the words, "Wait for the gin."

When her drink arrived, Lucy gulped it down in about three seconds and promptly ordered another.

"Attagirl, Luce," Tom said encouragingly. "There's never been a broken heart that alcohol hasn't been able to mend."

Lucy was blowing her nose so loudly that she didn't register what Tom was saying. Comprehension suddenly dawned on Chloe's face, and, eager to help, she said, "I never really liked Taylor, you know, Luce. And I don't think he was right for you in the long term. Far too serious." She thought some more and then added, "And dusty."

Tom nodded encouragingly at Chloe for these words of wisdom and comfort but Lucy, who had finished blowing her nose, lifted her head and eyed Chloe evilly.

"You never liked Taylor?"

"Couldn't bear him," Chloe admitted happily. "Gave me a headache with his boring conversations about archaeological digs in Syria and the Mesozoic era. Best thing you could have done, breaking up with him."

"I haven't broken up with Taylor," Lucy said icily. "Yet," she added conscientiously, "I did leave a message on his cell but I don't think you can say a relationship is over until the hate mail arrives."

"Oh." Chloe shifted uneasily in her seat and appealed to Tom for help, but Tom, extremely uncharitably, refused to catch her eye and continued to pat and soothe Lucy instead.

"Well, what are you crying about then?" Chloe asked in exasperation.

At this point the cell phone suddenly beeped, indicating that someone had left a very long and detailed message. Lucy jumped, visibly shuddered, and clung tighter to Tom for support.

"It's the ad . . . ," Lucy wailed, tears starting to trickle down her face again.

"What ad?"

"The ad that I put in the paper to find a new roommate. My phone hasn't stopped ringing for days now. And it started again at six thirty this morning."

"Well, that's a good thing. You'll find someone in no time."

"You don't understand!" Lucy said in exhausted frustration. "They're all psychopaths. And they all have my telephone number and know where I live. I haven't slept for three days."

"They can't all be that bad," said Tom, who was long used to Lucy's tendency to overdramatize everything.

"They're worse than bad," Lucy said tragically. "I put in what I thought was a simple and straightforward ad asking for a male or female, nonsmoking, professional roommate. What I've *seen* is a parade of chain-smoking itinerant workers. Nonsmoker does *not* mean that you smoke six packs a day but promise not to do it inside the house when I'm at home."

"They can't *all* be smokers."

"If it was just that I could almost cope. But that's not it!" Lucy's voice started to rise hysterically. "You don't understand! The only people who answer share accommodation ads are either students, financially insecure, or emotionally damaged. I've met a whole new demographic who are from broken relationships, in witness protection schemes, or are just generally highly strung psycho stalkers who have their eyes screwed in too tightly. And one man was wearing chain mail. I know I live in St. Kilda but there is such a thing as limits. I can't take it anymore."

Tom thought it prudent to intervene at this point as some small children, dining with their parents at a nearby table, had started to cry.

"Er . . . Luce?"

"What?"

"*You're* sounding psycho. *I* wouldn't move in with *you*."

At this inauspicious moment Lucy's cell phone started to ring once more, and Lucy promptly collapsed into wails again. To the immense relief of Chloe and Tom, Meg entered the beer garden and, without greeting anyone, peremptorily demanded, "Lucy, why aren't you answering your phone?"

"Don't want to," she said dismally, unable to relive the horror through another long explanation.

Meg looked enquiringly at Chloe, who shook her head and mouthed, "Wait for the gin." Thankfully the waiter arrived with Lucy's second gin and her pot of chamomile tea and asked whether they wanted anything to eat.

"Nothing for me," said Tom. "And Lucy is on a strict liquid diet."

"I had a big lunch, so I think I'll just have the chicken salad and a glass of the house red," said Chloe. "Meg?"

Meg shook her head, and the waiter departed. "I'm only here briefly.

I'm meeting Blake in half an hour to return some of his things, so I'll have dinner then."

"I bet you Blake will order stew," said Tom, with the air of one who had given Blake's diet careful consideration.

"What's that supposed to mean?"

"He just looks like the sort of guy who would eat lots of stew. Or gravy. Or just brown things in general."

This comment did nothing to endear Tom to Meg, who said sweetly, "You really have to stop being jealous of Blake, Tom."

"I'm not jealous of *Blake*," Tom said, revolted.

"Yes you are," said Meg and Chloe in unison, and even Lucy lifted her head briefly from Tom's shoulder to nod her agreement.

"Why would I be jealous of Blake?"

"He's better-looking," Meg said smugly.

"And he has more money," Chloe added, far too quickly for Tom's liking.

"He's more emotionally developed," Lucy contributed from the depths of Tom's shoulder where she had drooped once more.

"And—"

"You're a bunch of shallow harpies," Tom interrupted resentfully. "Is that all that you judge us poor men by? Our looks, finances, and character?"

"What else is there?"

"What about our hobbies and interests?"

"Porn collections don't count," Meg said dryly. And before Tom could say anything Lucy quickly interjected in a muffled tone, "Not even if they include a vintage reel of *Swinging in the Rain*."

"You're a philistine, Luce. Just because it's not in a gallery doesn't mean that it's not art." Tom was about to pursue this point when Lucy's phone beeped again, indicating that another message had been left, and the sound caused Lucy to once again collapse into tears.

"What's wrong with her?" Meg asked, eyeing Lucy uneasily. Meg hated public displays of emotion.

"The ad that Luce put in the paper for a roommate has apparently brought out the lunatic fringe," Tom explained, resignedly sacrificing his shoulder and shirt once more.

Chloe picked up Lucy's phone and checked the display. "Lucy, you have five new messages. Oh—thank you," she said as the waiter placed her order in front of her. "You should listen to them. Maybe someone really nice has left a message."

Tom buried Lucy's head more firmly in his shoulder so that Chloe couldn't hear the smothered cry of "Ki-ill her . . ."

"Give me the phone," Meg said authoritatively. "I'll listen to the messages. They can't all be that bad."

"Who is it?" Chloe enquired with fascination as Meg listened intently to the first message.

"Someone called Gilda. She sounds sort of norm—oh." Meg's eyes widened.

"What's she saying?" asked Chloe, taking a bite of her chicken salad and trying to crane in closer to Meg to listen.

"She wants to know if Lucy would have any objections to her astral projection group using the living room once a week. She says that they only *look* dead for half an hour or so."

"Well, at least she's asking first. That's quite considerate really," said Chloe optimistically.

Without lifting her head from Tom's shoulder, Lucy started groping sightlessly for a knife. Tom hastily removed all sharp implements from reach and ordered another gin, this time minus the tonic. When her drink arrived Lucy revived sufficiently to lift her head from Tom's soaked shoulder. Downing the gin, she glared at Chloe and then eyed Meg, who was still listening to the messages. "Which one are you up to now?" she enquired morbidly.

"Damien. Calm down, Lucy," Meg soothed as Lucy started visibly. "I just want to hear all of it and then I'll erase it. I haven't had this much entertainment since I sent that company into receivership."

"What's wrong with Damien?" asked Tom.

Lucy snorted. "He's called Damien Thorn. As in Damien from *The Omen*. The man's bound to be devil spawn."

"You can't judge someone by their name," Chloe objected. "He could be a welfare worker for all you know."

"What did Damien have to say?" Tom asked.

"He said that he's been meaning to give up smoking for months now and this is the perfect opportunity. He's just come out of a long-term relationship, but since the restraining order has come into effect things are much better. He doesn't actually specify whether he's the restrainer or the restrainee."

Tom whistled thoughtfully. "I can see your problem, Luce. This is getting quite hard to choose. But I think I'm going to have to stick with Gilda. She sounds more social even if when she does get together with her friends they prefer to lie around unconscious. What about you, Meg?"

"I'm putting my money on Damien. He appears to have a practical understanding of the legal system, so we have something in common."

"You're a pack of ghouls, and if there's any justice in the world you'll all die from the bubonic plague," Lucy said acidly. "But Damien's an amateur. Wait until you reach Marlon."

"What's wrong with Marlon?" asked Tom.

"He's a chicken sexer," Lucy said morosely as Chloe promptly spat out her mouthful of salad. "And a stalker," she added with grim satisfaction. "He's called me an average of three times a day since the ad went in."

"What does he call you about?"

"The first time was to tell me that he really liked the sound of the apartment. The second time was to tell me that he really liked the sound of my voice on my voice mail. The third time was to tell me that he really, really liked the apartment *and* me. After that it got more specific. On the plus side, he'd bring his own iron. He likes to iron socks."

"You need a screening process," Meg said sensibly. "You need to develop a set of questions that will make sure you know the sort of person that you're getting."

"The sort of questions that I want to ask, that I *ought* to ask, aren't allowed," Lucy said glumly.

"Like what?" asked Tom, who had disposed of Chloe's offending salad.

"Like—Do you have a drug addiction? Or—Do you have a criminal record? That'd do for starters."

"Why can't you ask those questions?"

"Because you just *can't*. It wouldn't be polite."

"So you'd rather live with a drug dealer than offend a stranger?"

"You don't understand, Meg! If you're considering living with someone, your first conversation with them can't be all about how you don't trust them and are thinking the worst about them. That would make me look like some sort of clean-living, judgmental, suspicious right-winger, and if they were normal then *they* probably wouldn't want to live with *me*."

"What else would you ask them if you could?"

"The possibilities are endless," Lucy said, swallowing another mouthful of tea. "Let's see—well, it would be good if you could ask them whether they're religious and if their faith involves the words *Armageddon* and *spaceship*."

"How about—Are you for or against capital punishment for people who listen to boy bands?" Chloe suggested, getting into the spirit of things.

"Don't even get me started on that," Lucy groaned. "Even if by some miracle I do find someone to share the apartment who is vaguely normal and practices a decent level of hygiene, they'll probably have a huge collection of gangsta rap or want to put up a Pamela Anderson poster in the living room. And I won't be able to do a damn thing about it," she ended bitterly.

"It is kind of ludicrous that you meet someone for fifteen minutes and end up sharing your life with them." For Meg, who was intensely private, the whole concept was abhorrent.

Lucy agreed with a wholesale shudder. "And the initial conversation is completely contrived anyway. You're both saying one thing and meaning another."

"Like what?"

"Like—Do you have hobbies? With the subtext being—Does it involve dismembering equipment? And what it *really* means is—Will you always be home? Or—Do you have a partner? i.e., Is it human? Will they always be here? Will *you* always be here?"

"Well what are you going to do?"

"Dunno," Lucy said dully. "Move to a trailer park with Marlon. Kill myself. Become a chicken sexer. The world is my oyster."

"That's my girl," Tom said encouragingly, finally managing to get her to hold her head up without the support of his shoulder. "Look, if they really are all that hopeless why don't you go back to your original idea and try to find an apartment of your own to rent?"

"That's a great idea, Luce," said Chloe encouragingly. "Besides which, you know that the offer to stay with me is still open if you don't find something straightaway. Tell you what, we'll even come with you to help look."

Meg and Tom both started. "Eh? What?"

"Really?" Lucy said, wiping her tear-stained face, the first glimmer of hope shining through her misery.

"Really," said Chloe firmly, glaring Tom and Meg into obedience.

"And I won't have to live with Marlon?" Lucy asked pathetically.

"Not unless things get really desperate and he has a fridge," said Tom. "Or a cute sister."

"I wouldn't mess with Marlon's sister if I were you," said Lucy sinisterly. "He's a chicken sexer remember. He could probably castrate you."

Tom winced. "One word of advice, Luce. Don't ever, *ever*, EVER mention the c word in front of a male. As it is I'm going to have to sit with my legs crossed for the next forty-five minutes."

"There was a time when I thought that Marlon's biggest drawback was that he would leave substantial back hair in the bath," Lucy said darkly, as her phone began to ring again. "How naïve I was."

6.

the doorbell principle

The following Saturday morning Lucy opened the door to her flat to see a deputation consisting of Chloe, Meg, and Tom on her doorstep.

With a squeal of delight Lucy pounced on them one by one and planted resounding kisses on their cheeks. "You're all my heroes."

"Get off," Tom said, pushing her away and trying not to look pleased.

"We're all ready to help you apartment-hunt," said Chloe cheerily. "We're going to provide objective opinions and see if these places really are as hopeless as you say they are."

"If you are even *thinking* about saying 'It's amazing what a coat of paint can do' I swear I'll throw something with sharp edges at you, Chloe," Lucy said warningly, before adding in a completely changed tone, "But thank you for coming. It will be much more fun with all of us."

"Can't wait," said Meg dryly.

Lucy grinned at her and then offered them all coffee, which they declined.

"Let's get this over with," Tom said impatiently. "Have you looked in the paper yet?"

"Yep. There are about ten that sound good, but naturally five of them are all open for inspection within the same fifteen-minute time span. So that leaves six to look at, providing that I don't get depressed and start crying and give up after the third one."

"Stop being so pessimistic," Meg said bracingly. "They can't all be that bad."

"They really are all terrible," Meg said in awe. It was three hours later and they had stopped for lunch.

"Sshhh. Lucy's coming back from the bathroom. We have to sound positive to keep her spirits up," Chloe whispered.

"Positive?" Tom hissed back. "Chloe, the last place had holes in the wall. And there were *teeth* marks around the edges. I don't even want to think about what sort of rodent would chew holes that size in plaster."

Chloe hushed him and turned to smile at Lucy, who was wearing an expression of noble suffering.

Lucy summoned up an unsteady smile and then announced in a faint voice that she was ready to go home.

"Why are you talking like that?" asked Meg with a frown.

"Like what?" Lucy asked tremulously.

"Like you're in the final stages of consumption," Meg said impatiently. "Look, Lucy, you have to stop being so emotional about something that is just a practical decision. You need to find somewhere to live and that's all a house is. It's a shelter."

"It's not," Lucy said, her bottom lip starting to quiver. "It's going to be my *home*, and I want to fill it with candles and aromatherapy oils and my paintings and books and I want to be *happy*. And I *can't* be happy living in a building that looks like an Eastern bloc housing commission."

"You never even went inside to see the actual apartment," reproved Meg. "It could have been quite nice inside."

Lucy looked at her in disbelief. "What's that got to do with it? It would kill my soul to come home to that every night."

"You wouldn't even see it in the dark! And how much time are you planning to spend looking at the outside of your apartment anyway?" Meg argued practically. "I'd be more worried about the view from inside if I was you."

"She has no aesthetic sensibility whatsoever," Lucy complained to Tom and Chloe.

"Of course she hasn't," Tom said soothingly. "She's a corporate lawyer. She sold her soul years ago." Ignoring Meg's glare he continued, "But don't go home yet, Ginger. Let's at least finish off the ones on your list."

"Come on, Lucy—just one more. Just think—it might be the one," Chloe said encouragingly.

Lucy allowed herself to be dragged up and unwillingly she set off in the direction of Shelley Street. With a cynicism born from grim experience, Lucy started to look for the towering block of eight hundred apartments constructed from granite with a view of the sewage processing plant. Shelley Street was only a short road however, and all of the buildings appeared to be of normal size and reasonable aspect. Refusing to get her hopes up, Lucy let Tom and Chloe run ahead to find number forty-three.

Number forty-three turned out to be a small block of about eight apartments, painted cream and with a high fence. They pushed the gate open and a well-tended garden with a small fishpond greeted them.

"It's lovely, Lucy," Chloe said enthusiastically.

They entered the building and set off in search of Apartment Four, the sound of piano music following them up a flight of stairs. Meg located the right key to the front door. With bated breath they pushed it open, but unfortunately the first thing that Lucy saw was The Curtains.

"What's it like . . . oh my God," Tom's voice faltered as he erupted cheerfully into the room and was confronted by the horrible sight.

Everyone stared at The Curtains in horrorstruck awe. They were simply, magnificently, awful. Bright shapes and patterns swirled before their dazed eyes; Chloe noted several tassels, Meg tried to avoid the orange braiding while Tom and Lucy clutched at each other for support before the onslaught of color. The curtains were at least a half a yard too long for the windows, and the excess material had spread out on the floor like a malevolent pool of toxic waste.

"Where on earth do you think they bought them?" Chloe whispered, as though she were in the presence of a great evil.

"They weren't made by human hands. They were forged. In Hell," Meg responded, unable to draw her gaze away.

"By fallen elves who were exiled from Santa's workshop for putting penises on Ken dolls," Tom contributed in a voice of doom, entering into the spirit of the narrative. As they all glared at him he was heard to mutter, "We need another male in this friendship group."

"I can't believe that you used the word *penis* in the same sentence as Santa," said Chloe disapprovingly. "That's just sick."

"What—do you think Santa doesn't have one?" Meg responded. "He must. Mrs. Claus always looks quite jolly to me."

Chloe clapped her hands over her ears and started to shriek.

It was too much. Feeling exhausted and strangely light-headed, Lucy sank to the floor and burst into tears.

"Well, they are horrible but I can't see that they're worth crying about," Meg said, still eyeing The Curtains with morbid fascination. "You haven't even looked at the rest of the place, Luce—it could be quite nice you know."

Lucy lifted her head. "You wouldn't understand, Meg," she said brokenly. "You own your house. It's not the curtains that are making me cry, it's their ideology."

"Can curtains have an ideology?" Tom inquired. "I can see how they would have a view of course."

"*Must* you be clever, Tom?" Chloe asked tragically.

"Sorry, Clo. What's your point, Luce?"

"The point," Lucy said, starting to sob again, "is that these curtains were put in this rental property for one reason and one reason only—to remind me that as a renter I have an insignificant place in the world and am not allowed to protest about things like toilets in the kitchen or parrot-patterned wallpaper or an unidentifiable smell in the hall closet. As a renter I should not aspire to beauty or harmony in my home but should just be grateful if I can find somewhere to live in my price range that doesn't involve saying *hi* to Mom and Dad when I come home every night."

At that moment they heard someone behind them, and with the exception of Lucy, who had prostrated herself once more, they all turned in surprise to look at the person who had just entered the flat through the door that had been left open. A tall, fair young man who looked like a surprised schoolboy with naturally rosy cheeks, that were even redder now from being stared at by strangers, smiled bashfully and then looked at his shoes. "Dreadfully sorry to interrupt," he said, and his accent was pure Oxford rowing crew. "But I heard someone screaming and then I heard crying so I thought you might need some help?"

Chloe smiled at him. "Hello. Sorry about the noise. I was scream-ing, and then Lucy started to cry. And that's very kind of you to offer to help, but I think Lucy will be okay in a minute. This is Lucy by the way," she said, indicating the still weeping pile crumpled on the floor. "She might be your new neighbor."

Without lifting her head, Lucy waved feebly, and the newcomer smiled hesitantly and tried not to look too horrified by the thought of living next door to a clearly emotionally unstable woman who kept company with someone who apparently screamed for no reason. "I'm Chloe," she continued. She really was a very well-brought-up girl. "And this is Tom, and that's Meg."

The neighbor stepped gingerly over Lucy to shake hands with Tom and introduced himself as Perceval Hamilton-Bythorne. Turning to Meg he lifted his eyes shyly to her critical scrutiny and to everyone's amazement an absolute tidal wave of scarlet swept across his face.

"Are you okay?" Meg asked, somehow managing to keep any tone of gentle consideration out of this enquiry regarding Perceval's welfare.

"Fine, fine," he stuttered, looking at the light fitting.

"Well you look very flushed. Why on earth are you grinning at me like that, Tom?"

"No reason," Tom said, craning his head and also inspecting the light fitting in order to escape Meg's glare.

Perceval tried to regain his composure, failed miserably and now addressing himself to the wall behind Meg, he stuck out his hand and repeated his name.

"Pleased to meet you," Meg answered, trying to shuffle into his line of view. Perceval kept moving to avoid her gaze but didn't let go of her hand so that they ended up doing a rather charming little dance down the length of the room. "I'm Meg. Are you a number?"

"I beg your pardon?"

"You just seem as though you should be a number. Perceval Hamilton-Thorn the Third or something."

"Hamilton-Bythorne. And no, I'm not a number because it's not a family name. 'Perceval' was a whim of Mother's. After the Scarlet Pimpernel you know."

Meg went off into an unholy peal of laughter. When she recovered, she wiped her streaming eyes and choked, "Are you honestly trying to tell me that you're named after possibly the lamest hero in English literature?"

"Don't be rude, Meg," remonstrated Chloe. "Anyway, I loved the Scarlet Pimpernel books."

"I'm sorry but I *have* to ask—do you have a teddy bear by any chance?"

Rather than being put off by Meg, Perceval seemed to be strangely enchanted. "I did—" he began eagerly, but got no further because Meg had collapsed into hysteria again.

Without ceremony, Tom stalked up to Meg and, standing in front of her so that nobody else could see what he was doing, he smacked her lightly over the head. "Stop being so rude," he hissed. "We're used to you but he's not."

"Sorry, sorry," gasped Meg. "He's just so—so *Brideshead Revisited*. Has Lucy fallen in love with him yet?"

Tom glanced around to where Lucy was still curled up and whimpering on the floor. "Doesn't look like it," he said cautiously.

Not quite sure as to what was happening, Perceval smiled shyly in the direction of Meg's right foot and then looked swiftly away again.

Chloe, who had wandered off to inspect the rest of the apartment, now came back in and announced, "You know, Luce, it's really quite a nice place."

"They are nice apartments, aren't they?" said Percy eagerly. "They all have roughly the same layout you know. I say, would you like to come and have a cup of tea in mine? It might make you feel better."

"Yes, please," sniffed Lucy, who was feeling uncharacteristically woebegone and in need of comfort.

Locking the door behind them, they filed downstairs into Perceval's apartment, which was bright and spacious and simply lovely. The main room had enormous floor-to-ceiling French doors, which flooded the flat with sunshine, and the room itself was dominated by a baby grand piano.

Seeing their curious stares he blushed again and stammered, "I'm a pianist. Obviously. They put those doors in for me just to get the piano in here. You don't mind music, do you?" he finished anxiously, looking at Lucy.

"Of course not. That would be lovely actually. What sort of music do you play?"

"All sorts, but right now I'm teaching and playing with an orchestra, so primarily classical." And then, as though he felt that he was unfairly dominating the conversation, he turned to Meg and asked her left knee, "What do *you* do, Meg?"

"I'm a corporate lawyer," she said, with the bored manner she always used to deter would-be suitors. "I destroy the rights of the working class and maximize profits for ethically unsound global corporations."

"Oh. Right." Perceval collapsed into embarrassed silence again and instead bustled around the kitchen. When he came out proudly bearing a tray with a teapot, five matching cups and saucers and a milk jug and sugar bowl, Lucy and Chloe sighed while Tom and Meg eyed him in disbelief.

"How long have you been in Australia, Perce?" asked Tom.

Perceval winced slightly at the use of "Perce" but answered, "Six months." He added with a rueful grin, "I take that to mean that I haven't lost my terribly English accent yet?"

"You sound very Aussie," said Chloe encouragingly. "Except when you say things like 'terribly English,'" she added conscientiously.

"Did you have Horror Curtains when you first moved in too?" asked Tom, jerking one thumb over his shoulder to indicate Percy's mercifully curtain-free windows.

"Eh? What? No, I didn't get curtains," he shook his head regretfully. "I've had to make do with wooden shutters."

They all looked at him to see if he was joking. He didn't appear to be.

"You can't possibly *like* the curtains in that apartment?" said Tom incredulously.

"Well they're a bit bright and vulgar, but they're sort of cheery."

"Do you mean you don't think they were *specifically* put there to crush my spirit and remind me of my lowly place in the universe?" asked Lucy, setting her teacup down and clasping her hands tremulously.

Perceval looked at the others for support, but they all seemed to think that this was a reasonable question.

"Er, not really, no."

"So it's possible that some people just have terrible taste?" Lucy said breathlessly. "That it's not a cruel game of torture masterminded by landlords and real estate agents to inflict psychological damage on low-income renters in order to maintain the status quo and ensure that we never rise above the caste into which we were born, thereby maintaining the demand for rental housing and reinforcing an unfair social structure?"

There was a brief silence and then Perceval hazarded a guess. "Yes. Absolutely," he said firmly, wondering what he was agreeing to.

Lucy's face lit up with a smile, and she turned to Tom. "Give me the keys. I'm going to look at the apartment again."

"Good girl, Luce. I'll come with you."

Although the apartment turned out to be unsuitable (in addition to The Curtains there was no laundry, bloodstained carpet in the bedroom, and a bidet but no toilet), the trip to Shelley Street wasn't a complete loss. With her usual kindheartedness, Chloe decided to adopt Percy as soon as she discovered that he knew very few people in Australia. This suited Percy perfectly, as, for reasons that no one was ever able to fathom, he had fallen for Meg at that very first meeting, despite the fact that she had been so rude to him. Nothing that she or anyone else could say or do budged him from his stubborn devotion to her. Tom tried to ask Percy about it once, but all he would say is that no girl had ever shown as much interest in him as Meg had displayed at that first meeting, when she asked him about his name and his teddy.

7.

donald/bertie and hammie

Despite the setback of the horror curtains, Lucy's attitude towards solving her rapidly approaching housing crisis had become far more optimistic. Deciding to temporarily shelve the idea of finding something affordable and suitable to rent, she rang Chloe midmorning on Tuesday, hoping that her offer of accommodation was still available.

"Of course you can stay with me for a bit," Chloe said distractedly. "I've never met the owners, but they're friends of my parents and Mom e-mailed them to check that it was okay. They're overseas with their kids for another couple of months—so it's not a problem at all."

"Are you sure, Clo?" asked Lucy anxiously. "It's just—you don't sound too happy about it."

"What's that? No, don't be silly—it's absolutely fine. You've just caught me at a bad moment."

Lucy could hear the noise of several voices in the background and the sound of change clattering into a register drawer.

"Chloe, where exactly are you? And why are you sounding so stressed?"

There was further noise in the background and then the very clear sound of Chloe cursing. "What? Sorry, Luce. I'm in a café and I just spilled coffee on myself. I'm going to have to hang up. I can't juggle the cell and the coffees and my briefcase and the files all at once."

"But Clo—what are you doing getting the coffees? What's happened to your intern?"

There was a small silence. "She's very busy, so I thought I'd get them for a change. It shouldn't be a hierarchy thing anyway," Chloe rushed.

"Clo?"

"Mmm."

"You still can't make her do anything, can you?"

"Not really, no."

"Have you even asked her?"

"I *can't*," Chloe wailed. "She's so *cool*, Luce. I want her to like me."

"She's twenty-one, Clo. Even we were cool at twenty-one."

"No way we were as spankfest as Ariel."

"As *what*?"

"Spankfest," Chloe repeated, a trifle defensively. "Ariel said it means *cool.*"

"I hate to tell you this, Clo, but *spankfest* does not mean *cool*. It's a made-up word."

"It is not." Chloe sounded positively tearful. "She wouldn't *tease* me. She lent me her Drones CD."

"*Spankfest*. Did you lend her *The Best of George Michael?*"

"Shut up, Lucy. Look, I have to hang up. They've run out of blueberry muffins so I have to go across the road."

"But you hate blue—oh good grief. It's for Ariel, isn't it?"

"Sorry, Luce, can't hear properly," Chloe said unconvincingly. "Come over tonight at sevenish and you can check the room out."

"Okay. Oh damn, I can't. I'm going to the movies tonight with Tom."

"Well, bring him along. It will only take you ten minutes to look at the room and then we can all go to the movies afterwards. I'll invite Percy too. That is, of course, assuming that Percy and I won't be cramping yours and Tom's style?"

"Tom and I are *friends*," Lucy said sternly.

"Yeah, yeah. I've heard it all before. Hey, if everyone is going we should invite Meg too."

"No point. I spoke to her this morning and she has to work tonight."

"Do you think she's okay after breaking up with Blake?"

"Seems to be. But you know Meg—she's not exactly the sort to wear her heart on her sleeve."

"No, she's not," Chloe agreed fervently. "Meg's such a control freak that sometimes I think she's had her heart surgically implanted in a cavity deep within her."

"Clo?" Lucy began cautiously. "Meg wouldn't need surgery for that because her heart is kind of already inside her chest cavity."

"Oh you know what I mean. I just meant the opposite of wearing it on her sleeve. Consider it sewn into the gusset of her pantyhose if you'd rather."

"I'd really rather not."

"Okay, whatever. Luce, I *really* have to go now. See you at seven?"

Lucy agreed but couldn't help wincing as she hung up to the sound of something that sounded very much like Chloe's phone clattering to the floor.

"This place is great," Lucy said, as the four of them wandered through the three-bedroom apartment in St. Kilda that evening. The view from the living room windows overlooked the foreshore, and in the soft dusk of twilight, tethered boats in the marina gleamed while lights had just started to appear in the windows of the distant city skyline.

Chloe was looking slightly less harassed than she had sounded on the phone that morning, and as she had deliberately avoided the topic of Ariel, Lucy had wisely decided not to bring it up.

"I know—isn't it fantastic? And I hardly have to do a thing. I just have to remember to feed Bertie."

"Who's Bertie?" asked Percy.

"The goldfish. Come and meet him."

They wandered over to where a glass bowl filled with water was sitting, perched rather precariously on a bookshelf.

"Chloe?" Tom asked hesitantly.

"Mmmmm," Chloe answered, fondly tapping the side of the bowl and making little goldfish-encouraging noises.

"The name on the bowl says *Donald*."

"Yes, I know. That's *their* name for him. But it doesn't suit him at all. He's clearly a Bertie."

"Fair enough." Tom tapped the side of the bowl to see what Donald/Bertie would do and was rewarded by seeing him go around in another circle. They watched him some more. To Lucy, Tom, and Percy it looked like he kept going around in circles, whether they tapped or not, but Chloe was convinced that he did something special with his tail whenever she tapped.

"Why do people have fish?" Lucy wondered aloud after about five minutes of this.

"They're restful," said Chloe. "You can watch them for hours."

"Well, I could watch my own feet for hours but that doesn't make them interesting. I think they're the preferred choice of pet for lazy people."

"I'm just glad to have a pet," said Chloe wistfully. "I always wanted one more than anything in the world, but I was never allowed to have one."

"Me either," said Percy eagerly. "Although I did have some pet ham once."

"I beg your pardon?"

"I wanted a pig, but my mother wouldn't let me have one, so I kept some ham in a shoebox on my dresser instead." As they all continued to stare at him, he added defensively, "I was only seven."

"You know, it's quite amazing that you haven't turned into a serial killer, Percy," Lucy said admiringly. "I really think that anyone else with your background would have taken up dismembering by now. It shows tremendous strength of character."

Percy flushed with pleasure. "Thanks awfully, Luce."

"Did your ham have a name?" Chloe asked sympathetically. Tom turned to the wall and pretended to start beating his head against it, but they all ignored him.

"Not really," said Percy, with a faraway look in his eyes. "I just called him Hammie."

"What happened to Hammie?" asked Chloe, her tender heart moved by this story of childhood deprivation.

Percy snapped back to the present. "I ate him," he admitted guiltily.

Lucy and Chloe stared at him in horror while Tom collapsed into laughter.

"You *ate* Hammie?" Lucy asked, aghast.

"I was very hungry," Percy said defensively. "I'd been sent to bed without dinner. I forget what I had done, but I must have been very naughty to have been punished like that."

"You probably tried to chop up one of the chambermaids," Tom suggested, adding knowledgeably, "That's one of the first indications of disturbed behavior. First you're attacking the hired help, and next thing you're eating your pets. In the final stages you'll wear a wig and start calling yourself Little Lola, but then again, as a peer of the realm, in all likelihood no one will comment on it."

Chloe, who had edged away from Percy and was still eyeing him askance, turned to Lucy.

"Do you want to have a look at the bedrooms? I'm sleeping in the parents' bedroom, but the boys' rooms are spare."

Leading the way down the hall, Chloe pushed open a door, and Lucy peeked into the tidy bedroom. A crate of toys sat in one corner and the bed was adorned with a *Shrek* comforter.

Lucy stared doubtfully at the grinning face of the green ogre. "I'm not sure that I'd be able to sleep under that," she said, nodding towards the bed. "It might give me the heebie-jeebies."

"Come and see the other room then."

The second bedroom clearly belonged to the elder son. Instead of toys there was a football and a cricket bat in the corner and a poster of a muscular footballer was tacked to one wall. Casting a brief, approving glance at the poster, Lucy shifted her attention to the bed and let out a long, contented sigh. The *X-Men* comforter bore the image of Hugh Jackman, made up as Wolverine.

"I'll take this room," she said promptly.

"Do you think you'll be comfortable in that bed?"

"Trust me, Clo; with that comforter I'll be all tucked up in bed by eight o'clock every night."

"You need help," Tom muttered, poking his head over her shoulder and instantly apprising himself of the situation.

Chloe looked pleased. "So that's settled then? You're going to stay with me for a bit?"

Lucy flung her arms around Chloe. "Are you kidding? You're saving my life. I would have had to drown myself in Donald—sorry, Bertie's bowl if I didn't have anywhere to live by the end of next week. I promise it will only be for a little while, Clo."

"Don't worry—the owners are away for a couple of months yet. It'll be fun. I'll get some spare keys cut tomorrow. Do you want to move in this weekend?"

Lucy's face fell. "I'd love to, but I can't. It will take me at least a week to pack and sort everything. What about the following weekend?"

"Fine by me."

Lucy turned beseechingly to Tom. "Toooooom . . . ," she began.

Tom sighed. "Yes, we'll help you move in. Sorry, Perce, but you don't get a choice. If I have to spend the entire day explaining the mysteries of stereo cables to Lucy by myself then I'll probably end up drowning myself in Bertie's bowl."

As Percy nodded, Lucy clapped her hands with excitement. "That's settled then. Come on, let's go or we'll be late for the movie."

She led the way out of the room, followed by Chloe. Percy put out his hand to detain Tom for a moment.

"Is she always like this?" Percy asked, nodding his head toward Lucy's departing back.

"Like what?" Tom asked in surprise.

"So—emotional?"

"Was she being emotional? I hadn't noticed."

"She's always either jumping up and down with excitement or bursting into tears. Doesn't she get tired?" Percy asked, with genuine fascination, his classically English reserve the complete antithesis of Lucy's wild displays of fluctuating emotions.

Tom laughed. "Oh that's just Luce. You'll get used to her after awhile. And it can get exhausting, but I think more for other people than for her. Just don't ever let her drink red cordial."

"What happens when she drinks red cordial?" Percy asked fearfully.

Tom thought for a moment. "Try to imagine Lucy as a game show contestant."

Percy went pale.

"On speed," Tom added.

Percy shuddered.

"And the game show host is Hugh Jackman," Tom concluded darkly.

Looking completely horrified, Percy followed Tom out of the apartment, wondering, not for the first time, how Lucy ever made it past customs when she visited England.

romantic fiction

Cast adrift amidst an ocean of boxes on Friday night, Lucy was immensely relieved when she stumbled across something that gave her an excuse to abandon her somewhat haphazard attempts at packing and call Meg instead.

"What's the matter with you?" asked Meg, who could tell from her "Hello" that Lucy had a specific reason for telephoning.

"I'm packing up my house, and I just found the book that I bought Taylor for his birthday next week."

"Did you ever hear from him after you left that message?"

Lucy shook her head, quite forgetting that Meg couldn't see her. "No. It's kind of strange actually. I knew he'd be upset with me, but I always thought he'd call back. Anyway, the reason that I'm calling is that I need to ask a favor."

"Let me guess," Meg drawled. "You want my help returning Taylor's present?"

"Oh please, Meg," Lucy begged. "I can't find the receipt, and you know how much I hate returning things. Sales assistants always hate me, and they always bend over backwards to help you."

Meg sighed. "What did you buy him?"

"Vikram Seth's *A Suitable Boy*. I should have known we were doomed as soon as I bought it."

"Why? What's wrong with it?"

"The title is loaded with symbolism. And it's too big."

"What do you mean it's too big? I thought you said he was a reader."

"He is, but I wrapped it up weeks ago and it's just been sitting on the table *looking* at me ever since. I should have realized it was invoking fate in the first place. It's not just a Big Book—it's a Weighty Tome. We'd only just started going out, and I bought him a book reeking of commitment."

"Right. Of course." There was a silence during which Meg gave up all hope of making this a brief conversation. Instead she asked cautiously, "Um, Luce? How exactly does giving Taylor a heavy book translate to testing his commitment levels?"

"Well, firstly it was as though I was testing him to see whether he had the staying power to make it through something serious. And secondly, you always want to know what someone thinks of a present that you give them. So it was pretty presumptuous to assume that I was still going to be around in three and a half years when he finished reading it. *If* he finished reading it."

"Lucy, I really think you're overreacting a bit. It's just a book."

"This from the girl who once broke up with someone because he bought you a book that you didn't like."

Meg could tell by Lucy's tone that she was giving her a scathing look down the phone line. "If you're talking about Morris, he gave me *The Satanic Verses* and inscribed it with glued-on letters cut out of the newspaper."

"Look, it's all beside the point now that I've broken up with Taylor anyway. So will you come to the bookstore with me tomorrow?"

"No," Meg said flatly.

"Why not?"

"Because you're pathetic in bookstores. You fantasize that every male who walks in is a poet who is going to make you his Muse, and you spend your whole time reading the back covers of impressive novels with the front cover held up so that everyone will know that you're a serious reader."

"I am a serious reader," Lucy said sulkily.

"How's *Ulysses* going?"

"Shut up. I'll finish it one day." There was a silence, and then Lucy begged, "Please, will you come and return the book for me, Meg? I promise to behave."

"Do you promise not to talk loudly about how chick-lit is causing the downfall of feminism?"

"Promise."

"And you won't sniff loudly when you look at the Dan Brown stand?"

"I had a cold," Lucy protested.

"Liar. And you're not allowed to spend more than ten minutes in the cultural theory section. It's completely pretentious, and you never even finished the *Foucault for Fourth-Graders* primer that you bought about a year ago. And if I turn up and you're wearing some god-awful combination of striped stockings and a mohair cardigan and trying to look like Audrey Tatou in *Amélie* I swear that I'll buy the latest Jackie Collins and give it to you right then and there."

"You wouldn't," Lucy said, badly shaken.

"I damn well will. I'll read aloud from it if I have to. So do you still want me to come?"

"Yes," Lucy said meekly.

Meg sighed. "Oh fine. It's my Dad's birthday next week, so perhaps I could exchange your book for something for him. But Lucy, you do know that the odds of meeting the man of your dreams when you both reach for the last copy of *Madame Bovary* is pretty much out of the realm of nonexistent and into the domain of futile and sad?"

"Yes," Lucy said brightly. She could tell that Meg was still suspicious, but she didn't care. Anyway it wouldn't be *Madame Bovary*. It would be *Pride and Prejudice*, because that had a happy ending.

"What *are* you wearing?" Meg asked when she picked Lucy up the following day.

Lucy buckled her seatbelt and frowned at her. Which was less an expression of displeasure and more of a necessary reaction because she was wearing glasses, and as she didn't need to wear glasses she now had to squint in order to see properly.

"I need them. They're for reading."

"No they're not. You're trying to look intellectual. Lucy, you really should take a good hard look at yourself, my darling. You're dressing up as a librarian and hoping to meet someone at a bookstore. Please let me put an ad in the paper for you."

"Oh right. *I* need help," Lucy said, heaving the gift-wrapped copy of *A Suitable Boy* onto the floor of the passenger seat and becoming gloomily aware that its weight was causing the opposite side of Meg's car to lift up slightly. "I don't know what's worse—my inability to stay away from Tom or your inability to stay with anyone for more than a month." She tried to fix Meg with a critical look, but the lenses of her glasses were blurring her vision too much so she ended up looking sardonically at the gear shift instead, which didn't have quite the same devastating effect.

"Isn't it odd how we assume that people with glasses are intellectual instead of just lacking good vision?" Meg mused, as she swung expertly into the traffic.

"I don't know what it is about boys in glasses, but they just make me melt. They look so sensitive and intellectual."

"It's a residual Superman complex," Meg said authoritatively. "You imagine them turning into the man of your dreams when they take the glasses off. But I still think that it's illogical. It's not as though you attribute romantic qualities to someone with a hearing aid. Makes them a bit like a dog really—you can imagine them tuning into high-range frequencies beyond ordinary human hearing."

Lucy changed the subject hastily before Meg forever ruined her optical Clark Kent fantasies with an image of a howling Wolf-Man. "What are you going to tell the bookstore?"

"What do you mean?"

"Well, you want to exchange the book for no good reason. They won't let you, so you need to have a good story ready like you bought it for your terminally ill great-uncle but he passed away on his deathbed before he could unwrap it and now you can't bear to have it around as it reminds you of his final moments."

"Don't be ridiculous. I'm going to tell them that I bought it for a present and it's unsuitable."

"But you *can't*." Lucy sought words to explain to Meg the unwritten laws of conduct regarding retail exchanges and returns. Lying about your reason for returning something was not just common practice it was damn sure *expected*.

"Of course I can," Meg said comfortably, executing a hairbreadth lane change that landed them between a speeding semi-trailer and a bus. If it had been Lucy driving it would have been classified as reckless driving, but because it was Meg it was obviously a precision maneuver, so nobody honked or swore at her the way they would have done if Lucy had barged in like that. "I see no reason to lie when I'm—or in this case, you—are not at fault. It's a simple transaction, and it's sound customer service to keep me happy. I had to return some stockings the other day and they were quite reasonable about it."

"*You can't return stockings!*" Lucy said, completely aghast.

"Of course you can. I paid thirty dollars for the wretched things and they snagged as soon as I put them on."

"Yes, but that's what's meant to happen. You're not supposed to be able to do anything about it. Somewhere in the world there is a stocking magnate sitting in the throne room of his palace on his own private island, still chuckling with glee because he invented the only product in the world that is designed to fall apart as soon as you touch them and no one can do a damn thing about it and not only that, we just buy more when we rip them. It's totally evil and completely brilliant and you'll destroy the known world order if you start complaining about it."

Meg took her eyes off the road for a moment to look at Lucy curiously. "What do you do when you get a run in your stockings as soon as you put them on?"

"What every normal girl does. I swear a lot and then I race out and buy a three-dollar pair from the supermarket and spend the whole night feeling like an army of ants wearing little sandpaper shoes are parading up and down my legs and then I break out in a mysterious rash the following day."

The conversation would have continued, because Meg was clearly unable to grasp what Lucy was talking about, but they had reached the bookstore, which miraculously had a rock star parking space right outside. Meg parallel parked the car in one smooth move, somehow managing to avoid parking it completely straight but five feet away from the curb, which was Lucy's specialty. She clambered out of the car, and Meg watched in amusement as she tripped on her long, crocheted skirt and screwed her face into a scowl so that she could see the entrance. "Lucy, take those ridiculous glasses off. You can't see a thing and you're going to hurt yourself."

"I'm fine," she said, throwing her head back and looking at Meg defiantly.

"I'm over here, Lucy. You're looking about three feet to my left."

"I know that. I was admiring that potted plant."

"It's not a potted plant, it's someone's grandmother." She softened slightly and adopted a more conciliatory tone. "How about you take the glasses off now and slip them on if you see someone that you want to impress?"

Lucy allowed herself to be persuaded, because in truth the glasses were giving her a headache and if she had to keep screwing her face up to see properly, the only person that she was likely to attract would be an angry seventeen-year-old wearing a Che Guevara T-shirt.

As soon as they entered Lucy felt her spirits lift. It was one of those bookstore/coffeehouse/lounge/breeding ground for political dissension-type places that Melbourne specialized in. While Lucy headed straight for the cultural theory section, Meg strode up to the counter and told the assistant, who looked like Amélie, that she needed to exchange the book because, despite its title, it was unsuitable. Lucy honestly didn't know how Meg went through life being so forthright and honest. It would have driven her mad to be even half as direct as Meg. Clearly displeased, the sales assistant wrinkled her button nose and pouted delightfully, but intelligently realizing that arguing with someone who clearly had no conception of basic retail etiquette was bound to be futile, she wistfully told Meg to choose something else and then went back to staring dreamily out of the window at the antics of a playful butterfly with her dimpled chin propped on her little hand.

Picking up a copy of essays by Susan Sontag and seating herself on one of the leather couches placed between the shelves, Lucy held the book up high and stealthily looked around the store. A man wearing a beret brushed past her and excused himself, pausing for a moment to ascertain what she was reading. She positioned the book at a more advantageous angle, and Beret smiled at her. He had just opened his mouth to say something when Meg barged up and thudded down next to Lucy. Looking distinctly alarmed, Beret hastily turned to the shelf behind and busied himself with a copy of Post-Modernism for Pre-Schoolers.

"What is it with Indian authors and length anyway?" Meg asked irritably. "They've all got bloody Napoleonic complexes if you ask me. Not a single one of their books is under two hundred thousand words."

"The epic is an integral part of the Indian literary tradition," Lucy said loudly, as she sadly watched Beret move to the next set of shelves.

"Keep your voice down and stop trying to show off," Meg snapped. "He's gay."

"I can't believe you would stereotype a man as gay simply because he's in a bookstore."

"He's wearing a beret, Lucy."

"It's artistic."

"It's appalling."

"That still doesn't prove anything."

"He's wearing a Ricky Martin T-shirt."

"Damning, but inconclusive."

"I saw him snogging his boyfriend. It was disgusting."

"Because they were kissing?" asked Lucy, shocked that Meg was showing signs of latent homophobia.

"No, because they were kissing in front of a biography of the Queen Mother. She's both dead and grandmotherly. It just doesn't seem right to have a blatant display of sexual attraction in front of her."

Lucy thought it best to change the topic as Meg seemed decidedly cranky today.

"Did you find something for your Dad?"

"Nothing is right," she said moodily. "*On the Road* might give him a late midlife crisis and make him leave Mom to go and find himself. And I happen to know that *The English Patient* annoys him because he saw the movie and couldn't understand why Ralph Fiennes left her in the cave with cans of food but no can opener. And I can't buy him *The God of Small Things* because he refuses to eat or read anything that he can't pronounce."

"Which one syllable word in the title would he have a problem with specifically?"

Meg glared at her. "It's not the title—it's the author's name. It's the same reason that he wouldn't read *The Shipping News*. The x in Proulx just completely confused him. And don't even get him started on the initial *E* in her name. He can never remember where it's supposed to go."

"Well perhaps it would be good therapy for him if you bought him something challenging with difficult names in it. What about a science fiction book?"

Meg looked skeptical. "I don't know. I've never read any science fiction."

"Of course *you* haven't," Lucy said impatiently. "You're a girl. Girls don't read sci-fi."

"Why would a science fiction book be good therapy for Dad?" asked Meg.

"It's sort of like specialized boy's fiction," Lucy explained. "There are lots of parallel universes and the names of the characters are made up by hitting the keyboard with your fist so that they're all called things like Quarzog from Outer-Uterine."

"Why do they read it?" asked Meg curiously.

"For the same reason that girls read chick-lit. Escapism. And to feel superior. We end up feeling superior to men because of our greater emotional development, and men end up feeling superior to aliens because they don't have to fulfill exhausting destinies and can spell their own names . . ." Her voice trailed off as she spied a dashing male figure wearing a white shirt with the sleeves rolled up in a far corner. As she watched, he turned the page of the book that he was perusing and impatiently pushed a lock of stray hair off his forehead.

Meg glanced over at the science fiction section and looked doubtful as she watched a teenage boy select a book. The garish cover featured an intergalactic princess whose breasts were of cosmic proportions and who had clearly had to leave Earth to escape gravity as her nipples would otherwise now be situated somewhere between her toes.

"And the girls all wear rubber suits in those books," Lucy added, following Meg's gaze.

"It's probably very practical attire for parallel universes. Warm and resilient."

"Yes," Lucy said anxiously, wondering how she could get rid of Meg so that she could continue to watch the divine being who looked like he'd come straight from a casting session for *Don Juan DeMarco*. "Why don't you at least go and look at some of the sci-fi books?" she encouraged Meg.

Still looking unconvinced, Meg got up and methodically began to work her way through the science fiction shelves. Five minutes later she was firing questions about the history of the genre at the teenage boy, who was now looking terrified and as though he thought God was punishing him for looking through the book of Helmut Newton photographs.

Lucy looked back over to where the godlike man had been standing, but he had disappeared so was probably now tugging his forelock in a back corner somewhere. Sighing, she put the Sontag back on the shelf and made her way to the classics section where Beret and his boyfriend were reading aloud to each other from an Oscar Wilde novel. They both smiled at her and then watched her like a pair of judgmental hawks to see what she would select. Nervously, she pulled a copy of Stendhal off the shelf (too showy, as if anyone ever actually read him) and was surprised to see them look admiringly at her, which is when she looked down to see that she'd grabbed *Justine* by the Marquis de Sade by accident. There was no help for it though, so she sat down and tried to appear intellectually absorbed by a description of Justine's de-flowering.

Meg joined her again a few minutes later clutching a sci-fi novel. Cheerfully asking Beret and his boyfriend to shove up and make room for her, she wedged herself in beside Lucy and immersed herself in the book. Lucy was trying to read over her shoulder, because by now the Marquis and Justine had made her feel both nauseous and inflexible, when suddenly she saw Forelock Guy again. She nudged Meg hard and nodded towards him. Meg subjected him to a brief but penetrating scrutiny and then started to read her book again.

"Well? What do you think?" Lucy whispered, unable to drag her gaze away from the errant forelock, which was lying in a careless and charming manner over the bridge of his glasses.

"Chronic masturbator," Meg said firmly, without looking up from the second installment of *The Werigandelthornbrum Trilogy* (*Hervyagot-mead's Return*).

"You can't *know* that," Lucy said, irritated by her decisive tone of voice.

"I noticed him before. Gorgeous-looking, but he's been in the bookstore for half an hour and he's been back to the self-help section four times. He's used to doing things for himself, and he likes doing them often."

Lucy felt like telling her that at least Forelock Guy probably had a sex life whereas Meg had more chance of getting laid by a hen than a man the way that she was going, but she managed to restrain herself.

"I'll be in the poetry section when you're finished," Lucy muttered crossly, getting up.

"Why don't you go and talk to him?" she asked in that annoying Meg way that suggested she had absolutely no conception of the land mine–strewn terrain that such a course of action would involve negotiating. Sometimes Lucy wondered whether Meg really was a woman.

"Don't be ridiculous. I am not going to pick up someone in a bookstore. It's completely inappropriate."

"I thought that was the whole reason why you love going to bookstores?"

Lucy glared at her.

"Imagination is one thing. Accosting a man that gorgeous is quite another."

"Really, Lucy, stop looking at me like that and go and talk to him already. I'll come looking for you in ten minutes, and if it turns out he's a nutter and is reading something weird like . . ." She looked around for inspiration, and her gaze fell on the copy of *Justine* that Lucy was holding. "Then again, maybe we shouldn't judge people by the books that they read." And with that Meg got up and disappeared towards the front of the store, leaving Lucy to twist around, vainly searching for Forelock Guy. There was no sign of him, however, so after a few minutes Lucy went in search of Meg and found her at the register, completing the exchange of books.

"Are you going to pay for that?" Amélie asked, in a most un-Amélie snappy tone of voice. It was remarkable what Meg could do to a person in less than five minutes.

To her surprise Lucy realized that the question was directed at her. She looked down and saw the copy of *Justine* that she had absent-mindedly tucked into her handbag. "Oh yes, sorry. I just put it there and then forgot . . ." She fumbled in her bag for her purse while Amélie gazed at her thoughtfully, as though she was considering how to teach Lucy a lesson in the most mischievous way possible.

"You don't want to buy that," Meg objected.

"Yes I do. Shut up, Meg."

"You'll never read it. And if you do it will be incredibly bad for your self-esteem. You'll only end up feeling sexually unadventurous. You're only buying it because you're worried the girl thinks that you were trying to steal it."

"She was trying to steal it. All of the perverts try to steal the Marquis de Sade," Amélie informed Meg.

"Really?"

"Yes. But most of them are smarter than your friend. They try to smuggle it out inside copies of large novels by Indian authors."

Lucy, who was still flushed and feeling like a criminal, thrust some money on the counter and glared at Meg, while Amélie put *Justine* in a brown paper bag just to make her really feel like she was purchasing pornography.

"Don't look at me like that," Meg said, pushing the door open. "I'm not the kleptomaniac sexual pervert."

They wandered out into the street and Meg strode around to the driver's side of her car. Lucy was leaning dreamily against it, waiting for Meg to unlock the door, when she heard a hesitant voice say her name. She turned around and nearly fell over. Forelock Guy was standing in front of her, clutching a card in his hand.

"Are you Lucinda?" he asked, looking from Lucy to Meg and back again.

Lucy looked at the card that he was holding, which listed her contact details and the name of her agency, and she felt her cheeks start to burn.

She twisted around and glared ferociously at Meg, who was grinning at her.

"Meg!" she hissed.

"I gave Byron your card," Meg said placidly. "Lucy, meet Byron. Byron, this is Lucy. Lucy thinks that you're cute, by the way."

That was it. As of tomorrow Lucy was enrolling Meg in a Girl Etiquette course. She had absolutely no understanding of embarrassment thresholds and how blatant honesty could be an undesirable thing in certain situations. There was nothing for it though so she raised her head and looked at Byron and was startled to see that his cheeks were also faintly flushed. "I'm so sorry about this," she muttered. "I had no idea that my friend gave you my card. I'll just take it back and we won't bother you anymore."

"Oh for heaven's sake," Meg groaned. "He followed you out into the street. He would have thrown the card away if he wasn't interested."

Lucy smiled politely at Byron. "Will you excuse me for a moment?"

Striding around to Meg's side of the car, she opened the door and shoved her inside. "Afterwards," she hissed at Meg.

"What?"

"We do the interpretative analysis of his actions *after* he leaves. *Not* while he's standing in front of us." Lucy slammed the door on her and then, taking a deep breath, she walked back around to where Byron O'Forelock was standing.

"I'm Lucy," she said, holding her hand out.

He took her hand, but instead of shaking it he held it and looked into her eyes. "I'm Byron," he said softly, and she noticed that he had a European accent that she couldn't quite place. There was a slight pause as they smiled sheepishly at each other, looked away in embarrassment, and then both tried frantically to think of something to say. With a flash of inspiration he asked, "What book did you buy?"

Oh crap, thought Lucy, trying desperately to think of something, *anything* other than a book by the man who gave his name to a particular form of sexual deviancy. It was ridiculous. She had read hundreds of books. Only naturally the only titles she could think of now were *Justine* and *The Werigandelthornbrum Trilogy.* "I don't actually know what I bought," she fumbled madly. "I, er, chose something at random off the shelf without looking. I find that way my reading isn't restricted."

Byron's expression cleared, allowing the unruly forelock to fall engagingly over one eyebrow again, and he looked at her admiringly. "That is a wonderful idea. I will try that next time."

"What are you reading?" Lucy asked, wanting to divert attention away from her fib.

There was an audible groan from inside the car, followed by what sounded like "Of all the nerds . . ." but they both ignored it.

"*A Farewell to Arms* by Hemingway," he said eagerly, pulling the book out of its bag and showing it to her. "I've always meant to read it. It is set in Italy where I am from."

Inside the car and able to hear everything, Meg grinned. He was reading Hemingway, wore glasses, and had an Italian accent. She wondered whether she had sufficient time to ring Chloe to place a bet as to whether Lucy would faint or orgasm first.

"Could I call you on this number?" Byron asked suddenly, turning her card over in his hands as the words spilled out.

"I'd love you to," Lucy said shyly, unable to meet his eye.

"Would you like to take my phone number too?"

Lucy swallowed hard as she found a pen in her bag and handed it to Byron, who wrote his number down and handed it to her.

"It was nice meeting you, Lucia," Byron finally said, looking her in the eyes. "I will call you, and perhaps we can see each other next week?"

"Okay," she said breathlessly.

She watched him walk down the street and then, opening the car door, she collapsed into the front seat and squealed loudly.

"See?" Meg asked, with justified self-satisfaction, as she started the engine. "It's so easy when you're just straight with people."

Lucy smiled and looked at Byron's number. He had written it on the back of one of the complimentary bookmarks that the bookstore gave out. Turning it over she read:

Elizabeth's spirits soon rising to playfulness again, she wanted Mr. Darcy to account for his having ever fallen in love with her. "How could you begin?" said she. "I can comprehend your going on charmingly, when you had once made a beginning; but what could set you off in the first place?"

"I cannot fix on the hour, or the spot, or the look, or the words which laid the foundation. It is too long ago. I was in the middle before I knew that I had begun."

It was a sign.

9.

written in the stars

"Where's Luce?" asked Tom, as he entered Chloe's flat on the following Saturday, carrying a box filled with Lucy's clothes. Percy was close behind him, his cheeks and ears bright scarlet from having been made to carry a laundry basket with Lucy's underwear proudly displayed on top.

"She's gone to get another carload, and I think she's picking up her new man on the way," answered Meg from where she was kneeling on the floor, busily sorting through a miscellaneous heap of vases, shoes, and kitchen equipment.

"What on earth is all of that?" asked Percy, observing the jumble in fascination.

Meg looked up and grimaced. "Lucy's idea of packing. She was disorganized as usual. Half the stuff that she meant to put into storage has ended up here."

"So who is Luce's latest victim?" Tom asked breezily.

Entering the room with an armful of flowers, Chloe was in time to hear the question, and she sighed audibly. "He's gorgeous."

"Very interesting, Clo," Tom said disparagingly. "Does he have a name?"

"His name is Byron," said Chloe, beginning to arrange the flowers in a vase. She paused to consider the position of a stem and then added over her shoulder, "He's Italian."

"Byron?" Tom replied scathingly. "That doesn't sound very Italian to me."

"I think his father is Australian," said Meg, who found the transparency of Tom's instantaneous dislike of any competitor for Lucy's affections highly amusing.

"And what does Byron do? Gladiator? Gondolier?" Tom asked flippantly.

"Funnily enough, you're not that far off," Meg commented. "He roams the world acting as a cultural stereotype as far as I can tell."

"What's that supposed to mean?"

Chloe shot a reproachful glance at Meg and then said dreamily, "He's *very* romantic."

Tom groaned. "Oh lord. That means we're going to have to put up with Lucy in love-struck mode."

"What happens to her?" asked Percy curiously.

Meg, Chloe, and Tom shared a look.

"She gets a bit sappy," Chloe finally admitted, feeling disloyal.

"A bit? Clo, she *gushes*. She'll start hoarding everything he touches or gives her, including used condoms. Her answering service on both her phones will be blocked in about a week because she'll keep every single message he leaves even if it's a text message asking her what the time is. She'll buy a book on whatever star-sign he is—"

"She'll probably start learning Italian," Meg added, without rancor.

"Exactly." Tom sat back and folded his arms. "And then it will be over in six weeks, and that's if it's a long-term relationship, and then we'll have to go through Lucy in heartbroken mode. Which is possibly even more exhausting."

"I don't know, Tom," Chloe said thoughtfully. "I know that I've only met him once, but they really do seem made for each other. And Lucy is completely different with him than how she normally is in relationships. She's usually so desperate to be in love that she can be a bit subservient. But she's a lot more confident with Byron. You of all people ought to know what a change that is."

"What the hell is that supposed to mean? Lucy wasn't subservient with me! She drove me out of my mind most of the time."

"Yes, and you were always so impatient with her." Tom looked at her in surprise and opened his mouth to refute this, but Chloe continued, "Byron can be quite fiery but he's also very gentle."

"Fiery?" Tom asked, starting to feel slightly threatened.

"Mmmm. And gentle," Chloe reiterated, quite unnecessarily in Tom's opinion.

"Where did you say she met him?"

"In a bookstore."

Tom's anxiety increased tenfold. "So he's a bookish type? Good-looking but a bit thin and weedy and pale?"

"He's gorgeous," Chloe repeated, and Meg nodded in assent. "And he does read a lot but he has a body to die for. I think he plays soccer. He's not little *at all*." She caught Meg's eye and they dissolved into laughter.

"Penis allusion," Tom explained briefly to Percy, who was looking confused. "If you go out with an Aussie girl for more than ten minutes you may as well send all of her best friends a highlighted ruler. Nothing's sacred—just remember that, Perce."

"The first time you and Lucy were together, you went out for two months," Meg said sweetly to Tom's crotch while Chloe collapsed into giggles again.

"Yes we did, Meg. So everyone here knows how well-endowed I am. Happy now?"

"Not as happy as Lucy used to be when Mr. Binky came out to play."

"I do *not* call my penis Mr. Binky," Tom said, as scathingly as he could manage. He turned to Percy, who was now eyeing Tom's crotch askance. "Perce, stop looking like that—Meg just made that up."

"I thought you used to have a teddy called Mr. Binky?" Percy said doubtfully.

"I did."

"That's a bit sick, Tom."

"There's nothing sick about it. My teddy was called Mr. Binky. My penis is called—"

Meg and Chloe waited breathlessly, but Percy spoiled it by covering his ears and begging Tom to stop.

"Anyway," Tom said, recovering his composure slightly, "this Byron sounds like a phony to me. I could predict his standard M.O. from start to finish. He met Luce in a bookstore, right? He probably hangs out in them all the time just to pick up women. He would have watched Luce, seen her go for all the predictable Lucy-type books— *Madame Bovary, A Passage to India,* anything by Virginia Woolf. He probably started chatting to her, discussed literature in an informed and witty way, impressed her with a classical reference, swooned her with an allusion to an esoteric poet, and then got her phone number. Tragic."

"What's tragic about meeting a handsome stranger in a cultured environment and having a stimulating conversation with them?" Meg asked pointedly.

Tom was floored for a moment but then he recovered. "It's tragic because it's such a setup. It's all an act. Give him two weeks and he'll have dropped the pose and stopped taking her to independent theater and political lectures. He'll have her sitting on the couch watching soccer with him."

"Lucy really liked *Bend It Like Beckham,*" Percy said thoughtfully.

Meg and Tom ignored him. "For their first date he took her on a night-time picnic to the beach," Meg informed Tom.

"Amateur," Tom sniffed.

"He went to the trouble of ringing Chloe at home when Lucy was out to ask what all her favorite foods are, even though he'd never met Chloe."

"That's quite good," Percy said admiringly, making a mental note to use that in the future.

"He probably took her for a long walk on the beach in the moonlight," Tom said dismissively.

"He did actually. And pointed out all the stars to her."

"That's not bad," Tom conceded grudgingly.

"And Lucy said they saw a shooting star," Meg continued relentlessly.

There was an awed silence.

"He's good," Percy said in a hushed tone. "He's *really* good."

Tom, who had been looking apprehensive, recovered his composure. "There's no way he'll be able to keep it up. That's the problem with Ginger. She needs too much attention. If he's starting out at that level he's left himself no room for improvement. Schoolboy error," he concluded patronizingly.

"Why do you call Lucy Ginger?" asked Percy curiously. "She doesn't have red hair."

"Luce loves old black-and-white movies, especially all of those musicals with Fred Astaire and Ginger Rogers in them. And one time she told me how Ginger Rogers once said that she did everything Fred did, only backwards and in high heels. And it just seemed to apply to Lucy perfectly. She's always tottering around in high heels doing impressive things but somehow going about everything backwards."

"And she tries so hard to make life smoother for you," Chloe agreed.

Tom looked at her suspiciously, but there wasn't a hint of guile on Chloe's face. "Yes I suppose she does," he said, uncomfortably aware of a sudden sharp scrutiny from Meg, who had sat quietly through this exchange.

At that moment the front door opened and the sound of Lucy's sandals clattering on the floorboards could be heard. Flushed with the exertion of carrying a stack of books, Lucy entered the room, closely followed by a specimen who, even to the unadmiring eyes of Tom and Percy, was clearly up there in the eye-candy stakes. To Tom's disgust even Meg's hello to Byron had a touch of the simper about it, while Chloe watched him put down the box he was carrying and then flick away the troublesome forelock, with her mouth hanging open.

Before introductions could be made, however, Lucy spotted the vase of flowers that Chloe had arranged and pounced on her with a squeal of delight. "Clo—they're beautiful! Are they for me?"

Chloe returned her hug and smiled at her obvious delight. "Yes, they're your welcome present," she laughed. "Do you like them?"

"Of course I do!" Lucy stepped forward and buried her face in the bouquet.

"She's not going to eat them, is she?" asked Percy, genuinely alarmed by this disproportionate reaction to a bunch of flowers.

"No, but I want to," came Lucy's muffled voice. She raised her head. "Don't you think they're delicious enough to eat, Percy?"

The ever-present blush rose to Percy's cheeks as he felt the center of attention upon him.

"They're very pleasant," he finally managed, wondering suspiciously as he always did whether there was any history of mental instability or Italian heritage in Lucy's family. They were *flowers* for heaven's sake. There was absolutely no need for this kind of emotional outburst over flowers. Actually, he couldn't think of any situation that called for such an excessive display of joy. Excepting of course, a victorious cricket final. Or perhaps the successful insemination of a favorite thorough-bred horse. But *flowers*?

"*Pleasant?*" Lucy looked at him incredulously. "Percy, you can't be serious. Come and look at them properly. You need to smell them and feel them and—"

"Stop it, Lucy," said Chloe, seeing Percy's escalating horror and coming to his rescue. "I'm glad that you like them though. They are gorgeous, aren't they?"

The word *gorgeous* recalled Lucy to Byron's presence and she suddenly realized that she hadn't yet introduced him. She swung around to where he was standing uncomfortably near the door and, putting her hand out to him, she brought him into the center of the room. "Byron, you've already met Meg and Chloe. And these are my friends Tom and Percy," Lucy said nervously, praying that Tom wouldn't be rude as he invariably was to her new boyfriends.

Percy and Byron shook hands civilly. To atone for the exchange that Byron had just witnessed, Percy tried to smooth things over. "How do you do? I'm Perceval Hamilton-Bythorne. I've absolutely nothing against flowers, you understand."

"But of course I understand," Byron said courteously.

"What do you think of the Euro?" Percy asked, anxious to make a member of the European Union feel at home.

Byron looked faintly bemused. "I believe it is proving very effective," he said thoughtfully, in his charmingly accented and slightly halting English. "Although obviously the creation of a market of three hundred million people with a single currency means that the effect on prices in areas such as—Lucy, what is the word for Internet business?"

"E-commerce," Lucy supplied adoringly.

"Yes. The effect on e-commerce is yet to be known of course."

"Of course it is. Right. Very good," said Percy, immediately collapsing as what he had intended to be merely a friendly overture showed alarming signs of developing into an intellectual fiscal discussion.

Byron turned to Tom, who was sizing him up through narrowed eyes.

"What part of Italy are you from?" Tom asked, somehow managing to make this innocuous question sound like an expression of doubt regarding the authenticity of Byron's accent.

"Firenze. Florence," answered Byron politely, thinking *this man has slept with Lucy.*

"What are you doing in Australia?" probed Tom, rather more aggressively than was necessary.

"I am here to do research."

"Byron's a scientist," Lucy interpolated proudly.

Tom raised one eyebrow inquiringly at Lucy, wondering how she had romanticized science in order to find Byron attractive.

She saw the look and explained, "His field is astronomy. Which involves physics, but we don't have to talk about that."

"Ah. So where are you living?"

"Brighton. Just near the beach. It is very beautiful."

"How old are you?"

"Thirty-two," Byron said, looking faintly bemused at this interrogation.

Tom eyed him suspiciously, still looking for a chink in his armor.

"What's your football team?"

"The Italian national team of course."

"I meant Australian Rules," Tom said triumphantly, finally feeling as though he had scored a point.

"Carlton."

"That's your team too," Lucy said pointedly, as Tom instantly deflated.

"This is an interrogation, is it not?" Byron said gently but with a touch of annoyance.

"Yes it is," said Lucy irritably. "Tom, if you've *quite* finished asserting your position as the dominant male perhaps you could go outside and pick nits out of Percy's hair or whatever it is that the alpha male gorilla does after making an idiot of himself."

"I don't have nits!" Percy expostulated, horrified to have the integrity of his personal hygiene questioned in front of a stranger and Meg.

"You're welcome, Luce," Tom said nastily. "We just finished bringing all your stuff in, so I think I'll be going now."

He stalked out of the room. Lucy groaned and followed him out, leaving Meg and Chloe to smooth over the uncomfortable silence that ensued and Percy to fight the uncontrollable urge to scratch his head that had now arisen.

"Oh for god's sake," Lucy said, running after Tom. "I'm sorry. And I am truly grateful for your help—you know I am. But why did you have to be so horrible to Byron? I really like him, Tom, and you've actually got a lot in common—"

Tom held a hand up to stop her flow of words. "Alright, alright, Ginger, I'm sorry. But the guy's a jerk, and I do *not* want to hear that we could be friends if I just gave him a chance."

"Fine. Just don't be too horrible to him in the future. Please? For my sake?" She looked at him pleadingly but with a smile hovering around her lips.

Tom looked into her eyes and then broke into a rueful grin. "I'll try. Just don't get too mushy and romantic, okay?"

Lucy stood on tiptoe and gave him a swift hug. "I promise."

10.

life is but *a* dream

Lucy gazed dreamily at the wide blue canopy of the sky as she reclined against the cushioned stern of the rowboat that Byron was gently ferrying down the part of the Yarra River that meandered past the restored nineteenth-century Fairfield boathouse. The air was shimmering with the heat of a lazy summer's day and apart from the gentle splashing of Byron's oars, and some distant children on paddle-bikes, and the occasional cry from a heat-exhausted magpie, all was still and quiet.

Closing her eyes, she gave in to the perfection of the moment; a perfection that was only marred by the fact that she wasn't wearing her favorite floaty white cotton dress (which was positively *made* for Ophelia-like watery drifting) and was instead clad in an old pair of shorts and a T-shirt that bore the caption "I'm Afraid of Reality TV." If she was going to nitpick, she would have also preferred to be wearing a hat and sunscreen, as the midday sun was searingly hot. And ideally she could also have done without the mosquitoes that were happily feasting on her bare flesh. But there hadn't been the opportunity for prosaic considerations such as appropriate clothing, insect repellent, and sunscreen, for Byron had surprised her by turning up on her doorstop that morning with a hamper and a grand plan for an impetuous romantic picnic. Grabbing her hand, he had laughingly insisted that she come exactly as she was and, caught up in the moment, she had succumbed. Opening one eye and observing her beloved, she had the sneaking suspicion that he had not reckoned on the force of the Australian sun either, for he was looking distinctly hot and uncomfortable. Lucy sat up and smiled at him. "Shall I have a turn at rowing?"

Byron looked at her doubtfully. "Do you know how to row?"

"No," Lucy admitted cheerfully. "But it can't be that hard. Anyway, you'll get heatstroke if you keep going like that. Let's change places." The boat rocked perilously as Lucy stood up to maneuver herself into Byron's place, but although she held out her hand to help Byron up he didn't move.

"Perhaps I should give you a lesson in rowing?" he suggested. "Come and sit here, Lucia."

Liking the sound of this, Lucy sat on his lap and placed her hands on the oars while Byron's arms tightened around her waist.

"You must hold them firmly and then at the same time dip them in the water and pull." Byron nuzzled her neck and Lucy squirmed pleasurably. The boat turned in a small circle and began to drift with the current as Lucy was concentrating far more on Byron than she was on her rowing lesson.

"You're not trying," Byron reprimanded her teasingly, continuing to kiss her neck. Lucy twisted around to face him, they began to passionately kiss, and she lost herself in the ineffable romance of the moment.

They were brought back to the present by a most unpleasant juddering impact, which was immediately followed by a cry of outrage and a loud splash. Breaking apart and looking around in alarm, Lucy and Byron realized with dismay that their boat had crashed into one of the paddle-bikes, rented by a teenage boy who was now flailing in the water. They looked at each other aghast, and then, without thinking, they both promptly kicked off their shoes and jumped into the river.

It wasn't deep, and to their annoyance, once they were in the water, they both realized that the teenager could swim perfectly well and was now breaststroking fiercely towards them.

"You weren't looking where you were going!" he accused them angrily, as he drew level, his face red with annoyance.

"I know," Lucy said ruefully, treading water and pushing her plastered-down hair out of her eyes. "We're very sorry."

"You should be. Freakin' idiots."

"Wait one moment," Byron said, his temper starting to flare at this rudeness. "You can't have been looking where you were going either. Why did you not yell out to warn us?"

The boy looked at him slyly. "Didn't want to interrupt. That was quite a nice show you two were putting on."

"Eew." Lucy looked at him in horror. "Were you spying on us?"

The boy gave her a leering grin as he righted his paddle-bike. "I wouldn't call it spying exactly. You're in the middle of a public park. It's hardly private. That T-shirt fits you even better when it's wet by the way."

Completely revolted, Lucy crossed her arms in front of her but had to unfold them because it was too hard to tread water in that position. Byron, his expression dark and stormy, swam closer to Lucy and tried to place a protective arm around her, which was a little difficult as they were both bobbing up and down in the current.

"You will apologize to Lucia," he said sternly to the boy, who grinned unrepentantly.

"For what? Telling her she has nice tits? You had your hands all over them a minute ago, so you can't talk."

Byron started to advance towards the boy as menacingly as one could in an aquatic fashion, but was checked by Lucy asking a trifle wistfully, "Do you really think I have nice breasts? They're not too small?" she concluded anxiously.

"You know what they say—more than a handful's a waste," the boy said philosophically.

"You will stop discussing your breasts with this stranger, Lucia," Byron said, as commandingly as he was able.

"I reckon you should stop telling her what to do," the teenager said, looking at Byron with dislike. "By the way, your boat has drifted away."

Byron's thundercloud demeanor instantly disappeared as his head whipped around in panic. In silence, Lucy and he gazed at their rapidly diminishing boat, which was merrily floating down the river.

"Why didn't you tell us that our boat was drifting?" asked Lucy furiously, turning back to face the boy and fighting the childish desire to splash water in his obnoxious face.

"Why is everything my fault?" asked the teenager, swinging one leg over the bike and hoisting himself onto the seat. "You seem to think I have nothing better to do than bring you two back to reality all the time. Well it's been a pleasure. Have fun."

There was a brief, humiliated silence as Lucy and Byron looked at each other and took in the extent of their predicament. Lucy was the first to swallow her pride. "I don't suppose you could give us a ride back to the boathouse?" Lucy asked pathetically, knowing full well that she couldn't possibly swim that far in her waterlogged T-shirt and shorts.

The teenager smirked. "I could probably fit you on the back. Your boyfriend will have to swim."

Lucy looked at Byron in dismay. "Will you be okay?"

He gave her a brave smile and brushed the wet hair tenderly off her forehead. "I will be right here beside you, Lucia. Go now."

"For God's sake," the teenager said impatiently. "You're in the middle of the Yarra River within two hundred yards of the boathouse. Stop carrying on like Kate Winslet and Leonardo DiCaprio in *Titanic*."

Byron cast him a baleful glare but helped Lucy hoist her sodden self up behind their objectionable rescuer, who smirkingly admonished her to "Hold on nice and tight now."

As they slowly made their way back to the mooring point, with the boy making obscene comments the entire way, Lucy held gingerly onto his waist and shouted encouraging comments to Byron, much in the manner of a long-distance swimming coach instructing her shark cage–enclosed protégé. She was dolefully aware that this was *not* how their lovely romantic outing was supposed to have ended.

If only I had been wearing my floaty Ophelia dress, Lucy thought miserably, scratching at a bite on her arm, *he'd probably be feeding me strawberries underneath a willow tree right this very moment.* She paused and scratched a different spot. *Then again,* she reflected, ever the optimist, *Ophelia went mad and drowned.* She thought and scratched some more but couldn't help concluding enviously: *Why is it that lunacy and death in Denmark are so much more romantic than humiliation and wet underpants in the Yarra River?*

"How was your picnic?" called out Chloe, emerging from the kitchen where she had been baking a cake, and wiping her hands on a dishtowel, as an exhausted Lucy staggered in late in the afternoon.

"You mean apart from having third-degree sunburn, mosquito bites that are bigger than my breasts, and having to pay a fine to the park ranger to retrieve our rowboat?" Lucy asked sourly. Unable to contain her exasperation she added, "How *could* Byron forget to take insect repellent and sunscreen on a picnic in the middle of the summer?"

"He grew up in Italy," Chloe pointed out. "We're all conditioned to the climate, but he probably had no idea of how ferocious the sun can be here. *You*, on the other hand, should know better."

Lucy's face fell. "I know. But when I said I wanted to change he said that I was perfect as I was, and it just seemed stupid to start fussing about sunscreen and hats. Anyway, that wasn't the worst bit. We had a little accident and then our boat drifted away and we couldn't get it back."

"You lost your boat?" Chloe asked incredulously.

"Yes. We crashed into a horrid boy on one of those paddle-bikes and we jumped into the river to save him and then our boat drifted away."

"Why on earth did you both jump into the river? Why didn't one of you stay with the boat?"

"Because there wasn't time to stop and think!" Lucy said, growing grumpier by the minute, as Chloe, rather than being suitably impressed by Lucy and Byron's selfless and heroic act, was instead bemused that they hadn't followed some sort of stupid maritime safety drill that was apparently known to the entire universe. "It could have been a life-threatening situation," she added darkly.

To her annoyance, Chloe started laughing. "Luce, the only way anyone could get hurt in Fairfield Park is if they swallowed some water from the Yarra and ended up with their teeth stained brown."

Much aggrieved, Lucy adopted a haughty tone. "Well, I think I did swallow some of the water, so if you don't mind I'm going to brush my teeth and have a shower."

"By the way, Tom called," Chloe suddenly remembered, as Lucy started to make her way towards the bathroom. "He asked where you were, and I told him that Byron had taken you rowing down the river."

"Did he leave a message?"

"Not exactly. He started laughing so hard I had to put the phone down."

Lucy sniffed. "Typical. Tom has absolutely no conception of romance."

Chloe gazed pensively at Lucy's damp, slimy, sunburned, and be-draggled figure.

"No, Luce," she agreed doubtfully. "I don't suppose he has."

11.

in sickness & in health

The following week Meg and Chloe were spending the Thursday night quietly, with a bottle of wine and a DVD at Chloe's. Their tranquility was interrupted at about a quarter to nine, by the entrance of Lucy, who staggered in, sneezing and coughing violently.

"What on earth is wrong with you?" asked Meg, backing away slightly.

"Got a cuh-hold-ishoo!" Lucy explained, erupting into another sneeze.

"How on earth did you catch a cold in the middle of the summer?"

"Byron took me to Moonlight Cinema last night," Lucy explained between sniffs. "And by the time we left the Botanic Gardens it was quite chilly and the grass was damp."

"Why didn't you take a jacket?"

Lucy stopped blowing her nose and looked at Meg scornfully.

"Because I didn't know I was going of course. He surprised me straight after work. It was very romant-ishoo!"

"Sounds it," Meg murmured, edging further away from the force of Lucy's sneezes.

"Lucy, you have to tell him to stop," Chloe said firmly, pausing the movie with the remote control. "He's going to kill you."

"How is taking Lucy to Moonlight Cinema a murder tactic?" inquired Meg.

"He's killing her with romance. Last week he took her rowing down the river, and she got a terrible case of sunburn."

"I didn't know he was taking me rowing," Lucy said sulkily. "Otherwise I would have worn a hat and sunscreen."

"That's exactly my point. You're completely unprepared all the time. You never know what to expect, so you can't dress appropriately for the occasion. That's why you've ended up with sunburn last week and pneumonia this week."

"'S'not pneumonia. S'cold," Lucy snuffled, throwing herself into a chair and doing her best dying diva impersonation.

"I mean it, Lucy. Look how sick you are. You have to tell him to stop."

Lucy looked up from her sodden handkerchief contemptuously.

"Tell him to atchoo!-stop? Are you out of your mind? Apart from the fact that I don't *want* him to stop, what do you think Tom would say?"

"Tom? What's he got to do with it?"

"He'd never let me live it down. When we were together, all that I ever wanted was for him to be romantic."

"Lucy?" Meg said sweetly. "We were talking about *Byron*."

"I know we were," Lucy said irritably, resting her throbbing head back against the chair and closing her eyes. "But if I'm going to die from anything it might as well be from an overdose of romance. So leave me alone."

"You can still do all of those things with Byron. Just take out the surprise element so that you know how to dress or what to bring."

"The whole point of a romantic gesture is the fact that it's unexpected. It would ruin it if it was all planned out and I knew what was going to happen."

"So the ideal romantic relationship is one where you're in a permanent state of ignorance?"

"Meg, I have a killer headache *and* I still feel like I'm being barbecued from my sunburn. Please stop sounding like a lawyer," Lucy begged, hoisting herself out of the chair. "I'm going to bed."

As Chloe pressed play on the remote again, Lucy paused beside the couch and glanced at the television. "Is that *A Room with a View*? Can you leave it in the DVD player? I really don't feel very well, and if I don't go to work tomorrow I'd like to watch it again."

"Sure," Chloe said, ducking to avoid another of Lucy's gale-force sneezes. In silence, Meg and Chloe watched the forlorn figure of Lucy disappear down the hall to her bedroom. They looked at each other and then back at the television screen where the heroine was running across a golden field in Tuscany to passionately embrace her lover.

"You are going to return it first thing tomorrow morning, aren't you?" Meg asked.

"First thing," Chloe reiterated firmly. "The last thing Lucy needs is more romance. I don't want to be held responsible for killing her."

The sound of the telephone ringing dragged Lucy out of her uneasy slumber early the following evening. As she groggily reached for the receiver, she registered that it was six o'clock. Hazily she tried to remember what had happened since she had collapsed into bed the night before. Completely muddled, she realized that she must have slept for the whole day. She had a vague memory of calling in sick to work and going to the bathroom, but apart from that she must have slept for the past twenty hours. Which simply couldn't be right because she still felt ridiculously tired.

"Hello?" Lucy croaked into the phone.

"God you sound hideous." Tom's voice boomed cheerfully. She winced and held the receiver slightly further away. "I thought that Chloe said you had the flu. You sound more like you've got a bad case of *Deep Throat*. You don't have deep throat, do you?" he added hopefully.

"What do you want?" Lucy asked irritably, laying her pounding head back on the pillow.

"Well, that's what I was going to ask you. I'm coming around to do my Florence Nightingale bit so I thought I may as well be practical and call first to see if there's anything that you particularly need apart from the comfort of my presence."

"I don't want you to visit. I want to die alone."

"Stop thinking only of yourself. I've already put on my nurse's uniform, and if I do say so myself I look rather fetching. Also I've been practicing sticking my thermometer into things all day."

"Keep your thermometer to yourself. And don't you dare come around. I'm sick and I need a shower, but I don't think I can stand up long enough to have one so I probably smell and my hair is greasy. And there are used tissues everywhere. The last thing I need to see is you looking all healthy and scrubbed and shiny."

"I do not look *shiny*," he objected.

"Yes you do. It's sickening." She paused and blew her nose vociferously without bothering to hold the phone away.

"You really are the most unattractive person when you're sick. I'll see you in twenty."

He hung up before she could protest further and after cursing him for ten of the twenty minutes she decided that she just wouldn't answer the door when he rang the doorbell. Only of course he didn't ring the doorbell, he simply let himself in with the spare key while she was still sulking on the couch.

"I can't believe that Chloe keeps the spare key under the doormat," he said, strolling in, weighed down with shopping bags. "It's really not very safe."

Lucy glared at him. "Do the wishes of a dying woman count for nothing?" she demanded tragically.

"What are you planning on dying from? Drowning in the oil slick on your scalp?"

Suddenly she couldn't bear it anymore. "Please don't be mean to me. I know that I look terrible, but I feel even worse. You know how much I hate being sick."

Tom looked at her and she could have sworn that something very like sympathy crossed his face. He recovered himself, however, and started to open the shopping bags instead. "Here, catch."

Lucy caught a giant box of tissues, the ones with aloe vera in them that were soft on your nose.

"I figured you'd be using toilet paper to blow your nose by now so I bought you some more of that too." He grinned and held up the toilet paper triumphantly as he caught sight of the roll beside her.

"Thank you," she said gratefully, honking her nose into one of the gloriously soft tissues.

"You're welcome. I also brought fresh milk, orange juice, Tylenol, and trashy magazines. And chocolate cookies. Plain ones I'm afraid, but I thought that anything too rich might make you feel worse. Did I forget anything?"

"Did you bring me a get well card?" she asked hopefully.

He looked crestfallen. "Damn. Knew that I forgot something."

"That's okay. As long as you didn't bring your thermometer I'm happy." Lucy picked up one of the magazines and looked enquiringly at Tom. "You brought me *Maxim* magazine?"

"They have very good articles," Tom said with a seraphic air. "You can learn a lot about health issues from *Maxim*."

"Looking at pictures of venereal disease doesn't count," Lucy said dryly.

Abandoning his attempt to win her over he added, "Stop looking at me like that. I brought you *Vanity Fair* too."

The doorbell rang, and Tom looked at Lucy enquiringly. She shook her head.

Tom strode to the door, and as he opened it she heard him say, "Oh, it's you," in a tone of strong distaste, so she was unsurprised when Byron walked in, bearing an enormous bunch of flowers and two gift-wrapped packages.

"Hello, Lucia," he said stiffly, obviously displeased to find Tom there. "I thought you did not want visitors?"

"I didn't," Lucy said hastily. And then, feeling ungrateful because Tom had brought her everything she needed, she added, "Tom popped around unexpectedly."

"No I didn't. I called first," Tom said unhelpfully. As Byron looked even more put out he added, "I was just about to see how hot Lucinda is. Using my thermometer. I don't think you should watch."

As Byron tried to work out what this meant, Lucy stifled a giggle, and managing to glare at Tom she said, "Thank you for my supplies, Thomas. Now, don't you have to go home and make yourself a cheerleader's outfit to go with the nurse costume?"

"No. I'm staying to look after you." And he settled himself more firmly in the armchair.

"I brought you some flowers, Lucia," Byron said, deciding that the best course of action would be to ignore Tom.

"They're beautiful," Lucy said sincerely. And they were. They were also highly exotic and if she came within a foot of them she was going to sneeze her head off. She caught Tom's eye and realizing the danger he got up and offered to put them in water.

Byron handed them to Tom reluctantly but cheered up when Tom went into the kitchen, leaving him alone with Lucy. "I also brought you chocolates."

Lucy unwrapped them. They were her favorite imported truffles that at any other time she would have drooled over. However now, even the thought of rich chocolate was making her feel slightly queasy. "Thank you, Byron. I'd give you a kiss but I don't want you to get my flu."

He accepted this quite readily, which made her feel slightly rejected, and she couldn't help noticing that he sat in a chair a few feet away from her.

"And I have one more present for you." He handed her the last package, which was obviously a book.

"You're spoiling me," Lucy said weakly, trying hard to evince pleasure but wishing that her head would stop throbbing. She unwrapped the book as Byron watched her expectantly. Lucy pulled the final layer of tissue away to reveal a copy of *A Brief History of Survival Farming in Albania*. She looked at Byron in confusion as he watched her expectantly. His face fell at her obvious bewilderment.

"You do not like it?" he asked with concern. "I did what you always do and picked a book at random off the shelf."

Lucy groaned inwardly, remembering the lie she had told to avoid bringing up her purchase of eighteenth-century pornography. "It's wonderful, Byron," she said, mustering as much sincerity as was humanly possible while gazing at a front cover that featured a mournful-looking farmer with his arm around an equally doleful-looking goat.

Tom came back in and Lucy hastily shoved the book under her cushion before Tom could see it. Thankfully, before he had a chance to pick another fight with Byron, there was another knock on the door, and this time Tom came back followed by Percy.

"Hello, Luce," said Percy, in a hushed tone, as though he were in the presence of someone terminally ill. "How are you feeling?"

"Okay," Lucy mumbled, untying her greasy hair. The elastic was making her headache worse and she was beyond caring if Byron found her repulsive.

"I brought you a Chopin CD and some echinacea tea," Percy said. "I can't stand herbal tea myself, but it's meant to be good for the flu. And I always find Chopin very restful."

"Thank you, Percy," Lucy said smiling gratefully at him, touched by this gesture.

There was a short silence and then Percy politely asked Byron how his day had been. As they began to make stilted conversation, Lucy felt the nausea rise up inside her again and wished fervently that they would all go away and leave her alone.

The front door opened once again, this time to admit Chloe, who looked rather taken aback to find her living room so filled with people. "Hello," she said in surprise. "What's going on? Lucy, how are you feeling? You still don't look very well."

"I don't feel very well," Lucy admitted shakily. "Thank you all for coming to visit me and for my get well presents, but I think I need to go back to bed." She got up slowly, willing her stomach to stop churning, and Byron and Tom both immediately moved to her side to assist her.

"I can help Lucia," said Byron, glaring at Tom, and taking Lucy's arm firmly.

Tom held on to her other arm equally firmly. "I think you've done enough."

"What do you mean?"

"Tom, don't," Lucy said feebly. "Please, I really need the bath—"

Tom wasn't listening. "Why do you think she's so sick in the first place?"

"I do not know what you're talking about."

"Please, Byron—I really—" Lucy felt another wave of nausea rising in her stomach.

"It doesn't take a genius to figure out that if you sit on damp grass at night you'll probably catch a cold, particularly if you're not wearing much anyway because you feel so hot from sunburn," Tom said coldly.

That was it. She was going to throw up on both of them. In fact she was going to stick her finger down her throat just to make sure she threw up on both of them because they *deserved* to be thrown up on.

To Lucy's everlasting gratitude, Chloe saw the danger and came forward and detached her from both Byron and Tom's grip. "Tom, stop being ridiculous. Byron, let go of Lucy's arm," Chloe directed firmly. "She's about to be sick and I'm taking her to the bathroom."

Both Tom and Byron hastily let Lucy's arms drop, and once Chloe had installed her comfortably on the bathroom floor in front of the toilet bowl, considerately tying her hair back, she left Lucy alone to succumb to her queasiness.

After her nausea had subsided, Lucy hugged the toilet bowl and rested her cheek against the cool seat. She was happy, truly happy, sitting here hugging the toilet, she decided. This was where she wanted to be. And she was not going back out there until everyone had left. What the hell was going on that two men were fighting over the privilege of holding her hair back while she vomited? She wasn't that damn attractive.

Chloe tapped on the bathroom door and then pushed it open gently. "You okay, Luce?" she asked.

"Yes," Lucy said, hugging the toilet even tighter. "But I don't want to get up just yet."

"Are you going to be sick again?"

"No. I'd just rather stay here with my head in the toilet than see those two right now. Are they still arguing?"

"No. Byron has left. Don't worry about them, Lucy. But I really think you should get off the floor—it's very cold and it will probably make your flu worse."

Reluctantly Lucy let Chloe pull her to her feet, and then at Chloe's bidding she brushed her teeth and splashed water on her face.

"Come on," Chloe said, once these ablutions had been performed. "We'll set you up on the couch. You can watch television, and it will be good for you to be out of your bedroom for a bit. I can open the windows in there and let some fresh air in."

Lucy submitted to being coerced back into the living room and pointedly ignored Tom, who was looking rather shamefaced. Percy was bustling around, plumping pillows and arranging blankets on the couch, and Lucy gratefully curled up on the soft nest that he had prepared.

"I'm having dinner with my parents tonight," Chloe said in a worried tone of voice. "Are you sure you'll be okay by yourself, Luce?"

"She won't be alone," Tom said in surprise. "I'm staying to keep her company."

"No you're not," Lucy said, appalled at the prospect of a night spent arguing with Tom when she felt so unwell.

"Of course I am. I wouldn't leave you alone like this," Tom said nobly.

"Tom, I *want* you to leave me alone. You've been here for half an hour and I feel *worse*. Look, I really do appreciate everything you've done for me, but please, *please* all of you go away," she begged. "Take my credit card from my purse and treat yourselves to a night out on me. Just leave me alone."

"I was wondering how long it would be before she went all Greta Garbo on us," Tom said, in an audible aside to Chloe. He turned to Percy to explain. "She goes into recluse mode when she's sick. Gets all dramatic and wants to die alone."

"She always has been a terrible patient," Chloe said, in a fond tone of voice that made Lucy want to stick Tom's thermometer up her nose.

"I am still here and I can *hear* you," Lucy snapped, irritable at being discussed like this. But Lucy gave up, too exhausted to argue, and just nodded feebly instead. Seeing that she really was spent and wasn't just putting it on, Chloe set about ushering Tom and Percy out of the room. As they left she cast an anxious backwards glance at Lucy but she may as well not have worried. Lucy was already curled up with her eyes closed, reveling in the glorious, blissful silence.

The early morning sun woke Lucy up the following day. As she gulped down the glass of water that had miraculously appeared on her bedside table, she realized that she felt better. Light-headed and a bit wobbly still, but definitely better. The thought of the orange juice that Tom had brought the day before was definitely appealing and she staggered out of her bedroom, only to be brought up short by the sight of Tom's lanky form stretched out uncomfortably on the couch. It appeared that Tom had also just woken up, as he was yawning and stretching.

"What on earth are you doing here?' Lucy asked, shocked by the sudden wrenching of her heart caused by the sight of Tom in sleepy early morning mode. She quelled the memories of other mornings when she had woken up beside him.

"Looking after you. Chloe stayed at her parents' last night but she rang me at about nine. You were really sick last night you know, and she was worried about you. So we thought someone should stay to look after you. As it would undoubtedly annoy Byron more if I stayed, I volunteered."

"Oh." Lucy wondered why the thought of Tom sleeping over at the apartment so that she wouldn't be alone made her want to cry. "Why didn't you sleep in the other spare bedroom?"

"Have you seen the size of that bed? I would have been horizontal but bent at the knees with my feet resting on the floor. It would have felt like I was doing the limbo for eight hours."

"So you slept on the couch all night?"

"No. I hung from the ceiling like a bat for a few hours and then I curled up on the top shelf of the refrigerator."

"I wasn't going to tell you but if you will be sarcastic—you did know that it's a pull-out couch?"

He groaned and rubbed his lower back. "No, Lucinda, I did not. Why on earth didn't Chloe tell me that the couch pulled out?"

Lucy grinned. "She probably didn't think of it. You've always slept in my bed before."

"Mmmm." He eyed her speculatively and something in his look made her flush and look away.

"Stop looking at me like that."

"Like what?"

"Like you want to stick your thermometer into me. It's a breach of the doctor/patient relationship to look at me like that."

"I was playing nurse, remember? They get better uniforms. How are you feeling?"

"Much better, thank you. I was going to get a glass of that orange juice that you brought. Would you like one?"

"Yes. But you come and sit down and I'll get it."

Content to be looked after, Lucy padded over to the couch and curled up amongst the blankets. When she was sure that Tom was safely in the kitchen she closed her eyes and buried her face in his pillow. The smell of him brought back memories of intimacy and she stayed with her eyes shut as long as she dared.

Settled comfortably on the couch they started to read the magazines that Tom had brought as they sipped their orange juice in companionable silence.

"Look at this." Lucy held up the copy of *Vanity Fair* that she was reading and showed Tom a glossy advertisement for makeup featuring a stunning model.

"God, she's gorgeous—who is she?"

"Glad you asked. That's precisely my point. Haven't the faintest clue who she is. And yet they feel the need to tell us that Jody is wearing mango on her eyelids, apricot blush, and persimmon on her lips."

Tom rubbed his nick. "Jody appears to have an uncontrollable urge to stick her face in fruit salad. I take it that's not your point though?"

"Well, why do they always use their names now? It makes me feel like I'm meant to know who they are."

"I think it's nice. It's more personal that way. It's probably less objectifying for the models."

"They're gorgeous, they get paid to be made up and have their hair done, and get photographed in the most flattering light possible. I don't want to be friends with them. A little objectifying would probably do them good."

"Cranky little thing when you're sick, aren't you?"

There was a silence and then, apparently apropos of nothing, Tom said, "I ate some mango body cream once."

"I'm not in the mood to listen to one of your lurid sexual stories, Tom."

"Funnily enough it's not one of those stories. It will be the next time that I tell it though. No, I was in The Body Shop and I was smelling this jar of mango body cream. It smelled so good I felt like tasting some. So I did."

"You dipped your finger in and ate it?"

"Unfortunately not. It probably would have been alright if I'd done that, but I was already smelling it, my nose was right in the jar, so I just stuck my tongue out and licked a bit."

"That's disgusting."

"Yes I know that now. That's what the girl behind the counter and the security guard said too."

"What did you say?"

"The truth. That I really like mangoes."

"What happened?"

"I had to buy the jar of course. And about ten other things because they made me feel so guilty."

"I remember now. You gave me a lovely basket of Body Shop things for Christmas last year. Oh my god—Tom?"

"Don't worry. I gave the jar of mango body cream to Meg."

"Why did you give it to Meg?" she asked jealously.

"I couldn't give it to you—that would have been too much like temptation. Whereas I'm fond of Meg, but I do find the girl extraordinarily unlickable."

"This is sounding like one of your lurid stories again," she said, trying not to show how pleased she was that Tom didn't want to lick Meg, even when she was slathered with mangoes.

Tom rubbed his neck again. He caught Lucy watching him and grinned ruefully. "I still feel like a pretzel."

"Why don't you try yoga?" Lucy suggested.

Tom looked doubtful. "Would I have to wear tights?"

"Don't be silly. There's a beginners class at my yoga school this afternoon. You should go. Think of it as intensive stretching. You'll feel much better afterwards, I promise."

Tom was still looking unconvinced. "I won't have to chant and stuff, will I?"

"Well, there's ten minutes at the end where we sit in a circle and burn incense and clap along to a tambourine but you'll probably really like it. As the new person in the class you'll get to play the triangle." Lucy saw that Tom was taking her seriously and added in exasperation, "I'm joking. Look, there's a flyer stuck to the fridge with the timetable. Just take it and if you feel like going then go. I promise it will make your back feel better."

Tom looked unconvinced but dutifully went into the kitchen and removed the yoga timetable from the refrigerator door. Pausing in the living room he looked down wistfully at the untidy pile of magazines on the coffee table.

Lucy followed his gaze. "Don't worry about the mess. I'll throw them out when I'm finished with them."

Tom grabbed the copy of *Maxim* magazine and held it protectively to his chest. "You can't throw this out. It's an extremely rare collector's edition."

"Oh really? Why is that?"

"Because it doesn't have Paris Hilton in it."

Lucy sighed heavily. "You can keep it. I suppose you need to have something to take home to introduce to your parents."

Tom grinned but ignored the provocation. "Do you need anything else before I go?"

Lucy smiled gratefully at him and waved her hand, indicating her tissues, magazines, and orange juice. "No thank you," she said cheerfully. "I'm all set now. I feel much better than I did yesterday anyway. Thanks again, Tom. I'd kiss you but I don't want you to get sick."

"Screw that." He bent down and kissed her swiftly. "Call me if you need anything."

It was only after he'd gone that she saw the card propped up on the table. Made out of the white cardboard of one of her discarded tissue

boxes, he had decorated it using the makeup samples from the magazines. Opening the card, she read the brief lines of writing inside:

*Don't die, Ginger—I couldn't bear it if you left me. (But if you do I
promise I'll send the biggest wreath of plastic carnations that money
can buy to your funeral.)*

Lucy smiled wryly at this typically Tom comment.
And then she put her head on her arms and wept.

12.

things starting with *b-o-o*

On Saturday morning Tom opened the door to his apartment to admit Lucy, who greeted him distractedly and promptly pushed past him.

"Lovely to see you too," Tom said sardonically, closing the door and following her into the living room.

Lucy appeared not to hear him. She was standing in front of his bookcase, perusing its contents anxiously. Tom moved Lucy's beach towel, canvas bag, and a bathing suit from where she had flung them across his couch and sprawled himself in their place, watching her in amusement.

"Upset about the Dewey decimal system again, Luce?" Tom asked kindly, after a few more minutes spent watching Lucy chew her lip, pull a book from the shelf, and replace it again.

"Be quiet," Lucy said automatically, adding in a rush, "Would you find *The Impressionist* or *Atonement* more impressive?"

"I've only read the first one."

"That doesn't matter. What would you think of me if I was reading them?"

"Fucked if I know. That you can read? What am I meant to think?"

"I'm going to the beach with Byron and I need to know what book to take to impress him."

Tom looked at her and then down at the bathing suit lying next to him. "Lucy honey? You're going to be wearing this." He delicately picked up the scraps of material that comprised her bathing suit. "I guarantee he won't care what you're reading. He'll be looking at other things starting with B-O-O."

Lucy shot him a scornful look. "He's not as lowly minded as you."

"It has nothing to do with being lowly minded. You look hot in this."

"Really?" Lucy asked pleased.

"Really."

Lucy sighed suddenly. "I wish Byron—" She stopped and bit her lip.

"What?"

"Nothing," she said, banishing the disloyal thought from her mind. She turned to him suddenly as something occurred to her. "Aren't you going to ask me what I'm doing here anyway?"

"I assumed you wanted to borrow a book."

"Partly. But I also have something for you." Temporarily abandoning the bookcase she rummaged in her untidy bag. "Here, I brought you a present."

"What's this for?" Tom asked, starting to unwrap the oddly shaped package.

"It's a thank-you present for helping me move. And for being nice to me when I was sick."

Tom paused thoughtfully in the act of unwrapping. "I'm really very good to you, aren't I?"

"Very." Lucy watched Tom's face for his reaction as the final layer of paper fell away.

He held up a jar of scented oil, a tube of deep pore facial cleanser, and a plastic dinosaur. "Ah, Luce? I have absolutely no idea what I'm meant to do with any of these. And I'm slightly scared if they're in any way connected."

"It's bath oil," Lucy said reprovingly. "So you can have a relaxing bubble bath after yoga and because I'm sorry that you got a sore back from sleeping on the couch when you were looking after me. And they gave me the face mask for free when I bought the bath oil."

"Why don't you keep it? I don't think I'll be using it somehow."

"It doesn't suit my skin type. And there's absolutely no reason why you shouldn't use it. Skin is just skin, whether you're male or female. You should try it. Face masks are very refreshing."

"That still doesn't explain the dinosaur," Tom said, holding the plastic reptile up in order to inspect him more closely.

"I wanted to buy you a rubber duckie to go with the bath oil, but they were all sold out. So I got you a dinosaur instead. It was the most macho bath toy I could find."

"Oh. Well as long as it's a *macho* bath toy, that's okay."

"He growls if you squeeze him," Lucy added.

"Very handy for scaring off potential burglars," Tom said lamely, groping for a situation in which a growling plastic dinosaur could be of value.

"You don't like him," Lucy said, crestfallen.

"I do," Tom hastened to reassure her. "And it was very sweet of you to get me a present. Thanks, Luce."

Lucy brightened up immediately. "What are you going to call him?"

"I have to name it?"

"Of course. And it's a him, not an it."

"Why? It's not like it—he—can hear me."

"He's going to share your bath," Lucy said reprovingly. "You can't be naked in the bath with a strange dinosaur."

Tom eyed her with fascination. "Have you ever actually stopped and listened to the words that come out of your mouth?"

"Oh fine. I'll name him for you," Lucy said impatiently. She glanced around the room and her gaze fell on a CD resting on Tom's stereo.

"We can call him Stipey," she said triumphantly. "After Michael Stipe."

"I'm going to be taking baths with the lead singer of R.E.M.?"

"I think it suits him. He's sort of stripey too."

"Stipey it is then," said Tom, knowing when to give in. He looked around for somewhere to put Stipey and ended up placing him on the sunny windowsill.

They both looked at the dinosaur seriously.

"He looks happy there, don't you think?" asked Lucy.

"Yes," Tom agreed, deciding not to point out that a plastic dinosaur was hardly likely to have an extensive range of facial expressions. He put an arm around Lucy and kissed her affectionately on the top of her head. She instantly snuggled closer to him and rubbed her head happily against his shoulder. He let her rest against him for a moment and then firmly pushed her away. "Get away from me before I'm forced to do terrible things to you, wench," he said with mock anger.

She wrinkled her nose at him and a flirtatious response sprang to her lips. Dutifully remembering Byron, she bit it back and instead looked curiously at the copy of *Maxim* magazine that was lying on the top of a heap of newspapers by the door, ready to be thrown out.

"Why are you throwing that magazine out? You wouldn't let me throw it out! I thought you wanted to keep it?"

A look of almost physical anguish crossed Tom's face. "I don't *want* to throw it out. I *have* to throw it out."

"Why?"

"Because I've developed a relationship with Librette."

"Who on earth is Librette?"

"Pages thirty-eight to forty-three," he groaned.

Lucy picked up the well-thumbed magazine and turned to page thirty-eight, where she discovered that Librette was a lingerie model who liked down to earth guys with a good sense of humor and favored a seating posture generally reserved for equestrian events. Lucy looked up to see that Tom was eyeing the open magazine hungrily. "She's gorgeous. I think I'm a bit obsessed."

"Tom, you do realize that her name is not Librette? It's Doris. Or Pauline."

"Stop ruining my fantasy."

"Let me just get this straight. You're breaking up an imaginary relationship with a woman in a magazine whose alias sounds like a brand of tampon?"

"She was starting to get so *needy*," Tom complained.

"You are a very sad person, Thomas. You're going to end up old and alone, hooked up to a catheter, watching porn."

"Doesn't sound that bad to me. Would I have a cute nurse to change the catheter bag?"

"Tragic." Lucy shook her head. "Just tragic."

She checked the time on her cell phone and shrieked. "Damn. I'm late again." She stood on tiptoe and kissed Tom hurriedly on the cheek. "Gotta go. I'll see you on Wednesday night for dinner. We're all meeting at our place, remember?" Picking up her things, she dashed out.

"Luce—wait a minute, you forgot to take a book—" The front door slammed, and Tom was left holding the two books in his hand. He glared at Stipey and the picture of the smiling Librette. "It just proves my point—life is impossible with Lucy. She is completely impossible. We're much better off without her."

13.

camping with hank

"Ready to go?" asked Tom, striding impatiently into Chloe and Lucy's living room on Wednesday night. Meg and Percy were already assembled in readiness for their dinner at a nearby restaurant. Lucy, who was on her cell, made a shushing gesture, and Tom looked enquiringly at Meg.

"Byron?" he asked.

"Marlon," she sighed. "As in chicken sexer, stalker Marlon. Byron's not coming. He called and canceled five minutes ago, which was considerate as he should have been here twenty minutes ago."

Tom grinned. "Don't you wonder how he and Lucy ever manage to spend time together? They're both as hopelessly unreliable as each other. It must be like waiting for the moons of Saturn to align."

Lucy finished her call and tossed her phone carelessly onto a chair. "Hello, Thomas. I've told Marlon that I'm not looking for a roommate anymore but he keeps calling. We're just waiting for Chloe. We actually have heaps of time—Meg deliberately told me the wrong time so that I wouldn't be late. Is that Chloe now?" She cocked one ear at the sound of the front door opening. Clutching her briefcase and suit jacket Chloe entered the room full of breathless apologies.

"And where have you been, young lady?" asked Tom with a raised eyebrow.

Chloe looked surprised. "At work. It's seven o'clock on a Wednesday night. Where else would I have been?"

"Chloe, you *reek* of cigarette smoke," Lucy said. "You smell like you've been in a nightclub."

Chloe suddenly became intensely focused on hanging her jacket over the back of a chair and depositing her briefcase in a corner.

They all eyed her suspiciously, and then Meg suddenly snapped her fingers. "I've got it!" she said triumphantly. "Ariel smokes, doesn't she?"

Lucy's eyes widened. "Yes, but Chloe wouldn't let her smoke in the office . . . Chloe—you *don't?*"

Chloe looked defensive. "I did ask her to give up," she said plaintively.

"What did she say?"

Chloe's shoulders slumped. "She said that she's not a quitter."

"Well fine, but you shouldn't let her smoke in the office, Clo. You know that it's illegal."

"What did you say her name was?"

"Ariel."

"It's from Shakespeare," Percy said helpfully. "*The Tempest.*"

Tom regarded him disapprovingly. "I don't think you should know things like that, Percy. And if you do you shouldn't say them out loud."

"It's not his fault he had an English public school education," Chloe defended Percy.

"I've had about enough of this girl and I've never even met her," Meg said irritably, reverting back to the original topic. "Chloe—Ariel's a complete bully, but it's your fault too. You're her boss. You shouldn't *let* her bully you.

To everyone's surprise, Chloe smiled jubilantly and pulled a pamphlet out of her bag with a flourish. "I know. You're absolutely right," she said excitedly. "That's why I've signed up Ariel and myself for this course."

Lucy grabbed the flyer out of Chloe's hand and read aloud: "Camping with Hank—the healthy way to achieve workplace resolution."

"Who on earth is Hank?" asked Meg dubiously, eyeing the photograph of a camp leader seated cross-legged on a mountaintop against a virulently orange sunset.

"Hank's a facilitator," Lucy said, reading aloud from the inside of the pamphlet. "Specializing in the resolution of unhappy working relationships or environments."

"Did you speak to Hank when you signed up for the course?"

"No. I spoke to an assistant. Hank was off on a hike."

"A hike?"

Chloe looked even more nervous. "Yes. That's how the course is run. You spend a weekend hiking at Wilson's Promontory. It's all about letting your defenses down when you're vulnerable in the wilderness and seeing things in a different perspective away from the urban environment and letting the beauty and harmony of nature act as an inspiration for how to conduct ourselves with our colleagues and fellow human beings—why are you all looking at me like that?"

"Chloe?" said Tom sternly. "You've been a very bad girl. You joined a cult without telling your Uncle Tom."

"Oh shut up, Tom. It's not a cult. It's a facilitated camping trip. I think it will really do the trick with Ariel."

"Chloe—you *hate* camping. Why are you going to so much trouble to help this horrible girl?"

"Because I'm a professional recruitment consultant!" Chloe snapped. "And I refuse to fail with Ariel. She's the only one I've never been able to place."

"I still think you're mad. Just fire her. She has more than enough attitude to find herself another job. There's no way I would go through the torture of a weekend stuck in the bush listening to Hank's facilitated crap-speak just to help Ariel."

Chloe looked even more shame-faced. "Yes you would," she whispered.

"No, I damn well would—Chloe? What haven't you told us?"

Chloe's head practically disappeared, shrinking turtle-like back against herself. "You're coming with me. I signed you all up."

"*What?*"

"I *had* to," Chloe said despairingly. "Hank only runs the courses for ten or more, and he only had one other girl enrolled. So he's doing us a favor really because there's only four of you."

"I'd pay two hundred dollars *not* to go camping," said Percy, who was wearing a horrified expression.

"Chloe, we are not coming with you. We don't need to do this course," Lucy said firmly.

"Yes you do. Hank only specializes in workplace disharmonies. But he can help with personal problems too. He could sort you and Tom out."

"We don't need sorting out!" Lucy and Tom chorused indignantly.

"Yes you do," Meg said disparagingly. "Good idea if you ask me."

"See?" Chloe said eagerly. "And Meg, Hank can help you and Percy too."

"We don't need help!" Percy and Meg objected simultaneously. Lucy and Tom smiled at them sweetly.

"Yes you do," said Lucy. "Percy suffers from unrequited love, and Meg, you suffer from unrelenting cynicism."

Percy's ears burned, but Meg smiled gratefully at Lucy, as though she had just paid her a tremendous compliment, and then shrugged. "I'll go, Chloe. I like hiking."

Chloe clapped her hands in glee. "Excellent! That means Percy will come too." She turned beseechingly to Tom and Lucy. "Pleee-ase? Pretty, super, triple please with extra chocolate on top?"

Lucy gave in first. "Okay, okay. But only because you put extra chocolate on top. And I'm going to invite Byron too."

"Tom?"

"You're a pest, Chloe."

"Yes, but you love me anyway. And if you come I give you permission to tell the guys at football that you had a threesome with Lucy and I."

"I've already told them that."

Chloe frowned. "Oh. Well, you shouldn't have. That was very wrong of you."

"You told me I could last September when you needed help moving," Tom protested.

"Don't I get a say in this?' asked Lucy irritably.

"No," said Tom and Chloe in unison. "And anyway," Tom added, "you said I could tell them that too."

"I would not have let you say something like that simply to get you to lift heavy furniture," said Lucy haughtily, very much on her dignity.

"No, you probably would have offered me oral sex. You've no morals at all. But I think you read an article in *Vanity Fair* that said bisexuality was fashionable that month."

"Well okay," Lucy said, slightly mollified. "That does sound like me."

"Tom, I'm not going to offer you oral sex to come camping with us," said Chloe in alarm.

Tom still looked hopeful. "Can you get Lucy to do it?"

Chloe turned beseechingly to Lucy. "Luc—ow! No. Guess not."

"Oh fine. I'll come out of the goodness of my heart then," Tom sighed magnanimously.

Chloe beamed sunnily at them. "Good. So it's all settled then. Now I just need to tell Ariel."

"Where the fuck is Ariel?" Chloe, clearly agitated, strode up and down the pavement outside the apartment. The others exchanged glances. Chloe rarely swore. It was a quarter past ten and they had now been waiting for Ariel to show up for forty-five minutes.

"Maybe she stopped to help a little old lady cross the street," Tom suggested laconically.

"Yes, and then the assault and robbery of the little old lady took longer than expected," Meg added, looking up from the third install-ment of *The Werigandelthornbrum Trilogy* (*The Alliance of Hervyagotmead & Cristallon-Dawnarc*).

"Stop it, Meg. She's not that bad. Please don't say things like that to her or the trip will be a disaster."

Meg closed her book, rose from her seat on her backpack, and stretched. "I can say what I like about her, Chloe, because she's not coming."

Percy, who was engrossed in a book called *The Deadly Outback*, lifted his head at this point to inform them, in a tone that was both awed and petrified, that Australia harbored no less than seventeen of the world's most lethal species of snake. Everyone regarded him bleakly for a moment and then turned back to Chloe who was still pacing.

"She'll come," Chloe said tersely. "I made it clear that it was her professional duty to be here."

"Chlo—she's never once, not once, taken anything about that job seriously. She hasn't even called to tell you why she's running late."

Chloe looked stricken. "What if something terrible has happened to her?"

"The only bad thing that could have happened to her is if she argued with a giant piranha," Tom said. At the mention of the giant piranha Percy's head snapped up anxiously. "I'd back her to take on anything else that got in her way. And I'd give her pretty good odds against the piranha too. Come on, Clo, let's go. You've left about thirty-five messages on her phone and we still have a two-hour drive ahead of us. She has plenty of time to contact you, and she'll just have to find her own way there."

Chloe looked at him incredulously. "You mean you still want to go?"

"Chloe, it's the weekend. We're all packed up to go away and we've paid two hundred dollars for the privilege of spending the weekend with this guru. I, for one, intend to get my money's worth of enlighten-ment and life skills. He'd better be able to show me how to undo a bra with my teeth or I'm demanding a refund. Luce, will you please stop text messaging Byron for one minute and hand me your backpack?"

Lucy jumped to her feet. "Thank God. I hate waiting. Byron just sent us a message to wish us all a good trip by the way. He's so sad that he had to work this weekend."

"It's such a shame," Tom murmured wistfully. "But when we look at the stars we'll be thinking of him."

Lucy pointedly ignored him. "Chloe, do you want to come in our car?"

"No, I'll go with Meg and Percy," Chloe answered, still with a worried crease on her brow. "It will distract me if Percy keeps reading bits out of his book."

Meg groaned at this prospect, but Tom couldn't help remarking, "I must say I do feel a bit like a member of the Famous Five embarking on a camping trip. Lucy, do you want to be George or the boring one— what was her name—Anne?"

"I don't mind being Anne," Lucy said handsomely. "Meg is more like George anyway. And you can be Julian, Tom, which makes Percy Dick."

"That means I'm Timmy," Chloe wailed, as the others, happy to have this resolved satisfactorily, prepared to depart. "Why do I have to be the dog?"

With a considerable want of sympathy, her friends ignored her as they slammed the boot and car doors and headed off in the direction of enlightenment.

"Greetin's, greetin's, how y'all doin' on this fine day?" As they emerged from the cars, sticky and irritable after the drive, Hank detached himself from the cowering figure of a woman to whom he had been expostulating loudly. All wiry energy and oddly unplaceable, pseudo-American accent, he pounced on them one by one and enveloped them each in a hug.

"That's what Camp Hank is about you see," Hank enthused. "LOVE! HONESTY! SHARING! Hey missy, where do you think you're goin'?" This was directed at Meg, who had headed straight back to the car at the mention of love, honesty, and sharing.

"Home," Meg said flatly, over her shoulder.

Hank burst into a loud cackle of laughter and hauled Meg back to where the others were assembled. "Looks like we've found ourselves the group joker! Okay y'all, now listen up. I want you to introduce yourselves. Say your name—first name only—and then say one thing about the person standing next to you that you think is special. We want to break down those barriers from the word go. Remember—Love. Honesty. Sharing." He turned back towards the woman he had been haranguing. "You first, Janice. Shoot."

Janice stared at her feet miserably through a curtain of mousy brown hair. "My name's Janice," she finally managed, adding mournfully, "There's no one standing next to me. That's because no one likes me. No one likes me, because there's nothing special about me," she finished with a kind of savage pride.

Hank bounded over and hugged her. "Janice honey, you're just chock-full of special somethin's. And we're gonna find them all this weekend."

"Do you think that includes her G-spot?" Meg muttered to Lucy. Lucy choked and tried unconvincingly to turn it into a cough.

"I'm Marlon," said a barefoot man who was seated despondently on a rock next to Tom. He waved dejectedly. "Hi, Lucy."

"*Marlon?*" Lucy shrieked, dropping her sunglasses in shock. "As in chicken sexer, stalker Marlon?"

Marlon looked visibly offended by this description. "I'm not technically a stalker until you take out a restraining order. Until then I'm just an aggravated nuisance."

"What are you doing here? How did you know I'd be here?"

"I heard you talking about it with your friends the other night. You ought to be more careful about hanging up properly. Is that your boyfriend?" he finished, eyeing Tom resentfully.

"He's not my boyfriend," Lucy said impatiently, dealing with what she considered to be the most pertinent issue first. She surveyed him thoughtfully. "Do you know you look *exactly* how I pictured you?"

Marlon gazed at her glumly. "I thought you'd be prettier," he said

mournfully, as though Lucy was yet another in life's long string of disap-
pointments.

Before Lucy could recover from this, Hank, who seemed slightly irritated that he hadn't been the center of attention for the past two minutes, interjected in his annoyingly accented, booming voice once again.
"Marlon, you have to say somethin' about the person next to you,
remember? One of the keys to success is to deal with the task at hand
without getting distracted. Hey—how's that? Lesson number one and
we ain't even left the parking lot!" Hank beamed at them.

Marlon paused in the act of wringing out a pair of wet socks to survey Tom in bewilderment. "I don't know who this guy is."

"That's alright, Marlon," Hank said reassuringly. "Go with that
unknowingness. Feel the strange complexity of another human being.
Close your eyes and run your hands over his face."

"Eh? What?" Tom started nervously, staring in horror at Marlon's
damp hands, which were still holding his clammy socks.

"I don't want to," Marlon said, even more nervously.

Hank surveyed them both with a huge look of disappointment and
then, with a rapid change of mood, brightened up. "That's okay! We'll
break those barriers down—y'all'll see."

Tom introduced himself. "And this is Lucy. She's special because—
He stopped.

They waited.

"Go on," Lucy hissed.

He turned to her and whispered, "Can I tell them about that time
we went skiing and—"

Lucy blushed violently. "No, you can't!"

"But that was *really* special," Tom said wistfully. "Okay—what about
the time you went to that costume place and rented—"

"Can't you think of one special thing about me that doesn't involve
sex?" Lucy demanded furiously, forgetting to whisper.

"Of course I can."

They waited some more. While Marlon eyed Lucy with renewed

interest, Tom concentrated with the sort of mental intensity normally reserved for telepathic spoon benders.

Lucy finally lost patience. "I'm going to push you off a cliff. Hi, everyone, I'm Lucy. The special thing about my friend Meg is that she's going to help me throw Tom off a cliff."

"And I'm Meg. The special thing about me is that it won't be my first murder."

"You were meant to say something about the person next to you," Hank reprimanded her, looking slightly disconcerted that his getting-to-know-one-another introductory exercise had descended so swiftly into sex and murder.

"Oh yeah sorry. In that case Chloe plays the harp beautifully."

"I've never played the harp in my life," Chloe said puzzled.

"Whatever. It's not like anyone cares anyway."

Hank eyed Meg narrowly, and pulling out a notebook, he scribbled something down.

"I'm Chloe," said Chloe, throwing Meg a resentful glance. "This is Percy, and he really does play the piano. Beautifully."

Percy, unaccustomed to being publicly praised, blushed proudly. "I don't have anyone to say anything about either so I suppose I'm a bit like Janice." He smiled encouragingly at Janice and was rewarded by a viciously repelling look, which took him aback slightly.

"And I'm Hank!" Hank said with manic glee. "And y'all are special to me. By the end of this weekend we'll have solved all those issues y'all just raised."

"What issues?' Meg wondered aloud.

But Hank didn't pay her any attention. "Let's hike!"

In the midafternoon, they had a brief respite on a rocky plateau overlooking the cobalt waters of Bass Strait. The track had hugged the coastline for most of the hike so far but trees had obscured the view, so that only tantalizing glimpses of a sapphire blue sea could be seen. Now both the sparkling blue of the sky and water were spread out before them, and the cool breeze that blew was welcome on the hot and sweaty skin of the hikers. Content to rest and gaze, they pulled out their water bottles, and Percy rummaged in his pack and found a packet of raspberry candies to the great joy of everyone.

While Percy and Tom stretched out against their backpacks and sporadically swatted oversized March flies, Lucy and Meg rested on a higher ledge to the right. Chloe, who was sitting slightly to the side of the boys, pulled off her left boot and sock and dolefully inspected the blister that was forming on her heel.

"That's where we're headed," hollered Hank from the summit of the outcrop, indicating the crescent-shaped shoreline of Refuge Cove, which appeared to be only twenty minutes away but which they were all wise enough now to realize was probably still a good three-hour hike distant.

Chloe, who had been brooding in silence for some time now, suddenly announced to nobody in particular, "I want a shepherd."

Tom and Percy considered this request, which, although slightly out of context, didn't seem altogether unreasonable, especially when Chloe added bitterly, "Hillary had one. Why can't I?"

"No reason at all, Clo," Tom said soothingly. In an aside to Percy he muttered, "Who's Hillary?"

"Haven't the foggiest. Perhaps it's someone she went to school with. Seems an odd thing to give a shepherd to a schoolgirl though." After a bit more thought he added, "Pony I can understand. Shepherd, no."

"Do you want the last candy, Chloe?" called out Lucy, who hadn't heard a word of this but was feeling sorry for Chloe, who was looking more and more dismal with each passing minute.

Chloe shook her head mutely, and Percy, feeling that this generous offer required more of a response, shouted, "Thanks anyway, Luce, but all that she wants right now is a shepherd."

"I don't know why we don't just push Percy over the cliff," Meg said, looking at the hapless Percy with disgust.

"Why are you always so cruel to Percy? He's one of the kindest people I've ever met."

"Me too. Isn't it strange how I don't find it the least bit endearing?"

Percy, unaware that he was the subject of this conversation and who had evidently not taken Chloe's request lightly, now declared, "You know, Chloe has a point. It's bloody odd when you think about it. Millions and millions of sheep in Australia. Never met a shepherd in my life. What I want to know is—who's taking care of the flocks? Who's saving the innocent lambs from the wolves?"

"We don't have wolves in Australia," said Tom, who was only marginally interested in this conversation.

"We probably do have shepherds only they're not called shepherds. They have shepherds in Greece," Chloe contributed in her despondent tone.

"Well, there's something wrong with this country if you have to import shepherds, that's all I'm saying. There ought to be restrictions. Some sort of tax on Greek shepherds."

"What are you all blathering about?" Meg asked, curiosity getting the better of her as she edged over to join Chloe and the boys.

"Chloe wants a shepherd. Her friend Hillary had one so now she wants one. Percy thinks there ought to be an import tax on foreign shepherds. Got any water left?" explained Tom incisively.

"What on earth are you going on about?" asked Lucy, coming over to join them but refusing to look at Tom.

"I wasn't going on about anything," flared Chloe, in a most un-Chloe-like show of temper, brought on by exhaustion and the discomfort of her blistered heel. "Percy was the one who was crapping on about putting a tax on imported shepherds."

At this juncture, Marlon sidled up to Lucy. "Do you want to share my water?" he asked suggestively.

Lucy edged as far away as the rocky plateau would allow. "No thanks."

"So what sort of costume did you rent?" Marlon asked with a smirk.

"I beg your pardon?"

"From the costume place. Your boyfriend was going to tell us about the costume you rented."

"He's not my boyfriend," Lucy said flatly.

Marlon's leer grew. "So you're single then? Single and you like playing dress-up. That's quite a combination."

"Look, you lecherous toad, I do not like playing dress-up, and I'm not single."

Marlon didn't seem in the least bit offended by this appellation. "Yeah right. Where's your boyfriend then?"

"He had to work," Lucy said irritably, wondering why it sounded like Byron was imaginary even to her.

"Playing hard to get," Marlon said with satisfaction. "All you kinky girls do that."

Meg thought it prudent to step in at this point. "Marlon, I'll play dress-up with you if you like. I'll wear my cheerleader outfit and I can flay strips of flesh from your back to make my pom-poms."

Marlon backed away hastily and went to sit off on a side from where he continued to watch Lucy intently. Hank, who had overheard this exchange, pulled out his notebook again and scribbled something down on the rapidly filling page headed "Meg."

14.

the journey game

Three hours later they finally staggered into the campground and wearily set about putting up their tents. Hank continued to bound around, issuing directives and announcing plans for team-building exercises and games that evening, which would apparently be a high treat for them all.

Lucy, who was exhausted from both the hiking and fending off Marlon, wanted nothing more than to go to sleep as soon as possible. So, when dinner was over and Hank delved into a canvas bag and produced some brightly colored rubber balls, it was all that she could do to restrain a groan.

"Okeydoke," Hank said. "Here you go—catch!" He threw one of the balls at each of them, unfortunately hitting Janice in the head with hers.

"Sorry, J!" he called cheerfully, as Janice blinked several times and gazed cross-eyed into the campfire.

Everyone held their ball and looked at Hank blankly.

"What do we do with them?" asked Percy.

"What do you *want* to do with yours, Percy?" Hank asked meaningfully.

"Not sure," said Percy nervously, wondering if he was failing some kind of test.

"Do you see it as a symbol of fun? Do you wanna play with it? Or do you see it as a responsibility? It's important to lose your inhibitions and go with your primitive urges." Hank's tone had intensified.

Percy stiffened. "I went to a very exclusive boarding school," he said haughtily. "My parents paid a lot of money to ensure that I don't have primitive urges."

"I want to throw mine at your head," Meg said conversationally, tossing her ball up into the air and trying to calculate the exact angle needed to hit Hank between the eyes.

"I think the important thing to figure out in your case, Meg, is *why* you want to do that," Hank said anxiously.

"But you just told us we should act on how we feel," Meg objected, still tossing her ball up and down.

"In that case I want to kiss Lucy," Marlon suddenly piped up lasciviously.

"If you so much as try I'll put a tent pole through your head," Lucy said with a shudder.

"But Hank said we should be trying to help each other achieve our goals. My goal is to kiss you. You should be helping me, Lucy. Isn't that right, Hank?"

"I guarantee that if you touch me all my friends will help me achieve *my* goal, which involves the aforementioned tent pole and your head. Why do you insist on being so creepy, Marlon?"

Hank intervened. "What *you* see as creepy is just the expression of Marlon's unique personality. I think the important thing in your case, Lucy, is to understand why you're so uncomfortable with someone openly demonstrating their affection for you."

"Gee, I don't know, Hank," said Lucy sarcastically. "Let's see— maybe it has something to do with the fact that I only met Marlon face to face seven hours ago and he's already asked me what color panties I'm wearing and keeps trying to get me to drink from his water bottle in some kind of oral sex simulation."

"I'm sensing a lot of anger here, L," Hank said seriously. "Does sex make you angry, Lucy?"

"Yeah, does it, Lucy?" echoed Marlon eagerly.

"I'm sleeping in your tent tonight, Tom," Lucy muttered in despair, quite forgetting their earlier disagreement. "And as soon as we get back to civilization, I'm changing my cell phone number."

"You know, Lucy," Hank began confidentially, "when I was building mud huts with one of the lost tribes of Tanzania, they performed a ritual in which sex and anger were played out through dance and song. What I learned from that experience I later incorporated into my role as CEO of CEOs-Anon—a golfing/support group for one of the most marginalized segments of our society—" Hank was about to launch into another self-promoting monologue, when he realized that Meg was tossing her ball from one hand to another with increasingly restless and powerful throws.

"Blah, blah, blah," Janice suddenly contributed angrily. "No one cares what Janice thinks or feels."

"Why does she always refer to herself in the third person?" Lucy whispered uneasily to Tom. "It freaks me out. It's like camping with Gollum."

"I care, Janice," said Marlon suddenly.

Janice peered at him suspiciously from beneath her curtain of hair. "Why would you care about Janice?"

"Because I'm trying to make Lucy jealous."

Lucy groaned and instinctively moved closer to Tom, who put a comforting arm around her. Janice glared at Lucy and muttered something that sounded suspiciously like "Slut."

When Hank's activities were finally over, they sat around the campfire and gazed pensively at the flying sparks.

"This is what's so wonderful about being out in the bush," Hank said with a smile. "You feel invincible and vulnerable at the same time. It can help conquer your greatest fears. Hey—now there's an idea! Let's go round the campfire, one by one, and share what we're all most afraid of. You first, L."

From her seat on a log that she had made Tom check thoroughly for creepy-crawlies before consenting to sit on it, Lucy, who was very tired and in no mood for any more of Hank's pseudo-psychological insights, pretended to consider the question carefully. "Curtains," she said finally, primarily for Percy's benefit.

"Ending up alone," said Tom soulfully, for Lucy's benefit.

"Being put down," said Chloe, for Meg's benefit.

"Do you mean that metaphorically or literally, Timmy?" asked Meg.

"Don't be mean to Chloe, Meg. Anyway it's your turn. What are you afraid of?"

"Forgetting to feed Chloe," said Meg for Chloe's benefit.

"Percy? What are you afraid of?"

"French Canadians," said Percy with a slight shudder.

"What?"

"They're neither European nor American. I don't trust them."

Hank looked at the others inquiringly, but they all shook their heads warningly.

"And you know what their national sport is?" Percy continued bitterly. "*Ice-skating.*"

"I was asked out by an ice-skater once," Lucy said dreamily, instantly whisked back to the nostalgia of a bygone romantic interlude.

Tom snorted vociferously. "For the hundred and fiftieth time, Luce— he was asking *me* out. You just got in the way."

Lucy snapped out of her reverie and glared at him. "Rubbish. Gay men never fall for you. You're about the only man who couldn't score on Mardi Gras night." She paused and then added generously, "I think it's your aftershave."

"What's wrong with my aftershave?" Tom asked, affronted.

"Nothing. I just don't think it would be very attractive to a gay man."

"And that conclusion is based on what? You are neither male, nor gay, nor exceptionally nasally intuitive."

"No, Tom, it could be true," piped up Percy, who had been following the conversation intently. "I never have any luck with Scottish girls. I believe it has something to do with my hair."

Everyone regarded Percy cautiously for a few moments and then, as one, made an unspoken pact never again to return to that particular topic.

Clutching her sleeping bag, Lucy opened the flaps of Tom's tent and set about making herself comfortable.

"Can I help you?" Tom asked politely, regretfully putting aside the copy of *One Hundred Years of Solitude* that he had borrowed from Meg.

"Yes please. Can you hand me your fleece? I can roll it up and use it as a pillow," Lucy said without a trace of irony, as she kicked off her hiking boots and put them outside the tent.

"You're not really going to sleep in here tonight, are you?" asked Tom, handing her the fleece nonetheless.

Lucy paused in the act of smoothing her sleeping bag out and looked at him in surprise. "Of course I am. Marlon has freaked me out completely and Meg refuses to take it seriously. I know Meg—she'll go straight to sleep and I'll end up wide awake and terrified all night. And Chloe had already offered to share Janice's tent, and she didn't want to swap in case Janice saw it as rejection. We have a full day of hiking tomorrow—I couldn't bear it if I didn't get any sleep tonight."

"I was kind of hoping to go straight to sleep," Tom said wistfully.

"Well you can," Lucy said, climbing into her sleeping bag and punching

Tom's fleece into shape. "I just know that if I need to wake you up in the middle of the night you won't be horrible to me like Meg would be."

Tom groaned, foreseeing trouble ahead. "Luce? Can I ask what Byron is going to say about this?"

"Don't be silly," Lucy yawned, rolling onto one side and closing her eyes. "Byron is far too mature to get upset over something as trivial as us sharing a tent. He'll probably be grateful to you for taking care of me."

Tom was preparing to refute this highly dubious statement when he stopped at the sight of Lucy curled up beside him, her hair spread out on her makeshift pillow. Wondering how it was possible for one person to be so adorable and infuriating at precisely the same time, he switched off the flashlight hanging overhead and turned away from her, ruefully aware that with Lucy by his side, he was now wide awake.

Several hours later Tom was sleeping peacefully when he was woken by a strange swishing sound. Struggling to consciousness, he registered confusedly that the walls of the tent seemed to be swaying. With his eyes finally open and adjusted to the darkness he realized that Lucy was holding one of his boots in her hand as she threw herself energetically around the tent.

"What the hell are you doing?" Tom asked irritably.

"Ssshhh," Lucy whispered, laying a finger over her mouth.

"You can't tell me to be quiet when you've just been doing an indoor tornado routine," Tom argued, with some justification. "What's the matter? Is it Marlon?"

"Worse," Lucy said grimly. "I think I heard a mosquito."

"No you didn't. Go to sleep," said Tom automatically.

"I *did*. Listen—there it is again."

There was silence for a minute.

"I don't hear anything," Tom yawned. "Night, Luce."

Unconvinced, Lucy lay back down and closed her eyes. From out of the stillness of the night came the high-pitched hum, this time swooping close to her ear. "There is definitely a mozzie in the tent," she said sitting upright.

"Go and sleep with Marlon then. I'm sure he'd love to kill things on your behalf."

"Very funny. Sit up and help me look for it."

"I was asleep!

"No you weren't. Nobody falls back to sleep in two minutes."

"Not when they're sleeping next to you they don't," Tom muttered darkly, sitting up nonetheless. He turned on the overhead flashlight to reveal the sight of Lucy trying to stuff socks in her ears.

She cursed loudly as the socks fell out again. "Goddammit, they don't fit," she said in frustration.

"Were you expecting them to?" Tom asked with mild interest.

"I am trying," Lucy said haughtily, "to put socks in my ears so that I can't hear the mosquito. If I can't hear it, I don't care if it chews me to bits. It's the noise that drives me bonkers. And if I get to sleep then so do you. So stop looking at me like that, because in a way I'm actually doing this for you."

"I've never had a girl wear socks on her ears for me before," Tom said humbly. "Does it mean we're going steady?"

Lucy ignored him. Deciding on a fresh tactic, she pulled the socks over her ears, affecting a spaniel-like demeanor.

Tom considered her for a moment and then pointed out, "You might not be able to hear the mosquito now, but you'll still need to scratch if it bites you again."

"Good point." Locating the insect repellent, Lucy began to spray it liberally over herself and her bedding.

"Happy now?" Tom asked, after this operation was over.

"I think so. Sorry I woke you."

"That's okay. Can I switch the light off now?"

"Yes," said Lucy, who had started scratching madly at a bite on her wrist. The itch was driving her crazy and she put her wrist up to her mouth and started to gnaw at the bite to relieve the irritation.

Tom paused in the act of reaching up to the flashlight and gazed at Lucy in fascination for a moment.

"Luce? You do realize that you're wearing socks on your ears and eating your own flesh?"

"Mmmm. I'm itchy," Lucy explained.

"I think I might go and sleep with Marlon," Tom muttered. "You're getting really scary."

Darkness descended once again, and there was silence except for the small surreptitious sounds of Lucy scratching her various bites. Perhaps ten minutes passed before Lucy picked up Tom's discarded boot and started to swat the walls again.

Tom groaned. Rolling over, he turned on the flashlight for the second time. "Luce? It's a *tent*. It's made of *fabric*. Trying to squash the mozzie against the wall won't work because THE WALL WILL BEND."

"It's three in the morning. I've hiked for six hours today and had virtually no sleep. I can't be expected to think logically," argued Lucy, continuing to flail madly inside the tent, which was swaying alarmingly. Suddenly she sat stock-still and then her face crumpled.

"I can still hear it," she whimpered. "It's right in my ear." She started to scrabble feverishly at the sock on her left ear.

"This is getting far too *One Flew over the Cuckoo's Nest*," Tom muttered grimly. "Alright, I can see it. It's on your cheek near your ear. Stay perfectly still and on the count of three I'll squash it. Ready? One—"

"OW!"

Lucy rubbed the side of her head while Tom wiped the bloody remains of the mosquito off his hand.

"You never said three," Lucy said, adding aggrievedly, "or two."

"You would have moved. You can't stand pain. Now lie down and go to sleep. *Please?*"

Still rubbing the side of her head, Lucy climbed back into her sleeping bag, and Tom switched off the light. There was silence for perhaps five minutes and then Lucy spoke in a very small voice. "Tom?"

"Ugrhgh."

"I need to pee."

There was a loud sigh. "If you're telling me this it's going to involve me in some way, isn't it?"

"Will you come with me and hold the flashlight?"

"No. No no no no no."

"Stop being silly. I need protection from Marlon."

"Marlon is asleep. Marlon has been asleep for hours. I never thought that I'd say this, but I want to be Marlon."

"But there might be snakes in the bushes. You know how scared I am of snakes."

"Do you faithfully promise that if I do this you will go straight to sleep and not say a word for the rest of the night?"

"I'll try," Lucy said cautiously, aware of her own limitations.

Once Tom had ensured that the bushes were snake free and was stationed a short distance away, Lucy relieved herself as elegantly as she could under the circumstances.

"Thank you," Lucy said gratefully as they climbed into the tent once more and zipped the flaps up.

"You're not allowed to speak for the rest of the night, remember?" said Tom, softening this dictum by kissing her on the forehead. "Now go to sleep."

Lucy obediently turned over and curled up in a ball and closed her eyes. There was silence for several minutes, and then, to her complete horror, Lucy felt something snake across her stomach. She screamed and started to thrash wildly in her sleeping bag.

"What the hell's wrong with you?" yelled Tom, snatching his arm away. "Stop hitting me!"

"Oh my god," Lucy panted in fright. "I thought your arm was a snake."

"My arm is nothing like a snake," Tom said offended, nursing his battered arm. "You *hurt* me."

"Well, keep your damn hands to yourself. What exactly were you trying to do?"

"What do you think I was trying to do?" Tom asked angrily, his temper starting to flare. "I was trying to sleep with you, of course."

"Tom, *please*. It must be about three in the morning. I haven't had a shower. I smell like insect repellent. I'm scratching myself like a dog with fleas. I'm wearing socks on my ears. And you're still trying to screw me. You cannot possibly be this desperate."

"I could too," Tom said sulkily.

"Tom, I mean it. I'm not sleeping with you. I really like Byron."

"You really liked Taylor too," Tom reminded her.

"That was different," Lucy said uncomfortably. "I'm not cheating on Byron with you. Now please can we go to sleep?"

Perversely, Tom wanted her even more now that she was refusing him. It was always like this with Lucy. "We'll both sleep much better if we're *really* tired," he said suggestively.

"I am really tired," Lucy retorted, rolling away from him and putting her hands over her sock-covered ears in order to block out his words. "Tom, I have never managed to stay faithful to anyone but you and I don't want to be that kind of person. For the last time, I am not going to cheat on Byron."

"But then that means you're cheating on me," Tom objected.

"Fine. I'm cheating on you. I think we should break up. Good night."

"You used to be fun," Tom grumbled, giving up and turning away from Lucy.

Lucy sat upright, in indignation. "I can't understand you, Tom! Whenever we're together you make it clear that it's just casual but you never treat me like it's casual. You always call me and want to see me and take me to the movies and out to dinner and to see plays and do everything that people in relationships do but always with this constant reminder that it's 'only casual.' I never even know what that means."

"Well why do you have this need to put definitions on everything?"

Tom retaliated. "Why can't you just enjoy something and be in the moment without wanting it to fall under some conventional category label?"

"Because I never knew where I stood! I didn't know if it was okay to call you if I had seen you the night before or if that meant that I was being clingy. I didn't know if I should invite you to Meg's dinner party or if that was too much of a 'couple' thing to do. And if I went ahead and made my own plans for the weekend, you'd always call at the last minute and be a bit surprised that I hadn't intended to see you. I hated it, Tom."

"Your problem is that you think too much about things that are really quite simple, Luce. You complicate things that don't have to be that complicated. Look, just forget it."

You only ever want me when you think you can't have me, thought Lucy silently, as they both rolled onto their sides and pointedly turned their backs to one another. *Never again, Tom. I am never letting you do that to me again.*

Staggering out of Tom's car after the long drive back, Lucy, who was hot, dirty, and exhausted after the physical exertion of the weekend, was less than overjoyed to see Byron waiting on her doorstep.

"Lucia!" he said exuberantly. "You have returned to me." His gaze sharpened as Tom nodded curtly to him and proceeded to heft Lucy's backpack from the trunk.

"I thought there were many of you on this trip?" Byron enquired, with a touch of steel to his voice.

"Of course there was," Lucy said, fishing in her pocket for her keys. "Meg and Chloe are dropping off Percy first."

She opened the door wearily and led the way inside. "I'd like to kiss you, Byron, but I'd prefer a shower first."

He didn't object and instead looked measuringly at Tom.

"I'm getting a glass of water," Tom said, with the easy familiarity that never failed to infuriate Byron. "Does anyone else want one?"

"Yes please," said Lucy gratefully. Byron shook his head and waited till Tom had departed for the kitchen.

"So you enjoyed your expedition?"

"Yes. I'm horribly unfit though. And you'll never believe who else was there—" Lucy stopped short as it belatedly occurred to her that it was probably not a good idea to tell Byron about Marlon. She had forgotten that Byron had a ridiculously touchy streak of honor and for the first time she wondered whether sleeping in Tom's tent had been the good idea that it had seemed at the time. For some reason this annoyed her immensely. Determined to prove to herself that Byron trusted her implicitly and that her conduct had been above reproach, she declared airily, "The worst part was that I didn't sleep very well. There was a mosquito in the tent and it kept me up half the night until Tom killed it."

Tom, who had reentered the room in time to hear this, grinned inwardly. "Show time," he murmured to himself, proffering a glass of water towards Lucy.

Sure enough, Byron's face had darkened and he shot a poisonous look at Tom who smiled blandly at him. "You slept with him?" Byron asked dangerously.

Oh lord, Lucy thought, quailing before the look on his face. She sneaked a glance at Tom. Seeing his infuriating expression of I-told-you-so amusement she squared her shoulders and met Byron's furious gaze directly. "Byron, I did not sleep with Tom."

"Yes you did," said Tom, in an aggrieved tone of voice.

"Okay I did. Sleep with him. Technically. Meaning we lay side by side unconscious in our separate sleeping bags. But we did not have sex."

"It was intimate though," said Tom wistfully. Ignoring Lucy's furious look he turned to Byron. "I attended to her pink bits. And there was definitely swelling involved."

Byron looked puzzled. "What is he saying, Lucia?"

Lucy gritted her teeth. "He's talking about putting calamine lotion on my mosquito bites. Tom, you are *not* helping."

"I think it is better that we don't see each other, Lucia," said Byron, who was looking extremely grim.

"Byron, this is ridiculous. There was a horrible man who kept following me everywhere and that's why I had to share a tent with Tom."

"What man? How many men were on this trip?" asked Byron furiously, and Lucy realized that she had made a tactical error.

"He's no one. He was creepy, and that's why I slept with Tom."

"So you did sleep with him?"

"Oh for God's sake," said Lucy, starting to lose her temper. "We cannot break up over this because *nothing happened!*"

"Are you telling me that he did not try to kiss you?" asked Byron shrewdly.

A hot blush swept Lucy's face, and Tom looked away uncomfortably.

Byron surveyed them both in silence. "I thought so," he said simply. He strode to the door and paused beside it for a moment. "I love you, Lucy. But I do not like games." There was a silence as the door closed behind Byron and then Lucy promptly burst into tears.

"Oh Luce," said Tom, sitting next to her and pulling her into a hug. "I'm sorry."

"No, you're not," Lucy managed to choke. "You hate him."

"Well yes," Tom admitted, his innate honesty surfacing. "But I am sorry I made things worse."

Lucy collapsed into howls again and Tom decided that the wisest course of action would be to simply try and soothe her. After five or so minutes she was about to reach the disgusting snotty stage of crying so he lifted her tear-stained face from his shoulder. "Let's play the journey game."

"Don't want to," sniveled Lucy.

"Yes you do. It always cheers you up. Come on, Luce. Where do you want to go? The Belgian Congo?"

"Siberia," Lucy said dismally, still sobbing.

"You can't go to Siberia," Tom said firmly.

"Why not? It's a legitimate place."

"That's against the rules of the game and you know it. It has to be a historical place that no longer exists. So what about Gaul? Or Yugoslavia?"

Lucy thought for a moment. "Sardinia?"

"Sardinia still exists," said Tom in confusion.

"Oh. Well I don't think it should. It's a very silly name."

"What about Troy? East Berlin? The British East Indies?" Tom coaxed her.

"I want to go to French Botswana," Lucy said firmly.

"I don't think the French ever owned Botswana,' said Tom uncertainly.

"Oh *who cares?*" said Lucy exasperated. "Tom, I don't want to play right now. I know that you're trying to cheer me up but I don't *want* to be cheered up. I've just broken up with"—and Lucy started to sob again—"the love of my life and I'm miserable, and I *want* to be miserable so please, *please* just go away and leave me alone."

Despite himself, Tom started to laugh. "Fine. I'll leave then. But honestly, Luce—you have to stop being so melodramatic. Wallow over Byron if you must, not that he's worth it, but he's hardly the love of your life."

Lucy looked up from her wet tissue with loathing. "Tom?" she said in a very low, deadly voice. "Can you understand that for once this is not about you? That this is not about you competing with Byron?"

Ignoring her vitriolic tone, Tom kissed her on the top of her head. "Go into heartbroken mode if you must. I know you don't like to share your ice cream, and watching Hugh Grant movies is too much like spending hours on end with Percy, so call me when you snap out of it."

Lucy listened to him leave and then abandoned herself to sobs once again. But whether she was crying over Byron, Tom, or the fact that she smelled worse than she ever had in her life, she wasn't exactly sure.

15.

boys' night

After observing for a week Lucy's incessant moping and her alarming growing addiction to adult soft rock compilations, Chloe decided to mount a rescue mission. Inviting Meg and Percy around in order to distract Lucy from thoughts of Byron, she ordered Meg to select a DVD that contained absolutely no suggestion of romance whatsoever. This strategy proved only partially successful however, as unfortunately the film Meg selected was so violent and nihilistic that it left them all feeling shattered, fragile, and in desperate need of affection and the milk of human kindness.

"Where's Tom?" asked Meg finally, breaking the appalled silence that had followed the climactic scene of apocalyptic misery.

"Out with the boys," answered Lucy, in a distinctly pained voice.

Meg grimaced, and Percy, his curiosity aroused, asked, "What boys?"

"The term *boys* is probably a bit generous," Meg said derisively. "Mutant apes from the planet Dribble is probably more accurate."

"They're his old football buddies," Lucy explained, seeing Percy's bewilderment. "And just so you know—Meg was being kind for a change in her description."

"Still, why wouldn't he invite me to a boys' night?"

"Don't look like that, Percy," Chloe said consolingly. "Tom knows you would have hated every minute. They all have ridiculous nicknames like Bazza or Wazza or Ferret. And they spend the whole night getting drunk and throwing beer at each other and reminiscing about stag nights where they all got drunk and threw beer at each other."

"They're hideous," Lucy agreed with a shudder. "But every so often Tom has this need to go and play with them, and three days later when his hangover has worn off he's quite subdued and happy to be with us again."

Percy was still looking aggrieved but his expression changed considerably when Meg snapped, "For heaven's sake, stop looking like a kicked puppy, Percy. You ought to be grateful to Tom. You're both English and sweet. They would have shaved your eyebrows off, poured beer down your pants, made you eat marshmallows off a stripper's breasts, and left you tied to a tree wearing nothing but a fluorescent G-string."

"She's right, Percy," Lucy agreed. "They're devastatingly unoriginal."

Percy was so euphoric that Meg had called him *sweet*, however, that he was gazing rapturously at her and had quite forgotten Tom's treachery. Meg, who as usual was completely oblivious to Percy's adoration, continued to frown as she pressed the remote control in a vain attempt to escape from the labyrinthine extra features menu of the DVD.

"You know," Lucy said suddenly. "We could go to the pub."

"Why on earth would you want to hang out with Tom's friends?"

Lucy grinned. "It could be fun. Just think how annoyed Tom will be if we crash his boys' night. And anyway, I'm sick of staying in and crying over Byron. I need to get out of the house and have some fun."

"I'm in," Chloe said unexpectedly. Meg swung around and stared at her in amazement. "Well I can't spend my entire life with you two, and then wonder why I never meet any men."

"I'm still here you know," said Percy in a hurt tone.

"Sorry, Percy," said Chloe contritely. "But you know what I mean."

"Not really, no."

Meg was still protesting. "But Chloe—they're not men they're—"

"I know. Savages from the planet Penis-Head. So what? I may as well practice on them."

"Oh for heaven's sake. Alright, fine. I'll come with you two, but only because you need protection."

Lucy and Chloe jumped up eagerly from the floor, and they all turned to look at Percy.

"Aren't you coming, Percy?"

He flushed scarlet and looked imploringly at Meg.

"It's okay, Percy," Meg sighed. "I promise that I won't let them tie you to a tree. If anyone's going to humiliate you, it will be me."

Bazza whistled as Lucy walked into the pub. "Check it out, fellas. Tits at two o'clock."

Tom, who had his back to the door, turned around and his jaw dropped as he caught sight of Lucy, closely followed by Chloe.

"Wait a minute—isn't that the chick you used to screw, Tommo?" asked Wazza. "She's not bad. You don't mind if I have a crack, do you?"

Their appreciation was cut short by the entrance of Meg. Bazza paled and Wazza gulped. "*Sweet Jesus*," Wazza trembled. "Who let the Devil Queen loose?"

"Oh come on. She's not that bad," Tom defended Meg.

"*Not that bad?*" Mate, I've still got the scars from the last time I saw her." Working himself up as he remembered Meg's scathing comments the last time that they had crossed paths, Wazza continued, "She ain't a woman, Tommo, she's the Bride of Satan and—"

"Warren, how nice to see you again," Meg said amiably, standing directly behind him.

Wazza jumped violently and spilled his drink all over himself.

"Oh dear. Still no hand-to-eye coordination I see. That's probably why you always spend most of the season on the bench." Bazza laughed heartily. "Then again, it will save Bazza from having to throw his drink at you." As Meg pronounced his name and turned her gimlet gaze onto him, the blood drained from Bazza's face.

"How are you, Bartholomew?"

"The name's Barry," Bazza muttered.

Meg shook her head gently and laughed. "No, I don't think it is." As they all looked inquiringly at her she explained, "You have to register under your full name at the legal service where I do volunteer work. By the way, Bartholomew, what ever happened to your solicitous little friend—what was her name now? Heavenly something?"

"I was just giving her a lift!" Bazza hissed furiously, his face scarlet. "And the name's Barry!"

Tom grabbed Meg by the arm and led her away forcibly. "What are you doing here, Meg?"

"Having fun," she said, looking up at him with limpid eyes. "Lucy needs to get over Byron and Chloe wants to meet men, so we thought it would be nice for you if your different groups of friends could spend time together."

"Oh you did, did you?" asked Tom grimly. "Well, I'll give you a hundred dollars if you grab Lucy and Chloe and take them home right now. Oh dear god—you brought *Percy?*"

"Of course. Stop looking so frightened. They wouldn't dare to do anything to Percy while I'm here."

At this point, Chloe rushed up, her cheeks flushed from the unaccustomed attention that she was receiving. "Tom, your friends are *lovely.*"

"Who have you been talking to?" Tom asked, feeling that his night was beginning to spiral out of control, and not in the way that he had hoped it would.

"Someone called Porno," Chloe said happily.

"Chloe, listen to me," Tom commanded urgently. "I want you to stay right away from anyone with a nickname that doesn't directly relate to their real name."

"What do you mean?"

"For example, I'm known as Tommo. And that's Davo and Bazza and Wazza. We're all relatively harmless. But Porno is a very bad man. And the same goes for Horse over there."

"Does he ride?" asked Chloe innocently.

"No, Clo."

"Then why—*oh.*" Her eyes widened, and before he could stop her Chloe slipped out of Tom's grasp and made a direct beeline for Horse.

"*Do* something," Tom said helplessly.

"Lighten up, Tommo," Meg said breezily. "It's good for Chloe. She spends far too much time with Lucy and Percy. It'll do her good to be around some manly men for a change. Anyway, if I were you I'd be far more worried about Lucy."

Tom drained his beer and felt the acute need for another one. "Where's Lucy?" he whimpered.

"In a corner with Porno. I'm not sure but it looks like he's holding a bag of marshmallows—" Meg stopped talking because Tom had thrust his empty glass at her and vanished in the direction of Lucy.

Meg chuckled and decided that she hadn't had this much fun in ages. Looking around the room her gaze alighted upon Wazza, who was huddled in a corner pleadingly asking one of his teammates, "I wasn't really that bad, was I, mate? I mean, I know I had a few stumbles at the start of the season but I was coming off an injury." Meg's eyes lit up and she headed in the direction of the hapless Wazza.

Two hours later the girls and Percy had descended into cheerfully messy inebriation, while fear had rendered Tom completely sober.

"Cheer up, Tommo," Lucy sang, as she staggered towards him and plunked herself in the seat next to his. "You're looking very sad."

"You're plastered," Tom said sourly.

Lucy considered this comment and decided that it was fair. "Yes I am. Which is why I'm going to help you."

"I don't need your help. I need you to go home so that I can start enjoying myself."

"Why can't you enjoy yourself with us here? Your friends don't mind. Look, here comes Wazza now." She giggled. "I think he likes me," she confided in a loud whisper.

"Lo, Luce," said Wazza, who had taken Meg's comments on his lack of sporting prowess badly and proceeded to down half a bottle of scotch. He eyed Lucy, who was sitting close to Tom and resting her head on his shoulder. "Hey—I thought you two weren't together anymore?"

"We're not. But I still love him, don't I, Tom?" Lucy appealed, somewhat confusedly, to Tom.

"Yes, Luce," Tom said, gently disentangling her arm from his.

"I'm going to help now," Lucy whispered. She turned to Wazza. "Tom has a very large vocabulary, you know," she said, stumbling slight over the pronunciation of *vocabulary*.

"Eh? What's that then?" asked Wazza, his brow furrowed.

"Vocabulary," Tom explained briefly. "It's Latin for penis."

A leering smile cracked open Wazza's face. "You dirty dog," he said fondly.

"I helped, didn't I, Tom?" asked Lucy, entangling her arm through Tom's again.

"No, you didn't." As Meg came up he pleaded in anguish, "Please take her home, Meg."

"Well if your 'cabulary won't impress them, what will?" slurred Lucy.

"Will you say that I slept with you and Chloe at the same time?" Tom asked hopefully.

Lucy's brow creased. "Why would I say that?"

"Because that would confirm what he's already told them," said Meg. "Bartholomew told me."

"Bazza," said Tom through gritted teeth. "His name is Bazza."

"I wish I had a name," said Percy wistfully, who had followed Meg closely and was in turn shadowed by Chloe.

"You have one," said Wazza cheerfully. "You're the Pommy bastard." He started chortling but subsided when he caught Meg's eye.

"Your nickname will have to be linked to your proper name, Percy," said Chloe knowledgeably. "You're too sweet to be called Hand-Job or Maggot Breath."

"Chloe, I do not have a friend called Hand-Job," said Tom firmly.

"Yes you do," said Chloe in surprise. "That's him over there with Porno."

Tom turned and surveyed a redheaded guy who was trying to convince two unimpressed girls to let him suck shots out of their belly buttons.

"His name isn't Hand-Job," Tom said exasperated. "That's the Vomit Man."

"No, that's what he used to be called," Chloe said earnestly. "But last week the police pulled him over and—"

"I don't want to hear anymore," Tom groaned, covering his ears.

Chloe looked confused. "I don't get it. I thought that's what happens on boys' nights. I thought we were meant to stand around and drink and tell each other disgusting stories."

Tom let his hands drop to his sides. *"We do,"* he said in a tone of considerable torment. *"You don't.* Please go home," he begged. "This is unnatural. Lucy's drinking beer, Meg's calling everyone by their real names and lecturing Wazza on football tactics, and now you're telling me lurid sex stories. Don't you three have a book club meeting to attend or a Ben Affleck film to watch?"

"But we're having fun."

"While I'm miserable! Oh look, forget it." Abandoning his attempts to make the girls leave, Tom made his way over to where Porno and Horse were standing. "What do you say we get out of here? Let's go somewhere there's some decent talent."

"There's talent straight ahead, mate," said Porno lasciviously, indicat-

ing Chloe, who was now in animated conversation with a group of guys
and unaware that her top had slipped down to dangerously low levels.

"You can't perve on them," Tom said revolted. "They're Chloe and
Meg and Lucy."

The boys looked at him in silence, and Horse raised one overgrown
eyebrow.

"They're my friends," Tom said. He added lamely, "You shouldn't be
objectifying them."

"Dunno what's got into you, Tommo," said Porno, shaking his head
sadly. "I reckon it's all that standing on your head in yoga. It ain't natural." He moved away with an equally disgusted Horse in tow.

Tom groaned and looked around frantically for Lucy or Meg so that
he could send one of them in to rescue Chloe from inadvertent nipple
exhibitionism. He couldn't see either of them anywhere so, gritting his
teeth, he waded into the group surrounding Chloe. Grabbing her by the
arm, he lifted her out of her seat, nimbly managing to yank her top up
at the same time, to the immense disappointment of the boys. "Come
on, Clo," he said briskly, leading her away.

"Tom! Where are we going?" asked Chloe, a furrow appearing in her
brow as he removed her from the center of attention. "I was having
fun—what are you doing?"

"Saving you from embarrassment and regret," said Tom shortly.

"Meaning what?" asked Chloe, her temper beginning to show at his
high-handed attitude.

"Your top was falling down. You were about to flash every guy in the
place. And you looked like you were about to go home with the first
guy who asked you," Tom explained briefly, feeling an anticipatory rush
of pleasure at the gratitude that would undoubtedly be coming his way
once his noble behavior was revealed.

"So what?"

"*So what?*" Tom spluttered. "Chloe, are you out of your mind? These
are the football buddies. If you did go home with one of them you'd

instantly regret it, but you'd still end up being talked about for the rest of the year."

"I'm not sixteen years old you know. Has it occurred to you that I might feel like having a one-night stand?"

Tom looked around in horror to see if anyone was close enough to have heard this. "You can't be serious?"

Chloe was looking uncharacteristically obstinate. "Why not?"

"*Why not?* Because you and Lucy and Meg spend hours ranting about how much you despise these guys."

"What does that have to do with anything?"

Tom stared at her in disbelief. "Correct me if I'm wrong, Clo, but weren't you just talking about going home with one of them?"

Chloe grinned. "You seem to be confusing casual sex with a relationship, Tom, which is very funny coming from you. I don't have to be able to discuss politics and literature with someone in order to have a fling with them." As Tom, reduced to speechlessness, sought for a response, she deliberately pulled her top down to a cleavage-enhancing level. Smiling cheekily at him she went back into the fray.

"What is that *noise?*" Lucy groaned, rolling over in bed.

"It sounds like someone's cooking breakfast," said Meg, who had been lying dully on the other side of Lucy's bed, awake but unable to move her head, which felt like it weighed about a ton.

"I can smell bacon," said Chloe, suddenly sitting upright at the foot of the bed, with her hair all on end.

"I wondered what I had my feet on all night," Meg said, squinting at Chloe, obviously pleased to have the mystery solved. "It must have been your face."

"Why didn't you sleep in your own bed?" asked Lucy.

"I thought this was my bed," Chloe explained.

"I'm surprised you made it home at all," said Lucy, propping herself up on her elbows and eyeing Chloe with considerable interest. "I thought you were about to go home with Horse, you dirty tart."

"He asked me to, but I said no," Chloe said virtuously.

"Oh. How come?"

"Well, I didn't exactly say no," Chloe said sheepishly. "But I threw up on his shoes, which is sort of the same thing."

"Does anyone know what happened to Percy?" asked Lucy, struggling to piece together the night before.

"He was still going strong when we left. I think he was going to another bar with some of the guys," Meg said disinterestedly, still gazing listlessly at the ceiling.

"But it must have been four in the morning," Lucy protested. "The only bars that would have let them in would be strip joints or that horrible ravers' club full of seventeen-year-olds in sweatpants who are all on drugs."

There was an awed silence while the three girls tried to visualize Percy at a rave.

"Do you think he's alright?" Chloe asked finally.

"I'm sure he's fine. He's probably learning how to dance to progressive trance," Lucy said comfortingly. There was another silence while they all tried to picture this scenario and then Chloe caught Lucy's eye, Lucy glanced at Meg, and they collapsed into helpless screams of laughter.

"I think I'm still a bit wasted," Meg said, wiping her eyes and wishing that her head would stop pounding.

"Me too," said Lucy.

Before Chloe could make it unanimous, the door to Lucy's bedroom opened, and Tom stalked in bearing a pitcher of orange juice and three glasses. He was wearing Lucy's pink gingham apron and an extremely disapproving expression. "About time you three woke up," he said sourly, putting the pitcher and the glasses down on Lucy's bedside table and starting to pour the orange juice.

"What time is it?" asked Lucy meekly, trying to remember what she'd said or done last night to make Tom so cranky.

"It's *ten thirty*."

"That's not so bad," Meg said, accepting her glass of juice gratefully.

"Half the morning is gone," Tom said shortly.

"Really? Shame because I meant to get up early and do my taxes. Who cares if we slept in? And what the hell has got into you?"

Tom picked up the empty pitcher and turned on his heel. "Nothing. Breakfast is almost ready, so if it's not *too* much trouble perhaps you could get out of bed and eat it."

He shut the door censoriously after him, and the girls stared at one another and then collapsed into giggles again.

"Does anyone remember what happened to him last night?" Lucy whispered.

Chloe shook her head. "I know he wasn't being much fun. I think I remember something about him wanting to go home to watch a Ben Affleck movie."

"You must have imagined that," Lucy said accusingly, throwing off the comforter and stretching.

They tiptoed into the kitchen in their pajamas and silently sat at the places Tom had laid out for them. Tom, his mouth pursed primly, started to serve out scrambled eggs and bacon.

"What time did you get up?" Lucy asked in amazement. "And what are you doing here anyway?"

"Someone had to make sure you all got home safely last night and I was too tired to drive home afterwards," Tom said virtuously. He added sternly, "I had to go to the supermarket to get milk for my coffee so I bought breakfast things at the same time. You have nothing but eight bottles of champagne, half a tub of sun-dried tomatoes, and a block of chocolate in your fridge, Luce. You're a disgrace."

Lucy thought about protesting that it was Chloe's fridge too but then decided against it. "I know I am. Thank you for getting breakfast," Lucy said meekly. As soon as Tom's back was turned she lifted her eyebrows inquiringly at Chloe and Meg who both shrugged.

"You were all plastered last night. You ought to be ashamed of yourselves," Tom continued to scold as he aggressively doled out more scrambled eggs.

"Tom?" Lucy ventured, circumspectly waiting until after he'd served her food. "You're behaving like a Stepford wife. Yes we were very drunk, and we probably shouldn't have crashed your night with the boys, but it was a pub after all. It's not as though we crashed a private party. And your friends seemed to like us. Chloe was the hit of the night."

Chloe blushed modestly.

"I didn't *want* Chloe to be the hit of the night. I didn't want any of you anywhere *near* my night."

"Well it's probably a good thing for your friends that we were there, because you were being the biggest loser alive," Meg commented mildly. "These scrambled eggs are very good by the way."

"Loser?" Tom raised his voice in outrage, and all three girls winced and groped for their coffee. "I couldn't relax all night because I was too busy trying to look after you three. And do I get any gratitude for it?" He waited.

"No?" Meg supplied, in a bored tone of voice.

"No!" Tom said triumphantly. "Not a word. If it wasn't for me, Chloe would have woken up next to Horse, Lucy would probably have convinced Wazza to take out a library card, and you, Meg, would be running a betting ring on my sex life with all of my buddies."

There was a short silence as the girls pondered their alternative fates in a Tom-free parallel universe.

"So I would have had sex?" Chloe said in a thoughtful voice, stirring more sugar into her coffee.

"And I would have inspired Wazza to read?" Lucy said, forcibly struck by the romantic potential in playing an inspirational role to a Rainman-like Wazza.

"And I would have made a lot of money," Meg said, glaring at Tom through narrowed eyes.

Tom looked from one to another and started to feel slightly afraid. "I'm going to be late for yoga," he said, hastily getting up from the table and deciding to cut his losses and run before he was denied altogether the strategic advantage of being the wounded party.

There was a silence after he departed as the girls brooded on their hangovers, lost opportunities and the wrongs wrought by Tom. Several moments later, the front door opened again, and Tom, with his head held high, reentered the kitchen. Staring stonily into the distance, he untied the pink gingham apron that he was still wearing, deposited it on the kitchen table, and then left without a word.

16.

the duel

The following week Tom had recovered sufficiently from his hissy fit over the boys' night to join Lucy, Chloe, and Percy in their regular outing to see a film. Opening her front door, Lucy beckoned Tom and Percy inside.

"Come in," she said cheerfully, kissing them both on the cheek. "I'm not exactly ready," she added ruefully.

"How surprising," Tom remarked with a grin. "We've only been going to the movies and dinner most Tuesday nights for the past six weeks."

She wrinkled her nose at him. "Chloe's not back yet anyway, so just go into the living room and make yourselves at home. I'll be ten minutes. Tom, you can get drinks. And if you're starving have a look in the kitchen cupboard. I'm pretty sure there'll be something to nibble on."

Tom heroically restrained himself from making a comment along the lines of he knew exactly what he wanted to nibble on, and it wasn't in the kitchen cupboard, and instead followed Percy into the kitchen. Rummaging amongst the pantry shelves and the fridge they managed to find a couple of beers and a packet of peanuts, and thus fortified they went back into the living room to wait for Lucy. The comfortable scene was rudely interrupted by the sound of the front door crashing open and the eruption of Byron into the room.

Apparently unsurprised to see Tom and Percy in Lucy's apartment, Byron immediately launched into impassioned speech. "Where is she?" he asked, striding around the room.

"In the turret," Tom answered gravely. "Weaving her burial shroud out of rose petals."

Byron glared at him. "You mock me. But I need to see her. I can't sleep, I can't eat . . ."

"Have a peanut," Tom said charitably, proffering the bowl.

Byron flung himself into an armchair and put his head in his hands. "What am I going to do? I have ruined everything."

"Nothing for it, old chap," said Percy, in his best pip-pip, stiff upper lip voice. "You'll have to join the Foreign Legion. It's the only thing that will impress her now. Very high standards has our Lucinda."

"She is the love of my life," Byron said gloomily, absently helping himself to a handful of peanuts.

"You can't possibly know that," objected Tom.

Byron shot him a scornful look. "Of course I can know that. It is only men like you who do not understand true love."

"What I meant was your life's not over yet," Tom pointed out sensibly. "Logically speaking, you won't know whether she's the love of your life until you're dead. Morbid, and a trifle unfair, but there it is."

"It feels like my life is over. Without her I'm nothing."

"Probably right. Best to end it then. Now, are you a head in the oven sort of guy or would you prefer me to drive over you? Happy to oblige naturally—hate to see a fellow human being suffer. Ah—here's the girl now. Come in, Lucinda, we were just discussing Byron's suicide."

Lucy stopped in the doorway in shock.

"Byron? What are you doing here?" she asked faintly.

"To the immense disgust of both Tom and Percy, Byron flung himself on his knees in front of Lucy. Grabbing her hand he showered it with kisses. "Lucia! My love! I can't sleep, I can't eat, I can't do anything without you."

"Well that's a complete fib. You just scoffed half my peanuts," Tom said indignantly.

Lucy looked at Tom in confusion while Byron glared at him. "What *are* you talking about, Tom?"

"Ignore him," Byron said, clasping her hands firmly in both of his and holding them to his breast. "Lucia, you must listen to me. I am sorry, I will do anything to prove to you how much you mean to me . . ."

While Lucy secretly approved of this melodramatic form of address, the novelty of someone other than herself behaving in this manner had the effect of making her adopt a far more dignified tone and attitude than she was normally wont to do. "Stand up, Byron, you're being ridiculous. There's a perfectly good chair over there, and we can sit down and discuss this like rational human beings."

"Better do what she says," Tom said *sotto voce*.

Byron looked at him doubtfully and then, deciding that whatever advice Tom gave him couldn't possibly be in his best interests, settled himself more firmly on one knee. "I will not do everything you tell me to, Lucia. I am a man, not a lap dancer."

"Lapdog," Percy said helpfully. "I rather think you mean *lapdog*."

"I refuse to talk to you until you stand up," Lucy said haughtily.

Without looking at Tom, Byron sheepishly got to his feet.

"Right. Now sit down over there."

Byron sat.

"Stand up again," Tom said, interested to see how long this could continue.

"Shouldn't you be somewhere far away, Tom?" Lucy asked dangerously.

"No. Can you make him pat his head and rub his tummy at the same time?"

"Ignore him, Byron," Lucy said quickly, as Byron, realizing that he had been insulted, jumped to his feet.

"Oh look, Lucy, I can do it too. I made him stand up," Tom said, vastly entertained.

Byron cast a venomous look at Tom and then started to stride restlessly around the room. "Lucia, you must listen to me," he said urgently, "I will do anything you want me to—just name it. I want to prove to you how sorry I am."

"What about a duel?" Percy suggested, throwing a peanut into the air and catching it in his open mouth.

"Good idea, Perce," said Tom, forcibly struck by the violent potential of this plan.

"This has nothing to do with you. Keep out of it," Lucy snapped.

"It has everything to do with me. I want to kill him. The chap completely nauseates me. And he ate nearly all my peanuts."

"Tom, will you *please* stop going on about peanuts?"

"Not until he stops pretending to be starving for your sake. He ate more than half the bowl. Never seen such bad manners in my life."

"Well he could still be starving if that's all he's eaten. Peanuts aren't exactly nourishing."

"Rubbish. Nuts have very high fat content. They're very good for you."

"Stop it. You're ruining the most romantic moment of my life." Lucy paused, and then added in the sort of soppy tone of voice that made Percy want to bolt for cover, "I never thought that I'd have two men duel over me."

"It is not romantic," Byron said, nervously eyeing Tom's strong, fit frame. "It's ridiculous. This has nothing to with him."

"This has everything to do with me," Tom said decisively. "I've been in love with Lucy for years."

Byron choked on a peanut and swung around to look accusingly at Lucy. "Is this true?" he demanded.

"Of course it's not true. He's just very upset about his peanuts."

"Wretched fellow was at it again," Tom muttered darkly, looking at Byron with distaste.

"Would you use pistols?" Percy asked dreamily, his aristocratic heritage coming to the fore.

Byron was looking decidedly agitated. "Water?" he asked hopefully.

"Spring-loaded," Tom said with an evil grin.

"Tom, shut up. You're scaring him. And anyway, you are not going to have a duel over me. I won't be objectified in such a demeaning manner."

"Oh get over yourself, Lucy," Tom said impatiently. "It's not really about you. I just want an excuse to shoot him. Never met such a wet specimen in my entire life."

"Duel over *me*," Chloe said eagerly, entering the room just in time to catch the gist of the conversation.

"I am not dueling over Chloe," Byron said, finding his voice again, albeit a wobbly one. "Love is the only thing worth dueling over, and I do not love Chloe."

"Well, if not pistols then what?"

"Darts?" Chloe suggested, having just returned from a quick drink at the pub.

"I'm afraid of needles," Byron said dejectedly.

"Well you can't be afraid of everything. And anyway, that's where the whole courage and nobility part comes in. You're *meant* to be scared."

"Think of your namesake Lord Byron fighting the Turks," Percy said encouragingly.

"Yes, but in all fairness the Turks weren't trying to immunize the Greeks," Tom pointed out.

"I still think the concept of a duel renders the woman passive," mused Lucy, who had a tendency to not budge easily from issues concerning herself.

"Well you could join in," said Tom fairly. "But you'd have to decide whose side you're on, and then it wouldn't be fair anymore because it would be two against one."

"What would you call a duel with three people?" Chloe wondered.

Percy, who could become exceptionally peevish and reactionary whenever anyone suggested tampering with perfectly good English traditions such as fox hunting, dueling, and trying to annex Wales, now asked shortly, "Have you ever heard of a truel?"

"No."

"Yes, well that's because they don't exist. If Lucy wants to fight a duel she can jolly well start her own. In the meantime, Tom and Byron can't just show up and try to push each other over."

Unable to argue with the inherent truth of this statement, they all fell silent and applied themselves to finding a solution to the problem, while Byron, overcome by nerves, absentmindedly helped himself to another handful of peanuts.

"I know!" said Chloe, her brow clearing. "We'll have a contest where you both have to do something lovely and romantic for Lucy. And then she can choose who she wants to be with."

"But I already know who I want to be with," Lucy objected, which earned her a salty kiss from Byron.

"No you don't," said Percy, dampening the Spirit of Romance that had threatened to overtake Byron and Lucy. "You're just confused. Happens to girls all the time. They go off with one chap and then realize they were really in love with someone else. That's why the divorce rate is so high. All comes down to people not knowing their own minds and duels going out of fashion. If there were more duels there'd be less choice around. Divorce rate would drop. Stands to reason."

While the assembled company tried to absorb Percy's blueprint for social cohesion, Tom abruptly switched his attention back to the pertinent issue. "What sort of thing would we have to do for Lucy?"

Lucy opened her mouth to suggest a number of things, but Chloe got in before her. "She can't *tell* you," she said severely. "That's the whole point. You have to figure out something that will win her heart."

"And I'm not allowed to kill Bryan?" asked Tom, not even trying to keep the disappointment out of his voice.

"No!" Lucy said angrily. "And don't call him that."

"Well, it seems a bit lame to me. It started off all fights and guns blazing, and now it's some Chloe-conceived hearts and flowers treasure hunt. What's in it for me?"

"What do you mean, what's in it for you? You're the one who brought up the idea of a duel in the first place."

"No I damn well didn't. It was Percy's idea."

"Well fine. Percy can take your place."

Percy looked as horrified as if he'd swallowed some uncooked girello. "What? No. Absolutely not. No offense, Lucy, and hate to disoblige, but Byron's welcome to you. You're a lovely girl but not exactly my cup of tea if you know what I mean."

"How dare you insult Lucia?" Byron retorted, instantly flaring up on behalf of his beloved.

"Oh for heaven's sake, make him sit still, Lucy," Tom begged. "It's Tuesday night. Doesn't he ever take a break from the fiery lover routine?"

Although Lucy privately agreed that Byron was a trifle on the emotionally exhausting side, she wasn't about to let Tom know this. "He's Italian," she defended him.

"Well that's no excuse," said Percy, in an unexpectedly exasperated voice. "I don't go around behaving like an upper-class twit just because I'm English and have a double-barreled surname. Now if you'll all kindly excuse me, I'm going home, as it's obvious that we're not going to make it to the cinema tonight. I want to do my toe-touching exercises. It's extremely bad for the digestion if I leave it till after eight." And Percy made a hasty exit before anyone could bring up the idea of him participating in the duel again.

"The Latin lover pose is getting slightly tedious," said Tom in a bored tone of voice.

"You're just jealous because you don't have a romantic bone in your body," Lucy lashed back.

"Crap. I give you flowers all the time."

"Tom, you buy me the worst flowers you can find. You think it's funny to give me three-day-old daisies wrapped in purple cellophane with a miniature balloon saying 'It's a Boy!' stuck in the middle."

"Beauty is in the eye of the beholder," he said, refusing to give up. "Or do I mean 'It's the thought that counts'?"

"I think the phrase that you're looking for is 'I'm completely incapable of a genuine romantic gesture because I'm too busy being cynical and screwing lots of women,'" retorted Lucy with asperity.

"I can be as romantic as Don Juan over here. I just think it belittles the gesture if you go around being conventionally romantic all the time."

"Prove it."

"What?"

"If you honestly believe that you can be as romantic as Byron then prove it. Chloe has come up with a simple but effective challenge. You won't agree to the contest because you know that you haven't a hope of winning."

"Why can't we use the good old Aussie method of proving who's superior by comparing the number of women that we've slept with?" Tom grumbled.

"Byron's number starts with a one," Lucy said with a smirk.

Tom tried to hide his pleasure but failed miserably. "Well, some believe that your teenage years are the best, but I prefer the maturity of the late forties myself," he said, puffing his chest out slightly.

"And his number is triple digits," Lucy continued sweetly.

"What are the rules of the contest, Clo?" asked Tom, in an unusually small and humble tone of voice.

"There are none. You just have to do something romantic for

Lucy that displays an intimate knowledge of her heart's desire. It's simple."

"I don't think Hugh Grant is available for hire. I seem to remember that he prefers it the other way round."

"Joke all you like, Tom. You're going to lose," said Lucy, getting up from her chair. "Come on, Byron. I'll cook you dinner."

"So you forgive me, Lucia?"

"Of course I do. I can't stay mad at you if you're going to do something romantic for me. Let's go into the kitchen."

Byron arose obediently, and as he passed Tom he shot him a look full of pure malice. "Anytime you wish to withdraw from the contest just let me know. There is less dishonor in that than in losing."

"Oh chewy on your boot," Tom said sourly, as Lucy and Byron exited.

Chloe raised one eyebrow at him. "What on earth did you say that for?"

"Because I know it will take him at least an hour with a dictionary of Australian slang to work it out. Much more satisfying than calling him a wanker. I mean really—'there is less dishonor in that than in losing'?" Tom mimicked Byron. "The guy's a dickhead. I don't know what Lucy sees in him."

As Chloe started to answer, he hurriedly continued, "And don't tell me either. I don't care." Drawing his chair closer to Chloe's, he bent towards her conspiratorially and asked urgently, "Okay, Clo. So what do I do?"

"What?"

"What do I do for Lucy?" he repeated impatiently. "Tell me."

"I'm not helping you *cheat*," Chloe said indignantly.

"I didn't mean for you to tell me what Lucy specifically wants," Tom said, instantly changing tack and deciding on a strategic retreat. "I meant in a more general sense. As a woman, what do you consider romantic?"

"Not a chance, Tom," Chloe said, preparing to get up. "You have to figure it out for yourself."

"Fine," he said irritably, thinking that he could always ask Meg. She detested Byron, so she would help him.

"And if you're thinking of asking Meg I wouldn't bother," added Chloe cheekily, pausing at the door.

"Why not?"

Chloe arched an eyebrow. "Are you seriously trying to tell me that you've forgotten what happened when Percy sent Meg roses and a card?"

"Ah. That."

"Yes. That. She gave the roses to that guy at work who had a crush on her. And the card. And she didn't even bother to cross out Percy's name and add her own."

"What ever happened to that guy?"

"He joined Australian Volunteers International and he's living in Papua New Guinea or somewhere like that now. I'm not exactly sure. You could ask Percy. They still keep in touch. I believe he was very moved by the beautiful words that Percy wrote."

As Byron adoringly watched Lucy hurl spaghetti at the wall in order to test whether it was al dente, a smile lit up the young lover's face. It had just occurred to him what Lucy would like, more than anything in the world, and that was sure to win her heart.

17.

the neighbor

Despite all Lucy's entreaties, Byron refused to stay with her that night, which she couldn't help suspecting had less to do with her cooking than it did with the loud music that could be heard next door.

"Oh my lord," said Lucy, reentering the apartment after bidding Byron a passionate reconciliatory farewell. "It's not only loud, her taste in music is completely horrible." She grimaced at the wall, through which could be heard the mournful strains of a Celine Dion power ballad. "It's so damn loud and I have to get to sleep tonight. Do you think we should say something?"

Chloe looked nervous. "You know how I hate confrontations, Lucy."

"Well, do you want me to bang on the wall then?" suggested Lucy. "She'll get the message."

Chloe shook her head vigorously. "No, that's even worse I think. Let's just leave it. Maybe she'll go to bed soon and turn it off."

Lucy listened intently for a moment and then shuddered. "Oh God. I think she's singing along now. That's it. I'm going to bed."

"Me too," Chloe stood up and stretched. "I thought I had earplugs somewhere but I can't find them," she said disconsolately.

"Try socks," Lucy advised, with an authoritative air. "Although it's really hard to get them to stay in your ears."

At a quarter to three in the morning Lucy had reached the limits of her endurance. Rolling out of bed she pulled her bathrobe on and staggered blearily into Chloe's bedroom. Chloe was sheltering from the music underneath two pillows, and Lucy had to thump her quite hard to get her to come out from beneath them.

"I've had it. Come on, Clo."

Chloe noticed the martial light in Lucy's eyes nervously. "What? Where are you going?"

"We are going to bang on their door and get them to turn their damn music down. Failing that, I'm going to lend them some of our CDs. I can't listen to this awful trash any longer."

"Maybe they're having a party," Chloe suggested, unwillingly pulling on her enormous furry coat and almost snagging her earring in the process.

"I don't care. It's almost three in the morning, and they're still playing Celine Dion. I want to hurt them."

"Are you very tired?"

"No. I just really hate Celine Dion."

Together they stumbled into the dark hallway out onto the landing. The music was so loud that they banged on the front door for about five minutes before anyone heard them. Just as Lucy was about to start kicking the door, a woman, who was clearly getting towards the slobbery stage of inebriation, swung the door open so violently that Chloe, who had thrown her arm back to hammer on the door once again, lost her balance and accidentally punched the woman in the face, with the full force of her body weight behind her.

The neighbor promptly sank to the floor like the *Titanic*. It was a shame in a way that she wasn't conscious to appreciate her appropriate choice of background music.

Lucy stared in horrified fascination at the crumpled figure and at Chloe, who had pitched onto the floor next to her victim.

"Chloe?" Lucy said cautiously.

"Did I kill her?" asked a fearful, muffled voice.

"Of course not. Get up. I'll need help to lift her."

Chloe staggered to her feet, looking pale. As she surveyed the unconscious neighbor, she turned a shade whiter.

"I can't believe you decked her like that," Lucy whispered, awestruck.

"I didn't mean to," Chloe hissed.

"Of course you didn't *mean* to," Lucy said soothingly. "But it's damn impressive all the same." Lucy stepped over the prostate body in the hallway into the living room. "Luckily for us I think she was having a party for one," she said, surveying the empty room with one wine glass and several depleted bottles of red wine.

Chloe was tugging at the woman's arm and trying unsuccessfully to haul her up. "Aren't you going to help me?" she asked, turning her head to see what Lucy was doing.

"Wait a minute. I have to find the stereo. Ah—here it is. God, she's got the new Ben Harper CD. Why the hell couldn't she have been playing that for the last three hours? I've been dying to hear it." She pressed the stop button somewhat more viciously than was necessary, and thankfully Celine's heart stopped going on.

"Lucinda Millbanke, we have just rendered a defenseless woman unconscious and you're changing the background music. Will you kindly help me get her onto the couch immediately?"

"Oh calm down, Chloe, it was an accident. And I don't know where the 'we' part comes in. You were the one doing the Muhammad Ali impression."

Somehow they managed to pull the dead weight of the neighbor onto the couch. Chloe collapsed in a shocked heap on the beanbag near one end of the old-fashioned sofa, which had enormous scrolled legs that raised it high off the ground. Lucy, meanwhile, investigated the room. There were photo albums and CDs strewn everywhere including every contemporary adult rock compilation ever released, all of which seemed to prominently feature the song "It's Not Over till It's Over."

"I think we've walked into the aftermath of a bad breakup," Lucy said wisely, her recent tiff with Byron still fresh in her mind. "Look at this mess, Clo—photos, wine, tragic CDs, empty ice cream container—my God." She broke off in horror.

"What?" asked Chloe, from her position next to the couch. Mutely Lucy handed her *The Very Best of Mariah Carey*. Chloe turned it over and the terrible truth dawned. "She paid full price for it."

Lucy nodded grimly.

"This is a *really* bad breakup," Chloe said uneasily. "I think we should get out of here."

"Me too." Lucy paused and considered the awkwardly positioned woman on the couch. "I just feel a bit bad. She doesn't look very comfortable."

Chloe peered over the couch arm and then shuddered and looked away. "I can't believe that I was *violent*," she said in horror-laden tones.

"Oh stop it. It was an accident. By the look of these empty wine bottles she was well on her way to passing out anyway. You just sort of helped her along. Look, let's just shift her a bit. She's so drunk she probably won't remember a thing, and with a bit of luck she'll think that she passed out by herself."

Cautiously Lucy approached the prone and stertorous figure. "I'll grab her legs and you move her arms," Lucy instructed nervously.

Chloe assented with a nervous nod, and Lucy bent forward. Before Chloe could get into position however, the neighbor let out a tremendous sigh and rolled over. Her hand swung over the arm of the couch and came gently to rest on Chloe's yak jacket. Chloe froze.

"Lucy!" Chloe hissed in a voice of panic.

Lucy eyed the neighbor carefully. "It's okay, Clo," she whispered. "I don't think she's fully awake."

"Can I move?"

"Not just yet," Lucy advised.

The hand moved across Chloe's coat, and a slight frown appeared on the woman's face.

"Dog," she mumbled groggily. "Dog in my apartment."

The hand stroked the jacket again, as though trying to make sense of its hairy presence next to her couch. Chloe remained crouched on all fours, hardly daring to breathe. The woman opened one eye and looked directly into Lucy's face. "Who are you?" she asked, too confused to be alarmed.

"I'm your neighbor," Lucy said cheerfully, deciding that the best course of action was to bluff her way through.

The woman's hand patted Chloe again, and Chloe shrank down even lower, trying to make herself as small as possible. The woman tried to lift her head in order to look over the arm of the couch at the supposed dog, but the sudden action clearly made her feel nauseous and she sank back down into the comfort of the cushions. "Why are you in my apartment?" she asked irritably, focusing on Lucy again. "Why is your dog in my apartment?"

"My dog ran into your apartment," Lucy said, deciding that the briefest explanation would be the best. "I had to come and get it of course. We'd better be going now. I hope you feel better soon."

The woman eyed her suspiciously but she was plainly too drunk and confused to argue coherently. She waved her hand feebly at Lucy, and correctly interpreting this as a gesture of dismissal, Lucy bolted for the exit. Turning at the front door she looked impishly at Chloe, who was still crouched beside the sofa, looking beseechingly at her with what could only be described as puppy dog eyes.

Lucy put her fingers to her lips and emitted an ear-splitting whistle that caused the neighbor to groan loudly. "Oh I'm sorry," Lucy yelled solicitously. "Was I making too much noise?"

Chloe grimaced at her to stop, but Lucy merely grinned and clapped her hands loudly, this time making the neighbor wince.

"Come on, Timmy," Lucy crooned.

Chloe looked at her with upraised eyebrows.

"Yes, Timmy, it's time to say goodbye to the nice lady," Lucy said, enjoying herself thoroughly. To Chloe she mouthed the words "Start crawling."

Chloe looked at her in outrage.

"If you don't move I'll have to leave you here all night," Lucy said, in a playfully warning tone.

Glaring at Lucy with bitter hatred, Chloe started to cautiously crawl across the carpet towards the front door, the yak jacket trailing out behind her. Reaching the safety of the exit, she glanced quickly behind her and then shot to her feet and disappeared.

"Bye then. Sleep well," Lucy hollered cheerfully, conscientiously remembering to slam the door extremely hard as she left.

She entered the apartment and collapsed into laughter, fending off Chloe, who immediately started battering her with a cushion. "Oh God, I'm sorry," Lucy said, wiping her streaming eyes. "If you could have seen your *face* . . ."

"Yes, I'm sure it was extremely funny from an upright position," Chloe said sarcastically. She added in an injured tone of voice, "Why did I have to be Timmy again? Why couldn't I be a girl dog at least?"

"It's not my fault. Blame Enid Blyton. Or Meg. She's George, so I suppose that makes you her dog. Sir Timmy. Ow! Chloe, don't—" Lucy shrieked and ducked for cover as Chloe started pelting her with cushions again.

"Wait a minute—stop—what's that noise?"

They paused in the middle of the fray and listened intently.

"It's coming from next-door," Chloe said, her laughter bubbling out. "She's banging on the wall to tell *us* to keep the noise down!"

18.

when *a* fish chooses to die

"Good morning, Caro Lamb Gallery, this is Lucy speaking."

"Lucy, something terrible has happened!"

"Chloe? What's the matter with you?" asked Lucy anxiously, disturbed by the distress in Chloe's voice.

"Everything! That horrible neighbor left a note saying that she's coming around tonight to discuss our dog because it breaches the tenancy agreement. And on top of that Bertie's gone!"

Lucy tried to remain rational in order to calm Chloe down. "Chloe?"

"Yes," she said distractedly.

"How do you lose a fish?"

"I don't know!" she said hysterically. "He's just gone. He's not in his bowl. You don't have him with you, do you?" asked Chloe, a glimmer of hope in her voice as this possibility occurred to her.

"Chloe, why on earth would I take a goldfish to work?"

"I just thought—" Chloe started to sob again. "I can't believe I've lost him."

Lucy endeavored to think logically as Chloe was clearly panicking. "Have you checked the bowl carefully? Perhaps he's hiding under a little plastic shipwreck or in the treasure chest or something."

"Do you even know anything about Bertie? There's no shipwreck for him to hide under. There's just a round glass bowl with some rocks and grassy stuff. I'm telling you, the fish is gone."

"Chloe? Don't hate me but—you didn't try to walk him or anything, did you?"

There was an icy silence. "I'm going to hang up on you if you don't stop treating me like an idiot and start helping. Of course I didn't try to walk him. I didn't need to because I put the bowl on the windowsill for an hour yesterday afternoon so Bertie had lots of fresh air and sunshine then."

Lucy thought about this statement, decided it was a moot point, and struck to the subject at hand. "Have you checked the floor around the bowl?"

"Now who's being stupid? How would he get out of the bowl?"

"No, really. I remember hearing somewhere that fish commit suicide by jumping out of their bowls. People come home and find them dead on the floor all the time."

"Why on earth would a fish commit suicide? What the fuck has a fish got to worry about?"

"I don't know. Maybe they worry that their life isn't really going anywhere, that they're just traveling in circles."

"That's the stupidest thing that I've ever heard. They're not exactly crumbling under the weight of social responsibilities. It's not like they get asked to look after other fish when someone goes away," Chloe said bitterly.

"All I'm saying is that maybe you should check the floor. Bertie might still be alive somewhere, gasping for air." Lucy paused for consideration. "Or do I mean water."

"And another thing," Chloe said, clearly unmoved by this pathetic image and unwilling to budge from the topic of Suicidal Fish Syndrome. "How the hell would anyone know if it was suicide anyway? Maybe fish are like dolphins and they enjoy jumping playfully. Maybe they just lack coordination so they keep missing the bowl on their way down and die instead. Maybe none of it is premeditated, and it's more like whales stupidly beaching themselves than a genuine social crisis."

"I DON'T KNOW AND I DON'T CARE. JUST CHECK THE DAMN FLOOR," Lucy bellowed.

There was a short silence. "I'm going through a very hard time right now, Lucy," Chloe said icily. "It would be nice if you could be sympathetic instead of yelling at me."

"Sorry, Clo," Lucy said contritely.

"You don't think he's been kidnapped?" Chloe said, returning to her major preoccupation.

"Not really, no." Lucy checked the clock on the wall and wondered how much longer this conversation was going to take.

"I mean by the neighbor. The horrible neighbor that I punched," Chloe finished in a whisper, as though afraid that someone would overhear her admission of guilt.

"I'm pretty sure she hasn't stolen your fish," Lucy said reassuringly. "Clo—I'm sorry but I really have to go. The other line's ringing. I promise I'll help you look for Bertie when I get home tonight."

Chloe deigned to accept this olive branch, but she hung up with a sniff.

A fruitless hunt of the living room by Chloe, Meg, and Lucy that night failed to yield any sign of Bertie. Sunk in gloom, Chloe collapsed on the couch and ignored all offers of comfort: ranging from a gin and tonic from Lucy and a pledge to meet the financial costs of her dog obedience training from Meg, who had been vastly entertained by Lucy's account of the previous night's happenings. When the doorbell rang

Chloe's head shot up in fear, and she was visibly relieved when Lucy reentered the room followed by Tom. "Oh thank God it's you. Tom, you didn't take Bertie, did you?"

"Your fish?"

"Yes."

"Of course not. Why would I—" Tom broke off his query as Lucy and Meg simultaneously shook their heads at him and frowned.

"What have you done to Chloe?" Tom asked Lucy in an undertone, as Chloe relapsed into despair.

"I haven't done anything to her!" Lucy said outraged.

"You must have. She used to be reasonably normal until you moved in with her," Tom whispered.

Lucy glared at him. "She's very upset. It's not just Bertie. She spent a lot of money on her furry jacket and the neighbor mistook her for a dog. Which is actually quite unfair, because the coat doesn't feel rough at all. It's really quite soft."

"Perhaps the neighbor thought she was a soft-coated breed like a golden retriever?"

Lucy shook his head. "The jacket's brown. But that's not the point. The point is we're going to get thrown out of the flat unless we can prove that we don't have a dog."

"But you don't have a dog."

"Yes, but she thinks we do, and we can't tell her we don't because then we'd have to explain why Chloe was crouched on all fours next to her sofa."

"I don't want to ask, do I?" said Tom, in a tone filled with foreboding.

"I smacked her unconscious," Chloe contributed helpfully.

"Who?" Tom asked, looking bewildered.

"The neighbor of course. I wouldn't punch Lucy," said Chloe, looking quite hurt that Tom would ever entertain this notion. "She's my *friend*."

"Why on earth did you punch her?"

"It was an accident. Sort of. Anyway, I don't think I'm that bad. Lucy changed the CD *before* she helped me pick her up off the floor."

They all turned and looked at Lucy accusingly.

"It was Celine Dion," she said defensively. "You can't help someone while that woman's caterwauling in the background. Makes you want to kill things."

Everyone considered this and then nodded grudgingly.

"Well, what are you going to do about the dog?" Meg asked, getting back to the matter at hand.

"Perhaps we could buy one?" Chloe said hopefully.

"Right. So then we really *would* own one just to make sure that we *do* get kicked out of the apartment?"

"Why can't you just say that it ran away or died or went to live in the country?" suggested Meg sensibly.

"I've already lost their fish, I can't lose their dog as well. They'll think that I'm completely irresponsible," Chloe said hysterically.

They all regarded her quietly for a moment, but as Meg opened her mouth to respond Lucy caught her eye and mouthed the words "Better not." Thankfully Meg subsided, and they tried to think of another strategy.

Before anyone could voice an alternative plan however, an unpleasant banging on the door heralded the arrival of the neighbor. They looked at each other in horror.

"What are we going to tell her?" Chloe asked, completely panic-struck.

The banging grew louder.

"Best to face it," Meg said, striding to the door.

The neighbor, sporting a magnificent bruise from Chloe's right hook, subjected them all to a penetrating glare before singling out Chloe. "Where is it?" she demanded aggressively.

"Where's what?" Chloe answered feebly.

The neighbor's expression hardened. "Don't waste my time. I know that you have a dog—your friend over there," and here she glared at Lucy who shrank against Tom for protection, "let it loose in my apartment last night."

"It's not like it hurt anything," Lucy protested, trying to mount some sort of defense.

"It peed on the carpet," the neighbor said, staring her right in the eyes.

"I did not!" protested Chloe indignantly before anyone had time to shush her.

The neighbor ignored this interjection. "You're in breach of your lease by having a dog in the apartment," she said unpleasantly. "So I repeat—where is it?"

"Now," hissed Tom to Chloe.

"What?"

"Nothing for it. Thump her again."

"*I can't hit her!*" Chloe said, completely scandalized.

"Course you can. You've already done it once."

"I am not hitting that woman."

"Well, bite her on the leg then, Timmy."

Chloe punched him.

"That's the spirit," he said encouragingly, wincing and rubbing his arm. "Only harder, and this time aim for her."

And then they all heard a dog bark.

"Chloe, stop it," Meg said wearily. "She's not going to fall for it. And anyway, that was the cheesiest pretend bark that I've ever heard. It sounded like a cat trying to bark."

"It wasn't me!" Chloe said indignantly.

Everyone fell silent and stared very hard at Chloe for a few moments. In the ensuing hush they heard a gentle scratching sound, like a paw on a door, followed by a slight whimper. The silence lengthened, although now it was impregnated with a strange intensity. The whimpering and scratching increased in volume, and the endeavors of the dog that wasn't Chloe evidently paid off, as a few moments later a door was heard to give way and a puppy, looking excessively pleased with itself, excitedly wagged its way down the hall and erupted into the room, barking shrilly.

Unaware of the electric effect that his doggy presence had upon the gathered company, he promptly sat down in the middle of the room and started to bite and scratch at the big red bow that was fastened to his collar.

Lucy was the first to regain the power of speech, but she grossly misused this gift bestowed upon humanity by sinking to her knees, holding out her arms, and cooing "Come here, baby! Oh you gorgeous, scrumptious little muffin of a thing, aren't you *adorable!*"

The neighbor meanwhile was triumphant. "Ha! You see? It's a dog."

"Well of course it's a dog," said Meg, who disliked people who stated the obvious. "But it's not our friggin' dog."

"Yes it is," said Lucy, who had by now disentangled the bow and attached note from the collar of the disgruntled puppy. "At least, it's my dog. It's a present from Byron. Sorry Tom, but he wins the duel. Not that you had a chance anyway. But look at the liddle dumpling! How could anything ever be better than such a precious shnookums?"

"Any more of that, Luce, and we'll get Chloe to punch *you* unconscious," Tom snapped crankily, wishing that he'd thought of a puppy.

"Don't you listen to your bad Uncle Tom," burbled Lucy, who was ecstatically cradling the wriggling puppy in her arms.

The neighbor was regarding Lucy with a particularly nasty glare. "You are well aware that we are not permitted to keep animals in this building. I will be informing the owners when they return of your breach of the rules. Oh, and I suggest you get rid of that dog as soon as possible or I won't wait for them to return. I can get you evicted tomorrow if I want." She smiled unpleasantly and walked out.

"She must be lonely," said Chloe in the silence that followed the neighbor's departure. "Don't forget she's just been through a breakup."

"That's it!" Lucy's head snapped up. "Chloe, you're a genius. Tom, go over there and have sex with her. Now."

"Um, let me think about it. No."

"Chloe wouldn't hit her and now you won't have sex with her. I think you're all being very disobliging," Lucy said petulantly. "Considering that normally you'll sleep with anything with a pulse, I think it's very selfish of you to refuse when it's about saving the life of a puppy."

"Wait just a damn minute. The puppy is a gift from Byron. Why don't you get dear old Byron to sleep with her? Considering he's such an expert, having screwed half the universe anyway," Tom added bitterly.

"But actually, Tom, that's perfect," said Chloe, who had been thinking the situation through. "Byron bought Lucy the puppy, which, let's face it, you're not going to be able to top. Unless you sleep with the neighbor and convince her to let Lucy keep the puppy."

"Why do I have to sleep with her?"

"Because she needs sex. That's why she's so unpleasant."

"That's a dreadful thing to say."

"But true. Look how unpleasant Meg is. She hasn't had sex for ages now."

"Remind me why I allow you to keep both of your eyes, Chloe?" asked Meg.

"See?" Chloe turned to Tom and looked at him beseechingly. "Celibacy does terrible things to the human heart."

"Please sleep with the scary neighbor, Uncle Tom," Lucy said, holding the puppy up so that it was facing Tom and putting on her best pleading puppy voice.

"Stop it, Lucy, you're freaking me out. I've often heard little voices inside my head telling me to do strange sexual things, but having a puppy beg me to screw a woman that I don't know and who thinks that Chloe is one of its relatives is getting a bit weird even for me."

"Look, just go over there and talk to her then. Take her some of the scones Chloe made."

"Why me?"

"Because you're male. And you're handsome and can charm her and she'll love you and that will make us love you. Even more than we already do."

After another half hour of arguments and protests Tom could be seen sulkily crossing the landing with a plate of scones. The girls clustered in the doorway, wishing him luck, and then, as soon as he was out of sight, promptly abandoned him to his fate and went back inside to play with the enchanting puppy.

"What sort of dog is he?" asked Chloe curiously.

Lucy checked the note from Byron. "He's an apricot spoodle. Half spaniel, half poodle."

"It sounds like something you'd eat. And he looks more like a mutt than a designer dog," Meg said frankly, eyeing the squirming bundle of shaggy hair with trepidation. Meg wasn't overly fond of animals.

"She means that in a good way, muffin," Lucy hastened to reassure the puppy.

Meg groaned loudly. "Please, please tell me you are not naming him Muffin? Even you couldn't be that soppy."

"I probably could, but I'm not going to call him Muffin. I'm naming him George. After George Clooney," said Lucy promptly.

"But you *can't*," wailed Chloe. "Please don't be so mean, Lucy."

"What's wrong with you?" asked Meg in confusion.

"Lucy knows that I want to name my first-born son after George Clooney, and I can't if she gets in first and calls her dog George," Chloe explained.

"Chloe, you have to have sex to get pregnant," Meg reasoned patiently. "The dog will be well and truly dead of old age before you—ow!" She stopped as Chloe and Lucy hit her simultaneously.

"I can't believe you talked about dying in front of him!" Lucy said indignantly. "He's just a baby." Feeling more kindly disposed towards Chloe, she considered the problem of the puppy's name again.

"Perhaps I could call him Clooney," Lucy relented. She looked at the puppy. "Clooney!" she crooned. "Spoodle Clooney!"

The puppy trotted over to her, and Lucy crowed with delight. "He knows his name! What a clever, clever button you are."

Meg clicked her fingers. "Toilet brush!" she called. "Fridge magnet!"

The puppy promptly wriggled from Lucy's grasp and made its way towards Meg.

"Sometimes you're just evil," Lucy said with heartfelt sentiment, scooping her puppy back.

"Sorry, Luce. Couldn't resist. He sort of looks like a fridge magnet-sized toilet brush though, don't you think?"

"You'll have to be nicer to him if he's going to stay with you."

Meg stopped laughing abruptly. "What did you just say?"

"Oh please, Meg. He can't stay here or Chloe and I will get thrown out. And I can't give him to Tom or Percy because they're both in apartments too. You're the only one with a house and a backyard."

"Lucy, I don't like dogs."

"You don't have to like him. I promise I'll take care of him and do everything. He just needs a place to stay until I find somewhere permanent to live."

"Why can't he stay with Byron?" Meg objected.

"Byron's roommate has a cat."

"Well why the hell did Byron buy you a dog without first finding out if you were allowed to have one?"

"He's very impulsive." Lucy was prepared to defend to the death any giver of largesse in general and puppies in particular.

"That's just great, Lucy, but his romantic gesture has backfired a bit, hasn't it?"

"Please, Meg?" Lucy begged. "It'll just be for a little while, I promise."

Meg sighed as Lucy put Clooney into her arms to try to soften her heart. "Oh I suppose I can put up with him for a bit," she said ungraciously.

"He'll be no trouble at all," Lucy assured her anxiously.

Clooney yelped happily, and the deal was done as he started to gently pee on Meg's skirt.

19.

the bottom thing

Meg closed the kitchen door firmly behind her, so that Clooney couldn't escape into the carpeted areas of her house, and then un-clipped his lead. Yelping with excitement at being unrestrained, he ran eagerly around the kitchen, investigating corners and sniffing tenta-tively at stray crumbs.

Trying not to feel dismayed by having to assume responsibility for this small, overexcitable creature, Meg let him rampage happily for a few more minutes before deciding that she had to lay some ground rules. She cleared her throat. "Clooney!" she said sternly.

He didn't so much as raise his head.

"Spoodle Clooney!" she said, in a tone that was inappropriately harsh.

The puppy's head snapped up as his body cowered down. Lifting big, scared eyes to her face, the expression on his face clearly read "What have I done?"

Meg groaned. "Oh for heaven's sake don't look like that. You haven't done anything wrong. We just need to lay some ground rules if you're going to be staying here." The puppy sat on his haunches and regarded her with an intelligent, inquiring look.

"I don't like dogs. I don't want a dog. You belong to Lucy, not me. So rule number one—no peeing indoors or on me. You will sleep in the laundry room and I'll put newspaper down for two weeks. After that you'd better be housebroken or there'll be trouble." Meg paused and eyed Clooney severely, but he appeared to be listening intently.

"Rule number two—no jumping up—especially when I'm wearing a suit. No slobbering, no shrill barking, and your areas are the kitchen, laundry room, and the backyard. If I find a single dog hair on my couch I'll have you neutered without anesthetic. Understood?"

Clooney yelped.

"Right," said Meg, feeling quite pleased that her rational discussion with Clooney was yielding such positive results. He was so absurdly small that Meg felt ridiculous, towering over him like a giant from her standing position.

She crouched down awkwardly to make her final point. Before she could open her mouth however, Clooney, interpreting her movement as the instigation of a game, barked joyously and launched himself at her. Taken completely by surprise, Meg fell backwards as Clooney began to lovingly lick her face and hair. While trying futilely to fend him off, Meg made a mental note to kill Byron and Lucy, in that order.

"Hello, Percy!" Chloe said with genuine pleasure, opening the door to admit him into the apartment, which was filled with midday Saturday sunshine. "What are you doing here?"

Percy kissed her warmly on the cheek. "Looking for playmates," he confessed. "Would you like to go out for lunch?"

"I'd love to, but can we just wait till Meg and Lucy get back? They took Clooney for a walk on Elwood beach and Lucy didn't take her keys. They left over an hour ago so they shouldn't be too much longer."

"In that case, shall we call Tom and invite him too?"

Chloe grimaced. "I wouldn't bother. He's probably with that horrible neighbor. Even Lucy hasn't seen him for the past week."

"Do you think he really likes her?" asked Percy, who was yet to meet her.

"I think he probably really likes having sex with her," Chloe said cynically. She sighed when she saw the reproving expression on his face. "I'm sorry, Percy. But it's true. Tom has absolutely no problem having relationships based on nothing but physical attraction. They're usually over in about two weeks, which is just enough time for the girl to spend the next two months wondering what happened or went wrong. Although in this case it's more than likely that our neighbor is on the rebound after a bad breakup, so maybe Tom is the one being used."

Before Percy could reply they heard the sound of the front door opening, followed by a clattering of paws and shoes on the floorboards. Yelping with excitement at seeing Chloe and Percy, Clooney launched himself at both of them, wiggling and tumbling in an ecstasy of attention and affection.

"Hello, Percy," Lucy said in surprise, kicking her shoes off and scooping Clooney into her lap, where he barked indignantly at being restrained. "What are you doing here?"

"We're going out for lunch," Chloe answered for him. "Do you want to come?"

"I'd love to but I can't," Lucy said regretfully. "I have to drive Clooney to the doggie day spa. He's having the works—herbal shampoo and conditioning treatment, manicure/pedicure, teeth and ears cleaned, and some horrible bottom maintenance thing that I didn't ask too much about. And he gets a massage and a haircut. All for fifty dollars. It's a bargain."

"Sounds wonderful," Chloe said enviously. "I wonder if I could book myself in?"

"I don't think you'd enjoy the bottom thing, Clo."

"How on earth would you know whether or not a dog had been given a massage?" Percy wondered aloud.

Lucy frowned at him. "Some things you just have to take on good faith. But maybe Clooney will look relaxed afterwards."

Percy looked doubtfully at Clooney, who had escaped from Lucy's lap and was now chasing his own tail frenetically in the middle of the living room. Before he could voice his firm opinion that it would take nothing short of a horse tranquilizer to calm Clooney down, Meg spoke up.

"Talking of haircuts, I'm thinking of getting my hair cut short," she announced casually.

Lucy and Chloe looked at her in amazement. "But you never do anything to your hair," Lucy said, in a tone that was almost accusing.

Meg flushed, and Lucy hastily tried to backtrack from her tactless comment. "What I mean is you have such lovely long hair, and you only ever get it trimmed. I just can't imagine you with short hair."

"Well, maybe I won't cut it all off. Maybe I'll just get some highlights put in or something," Meg said defensively.

Lucy looked at Meg curiously, but Percy, sensing that Meg needed encouragement, and anxious not to let the conversation swing back to Clooney's bottom maintenance, intervened enthusiastically. "I think you'd look wonderful with highlights."

This earned him no points whatsoever with Meg, who regarded him disparagingly. "Percy, you wouldn't have the first clue what I'd look like with highlights. You probably don't even know what highlights are."

"I do so," Percy said, stung by this criticism of his general coiffure knowledge. He turned to Chloe, who could generally be relied upon to support him but even she was shaking her head ruefully.

"I'm sorry, Percy, but you really shouldn't take part in this conversation."

"Why not?"

"Because you're a boy, so you suffer from genetic Haircut Blindness. Meg could have her head attacked by Edward Scissorhands and you probably wouldn't notice."

"I jolly well would," Percy protested, feeling that his devotion to Meg was somehow in question.

"You want me to prove it to you?"

"How?"

With a flash of inspiration, Chloe covered Percy's eyes with her hands. "Okay. Now tell me—what color is my hair?"

There was a pause, and then Percy said cautiously, "Blondey-brown. With red bits."

"Wrong!" said Chloe triumphantly, not taking her hands away. "My hair is caramel with russet highlights. See—you're color-blind when it comes to female hair," she stated satisfied.

"Oh don't be ridiculous, Chloe," said Meg impatiently.

"Well, we'll try it again then. Percy, what color is Meg's hair?"

This time there was no hesitation.

"Brown."

They all turned to survey Meg.

"It is really," said Chloe, disappointed.

"Yes it is. There's really no other word for it. It's brown," said Lucy, staring at Meg thoughtfully.

"So I have brown hair. What's the big deal?" snapped Meg.

"I don't know. I guess I've never paid much attention to your hair before, but now that I look at it . . . it's just so *brown*."

"You're all being ridiculous," retorted Meg, unfeasibly annoyed that her hair color merited only one appellation.

Before anyone could respond to this, Tom's voice could be heard on the landing, cheerfully calling out Lucy and Chloe's names.

"Come in—the door's open," Lucy hollered back, trying to suppress a sudden rush of delight at hearing his voice.

Her delight was short-lived however, as Tom strolled into the room closely followed by the unpleasant neighbor. Even on a Saturday she was wearing full makeup, Lucy noted with horror. What was Tom *doing* with this awful creature?

"Hey there," Tom said, with a nonchalance that was perceptibly forced. "What's going on?" Clooney shot off Lacy's lap and to everyone's horror headed straight for the neighbor. Before he could expend his puppyish enthusiasm on her, Tom deftly lifted him up with one hand and held the excited puppy to his chest. The neighbor, whose face had hardened at the sight of Clooney, closed her mouth angrily as Tom stroked and calmed the effervescent bundle.

"He's not living here," Lucy said hastily, feeling as though she had just been caught out in an act of wrongdoing. "He's staying at Meg's. We just took him for a walk."

The neighbor clearly didn't believe her, but with Tom cradling the object of her disapproval she contented herself with saying, "For God's sake, put him down, Tom. I can smell him from here, and we don't have time for you to go home and change your shirt before we go out to lunch."

Meg, who was about as fond of dogs as the neighbor, nevertheless took an immediate, irrational dislike to her for objecting to Clooney and decided to come to Lucy's rescue. "Aren't you going to introduce us properly, Tom?" Meg asked sweetly.

He shot her a mistrustful look. "This is Meg, Lucy, Chloe, and Percy," he said, waving his hand at the interested gathering. "This is Delilah."

"That's D-E-E-L-Y-L-A-H," Deelylah clarified as she held out her hand to Percy.

"Eh? Oh, very pleased to meet you. I'm P-E-R-C-Y," Percy spelled politely as he shook her hand, wondering if this was another strange Australian formality that he hadn't previously encountered, like the way men who were intimate friends abused one another and thumped each other as hard as they could whenever they met.

Deelylah's immaculately made-up face hardened. "Are you taking the piss?"

As he always did in situations where he had no idea what was happening, Percy turned imploringly to Meg.

"She's asking if you're here to take a sample of her urine," Meg explained kindly. Before anyone could comfort the stricken Percy she extended her hand to Deelylah. "Hi. I'm Meg. But my middle name is Polleeannah. Spelt P-O-L-L-E . . ."

"Why don't you come into the kitchen, Deelylah?" interrupted Chloe hurriedly. "I was just about to make some tea."

After casting a darkling glance at Meg, Deelylah followed Chloe into the kitchen.

"You really are obnoxious sometimes, Meg," Tom said, without rancor. "Deelylah has an extremely unique name, and she simply likes to let people that she's meeting for the first time know that she's not an ordinary Delilah."

"Tom, she's ghastly," Meg said, without preamble. "She's completely affected and her *real* name is probably Agnes."

"Probably," Tom agreed, unperturbed. "But don't go putting ideas like that into my head, or knowing me, I'll call out Agnes at a crucial moment and get into all sorts of trouble. You're being very quiet, Luce," he continued, swinging around to observe Lucy, who was flicking through a magazine and apparently taking no interest in the conversation.

Lucy lowered the magazine onto an unprotesting Clooney, and regarded him steadily. "What would you like me to say, Tom?"

"What you think, I suppose."

"I don't know the girl. But I have to say it doesn't look promising. And I, for one, intend to call her Delilah not Dee-ly-lah."

"How will she know?" asked Percy, trying to remember all of this and wishing that he was carrying a notebook.

"She just will," Lucy said with a sudden grin. "Girls have a sixth sense when it comes to veiled bitchiness."

Before Tom could retort, Chloe and Deelylah came back into the room. To Lucy's immense disgust, Deelylah snuggled up to Tom and purred into his ear that they had better be going because, with a secretive smile, he had already made them late.

"Sick her, Clooney," Lucy muttered fiercely into Clooney's attentive ear. "Or even better, *be* sick on her." Clooney licked Lucy consolingly, which didn't make her feel any better, particularly when she looked up to see that while she was getting covered in dog slobber, Deelylah was getting a kiss on the cheek from Tom.

"Sorry we can't stay for a cup of tea, Clo. But we'll see you all later," Tom said, draping an arm around Deelylah's admirably toned shoulders.

"Bye," everyone, with the exception of Lucy, chorused unenthusiastically.

Deelylah gave them all a cold smile and allowed Tom to escort her out of the apartment. After their departure there was a small silence.

"K-L-O-W-E-E," said Chloe suddenly.

"Beg pardon?"

"I was just experimenting to see how I could spell my name in a different way. Lucy, you could be L-E-W-S-I-E."

"And Meg could be M-E-G . . . Damn, it doesn't really work for Meg, does it?"

"She could be double G, I suppose," said Chloe doubtfully. "But it's not very funny."

Bright color suddenly flushed Meg's cheeks. They watched in surprise as she grabbed her handbag and fastened Clooney's lead. With a quick "I'll drop Clooney off at the spa," she left the room, towing an equally surprised Clooney and slamming the door harder than was necessary behind her.

"What's got into her?" asked Chloe in surprise.

"I'll go after her," Percy said eagerly.

"No, don't, Percy," Lucy advised. "I know that you mean well, but when Meg gets into these moods it really is best to leave her alone. She'll only turn on you if you go after her now. She hates people knowing when she's upset."

There was another short silence and then Percy asked cautiously, "Do you think Tom really likes Deelylah? It's just—she doesn't seem like his type."

Lucy snorted. "When Tom's been single for awhile RuPaul would be his type provided he was a good lay."

"There is no way RuPaul would wear as much makeup as that horrible girl," Chloe protested. "Do you think she wears makeup to bed?"

"Probably," said Lucy, uncharitably happy to launch into a bitch session about Deelylah. She paused and added viciously, "I bet you she has *weekly* bottom maintenance."

Percy groaned and hoped fervently that Tom's affair with Deelylah would meet a swift end. He wasn't sure that he could cope with too many more exclusively girly conversations.

20.

hide & seek

Several hours later, Lucy was staring into space, unconsciously chewing her bottom lip as she pondered Meg's outburst. She came out of her reverie to see Chloe standing a few feet away, regarding her with a hang-dog and furtive expression. "Hey, I didn't hear you come back from lunch," Lucy said surprised. "Where's Percy?"

"He's gone home." Chloe shuffled her feet, and Lucy looked at her suspiciously.

"Clo? Why are you looking at me like that?"

"I think I've lost my earring."

Lucy sighed. "Chloe, you're always losing earrings because you wear clip-ons. Why don't you just summon up your courage and have your ears pierced? I've said that I'll come with you."

Ignoring this offer, Chloe said in a slightly panicked voice, "You have to help me find it. It's not the earring that I'm most worried about, it's where I lost it."

"I don't want to know, do I?" Lucy said, with a strong feeling of foreboding.

"I think I lost it in Deelylah's apartment."

There was a silence and then Lucy groaned. "Chloe, you *didn't*."

"I really think I did," Chloe said tearfully. "I've been looking for it everywhere, and the last time that I remember seeing it is that night. I'm sure that I was wearing it when we went to knock on the door, because I remember that when I pulled on my coat it almost snagged the earring."

"Which earrings were you wearing?"

"The big dangly ones with the purple bits."

"So there's a fair chance that she's already found it?"

"Maybe. Do you think we should just go over there and confess?"

"Probably. But I don't think I understand what happened anymore, so I'm not exactly sure that I can explain it to her."

Sunk in the gloom of her own thoughts, Chloe ignored this and instead said, in a depressed tone, "We can't tell her the truth now that Tom's seeing her. She'll think we're maniacs and probably have us arrested, and that will cause a fight between her and Tom and then it will be all our fault if they break up and Tom will be furious with us."

Lucy brightened noticeably for a moment, but after weighing up the benefits of Tom and Deelylah breaking up against Tom's probable anger with them for causing the breakup, she decided regretfully against pursuing a confessional course of action. "Look, even if she does find it she probably won't worry that much about it. Why don't you just buy a new pair of earrings?"

"I can't just leave it there," Chloe said distressed. "Percy gave them to me for my birthday. I love those earrings, and he'll notice if I stop wearing them. I don't want to hurt his feelings and besides, I want my earring back."

"Well there's only one thing we can do then," Lucy said sensibly. "We'll have to get into her apartment and look for it."

Chloe shuddered at the thought of returning to the scene of her crime. "How are we going to get invited into her place? She hates us. Even me. And I gave her a plate of scones," she finished in a wounded tone of voice, as it occurred to her that her baked-goods generosity had been greatly abused.

There was a small pause, and then Lucy said cautiously, "I wasn't thinking that we would be *invited* exactly . . ."

"No, Lucy. Absolutely not. I am a committed pacifist."

"What are you talking about?"

"You're going to ask me to hit her again. I told Tom that I won't and I mean it."

"Chloe, don't be ridiculous. I'm not asking you to hit her. What I was thinking was maybe just slipping in when she goes downstairs to use the laundry. She leaves her front door wedged open all the time so that she doesn't have to take her keys."

Chloe turned this plan over in her mind and conceded that it might work. "Okay," she agreed, albeit a trifle unwillingly. "When are we going to do this?"

"She always does her laundry on a Saturday afternoon. We can do it as soon as she gets back from lunch with Tom."

Chloe's anxiety increased tenfold at the thought of executing their plan so soon. "I don't know, Luce . . ."

"Fine. Leave your earring there then," Lucy said impatiently. "It's really not a big deal, Clo. We'll duck in, have a quick look—it can only be in the living room or hallway—and nip out again. End of story."

Put like that it didn't really seem like that big a deal. Chloe agreed, feeling vaguely comforted.

Wearing a distinctly harassed air, Chloe responded to Lucy's peremptory command forty-five minutes later. Lucy, who had been keeping a watch for signs of Deelylah's return, was about to issue the command to change strategic positions when something else caught her attention.

"Clo?"

"Yes?"

"You're dressed like a burglar, aren't you?"

Chloe looked down at her black leggings and black top. "Too much?"

"Well no, you look great. But it's daytime."

"I didn't think of that," Chloe said crestfallen. "I'm so nervous I can't think properly."

"Don't worry, you won't have to think about it for much longer. She's back, and she should be going to the laundry any moment now. Come on, let's wait at the front door so we can hear her." Lucy led the way to the front door. Propping it open, she listened intently for sounds of activity from next door.

"Lucy?" Chloe whispered, as she hung back.

"Mmmm?"

"I think we need a lookout. I think *I* should be the lookout," she said hastily, before Lucy could claim the position.

"Don't even think about it, Chloe. You're coming in with me." The sound of Deelylah's door opening, followed by footsteps going down the stairwell, galvanized her into action. "It's now or never. Move. We only have a few minutes."

Taking a deep breath, Chloe followed Lucy as she scooted across the landing and entered Deelylah's apartment. Just inside the living room, Lucy stopped abruptly in amazement, causing Chloe to collide into her.

"What is it? What's wrong?" Chloe whispered, terrified that they had already been caught. She followed Lucy's line of vision. The silver frame that they had last seen facedown on the coffee table amidst empty wine bottles had been resurrected and was now positioned in the center of the mantelpiece, proudly displaying a photograph of a smiling Tom.

"What the hell is that?" demanded Lucy furiously, forgetting to whisper. Chloe nervously shushed her, and she dropped her voice to an angry whisper. "The woman's a psychopath. They've been going out for about three seconds and she has a photograph of him on display! Doesn't she understand Tom at all? He'll run a mile when he sees that."

"Well that's good then, Lucy," Chloe said anxiously, not wanting to get sidetracked from their mission. "They'll break up, and you won't have to be jealous anymore."

"I am not *jealous!*" Lucy said indignantly, forgetting to whisper again and getting shushed by Chloe once more.

"Okay, you're not jealous. You're just pissed off. Can you please help me look for the earring so that we can get out of here?"

"I am not pissed off!" Lucy seethed, sounding as pissed off as was possible at such a low volume.

"Yes you are. You don't want Tom, but you don't want anyone else to have him either. You look on the floor over there and I'll search around the couch."

"That is completely untrue," Lucy hissed. However, Chloe now had her head stuck under the couch and either didn't hear or was ignoring her, so Lucy had no choice but to start searching for the missing earring. Lucy was feeling around the floor near the window when she suddenly heard a voice that she knew very well indeed. "Chloe!" she whispered, as loudly as she dared. "They're coming."

Chloe popped her head over the back of the couch. "What did you say?"

Lucy heard Tom's voice again and the sound of footsteps on the stairs. "Hide!" she commanded brusquely and promptly vanished behind the curtains. Chloe stared at her, and then, as the front door was pushed open to its full extent, she executed a surprisingly neat commando roll and disappeared under the couch, where she lay, barely daring to breathe.

A moment later Tom and Deelylah entered the room, and Lucy and Chloe heard the sound of an empty laundry basket being dropped onto the floor.

"Would you like a drink?" asked Deelylah, and Lucy would have sneered at the breathy sexiness of her voice if she hadn't been trying so hard not to breathe in the dust that lay thickly on the curtains.

"A juice would be great," said Tom, settling himself comfortably on the couch. His weight caused the cushion to sag to just above Chloe's face but she shut her eyes and tried to pretend that she was lying on a beach on a Greek island instead of being under a hostile woman's couch in dangerously close proximity to Tom's rear end.

Deelylah went into the kitchen, and Lucy was just considering the best way to attract Tom's attention when Deelylah suddenly popped her head back into the living room and said, "You can put on some music if you like. My CDs are all over there."

"Oh. Okay." To Chloe's immense relief Tom got up and went to investigate Deelylah's CD collection. Cautiously putting her head around the edge of the curtain, Lucy watched as Tom, who had his back to her, picked up a couple of CDs and shook his head in disbelief as he read their titles. Before she could hiss at him, Deelylah reappeared carrying two drinks, and Lucy took a deep breath of fresh air and retreated behind the curtain once more. Hoping desperately that she wouldn't sneeze, Lucy couldn't help but feel that she was in a better position than Chloe, who now had to cope with the weight of both Tom and Deelylah sprawled on the couch on top of her.

"What are your plans for the rest of the weekend?" Tom asked Deelylah.

"I went to the gym first thing this morning. And I'll probably go for a run later this evening when it cools down."

"Very impressive. So you're into fitness then?"

"I'm passionate about it," Deelylah said passionately. "I can't stand couch potatoes. I think it shows that you don't love yourself if you don't love your own body."

"I prefer to let other people love my body," Tom joked, but Deelylah didn't appear to find this funny.

"I take health and fitness very seriously," she said seriously. "I mean, really, Tom, if you don't look after yourself who will? We all know that we can't depend on being with anyone else for a lifetime. It's more than likely that we're all going to end up alone, so it's imperative that we treat ourselves well."

Lucy had previously estimated Deelylah's relationship expectancy with Tom at about three weeks, but hearing this she began to wonder. Although Deelylah's self-sufficient philosophy was couched in the sort of language that appeared in the Sunday newspaper's Life Coaching section, ironically Tom and Deelylah's shared cynicism about the longevity of relationships meant that, in one way at least, they were ideal for each other.

There was further desultory conversation and then an ominous silence preceded some muffled squeaking noises. As the couch springs moved and the sound of heavy breathing became audible, both Lucy and Chloe realized with horror that Deelylah and Tom were kissing.

"Dear God," prayed Lucy. "I know that I haven't prayed since I was thirteen when my dog Miffy died and I stopped believing in you, but please, please, if you exist, please don't let them have sex now."

"Dear God," prayed Chloe. "Please don't let me die like this. I don't want to suffocate under a couch, crushed to death by two people having sex, one of whom thinks that I'm a dog. I'm not a bad person, truly. I just wanted to find my earring."

The breathing and squeaking got louder and Lucy had already made up her mind that if she heard a single moan she was going to jump out from behind the curtains, say how do you do politely, and run away, when a familiar voice called out from the front entrance.

"Hello? Hello? Anyone home?"

Percy! thought Chloe and Lucy simultaneously, with a rush of relief.

The squeaking abruptly stopped and Deelylah swore. "It's that English twit. Ow!" she exclaimed, as Chloe, unable to restrain herself, jabbed her indignantly through the cushion.

"What's the matter?" asked Tom.

"I must have sat on something sharp," Deelylah said, inspecting her seat in confusion.

Tom was unmoved. "Percy's a good friend of mine," he said, in a decidedly annoyed tone of voice.

"Oh right. Sorry I forgot. But you must admit, he's not too bright," Deelylah said, sitting up straight and smoothing her clothes.

Before Tom could further defend Percy, the subject of their conversation entered the room.

"Sorry to barge in like this," he started shyly. "Oh—Tom! You're here?"

"I seem to be, Perce. What's up?"

"Well, as I was saying, awfully sorry to barge in like this, but I don't suppose either of you have seen Chloe or Lucy? I just had lunch with Chloe and I was halfway home when I realized that she'd left her sunglasses in my car. It's very odd because the door to their apartment is wide open but . . ."

Whatever Percy had been going to say was swallowed as Chloe, deciding that desperate times called for desperate measures, rolled out from under the couch, popped her head up behind Tom and Deelylah, who remained unaware of her, silently mouthed the word "Help!," mysteriously pointed to the curtains, and then disappeared back under the couch again.

"What on earth is the matter? You look like you're having a fit," Tom asked, eyeing him curiously.

"What?" answered Percy wildly, completely at a loss as to what was going on but retaining enough prudence to be aware that he needed to tread carefully. "A fit? A fit? Yes I might be having a fit." Summoning every last ounce of ingenuity, he added, "They run in the family I believe. Mother had a labrador that used to have fits."

"You were looking for Chloe," said Deelylah, in a tone that indicated that she thought Percy should probably be institutionalized but that the issue didn't interest her overmuch. "She's not here."

Percy was standing on the far side of the room, which enabled Lucy, who had been peeping out, to have gained a fair idea that he must have caught a glimpse of Chloe. Taking a deep breath, and trusting that Tom and Deelylah wouldn't look over to their left, she pushed the curtain out slightly, just far enough so that Percy could catch sight of her. The small movement caught his eye, he glanced over, saw Lucy mouth the word "Help!" and then the curtain fell back into place and he snapped his head back to look at Tom and Deelylah again.

By now Percy was wondering if he was in fact a bit delusional. Clearly the girls had gotten themselves into another mess involving the neighbor. "Would you mind leaving us alone for a few minutes, Deelylah?" Percy asked politely. "I need to have a word in private with Tom."

"But this is my apartment."

"Daresay you're right," said Percy dismissively, his aristocratic hauteur aroused by Deelylah's crude manner. "Noticed the photo of Tom up there. Can't think of anyone else who would have a photo of Tom on the mantelpiece." He thought hard for a moment and then added conscientiously, "Except Tom of course."

Tom eyed Percy and decided that even though he was clearly in one of his nuttier moods, he was obviously in earnest. Turning to Deelylah he wheedled, "You could check on your laundry. It might be ready to put in the dryer."

She shot him a filthy look. "If *you're* going to kick me out of my own apartment too then I suppose I may as well go." In high temper she picked up the laundry basket, and made her way down the stairs.

"Okay, Perce, what's up?" Tom asked benevolently.

Before Percy had a chance to respond, the curtains began to kick. Tom spun around and stared in horror, while to his amazement, a completely unfazed Percy rushed forward and helped unravel Lucy, who fell into his arms with her eyes red and streaming and promptly started to sneeze violently.

"Please stop sneezing, Lucy," Percy begged. "Deelylah might come back at any moment and she'll hear you."

"I can't—ATISHOO!—help it ATISHOO! Those wretched curtains are filthy."

"Bless you. But Lucy, I've told you a million times—if you leave curtains alone, they'll leave you alone," scolded Percy, helping to unwind Lucy from the clinging drapes, which seemed reluctant to let her go.

"What on earth are you doing in Deelylah's apartment?" asked Tom in complete bewilderment. Feeling as though his head was about to explode, Tom sank back down on the couch and then leapt up again as the couch politely requested him not to sit on its head. "What was that?" asked Tom, eyeing the couch in alarm.

"Not what. Who." Percy said punctiliously.

"What?"

"Chloe. She's a *who*," Percy explained patiently. "Not a *what*."

"Percy, why are you going on about Chloe? You're meant to be in love with Meg. God you English are fickle."

"There you are," Percy clucked appreciatively. "An Englishman would still be stuck on the talking couch but you Aussies put your mates first. Admirable. Really very admirable."

Chloe stuck her head up cautiously from behind the couch. "I found my earring!" she said in delight, holding up the missing accessory for Lucy to see. "Hello, Percy. Hello, Tom," she added, well-mannered as always.

"Why are you dressed like a burglar?" Percy asked curiously, as Chloe emerged fully from underneath the couch.

Recovering from the heart failure caused by Chloe's appearance, Tom swung around to face Lucy.

"This is your doing, Luce," he said grimly. "Were you watching us kiss?"

"Of course we weren't watching," Lucy said in disgust. "It was bad enough having to listen to it."

"How long have you been here?" Tom demanded, ignoring this provocation. "Have you been here since I arrived?"

"Have you been out in the sun, Thomas? Brains gone a bit soft?" Lucy asked sympathetically, still blowing her nose. "Of course we were here before you. Or did you think we magically materialized in the Dr. Spock tube after you came in?"

"Transporter," said Percy, who couldn't abide incorrect references. "It was called a transporter. And Spock wasn't a doctor. Very common misconception."

Both Lucy and Tom ignored this interruption.

"Lucy, you had better give me a straight answer in the next five seconds or I'm going to put you over my knee and spank you extremely hard."

"Promises, prom—oh okay then, I'll stop. I'm stopping. I've stopped now." Lucy subsided at the look on Tom's face.

"Were you spying on Deelylah and me?"

"Were we *what?* No we were *not!* Why on earth would we do that?"

"I don't know, Luce. I have absolutely no idea why you would be hiding behind the curtains in Deelylah's apartment either. Why don't you help me out and tell me?"

Seeing that Lucy was looking mutinous and prepared to engage in full-scale verbal warfare, Chloe hastily intervened. "It was my fault, Tom," she said contritely. "I lost my earring and Lucy came with me to help me look for it."

"You lost it that night you hit Deelylah?" Tom said, grasping the situation with an immediacy that even Lucy had to concede was impressive.

"Yes. So we had to sneak in to look for it. Can we go now? Deelylah will be back at any moment."

"And before you ask, we don't want to confess for your sake. We thought she might break up with you if we told her what happened that night," Lucy said. "So get back on that couch and be grateful."

"Can we *please* go now?" begged Chloe, shooting another anxious look at the open front door.

"Wait a minute. Why didn't you ask me to look for the earring?"
There was a short silence.

"Didn't think of that," Lucy finally admitted sheepishly.

Tom shot her an appraising look that was very far from affectionate.
"I don't suppose you did. You know, you're not going to turn this into
sides, Luce," he said, in a conversational tone of voice that didn't fool
Lucy for a second.

"What *are* you talking about?"

"I know what you're doing. You didn't ask for my help because in
your mind you've already put Deelylah and I on one side and you're
turning us into the enemy."

"You really are the most paranoid, conceited—" Lucy broke off
as Deelylah reentered her apartment, looking completely taken aback
to find her living room full of people, the majority of whom she
didn't like.

"Afternoon," Percy said, to break the silence that had fallen.

"I've already seen you this afternoon," Deelylah said unkindly, adding bluntly, "What are you all doing in my apartment?"

"We had to ask Tom something," Chloe said, shooting a pleading
look at Tom.

Lucy held her breath. Tom couldn't be relied upon to back up their
story if he was truly angry.

There was a short pause and then Tom said, "Yes, they came to
ask me something." As Lucy and Chloe slowly let their breath escape
in relieved sighs he added pointedly, "And you were just leaving,
weren't you?"

Chloe assented and made for the door, while Lucy muttered
"Gladly" under her breath.

With Percy in tow Chloe made her escape but Lucy stopped and
turned at the door. "Atlantis," she said, looking directly at Tom.

Deelylah looked at her in confusion. "What did you say?"

"Atlantis. City under the sea. And Pompeii. Nice places for a holiday, don't you think, Tom?" Without waiting for an answer she turned and closed the door behind her.

"What did she mean?" asked Deelylah curiously, looking at Tom, whose expression had darkened.

"Nothing. It didn't mean anything," Tom said, trying to regain his composure. But he knew what it meant. Lucy was wishing that he was ten thousand miles under the sea or at the mercy of an erupting volcano. Which was basically Lucy's way of telling him to drop dead.

21.

girls' night

Byron's exuberant voice came through Lucy's cell phone. "Lucia! Where are you? There is a preview screening of that film we wanted to see tonight and the director is giving a talk afterwards. You must meet me there in half an hour."

"Oh Byron, I'd love to but I can't. I'm on my way to Meg's to take Clooney for a walk and then the girls are coming around," Lucy answered regretfully.

When he answered, Lucy could exactly conjure up the sulky expression on his face. "But I have booked tickets."

"That's very sweet of you, Byron, but I have to walk Clooney. He's been cooped up all day," Lucy explained patiently.

"Why can't Meg walk him?" Byron asked petulantly.

"Because he's my dog," Lucy said, trying not to sound shocked. "Meg's doing me a huge favor as it is letting him stay at her place." Telling herself that Byron couldn't have realized what he was saying, she attempted a compromise, "Why don't you meet me at Meg's and walk Clooney with me?"

"I wish to see this film."

"Oh. Right." There was a silence, and then Lucy said, "I am sorry, really I am. Just give me a bit more notice next time."

"I wanted to surprise you."

"Well you did." Lucy tried to sound light-hearted, but it didn't quite come off. She tried to think of something else to add, but realizing that she didn't really have anything further to say, they said goodbye awkwardly.

Letting herself into Meg's house, Lucy was far too busy dealing with Clooney's joyful hysteria at her arrival to spare a second thought for what had seemed to be a petty and minor argument. She was nonetheless pleased when her phone rang again a moment later, but picking it up eagerly she hesitated when she saw Tom's name displayed rather than Byron's.

Tom, on the other hand, felt his mood lift as soon as he heard her voice. "Luce, it's me."

"Hello, Thomas, how are you?" Lucy asked coolly.

"Going out of my mind with work. Listen, what are you doing tonight? Do you want to go and see a film or something?"

There was a pause. "I can't," Lucy said. "I already have plans."

"Oh come on, Luce. You cannot seriously be angry with me for seeing Deelylah. May I remind you that *you* were the one who wanted me to go and charm her in the first place?" Tom asked pointedly, deciding to cut to the chase.

There was a brief silence, and then the innate honesty in Lucy's nature overcame her annoyance from the previous week. "Look, Tom, I'm sorry about what I said the other day. I didn't mean it. But I just don't understand what you see in that girl."

"Well that makes two of us, because I haven't the faintest idea what you see in Bryan."

"Stop calling him that. Anyway, I really do have plans for tonight."

"Oh." The disappointment he felt was out of all proportion and he knew it, but something prompted him to say recklessly, "What are you doing? Can I join you?"

There was another silence.

"Sorry, I shouldn't have asked," Tom said, embarrassed. "You're probably seeing Byron."

"I'm not actually," Lucy said hastily, feeling his humiliation. "It's just that I'm having the girls around . . ."

"That's perfect then," Tom said, brightening. "You owe me one for crashing my boys' night. What time shall I come around?"

"Are you sure you want to come?" Lucy asked uncertainly. "You might be bored. It's not like we're out at a pub or anything."

"Why? What do you do?"

"Watch a DVD and have some drinks."

"That's not gender exclusive. Sounds exactly what I feel like."

"Sometimes we paint our toenails and give each other facials," Lucy continued.

"Do you have pillow fights in your underwear?" Tom asked hopefully.

"No. But we compare the penis lengths of all the men that we've slept with," Lucy said crushingly.

"In that case, I'm hoisting Mr. Binky over my shoulder and we're definitely coming."

Lucy sighed. "Oh fine then. I suppose I do owe you one. It's about six thirty now, so come around in about an hour."

"Seven thirty?" asked Tom, startled. "That's a bit early, isn't it?"

"We have dinner together. We don't just get together and drink."

"Oh." Tom absorbed this novel concept and then rallied to ask, "Speaking of drink, shall I bring a keg?"

"Tom, there's only four of us and it's midweek. A bottle of wine will be fine."

"Can I bring Percy?" asked Tom in a small tone of voice, suddenly afraid of what lay before him.

"Yes, you can bring Percy. But no one else. It's about spending time with your closest friends, not having the rent-a-crowd over. I'll see you at our place at seven thirty then."

Tom hung up from Lucy, and five minutes later he remembered to call Percy.

"What are you doing tonight, Perce?"

"I'm going around to Lucy's."

"How can you already know about that?"

"She just called to invite me."

"How do you reckon girls go through life being so organized?"

"Not sure. I have to go, Tom—a student just arrived."

"Wait a minute. Uh, Perce?"

"Yes?"

There was a short silence, and then Tom cleared his throat. "What are you going to wear?"

"What do you mean, what am I going to wear?"

"What do you mean what do I mean?" asked Tom growing increasingly frustrated. "It's not a complicated question. What are you going to wear to Lucy's tonight?"

"Are you feeling okay, Tom?"

"Shut up. Look I've never been to a girls' night before—"

"And you think I have?"

Tom ignored him. "And you know what Lucy's like. She's probably invited Byron now too, and if I turn up in jeans and Byron is in a shirt and pants I'll never hear the end of it. So what do you think I should wear?"

"Tom, we're going to Lucy's to watch a movie. I really don't think it matters."

"So you think jeans will be okay?"

Percy looked wistfully at his watch and wondered how long this was going to take. "I'm sure jeans will be fine."

"But what if we go out afterwards?" Tom pondered in a worried tone of voice. "I don't want to have to go all the way back home to get changed again."

"Wear trousers then."

"My navy ones?"

"Yes, Tom. Wear your navy trousers," groaned Percy.

"With what shirt?"

There was a silence.

"Tom? I'm hanging up. You're getting creepy."

"Well, what are you going to wear then?"

"I don't know. I hadn't thought about it. My jeans I suppose."

"But then I'll look overdressed."

"Fine. If I promise to wear trousers can I hang up now?"

"Promise."

"I promise." Percy hung up the phone and turned to see his student surveying him doubtfully.

Lucy, Meg, and Chloe had already opened the first bottle of wine and were curled up gossiping in the living room when the doorbell rang.

"That'll be Tom," said Lucy, unfurling herself from the couch. "Now remember—be nice. He was so cranky after the boys' night and that scene in Deelylah's apartment that we have to make it up to him now."

Meg rolled her eyes, but Chloe solemnly crossed her heart as Lucy departed to answer the door.

"It's Tom," Lucy announced unnecessarily, as she led the way into the living room.

Tom greeted the girls, handed a bottle of wine and a six-pack of imported beer to Lucy, and then inquired after Percy.

"He's on his way. He called to say that he's running late."

Tom thought for a moment and then, with a notable lack of enthusiasm, asked, "Where's Byron?"

Lucy's face fell. "He's not coming. He had tickets to see a film."

"Oh." Tom brightened perceptibly and then looked thoughtful. "What do you think he would have worn if he *had* come?"

Lucy eyed him warily. "Tom? Are you feeling okay?"

"Of course I am." Hastily he changed the subject. "Would you like help with anything?"

"Come and sit down next to me, Tom," Chloe invited cheerfully. "You can help keep Clooney away from the antipasto platter while I finish it."

Tom perched on the arm of the sofa next to Chloe and gazed in awe at the colorful arrangement of food on the large white platter. "Who else is coming?" he asked, trying to quell the eternal hope that Lucy might have recently made friends with a beautiful dental nurse.

Lucy looked at him in confusion. "No one. I told you on the phone that it was meant to be a girls' night."

"You mean you do all this," Tom gestured towards the antipasto platter, "even when it's just the three of you?"

"It's a plate of food, not *Vogue Entertaining*. It's not exactly a big deal unless your idea of hospitality comprises offering your friends chips straight from the bag."

"I buy chips *and* salsa," said Tom offended.

"I don't care if you're lazy, but you don't have to be such a cliché of a single guy," Lucy retaliated.

"I'm not a cliché, I'm the archetype."

"Oh for God's sake, will you two stop bickering for three seconds?" Meg complained while Chloe nodded assent.

Tom and Lucy looked at them in surprise.

"We weren't bickering," Lucy said uncertainly.

"That was just normal conversation," agreed Tom.

"It was bickering. That's all that you two ever do. You argue. I don't care if you do it in private, but it's extremely boring for other people to listen to. So please shut up. Let's talk about something else."

There was a silence, which Tom contemplated breaking by relating an inappropriate joke, but before he could open his mouth, Meg spoke.

"By the way, were either of you responsible for forwarding that chain e-mail that says you have to buy knickers for ten people?"

"Where you have to what?" asked Tom, completely bewildered.

"You get an e-mail that asks you to buy a pair of knickers for the last person on the list," Chloe explained. "If everyone does it and no one breaks the chain you'll supposedly receive ten pairs of knickers in return."

Tom looked mystified. "But I don't understand. *Why* would you want strangers to buy knickers for you?"

"I don't want them to!" Lucy said, pleased that he had caught on to her objections to the chain e-mail so quickly. "That's exactly my point. And I don't want to have to buy them for anyone else either. Knickers should reflect personal taste. One woman's red lace G-string heaven is another woman's full cotton brief with girdle support hell."

"Hello!" said Lucy cheerfully as Percy shyly entered, bearing a bottle of wine.

"You look lovely, Percy," said Chloe warmly.

"Thank God you're here," Tom said, immediately dragging Percy into the kitchen. "So far they've talked about girdles and G-strings. In the same sentence. They're ruining everything for me."

Percy paid no attention to Tom's litany of woes, having a greater injustice on his mind. "You told me you were going to wear trousers!" said Percy in an outraged whisper.

"I changed my mind. I felt too overdressed," Tom muttered.

"You promised!"

"Actually I didn't," said Tom meanly. "I made you promise."

"I can't believe you would be so underhand."

"There's no need to make a big deal of it, Perce." Tom eyed Percy, who was still gazing at him mutinously. Feeling that more was called for he added charitably, "You look very nice."

Percy looked down at his crisply ironed shirt and trousers. "I'm overdressed," he said miserably.

"No you're not. You heard what Chloe said when you walked in. You look good. Really good."

At this inauspicious moment, Meg walked into the kitchen. Tom and Percy both promptly flushed beet red to the roots of their hair and concentrated their combined efforts on opening one bottle of beer.

Meg eyed them suspiciously. "What's going on?"

"Nothing," said Tom, wishing that his voice hadn't squeaked on the first syllable.

"Are you two feeling alright?"

Percy cleared his throat. "Fine."

"Absolutely fine," Tom concurred a little too heartily. He held up the bottle of beer, with the air of a man successfully engaged in a masculine pastime. "It's open," he said proudly.

"Let's do another one," said Percy eagerly.

Meg cast them another piercing glance that reduced them to incoherence once again, and then, picking up the bottle opener, she went out to the living room.

"Where are the boys?" asked Lucy, who was putting the disc into the player. "I want to start the movie. What are they doing in there?"

"Talking about their clothes," Meg whispered, trying to control her laughter.

"You're making that up," accused Lucy, swinging round to look at Meg.

"I swear I heard them arguing about what they were going to wear tonight."

"You must have misheard them," Lucy said dismissively. "Tom's idea of dressing up involves—well never mind what it involves," she finished lamely.

The other two eyed her with interest. "I always picked Tom for the sort who'd try your underwear on," Meg said knowingly. Before Lucy could protest, Tom and Percy reentered the room and took their places at opposite ends of the sofa without looking at each other.

"What film are we watching?" Tom asked.

"*Dirty Dancing,*" said Meg, Lucy, and Chloe in unison.

"But that's ancient," Tom said, appalled. "Why didn't you get a new release? And haven't you seen it before?"

The girls regarded him pityingly. "*Of course* we've seen it before. About fifty times. That's the whole point."

Tom looked inquiringly at Percy, but Percy shook his head helplessly. "What's the point of seeing a movie you've all seen before?"

"It's fun seeing your favorite bits over and over again."

"Oh," Tom said enlightened. "It's like when I watch *Bobbi and Bambi's Spring Break*. You just fast-forward to the shower scene and the bit with the German backpackers."

The girls' expressions ranged from withering to icy.

"If you so much as *hint* that *Dirty Dancing* may in any way be compared with a porn film you can leave right now," said Lucy.

He turned to Meg for support and was surprised to see her looking at him sternly.

"Some things are sacred," said Meg. "And we don't fast-forward. We watch the whole movie."

Lucy pressed play and jumped back to nestle on the couch beside Tom, who fought the urge to put his arm around her.

"Cos I've—had—the time of my life—" Chloe sang, and Lucy and Meg immediately joined in.

"What—what are you doing?" Tom asked in alarm. "What's going on?"

"We're singing," said Lucy, not pausing for breath, "And I never felt like this before . . ."

"Nobody puts Baby in a corner," Chloe said mysteriously, and the singing abruptly stopped as the girls collapsed into giggles.

"I carried a watermelon," offered Meg unsteadily, and the shrieks escalated.

"I need another drink," said Tom, wondering what in hell was going on.

"Me too," said Percy hastily, following him into the kitchen.

"What the fuck is going on out there? I feel like I've joined a cult."

"I have absolutely no idea. Unless . . ."

"What?" prompted Tom.

"Do you think they're on drugs?"

"Lucy takes half an E about once a year. Usually on New Year's Eve. There is no way she would be on anything on a weeknight."

"Have they stopped singing?" asked Percy, straining to listen.

"I think so. You know, there's only one way to get through this, Perce."

"Get drunk?"

"You got it."

"Let's go."

"Patrick Swayze is a schmuck," Tom announced, as the movie ended, with the air of one who had thought long and hard about this particular topic.

"He is not a schmuck," Lucy said grumpily.

"Anyone who appears in a movie that ends in a dance-off is a schmuck," said Tom firmly. "And he has a goiter."

"Patrick Swayze does not have a goiter."

"He does. Or else it's an abnormally large Adam's apple."

"You're just jealous because you've never held a girl over your head while standing in a lake," Lucy said, somewhat inconsequentially.

Tom looked at her dubiously. "Why the hell would I be jealous of a thing like that?"

"Because it's romantic."

"So that's what women want? To be held in the air like a prize trout by a guy up to his waist in water?"

"Yes," said Lucy uncertainly, wondering why it didn't seem so appealing when it was put like that.

"And what happens next?"

"What do you mean, what happens next?"

"Well, he'd have to drop her in the water," said Tom reasonably.

"No he wouldn't. He could carry her back to the shore."

"He could not," Tom said firmly. "Have you ever tried to lift someone over your head? I did weights at the gym once. It was exhausting. There's a reason why weight lifters let the barbell crash to the floor."

"That doesn't mean you'd have to throw her in the water," Lucy said irritably. "She could do an elegant dismount sort of a thing like ballet dancers and ice-skaters do."

"Don't mention ice-skaters, you'll scare Percy. But according to your definition of romance, your ideal man would be a ballet-dancing trout fisherman?"

"I never said anything about trout fishing. You're the one who brought that up," said Lucy resentfully.

"He'd need experience in wading," Tom said thoughtfully. "Would he have to wade out holding her, or could she swim until he reached the proper water level for lifting her over his head?"

"She'd be lighter if she wasn't waterlogged," Percy contributed helpfully.

"Good point, Perce. But that's a frickin' lot of effort to go to by the time you've waded out carrying her and then held her over your head. Does the water have to be waist-deep, Luce? Is it just as romantic if the water is only up to his ankles?"

Before Lucy could have a verbal aneurism, Percy said in a deeply perplexed tone, "But *why* would you swim out to the middle of a lake, hold your girlfriend over your head, and swim back again? What's the point?"

"No idea," Tom said cheerfully, refilling everyone's depleted glasses. "Proves my point. Sort of thing only a schmuck would do."

"Nice bunch of flowers." Percy nodded. "Far more sensible. Less effort too," he added thoughtfully.

"As if Tom would recognize a nice bunch of flowers," Lucy said, with an edge to her voice.

Tom grinned affably at her but was undeterred. "I think it's an interesting philosophical question. If you stop and think about most of the things that are meant to be romantic, what do they actually mean?"

"What *are* you talking about?" asked Chloe curiously.

"Well, take picnics for example. It's practically an unwritten rule that if you start dating a girl in summer you have to take her on a picnic. Now I have a theory—"

"Oh no," groaned Lucy. "Please God, save us from Tom's theories."

"I have a theory that all of the conventional romantic gestures and traditions hark back to the caveman era, and most of them actually have extremely practical origins."

"You know, Tom could be right. I believe there's a painting on one of the cave walls at Lascaux that depicts a caveman stowing a wicker basket and rubber-backed tartan rug into the trunk of his four-wheel drive," Meg said thoughtfully.

"As I believe I have repeatedly told you, Margaret, sarcasm is the lowest form of humor," Tom said with dignity. "What I meant was, the desire to be taken on a picnic probably has something to do with an ancient impulse to find a mate who has the ability to provide food in the wild."

"The Botanic Gardens are hardly the wilderness."

"Stop nitpicking. The theory is sound. The ability to provide nourishment in an al fresco setting harks back to hunter-gatherer days."

"Someone please shut him up," Lucy moaned, throwing herself facedown on the couch and putting a cushion over her head to block out the sound of his voice, "or I'll never be able to go on a picnic again. I'll be too worried that Tom is going to pop up out of the undergrowth wearing a woolly mammoth loincloth with a bone stuck through his topknot to enjoy myself."

"Now hold on," said Percy, who had been listening intently to Tom's exposition. "Tom could be on to something here. What about intimate nights by blazing fires?"

"The provision of heat and shelter," Tom answered promptly. "Too easy. Give me another."

"Candlelit dinners?" Chloe suggested.

"Fire, food, and night vision."

"Dancing with a rose between your teeth?" Lucy flung out, determined not to allow her cherished notions of romanticism to be tainted by mundane practicality.

Tom considered for a moment. "Coordination and agility are major physical characteristics needed for survival. Good dentistry means a mate who can chew and digest their food better, leading to improved strength and fitness. The ability to identify and pick a rose means a partner who knows his vegetation and won't poison you by picking poison ivy to garnish the saber-toothed tiger roast. But this is all purely theoretical anyway, because dancing with a rose between your teeth isn't romantic, Luce, it's just plain sad."

"It is not," flared Lucy, a trifle more defensively than was warranted.

Tom cast her a shrewd look and then collapsed into laughter. "Oh God I can see it now. Byron tried to teach you how to tango with a rose between his teeth, didn't he? Please, please, tell me that a) he forgot to remove the thorns and b) someone videotaped it?"

"Just because your idea of a tender moment involves hugging the football guys after your team wins doesn't mean that you have to spoil things for other people," Lucy retorted acidly.

"Don't start bickering again," Meg said in a warning tone. As Lucy and Tom both subsided, Meg suddenly turned to Percy. "That reminds me—I've been meaning to ask for ages, Percy—how did you come out of the boys' night unscathed? I can't believe those apes didn't do anything atrocious to you after I left."

Percy blushed and looked away. "Not sure. Would anyone like another drink?"

"Yes, that is odd," Chloe said thoughtfully. "You still have both of your eyebrows and they didn't take your wallet and your keys and leave you in a hotel room with a stripper—"

Lucy snapped her fingers. "I've got it. They dyed your pubes, didn't they?"

"They *what?*" gasped Percy, completely horrified. "No, they did *not.*"

"Did they dack you?"

"Did they *what* me?"

"Dack you," Lucy said impatiently. "Pull your pants down?"

"Do you mean to tell me that this country has invented a verb for the action of pulling someone else's pants down?"

Lucy's eyes lit up mischievously. "Do *you* mean to tell *me* that you've never been dacked?"

Percy looked at her nervously. "Of course I have. I went to boarding school."

"Doesn't count," Lucy said wickedly, moving closer to Percy. "It's not dacking unless it's done in Australia."

"Tom, help me," Percy appealed. "She's starting to scare me."

Tom shook his head benevolently. "Sorry, Perce, but I agree with Luce. It's like an initiation. Should be part of the naturalization process if you ask me. Sing the national anthem, swear allegiance to Australia, and finish off with a dacking by your buddies."

"Lucy—if you so much as try to—get her off me!" Percy tried to fend off Lucy as she pounced.

"Help me, Chloe!" Lucy shrieked as Percy started to struggle in earnest, still too much the gentleman to use real force against the girls.

Meg, Chloe, and Tom promptly abandoned their drinks and joined the fray while Clooney circled them, barking excitedly. The giggles and shrieks from the squirming bodies grew louder so that it was some time before they heard the sound of someone clearing their throat.

The struggle promptly stopped, and Lucy, Chloe, and Meg raised their heads cautiously to peer over the back of the couch, straight into the censorious eyes of Byron and Deelylah. Lucy was the first to recover. "Byron!" she said cheerfully, still straddling Percy and trying to straighten her top. "What are you doing here?"

"I went to the movie and then I wanted to see you," Byron answered. "Why are you sitting on Percy, Lucia?"

Lucy groaned, recognizing the jealous look on his face. "Meg and Chloe are sitting on him too," she said defensively.

"Evening, Biro," Tom hollered cheerfully from the bottom of the pile where he had somehow ended up.

"Tom?" gasped Deelylah. "Is that you?" She stepped forward to peer over the couch, and Tom waved feebly at her from underneath Chloe's armpit, his bravado rapidly diminishing at the sight of her. "What on earth are you doing?"

"Trying to dack Percy," said Tom, attempting to inject a note of pride into their mission. "What are you doing here?"

"I came to tell your friends to keep the noise down. Why you insist on keeping the front door open and screaming at the top of your lungs I have no idea," Deelylah said icily, casting a poisonous look at Chloe and Lucy. She looked down at her bare leg, where Clooney was licking her ankle. "Will someone please get this mutt off me immediately. I'll have to take another shower now."

Lucy and Meg scrambled off while Tom managed to shove his way out from underneath Percy and Chloe, who collapsed on the couch still trying to control their laughter. Feeling as though they had to atone for their behavior, Tom put a conciliatory arm around Deelylah, Lucy snuggled up to Byron, and Meg gathered up her bag and clicked her fingers commandingly to summon Clooney.

"I have to take Clooney outside, so we may as well go now," Meg said. "Thanks for a great night."

"I'll call you tomorrow about tickets to the fundraiser ball," Lucy said, dropping to her knees to bid Clooney farewell. Sadly she watched Meg and the puppy depart.

"You're drunk," Deelylah said accusingly to Tom.

"Not drunk," Tom protested. "Just happy."

"Well you can't drive home. Come on, you can stay at my place."

For a fraction of a second Tom hesitated as he looked at Lucy, who refused to meet his eye. And then he saw Byron by her side. Kissing Lucy on the cheek, he waved farewell to Chloe and Percy and then left with Deelylah.

Feeling suddenly flat, Lucy half-heartedly started to clean up.

"Come to bed, Lucia," Byron coaxed her.

"Leave it, Luce," Chloe said. "I'm going to stay up for a bit. You go to bed."

"Really?" asked Lucy gratefully.

Chloe nodded. Lucy kissed her and Percy good night and then followed Byron meekly into her bedroom. The door closed behind them, and Chloe and Percy looked at each other.

"Let's watch the bit where he teaches her to dance again," Percy suggested, seeing that Chloe looked downhearted at the abrupt departure of Meg and Lucy.

Chloe smiled gratefully. "You're the best, Percy." She pressed a button on the remote control and they settled back to enjoy the rest of their girls' night.

22.

one day my prince will come

Lucy checked the time again. It was now eight o'clock. Byron was supposed to have met her at the apartment half an hour ago so that they could have dinner, just the two of them, before leaving for the ball with Chloe and Meg. He didn't own a cell phone so she couldn't call him to find out why he was delayed. She had therefore been reduced to pacing restlessly in the living room, experiencing the unwelcome novelty of being the first to be dressed and ready to leave.

"He still hasn't called?" Chloe asked, emerging from her room in yet another different frock.

Lucy shook her head, compressing her lips tightly to stop herself from saying something irritable. Instead she looked Chloe over critically and then shook her head. "It's a beautiful dress, but that color doesn't do anything for you, Clo."

Chloe grimaced and vanished once more into her room, which was beginning to look as though her wardrobe had thrown up on her bed.

Another ten minutes dragged past, and Lucy was now past being angry and had become genuinely concerned. When, twenty-five minutes later, Byron rang the buzzer, she threw herself upon him as he walked through the door, looking excessively handsome in his formal attire.

"Lucia!" he said, lifting her up and hugging her, pleased with her effusive welcome. "Have you missed me?"

"I thought something had happened to you," Lucy said, clinging tightly to him. "I was going out of my mind."

"Why?"

Lucy's grip on Byron slackened. "What do you mean why? You're over an hour late, that's why!"

Byron laughed. "What is it that your friend Tom calls you? A drama queen?"

Lucy increased the distance between them, so that they were now at arm's length. "Why *are* you so late?"

Byron shrugged and gestured expansively with his hands. "I lost track of time."

Lucy felt her anger return. "We spoke three hours ago and made a definite plan to meet at seven thirty to have dinner together."

Byron gave her his most captivating smile. "I know, I'm hopeless. I am always running late."

"That's not really a very good excuse." Lucy tried to keep her voice even but a note of resentment crept in.

"Lucy, I have said that I'm sorry. What more do you want me to do?"

"Well for a start you could try not to be so arrogant."

Byron raised his eyebrows, trying to ascertain whether she was joking. "Arrogant?" he said uncertainly. "I haven't been arrogant."

"What would you call it? You obviously think your time is far more important than anyone else's and that I have nothing better to do than to sit around waiting for you to show up."

"Lucia!"

"Don't you Lucia me! I'm sick to death of you canceling, postpon-

ing, and changing plans. And even when we do make a firm arrangement you're always late. It's just plain rude."

"Lucy, I said that I'm sorry."

"Well don't! Don't be sorry and just show up on time for a change."
Lucy stopped and realized that she was shaking.

"Lucy, you are overreacting," Byron said in a coaxing tone, putting
a hand out towards her. He stopped, startled by the ferocious anger in
her eyes.

"I think you should leave, Byron," Lucy said levelly, looking him
straight in the eyes.

"But what about the ball?"

"I'm going with Meg and Chloe. Feel free to go, but quite frankly I
really don't want to spend time with you right now."

The persuasive look in Byron's eyes faded, to be replaced by something far colder. "That is not such a big change, is it?"

"What's that supposed to mean?"

"It means you hardly have time for me anyway."

"If you're talking about the fact that I now seem to spend most of
my life racing from work to Meg's to look after Clooney then no, I suppose I don't have as much time for you as I used to. But can I just
remind you that *you* gave me Clooney?"

"I wouldn't have if I had realized that it was going to take over your
entire life."

"Clooney is a he. Not an it," Lucy said through clenched teeth.

"Well you've become very boring since *he* came along. We used to
be able to be spontaneous."

"Can you even hear yourself? Do you have any idea how childish
you sound?"

"Can your hear *yourself*? Can you hear how boring and responsible you
sound? You're becoming like your friend Meg. You used to be fun, Lucy."

Lucy's voice dripped ice. "Don't you dare say a word against Meg."

"I would not bother. It puts me to sleep just thinking about her."

"I want you to leave. Right now." Lucy kept her voice deliberately calm, knowing that this would infuriate Byron more than if she screamed at him.

Byron glared at her, and turning on his heel he left, slamming the door viciously behind him. Lucy sat down trembling on the couch and tried to work out what had just happened.

Clad in yet another dress, Chloe came cautiously into the room and sat down beside Lucy, putting an arm around her. "Are you okay?"

Lucy nodded. "Sorry you had to hear all that, Clo."

"Don't worry about me. It was quite entertaining really," Chloe said, trying to make Lucy smile.

"Did you hear what he said about Meg?"

Chloe nodded. "I'm sure he didn't mean it. He was just angry."

"He has nothing to be angry about! He was late as usual, and he's jealous of a dog! He couldn't be more ridiculous if he tried."

Chloe hesitated before speaking. "Luce? Why did you get so angry?"

Lucy stared at Chloe in amazement. "Are you serious? He was late. Again. For about the fiftieth time. With no excuse."

"But Luce—*you're* always running late."

Lucy looked shamefaced. "I know I am. But I've been trying very hard to be on time for ages now. I never realized how annoying it is."

"You can say that again," concurred Chloe, thinking of all the times she had sat alone, waiting for Lucy to show up.

Lucy gave a wan smile. "I always thought I was charmingly irresponsible. Now I realize I was just rude."

"And arrogant," Chloe agreed cheerfully.

Lucy perked up slightly. "Did you hear that bit? I was quite proud of that."

"You should be. You were fabulous. All ice-cold and calm in a nasty way. It didn't sound like you at all. I kept waiting for you to start screaming at him or throwing things."

"Clo?" Lucy asked, struck by an awful thought. "Do *you* think I've become responsible?"

"Being responsible isn't necessarily a bad thing, Lucy," Chloe countered, aware that Lucy had hitherto equated responsibility somewhere next to accounting proficiency on a table of desirable virtues. "If you weren't responsible for Clooney he'd be miserable and uncared for."

"I would never do that to Clooney," protested Lucy vehemently.

"I know you wouldn't. But all I'm saying is it's a good thing you don't share Byron's views about being responsible and being boring going hand in hand."

Lucy sniffed while she digested this novel idea. "Byron and I are breaking up, aren't we?" Lucy suddenly said bleakly.

"Lucy, stop it!" Chloe said exasperated. "You had a fight, that doesn't mean you have to call your whole relationship off. Why do you always have to be so extreme?"

Lucy looked startled. "But I don't see the point in continuing. We're always arguing and we never do the romantic things that we used to."

"Like catching the flu and breaking up over nothing because of Byron's jealous streak?" Before Lucy could defend Byron Chloe added, "Sorry, Luce, I couldn't help it. Look, before you call it all off or decide that you can't live without him why don't you make a list of all the qualities that you want in a partner? You need to calm down and start thinking clearly and sensibly about what you want from a relationship."

"You mean like a list of pros and cons?" asked Lucy, trying to quell the innate horror that the organized orderliness of any sort of list inspired in her.

"Sort of. But you could leave out the negative things. Just make a list of all the qualities and attributes that you would like your ideal man to have. Then see how Byron matches up."

Lucy looked doubtful. "Does it work?"

Chloe gave a sudden mischievous smile. "Well, I tried it recently."

Lucy looked at her curiously. "So who's your perfect man then?"

Chloe's smile turned mysterious as she stood up and prepared to return to her bedroom to change her dress again. "I'm not exactly sure. But maybe tonight I'll find out."

23.

the ball

Lucy felt her anger fade and her excitement grow as they exited the taxi and made their way towards the St. Kilda Town Hall. The white neoclassical façade was bathed in hot pink lights for the occasion and a red carpet ran from the entrance to the main room, which was ablaze with lights and loud chatter. Showing their tickets of admission, they checked their bags and coats into the cloak room and then entered the ballroom. A stage had been set up to the right where different acts would perform all night, while a drag queen with an exquisite sense of comic timing and dress sense was acting as MC.

A number of tables and chairs had been loosely placed around the stage but the majority of the room was already filled with people. To the left, a second, slightly smaller room held the dance floor and was where the band would later perform.

"Quick, Chloe, we have to get Lucy out of here," Meg murmured, surveying the chattering throng.

"Why?" asked Chloe in surprise.

"It's a crowded room. She's bound to glance across it and fall in love with someone and then we'll have to endure Byron going on another rampage."

"Very funny," Lucy said witheringly. "Come on, let's try to make our way over to the bar."

They started to make their way slowly through the crowd. When they finally reached the bar, Chloe volunteered to get the drinks. Meg and Lucy stood slightly to one side, and while Meg watched the actor on stage recite a Shakespearean sonnet interspersed with Tourette's syndrome, Lucy's black mood descended once again as she searched the room in vain for Byron.

"Do you think I've left it too late to become a chicken sexer?" Lucy asked morosely, obviously having fast-tracked from the particulars of her relationship doldrums to an all-encompassing malaise regarding her entire life and future in general.

"No, but if you do that now you won't have a hobby to look forward to in your retirement," Meg said briskly, refusing to indulge Lucy's evident desire to wallow in her despair. "Is Chloe any closer to being served, do you think?"

Lucy stood on tiptoe to try to catch a glimpse of Chloe at the crowded bar and then exclaimed in annoyance as a passerby practically shoved her into an actor who was wearing nothing but a large bunch of balloons, from which he occasionally plucked one and twisted it into a funny shape for a small donation. "Ow!" Lucy exclaimed irritably. "He almost made me burst that man's codpiece."

"Are you okay?" Meg asked, helping her to right herself.

"I'm fine. I can't see Chloe anywhere. I knew you should have been the one to go after drinks. You always get served straight away. Can you see the boys?"

Meg surveyed the crowd and sighed. "There are so many people here we could spend the entire night circling around looking for each other. Look, do you mind waiting here while I help Chloe with the drinks? If one of us goes off looking for the boys now I really think we'll end up losing each other."

Lucy waved her away. "Don't worry about me. I'm going to get a balloon while I wait, so I'll be fine."

Meg headed towards the bar while Lucy approached the balloon man. Recognizing her as the girl who had practically hurled into him a moment ago, he refused to be disarmed by her friendly smile.

"What'll it be?" he asked, after she had handed over her donation.

Lucy looked at him hopefully. "Can you make a spoodle?"

"What the hell is a spoodle?"

"It's a breed of dog. It's a cross between a spaniel and a poodle."

"Look lady, it's a frigging balloon. You can have a heart or a flower. Make your choice."

Lucy submitted to owning a heart-shaped balloon but was somewhat mollified by being granted her choice of a pink balloon. She was eagerly watching the heart take shape when she happened to glance up and spot a familiar figure. Byron was standing not ten meters away from her. And he was kissing another girl.

Lucy felt her heart lurch and a violent wave of disbelief shot through her. Muttering a quick "Thank you" to the balloon man, who was presenting the finished heart to her, Lucy blindly pushed her way through the crowd towards the exit, ignoring expostulations from the audience, who were appreciatively watching a reverse stripteaser provocatively pull on a pair of earmuffs. Reaching the entrance, she took deep breaths of fresh air and wrapped her suddenly goose-pimpled arms around her waist.

A crowd of smokers was looking at her curiously. Wanting to be alone, so that she could give way to the tears that she knew were imminent, Lucy moved further down the marble steps and then slipped. With one hand clutching her balloon, Lucy was unable to save herself and she landed heavily on her bottom on the lowest step. It was the final indignity in a very trying evening. She burst into tears.

After her tears abated, Lucy tied the ribbon of the balloon around her wrist so that it couldn't escape, resolutely concentrating on the mundane task so as not to think about Byron. When she had finished she looked up at the stars, wanting a distraction so that she could remain in the present; so that she didn't have to think about the stupidity of jealousy and love and the way one always thought one's bottom was too big until it came into sudden contact with marble, when one was forced to acknowledge that there really wasn't much padding there at all.

Lucy was hidden in the shadows, so that when Tom, Deelylah, and Percy arrived, she was able to observe them without them seeing her. The sudden rush of gladness and relief when she saw Tom overwhelmed her, and her first instinct was to throw herself into his arms so that she could sob her heartache out onto the comfortable familiarity of his shoulder. But then she saw Deelylah at his side, wearing a floor-length emerald green gown. She looked striking and—there was no other word for it—*grown-up*.

Lucy suddenly felt stupid and childish, crying on the stairs in her bright pink dress. With a brief flash of wry humor she couldn't help acknowledging that a novelty balloon probably wasn't the best choice of accessories either. Holding her breath she sat completely still and silent until they had passed by.

Fifteen minutes later, with red eyes and her makeup slightly smeared, but with her dignity very much restored, Lucy reentered the ballroom in search of Meg. She found her patiently sipping her drink and standing where Lucy had promised to wait for her.

"Where have you been?" asked Meg, her tone softening considerably as she recognized the unmistakable signs of Lucy's tears.

"Outside," Lucy answered briefly, not trusting herself to meet Meg's gaze in case she burst into tears again. "Where's Chloe?"

"Snorting coke in the men's room."

"*She's what?*" exclaimed Lucy, completely startled out of her misery by this information. "Since when does Chloe take drugs?"

"Well, I don't know that she's actually snorting coke," Meg admitted. "She was using the men's bathroom because the queue for the women's went on forever and I think she just lent some guys her credit card to chop it up. You know what Chloe's like—she's always trying to help other people. I just saw Tom and Percy and Agnes, buy the way."

Lucy gave her a small smile that faded almost instantaneously. "Megs, I have to leave now. Can you tell the others that I said goodbye?"

"You want to leave? Why?" Meg asked in surprise. She looked closely at Lucy's face and then asked with her usual sharp acuity, "Where's Byron?"

"Kissing another girl," Lucy answered tersely.

There was a pause, and then Meg asked carefully, "Are you okay, Luce?"

"Perfectly fine."

"You're sure you want to leave?"

"Yes. You stay though. All I want is to go home and get into my pajamas so you really can't do anything for me. I'd be much more upset if I ruined your night too. Please stay and have a good time."

Meg looked at her doubtfully and then sighed. "Okay, Luce. I'll see you into a cab though. But before you go don't you want to—" She hesitated.

"What?" prompted Lucy.

"I don't know. I just thought you might want to find Byron and throw a drink at him. Or scream at him in front of everyone. Or hit him. Or—well, basically create a scene I guess."

Lucy considered for a moment. "Do you know that is weird? Because all I really want is to go home. But I'll probably be back to normal tomorrow and then I can set fire to his photograph and act like Betty Blue for the next week and a half."

Collecting Lucy's things from the cloak room, they walked out to St. Kilda Road and hailed a passing taxi. Meg gave Lucy a swift hug and a kiss on the cheek and then closed the taxi door behind her. Lucy slumped against the backseat and felt a wave of extreme tiredness wash over her. As the taxi moved off she watched her heart-shaped balloon bob gently against the ceiling.

It was with an immense feeling of satisfaction that she pulled the brooch off her coat, and, conjuring up the image of Byron's handsome face, proceeded to stab the pin viciously, right through the center of the plastic heart.

24.

the shepherd

At a little after two in the morning, Lucy, who had been unable to fall asleep despite a prolonged and vigorous bout of tears, heard the front door open and the unmistakable sounds of several mildly inebriated people clattering into the apartment, fondly believing that they were being very quiet. Getting out of bed, Lucy padded into the living room in time to see Tom and Meg collapse on the couch, while Chloe admonished them to hush in a voice that was considerably louder than her normal speaking tone. Lucy couldn't help feeling a mite envious as she realized that by the looks of things they had had a fabulous night.

"Hey! What are you still doing up?" Meg exclaimed, catching sight of Lucy's pajama-clad figure in the doorway.

"Couldn't sleep," Lucy said briefly. "Where's Deelylah?"

"Next door," Tom answered. "She wanted to go straight to bed so I've just come over for one last drink."

Lucy curled up in an armchair and hugged a cushion to her.

Determined to maintain her dignity and show how little she cared, she fought the urge to ask after Byron. "Did you have fun?" she asked wistfully.

Chloe tottered over to her and gave her a squeeze. "Yes. But it would have been much more fun if you were there," she said.

Deciding that not asking about Byron *first* constituted maintaining her dignity, Lucy promptly asked, "Did you see Byron at all?"

There was a pause and Chloe giggled. "Poor Byron. I don't think he had a very nice night."

"He looked like he was having a nice night when I saw him kissing that girl," Lucy said bitterly.

"Mmmm. Unfortunately that wasn't the only attention he received," Tom said blandly.

"What do you mean?" Lucy asked sharply.

Meg looked slightly guilty. "Ah, Luce? You know how there was a drag queen acting as MC?"

"Yes," Lucy said impatiently.

"Well, he kind of ended up chasing after Byron."

"*What?*"

"I told him Byron really liked him but that he was too shy to talk to . . . her," Meg confessed, somewhat confusedly.

Lucy looked at Meg stunned, and then, as Meg gave her a lopsided grin, it suddenly dawned on her exactly how drunk Meg was. It was always difficult to tell with Meg because she never seemed to lose her self-possession.

"You're not mad at me, are you?" Meg asked cautiously.

"Mad at you? I love you so much right now I think I want to marry you. And to think I wasted time taking my anger out on a balloon. Your way is much better. So what happened?"

Chloe interrupted, her words tripping over one another in her eagerness to share the story. "He spent the whole night chasing Byron around the room and dedicating Edith Piaf songs to him. Byron was utterly terrified of her. Or do I mean him?"

Lucy burst into a peal of laughter and flung herself across the room to hug Meg. Collapsing back into her armchair and surveying her three friends, Lucy, who was feeling lighter after these revelations, couldn't help thinking that there was still something wrong niggling away at the back of her mind. As it occurred to her what it was she emitted a deep sigh. "Oh no. Have we lost Percy again? This is becoming a habit on big nights out."

Chloe looked around, slightly startled. "That's odd. He was outside with us when we were leaving. I wonder where he went?"

As though on cue, at precisely this moment, Percy entered the room with a rather scruffy stranger in tow. His face flushed, Percy took off his jacket and threw it over the back of a chair and then beamed at the assembled company.

"Oh there you are, Percy," Lucy said with relief. She smiled warmly at the stranger. "Hello, I'm Lucy. Are you a friend of Percy's?"

Before the stranger could respond, Percy, who appeared to be bursting with both pride and a dangerously high level of mood-altering substances, answered. "He's a shepherd. I brought him home for Chloe."

"Did you really, Perce?" said Chloe vaguely, as Meg collapsed into helpless laughter and Lucy and Tom eyed the shepherd doubtfully. "How lovely of you. But I don't need one anymore. It was just while we were camping."

"What did you want a shepherd for, Clo?" asked Tom, his curiosity overcoming him.

"To carry my backpack of course."

"Percy's being thick as usual," Meg said, regaining her composure and hiccuping slightly. "Chloe wanted a sherpa. Like Tenzing Norgay who accompanied Sir Edmund Hillary up Mount Everest."

"Yes," said Chloe happily. "I wanted one of those."

"Well why the hell couldn't you say so instead of going on about shepherds?" asked Percy, justifiably aggrieved that he had been unfairly made to look like an idiot. "I went to a lot of trouble to find him."

"He doesn't look like a shepherd to me," said Tom, eyeing the lounging figure critically.

"Well he jolly well is one. I went to that place that Meg told me about and I asked for a shepherd, and he came up and said that he was what I was looking for."

At this point the shepherd decided to speak for himself. "Man, you want to dress me up as a shepherd, that's fine by me, but I'm not doing anything weird with sheep. I do most things but sheep ain't one of them."

A short silence greeted this speech and then Tom, who was rapidly sobering up and looking a bit grim, said, "Percy, where *exactly* did you say you found him?"

"In St. Kilda. Near the town hall."

As one, Tom, Lucy, and Chloe spun around and glared at Meg who had started to laugh again. "Oh God, alright I'm sorry, I just thought it would be funny. I didn't think for a second that he would actually bring home a prostitute."

"*A prostitute?*" Instead of his usual beet red, Percy had gone white and looked as though he was about to faint.

The shepherd cleared his throat. "I prefer the term *sex worker* actually."

"What? Oh, sorry. Sex worker then," said Meg agreeably.

Percy was looking at the shepherd in horror. "You said you were a shepherd."

"Man, I'll be anything you want me to be, but like I said before I'm not doing anything sick with farm animals. Unless it's a pig," he added, almost as an afterthought. Meeting their blank stares he elaborated, "They're actually very clean animals. Everyone thinks they're dirty but it's a misconception."

"You needn't look so shocked, Percy," Meg said kindly. "You're English. You come from a very long and distinguished race of sheep-shaggers. I believe it's a well-known fact that during the medieval period the peasants cuddled up to cows and sheep for warmth and relationships ensued from there. But you aristocrats just did it for fun."

Percy threw his head back. You could almost see the family coat of arms and hear the herald's trumpet as he hotly declared, "No Hamilton-Bythorne has ever shagged a sheep!"

"To the best of your knowledge," Meg pointed out cruelly.

"Yes, to the best—no! Never!" And then Percy did something that he had never done before. He looked Meg directly in the eyes and said disdainfully, "The tone of your mind is actually very low, isn't it, Margaret?"

The unaccustomed ice in Percy's voice floored Meg for a moment, but then she rallied. In a deadly tone she said, "Perhaps, but then again I'm not the one who brought home a prost—sorry, sex worker for Chloe."

Percy held her gaze for a long moment, and for the first time ever, Meg was the first to look away. And then Percy turned and walked out of the room, forgetting his manners enough to slam the door violently behind him.

"The thing with Byron and the MC was inspired, but you probably did go a bit far this time, Meg," Tom said, in a conversational tone of voice.

Meg bit her lip and then, gathering up her things, she walked out of the apartment without saying a word, and the front door slammed once again.

Chloe, who was looking completely distraught, suddenly burst out, "It's all my fault!"

"What? Don't be silly, Chloe, of course it's not your fault," Lucy comforted her. "Tom's right—Meg overstepped the mark big-time. She forgets sometimes what a complete innocent Percy is."

"But if I hadn't asked for a shepherd, I mean a sherpa in the first place . . ."

At this point the shepherd spoke up. He sounded bored. "Look, if no one wants me for anything, how about someone just pays me and I can leave you all to it?"

"Sure," said Tom, glad to be given an uncomplicated task. He pulled out his wallet. "Lucy, have you got a camera? Can you take a picture of me paying a male sex worker? It's not something that I ever thought that I'd be doing, so it would be nice to have a photo to remind myself of the surprises that life can have in store." He eyed the stranger regretfully. "Shame you're not dressed as a shepherd. That would make a far better photo. And Mom would be so proud."

"Yeah, yeah whatever. Two hundred bucks."

Tom almost dropped his wallet. *"Two hundred dollars?"* he gasped.

Even Chloe looked up in surprise. "But you didn't do anything!"

"Not that we want you to earn it," Lucy said hastily.

"Two hundred bucks," repeated the shepherd stubbornly. "You wanted to play dress up, it's always gonna cost you more. And no one told me it was going to be a group thing."

A collective shudder went through the room.

"But you didn't have to dress up," Lucy pointed out sensibly.

"I was hired on the understanding that I would. Pay up, Miss Muffett."

"I think you mean Little Bo Peep."

"Oh for heaven's sake, Lucy, let it go. Now is not the time to be correcting the nursery rhyme references of a sex worker. Here, I've got fifty." Tom pulled out the bill and showed the shepherd the inside of his wallet so that he could see for himself that he didn't have any more money. Before he handed over the money he paused and said thoughtfully, "Look, seeing as I'm paying you and we haven't really asked you to do anything . . ." His voice trailed off and they all looked at him speculatively.

"Yes?" prompted the shepherd impatiently.

"Would you smell me?"

"Excuse me?"

"I just want you to have a quick sniff of my aftershave and tell me if it puts you off."

"Man, you are the weirdest bunch of people I have ever met and I thought that I had met some pretty weird people." He shook his head but obligingly leaned forward and took a deep whiff of Tom's neck.

"Issey Miyake—am I right?" He grinned.

"Yes," said Tom eagerly. "Does it put you off?"

"God no. I love the stuff."

"So you find me reasonably attractive?"

The shepherd took a step back and looked Tom up and down. "You know," he said finally. "It's strange because you're not the worst-looking guy that I've ever seen and you're clean and fit. Obviously a bit of a smart ass but I don't mind that generally. But I can't say that I find you attractive. Dunno why really. Just don't."

"See, Lucy?" Tom said triumphantly. "It's not my aftershave that puts gay men off."

"That's wonderful news, Tom," Lucy said encouragingly. "That means that it's just you then."

Tom instantly looked crestfallen but while he tried to think of a response the shepherd repeated in a bored tone of voice his desire to be paid and to leave.

"I've got twenty," said Lucy, hunting through her bag that she had discarded next to the couch.

They turned to Chloe. "I spent all my cash at the ball," she said mournfully. "But I baked some fruit buns yesterday. Perhaps you'd like a plate of those to take away?"

Thankfully the shepherd seemed to like this idea. Pocketing the seventy dollars, and giving Lucy and Tom a very hard stare, he followed Chloe into the kitchen and could presently be heard informing her that he preferred his buns buttered. Tom opened his mouth to say something, thought better of it and they sat there in silence again.

"Anyway, it could have been worse," said Tom, after a while, trying to make the best of things.

Lucy looked disbelievingly at him. "How exactly?"

"He could have brought home a German shepherd."

Lucy threw a cushion at him, but Tom was conscious of a dart of pleasure at having been able to make her smile.

There was another small silence and Lucy couldn't help feeling unaccountably strange at finding herself alone with Tom in the early hours of the morning. To break the tension, she cast her gaze around the room, looking for something about which to make idle conversation.

"Oh no," she said in dismay, standing up to investigate further. "Percy's left his coat here." As she shook it out and laid it neatly over the arm of the sofa she became aware of a jangling noise and a weight in one of the pockets. She groaned. "His keys and his wallet are still in his coat. He won't be able to get into his apartment."

"He'll be alright. You can't call him because I know he didn't take his cell phone out tonight. He'll just turn around and come back when he realizes." Tom paused and then added in a gentle tone of voice, "More to the point, are you okay, Luce?"

Lucy, who was overtired and drained from her protracted crying session, simply nodded. She looked so small and lost, curled up in the oversized armchair in her pajamas, that Tom had to fight an almost unbearable need to gather her up in his arms and comfort her. Knowing that the last thing he wanted to do was to complicate matters further, he abruptly arose and kissed her on the top of her head. "It will all work out, Ginger," he said, tilting her chin up so that she was forced to look directly into his eyes. "I promise."

In that moment, Lucy wanted very badly to believe him. But as Tom left the apartment to join Deelylah, she couldn't for the life of her imagine how her fairy godmother was going to sort this one out.

25.

secrets

Pulling herself morosely out of bed the following morning, Lucy walked bleary-eyed into the kitchen to make herself a cup of tea.

"Morning, Percy," she said absently, faintly registering that Percy was sitting at the kitchen table wearing a shirt and boxer shorts and eating a slice of toast. Switching the kettle on she suddenly swung around.

"Percy? What on earth are you doing here at this time of morning? Oh my God!" Lucy clapped her hands to her mouth in genuine shock as Chloe walked in, wearing a distinctly satisfied freshly-shagged expression. "What's going on?" Lucy asked weakly, sliding into a chair.

"We slept together," Chloe said briskly, realizing that acute embarrassment coupled with an innate fear of Lucy's histrionics had rendered Percy mute. "Do you want some toast?"

"Don't you 'Do you want some toast' me, Chloe Clairmont," Lucy said indignantly. "What? When? How? *Why?* Immediately."

"Maybe I should go," mumbled Percy, swallowing his last mouthful of toast. He stood up to make his escape and in front of Lucy's disbelieving eyes, Chloe kissed Percy passionately on the mouth.

Lucy shrieked and clapped her hands over her eyes this time. *"Stop it! Stop it this second!"*

"Shut up, Lucy," said Chloe, seating herself at the table and serenely pouring herself a cup of coffee. "And Percy's gone so you can uncover your eyes."

"Don't think you're getting off scot-free, Mr. Pants Man," Lucy called after his hastily receding back.

Chloe took a sip of her coffee and met Lucy's incredulous gaze with a cheeky grin. They waited until they heard the front door close and then Lucy spoke.

"You shagged Percy," Lucy stated, in the flat tone of one who was trying to remain very calm and rational.

"Correct."

"Why?" screeched Lucy, unable to maintain her controlled demeanor for more than three seconds.

Chloe shrugged. "Not sure. It just sort of happened."

"Were you drunk?" demanded Lucy.

"No. We'd had a lot to drink at the ball of course, but by the time he came back to the apartment to get his keys we definitely weren't drunk."

Lucy thought for a moment. "Did you take drugs?"

"No, Lucy, I did not take drugs," Chloe said coldly. "And for your information he was fantastic."

Lucy shrieked again. "Stop it! I won't hear Percy spoken about like that."

"Why not? He's absolutely great in bed. Oh calm down and stop screaming. I'll stop saying it."

"Percy is not some hot stud that you've picked up," Lucy scolded. "Percy is our *friend*. And you shouldn't sleep with your friends."

Chloe choked on a mouthful of coffee. "Excuse me? I'll give you one chance to take that back before you go down in history as the world's biggest hypocrite."

"Tom and I are different," Lucy said impatiently. "It's not at all the same thing if you *begin* as lovers. But I am *shocked* at you and Percy."

Chloe stretched out her arms and smiled at Lucy. "Be as shocked as you like, Luce," she said sweetly. "But you'd better get over it, because I don't think it's going to be a one-night stand. Do you mind if I jump in the shower first?"

"No, of course not," answered Lucy, trying to digest shock after shock.

As Chloe departed the kitchen, humming a song, Lucy got up to switch on the kettle again. Waiting for it to boil she suddenly paled as something else occurred to her. *Meg.*

Tom slid into the seat next to Lucy at the Galleon Café, suppressing a grin as he took in her air of suppressed melodrama. "Okay, Luce. What's the emergency?"

She took a deep breath, and then, abandoning any attempt to lead up to the subject gently, she blurted, "Percy and Chloe slept together." She sat back and watched him expectantly, waiting for a suitably stunned reaction. Tom's brow furrowed as he looked at her.

"I know," he said gently.

"You know? How could you know? Who told you?"

"Percy of course. Why are you looking like that?"

"I don't believe you. Percy would never do anything so ungentlemanly as to betray a secret, especially one concerning a lady."

Tom looked irritated. "Stop talking like an outraged heroine from a bad nineteenth-century novel. I thought you were about to use the word *milord* then." Before Lucy could protest, Tom continued on, "As a matter of fact I happen to agree with you. Percy *wouldn't* discuss it if he thought it was a secret. But from the way that he spoke about Chloe I don't think they're going to be a secret for much longer."

Lucy looked aghast. "But it *has* to be a secret! What on earth is going to happen if Meg finds out?"

"What does Meg have to do with it?"

Lucy started to sputter. "What does Meg have to do with it? Are you *completely* stupid, Thomas? Meg is extremely proud. She'll never give Percy a chance if she knows that he's been with Chloe."

"I hate to be the one to point this out to you, Lucy," said Tom at his driest, "but Meg has never given Percy a chance anyway. I doubt very much if Meg will care."

Lucy was speechless.

Tom looked at her and suddenly laughed. "Oh Luce. I wish you could see your face. This is exactly why I love you so much. You really are a true romantic. Even after that scene last night, you still really thought and hoped that Meg and Percy would get together one day, didn't you?"

"Why shouldn't they?" Lucy said defensively.

"Why should they?" Tom retaliated. "I mean honestly, Luce. Think about it. They're complete opposites. Percy is sweet and humble. Meg is ruthless and determined. Percy plays classical piano and spends his days with Chopin and Mozart. Meg spends her days with white collar criminals and captains of industry. Percy's reading the biography of the Mitford sisters. Meg takes kung fu classes—"

"But he loves her!" Lucy burst out, unable to bear this tirade any longer.

Tom looked at her sympathetically but shook his head. "I really don't think he ever did, Luce. I think initially he was attracted to her because personality-wise she reminded him of the girls at home that he was brought up with—he's shown me photos and told me stories, and they all seem like strident English hunting gals who know their own minds. But how much time have Meg and Percy ever spent together by themselves? On the other hand *Chloe* and Percy have always gotten along famously. He's forever doing sweet things for her, even," and here Tom stopped and smiled ruefully, "bringing home a shepherd for her. I think last night the scales finally fell from his eyes and he saw what's been obvious for months."

"What are you talking about?"

Tom looked at her in surprise. "Chloe of course. She's had a soft spot for Percy since she first laid eyes on him. Are you telling me you didn't know?"

Lucy looked dumbfounded as several things clicked into place at once. "So that's why she hasn't had a date for so long," she said slowly. "And she never would have said anything because of Meg . . ." Her voice trailed off.

Tom watched her. Lucy was looking down at the table but she appeared to be listening intently. "Sometimes it can take a while to figure out what you really want, even when it's right in front of you." Tom stopped and looked at Lucy again, with an unusually soft expression in his eyes. "Lucy?"

"So what are we going to do?" she burst out, obviously having paid no attention at all to his last few comments.

Tom sighed. "I can't begin to tell you the problems I have with your use of *we*."

"But we have to do something! Meg's self-esteem is at rock bottom right now and if she finds out about Percy and *Chloe* . . ." Lucy made a gesture with her hands that tried to convey the damage this would do to Meg's understanding of the known world order.

"Meg's a big girl. She can take care of herself," Tom said firmly.

Lucy looked at him despairingly. "I don't know what's wrong with everyone! Byron and I are breaking up. You and I hardly talk anymore. Percy's mad at Meg. And now Chloe and Percy are sleeping together. *What is going on?*"

Tom smiled at her ruefully. "Oh calm down, Luce. You and I are fine—we always are, more or less. And I really don't think Percy was with Chloe because he's on the rebound from Meg." Tom looked at her for a long moment. "Lucy, we are not going to meddle in Percy and Chloe's relationship."

She leaned forward to convey her earnestness. "Okay, but promise me that you won't say anything about Percy and Chloe to Meg. And you have to get Percy to hide it from her too. Just for a little while. Please? For me?"

"Alright, alright," Tom said, putting his hand over her mouth to silence her. "I won't say anything and I'll speak to Percy too. Not that I think you need to worry that much about him saying anything to Meg anyway. He's furious with her over the whole shepherd thing, so I doubt very much if he'll be speaking to her for a while."

Lucy wiggled away from his clasp but only in order to move closer and hug him joyously. "Thank you, Thomas," she said, looking at him gratefully.

He looked down into her upturned face and there was a fraction of a second when something flared between them. Then, as Lucy remembered Deelylah, Tom recalled Lucy's distraught face over Byron from the night before. Fighting the impulse to hold her, he stuck out his hand instead. "Deal?" he asked, with a wry smile.

Lucy ignored his outstretched hand and flung her arms around his neck. "Deal," she said happily, kissing him resoundingly on the cheek.

And Tom felt a curious sensation surround his heart, as his arms tightened around her.

26.

flea powder

While waiting in the queue to purchase the mid-morning coffees for herself and Ariel, Chloe opened her purse and saw with dismay that as usual, she had absolutely no cash. Sighing, she extracted her credit card, realizing as she did so that she would probably have to purchase ten dollars' worth of muffins in order to pay by credit. Turning the card over idly in her hands she suddenly noticed a film of white powder along one edge, some of which had settled onto her fingers. Curious, she raised the card to her nose and sniffed gently.

"I did it!" Chloe shrieked over the telephone to Lucy, approximately two hours later.

"Did what?" asked Lucy confusedly, holding the receiver away from her ear.

"Ariel just received the most damning, the most blistering, the most *wonderful* set-down of her life!" Chloe said excitedly.

"About goddamn time. But what happened?"

"I don't know," Chloe said honestly, subsiding slightly as a puzzled note crept into her voice. "All I know is that I felt invincible and the words just kept coming and I didn't let her get a word in edgeways for about forty minutes. I was fantastic," she finished, in awe.

"Did you fire her?"

"No," Chloe giggled. "I don't think I have to. You should have seen her face, Luce. I don't think anyone has ever told her off in her life. I could be wrong, but I have the feeling that she's going to be a very obedient intern from now on. She was literally terrified of me."

"Where is she now?"

"Picking up my dry cleaning," Chloe said airily.

"Chloe, you take your dry cleaning to the place just near the apartment. It's more trouble for you to bring it home from the office."

"I didn't think of that," Chloe said, in a slightly chastened tone of voice as she blew her nose noisily. "I just knew that I had to give her something menial to do to drive the lesson home, and that was the first thing I could think of."

"Oh. Well anyway, I'm very happy for you."

"Thanks," said Chloe happily. "I'm going to call Percy and tell him the good news. And then Meg. And Tom."

"Clo?" asked Lucy, as Chloe sniffed again. "Are you getting a cold?"

"Don't think so," Chloe said. "Do you know, Lucy, I haven't felt this good in ages? I was looking at myself in the mirror before and I think I look positively spankfest."

"That's great, Clo," Lucy said supportively. "I'll see you later okay?"

"Bye," Chloe sang. She hung up and rearranged the papers on her desk for the fifth time. As she heard the door to the outer office open, announcing Ariel's return with her dry cleaning, a smile lit up her face. There was photocopying to do, she decided. Lots of it.

———

Two weeks later, Meg let Clooney off the leash when they got to the beach and watched, smiling, as he raced towards the water's edge, barking excitedly at the seagulls. Linking her arm through Lucy's, they strolled along the sand, keeping an eye on Clooney's antics. "How does it feel to be single?" Meg asked Lucy, when they were satisfied that Clooney wouldn't run off.

Lucy grimaced. "Would you believe that Byron actually tried to convince me that he kissed that girl because he was so passionately worked up about *our* fight?"

"Sadly I would believe it. What did you say?"

"That I hoped he'd taken her number because we were about to have an even bigger fight. Let's not spoil a beautiful day by talking about him. How are *you* feeling, more to the point?"

"Better since I called Percy and apologized to him."

"What did he say?"

Meg gave a slight smile. "What do you think he said? It's Percy. He was perfectly sweet and polite of course. Only—" she hesitated and then continued, "his voice was different."

"How?" asked Lucy, feeling her way tentatively.

Meg shrugged. "I don't know exactly. He's just always had—I suppose it was a *special* tone when he spoke to me," she said, flushing slightly as she revealed this, "and he doesn't sound like that anymore."

Completely tongued-tied, Lucy looked around frantically for something to change the subject. To Lucy's immense relief, Clooney came bounding back at this point and while she fought off his wet and sandy elation, she tried to gather her thoughts. However, Meg didn't seem to require a response because now, looking at Lucy curiously, she changed the subject.

"I know you don't want to talk to him but I have to say that you don't seem very upset about Byron," she commented.

Lucy smiled ruefully. "I'm not. I know that I should still be heart-broken, but I've been so busy I've hardly thought about him." She hes-itated and then added, "I've been seeing quite a bit of Tom these past few weeks."

"Ah," said Meg, somehow managing to inflect a world of sarcasm into that one syllable. "Your relationship ends so you start spending all your spare time with Tom. How unusual."

Lucy shook her head vigorously. "You don't understand, Meg. It's different this time. He's still with Deelylah so we really are just friends. But this week we went shopping for a new suit for Tom. He's taking me to the football game on Saturday and he e-mailed me today to see if I wanted to go out for dinner afterwards."

"Lucy! I hate to tell you this, but even if Tom thinks he's not in a relationship, you are."

"But we're not! Obviously we're not sleeping together. We don't even kiss each other anymore except on the cheek."

"Sounds right. Tom would have to remove the sexual element in order to be able to do all of those other things with you. Otherwise, you really *would* be his girlfriend. I have to say—he is one wildly confused boy but there is a certain logic to his twisted behavior."

"Meaning what?"

"Meaning that in his own warped way Tom is trying to be honest with you. He has to withhold on some level or else he knows that he's not being fair to you."

Lucy thought this through. "So you mean, he's not using me for sex."

"Yes."

"But we're not just good friends either?"

"Not really, no."

"Well, what the hell are we then?" asked Lucy, completely exasperated.

Meg thought for a moment. "Confused."

"Meg, he's given up football and he's doing yoga three times a week. I'm telling you, there's something really wrong with him."

"It sounds to me like there's something really right with him. Lucy, has it occurred to you that Tom might have actually changed? And why on earth are you complaining? It sounds like he's finally behaving how you're wanted him to for a long time now."

"He won't sleep with me!" Lucy burst out.

"So *that's* why you're so upset."

Lucy ignored her and rushed on. "I practically *threw* myself at him last night and he *hugged* me and then kissed me on the *cheek* and told me that he *loves* me and then"—Lucy's voice rose higher in indignation—*"he left!"*

"I seem to remember you always being furious with Tom for wanting to have casual sex with you," said Meg, trying not to let Lucy see how much she was enjoying this turn of events.

"Well yes but—"

"But what?"

"This is unnatural! Tom has *never, ever* rejected me in his life. What if he hates me?"

"He said that he loves you," Meg reminded her.

"Well then, what if he loves me in a Brady Bunch kind of way?"

"Do you mean in a Mrs. Brady and Greg type of way or a Bobby and Cindy in the kennel kind of way?"

"They really were a disturbed family, weren't they?" said Lucy, temporarily sidetracked.

"Extremely. But, as Chloe firmly believes, potentially helpful. Do you remember the episode where Marcia's nose swelled up right before the school dance and the class hunk rejected her and the sweet boy stood by her?"

"Yes. What does that have to do with Tom and me?"

"Nothing. It was just a really good episode. You and Tom are more like the time the Bradys had to get rid of their dog Tiger because Jan was allergic to him."

"But she wasn't really allergic to him in the end," Lucy remembered. "She was just allergic to his flea powder."

"Exactly."

Lucy thought this through. "Are we talking about Tom's after-shave again?"

"No. Although I wish someone would talk to him about it. My point is that there's nothing fundamentally wrong with Tom and you being in a relationship. The two of you are completely compatible—anyone can see that. There's just something else that you haven't quite figured out yet that is stopping you from being together."

"Like what?" asked Lucy, completely frustrated.

"Well, like Deelylah for starters," Meg said bluntly.

Lucy's face darkened at the mention of Deelylah. "He can't possibly be serious about her, can he?"

"I don't see how. She's repulsive. But Tom is very good at separating things. It's quite conceivable that he's in love with you and sleeping with her. It's one of those things boys and overachieving girls seem to be able to do with no problem at all."

"Margaret Li," Lucy intoned, with grim loathing, "you are a *terrible* counsellor. Not only have you not solved my problems for me, I think you've made me more confused."

Meg laughed and whistled to Clooney. "As I said, Luce—you need to figure it out for yourself. And anyway," she added cheekily as she bent down to fasten Clooney's leash, "is it really such a bad thing being the best friend of the new and improved Tom? It seems to me that the problems start when you try to be friends *and* lovers."

Lucy stared unseeingly at the horizon and unconsciously chewed her lip as she thought over what Meg had said. Maybe Meg was right. Maybe they were better off as friends. *Damn him,* she thought, lifting her head defiantly. If he wanted to play games so could she. She was going to be the best friend that Tom had ever had, and it would hurt him far more than it would hurt her not to be lovers as well.

Meg was in the worst possible mood for receiving a visitor that evening. She was tired, emotional, and for months now she had been unable to escape from Blake's cutting comments about her propensity for solitude. She was also far too astute not to have noticed the withdrawal of Percy's affection towards her, and although she would never in her life have admitted to it, her pride, if not her heart, was certainly bruised. Needing someone to take her frustrations out on, she was subjecting a cowering Clooney to a violently vigorous brushing when the doorbell rang.

Thankful to be granted a reprieve, Clooney wriggled out of Meg's grasp and subjected Tom to a rapturous greeting that befitted his savior-like status.

"Why do we never hang out at your place, Meg?" Tom asked, strolling in once Clooney's enthusiasm had slightly subsided and looking around appreciatively at the stylish living room.

"Because you'd mess it up," Meg replied tartly, closing the door behind him.

Tom merely grinned at this acerbic comment and then threw himself down on Meg's big white couch. Sprawling out with Clooney on his chest he looked around. "Hey—those lilies look great. They're Christmas lilies aren't they?"

Meg folded her arms and regarded him suspiciously. With her characteristic directness, compounded by the fact that she was spoiling for a fight, she proceeded to cut straight to the point. "Tom? You're still in love with Lucy aren't you?"

"Why on earth would you say that?"

"You just commented on my *flower arrangement.*"

"So what does that have to do with Lucy?"

"Don't be deliberately dense. Lucy loves flowers more than anyone in the world. *I* think of Lucy when I buy flowers. But my point is, you would never have noticed my flowers unless Lucy was affecting you."

"Meg, it was a simple comment. If I praise your couch it doesn't mean I'm thinking of Chloe."

"What does Chloe have to do with my couch?"

"I didn't mean your couch specifically. She just likes to hide under couches sometimes."

"This is the first time I've heard of Chloe's couch fetish, whereas everyone knows how much Lucy loves flowers," Meg maintained implacably.

"Of course I know that Lucy loves flowers," Tom said, starting to get irritated. "Anyone who spends more than a day with Lucy knows that."

"Oh you did know then? I often wondered. In that case can you explain why you were so unnecessarily cruel to her buying all those cheap, ugly flowers?"

"Lighten up, Meg. It was a joke. Lucy understands me."

"Pity you never bothered to understand her. And if it was a joke it was a nasty one. How would you like it if someone who is supposed to care for you continuously made fun of something that you love? But then again, I'm not exactly sure what it is that you do love."

"You know, Meg, if you're in this sort of mood it would be more polite of you to not answer the doorbell," Tom said, sitting upright and depositing an indignant Clooney on the floor. "I'm leaving."

"Do," Meg said cordially. "You always leave when things get hard, and I'd hate you to break the pattern of a lifetime."

"Yes I know I do. Happily, I don't have your callous streak, which means that you never give anyone a chance. Personally I don't see the point of avoiding relationships altogether just because I have to prove that I can't fail at anything."

Meg's face went white. "That's completely untrue."

Tom laughed scornfully. "Don't play dumb, Meg—it doesn't suit you at all. Why don't you call up Percy right now so that you can walk all over him? It will make you feel much better."

"Why don't you run along to Lucy like you always do and then go and sleep with someone else just to prove to yourself that you're not in love with her?" Meg retorted venomously.

The door slammed behind Tom and Clooney barked anxiously as Meg fought to quell the familiar terror that was rising within her.

She wouldn't fail at anything. She couldn't fail. She just couldn't.

Yoga wasn't helping. Tom tried hard to concentrate on his breathing and the poses, but he was still too worked up after his fight with Meg, which he kept mentally replaying. Giving up, he flopped back onto his mat and stared at the ceiling of his living room.

Why, all of a sudden, did giving Lucy terrible flowers appear churlish and cruel? He had always seen it as a private joke between the two of them, something that demonstrated how close they were because only he could have got away with doing that for so long. There was an uncomfortable awareness looming in his mind and he knew that if he kept thinking he'd have to face it. He wanted to shy away from it, but if nothing else, Tom wasn't a coward, so he forced himself to remember the look on Lucy's face every time he had entered the room carrying a bunch of flowers. She had always been hopeful, he realized with a shock of self-disgust. The look on her face had never been that of a person sharing a joke, her welcoming smile had never held a hint of sarcastic awareness. She had always hoped that this time he was bringing her flowers she would like.

And he never had.

But she *knew* that he loved her, he argued with himself. She didn't need flowers to reassure her. This argument didn't stand up for more than a second. That wasn't the point. He had taken something she loved and turned it into a joke.

Feeling angrier with himself than he could ever remember being, Tom got up and stalked restlessly into the kitchen, where he filled a glass of water and drank it, looking blankly out of the window. All of a sudden he desperately needed to *do* something. What he wanted, more than anything, was to see Lucy. He thought back to what Meg had said about how he always used Lucy to make himself feel better. Well, if that was all that was driving the impulse then he could do that himself.

Walking into the bathroom he undressed and ran a bath. With a wry smile he saw the jar of aromatherapy bath oil that Lucy had given him. He poured some of it in. A warm, floral scent instantly permeated the air, which reminded him uncomfortably of Lucy once again. Grabbing a book and about to unwrap the towel from his waist, he suddenly caught sight of Stipey looking at him from the side of the bath. Tom abruptly stopped and glared back at the dinosaur, who was looking at him mournfully.

"Oh for Pete's sake," he muttered. He tried to ignore the dinosaur but then relented as he lowered himself into the bath. "Okay mate," he sighed, putting Stipey into the bubbles with him. "You can have a swim." He was definitely going insane. He was positive that Stipey looked happier already. Two minutes later he let his book drop to the floor and rested his head back against the side of the bath. Stretching out one hand, he idly picked up the tube containing the face mask. He read the instructions on the back and then, with a shrug, smeared the paste over his face. It felt cool against his skin. The instructions said to let it set for ten minutes, so Tom closed his eyes and started to drift slowly to sleep in the warmth.

His blissful state was rudely interrupted by the sound of his front door opening. Hearing the sound of footsteps, for one joyous moment he thought it was Lucy. As the footsteps came closer to the bathroom door he knew that it must be Deelylah. And he further realized that this knowledge didn't make him in the least bit happy.

Deelylah's voice called through the bathroom door. "Tom? Are you in there?"

"Yeah. Just give me a min—"

It was too late. Deelylah pushed the door open. She stared at him in disbelief. "What on earth are you doing?"

"Giving myself a facial," Tom said defiantly. Recalling the instructions on the tube he added, "It sinks deeper into the pores if you put it on while you're in the bath."

Deelylah stared at him in confusion, and Tom knew that there wasn't the faintest hope that she would laugh or make a joke. Lucy probably would have promptly climbed into the bath with him fully clothed, he thought resentfully. And that's when he realized: Deelylah just wasn't that much fun.

"Giving yourself a facial?" Deelylah repeated, with no attempt to keep the scorn out of her voice.

"Yes," Tom agreed. He saw Deelylah's gaze wandering to his left leg where he could feel something bobbing gently against him. He looked down and saw Stipey, covered in bubbles, gently hitting against his knee, as though asking for attention. "And I'm playing with my dinosaur," he said, giving in to a sudden urge to go too far. He held up the bubble-covered dinosaur. "This is Stipey." He squeezed Stipey gently and Stipey let out a faint, watery growl. "He's a manly sort of bath toy, don't you think?"

Deelylah was staring at him blankly. "What's got into you?"

"What do you mean?" Tom asked, with a reasonable simulation of innocence.

"I mean that you're always doing yoga or hanging out with those girls next door and now you're in the bath giving yourself a facial? I feel like I'm going out with one of my girlfriends."

"I can't help it if I'm a SNAG," Tom said. As Deelylah continued to look contemptuous, he added helpfully, "Sensitive New Age Guy."

"I know what it means!" Deelylah snapped. Her disdainful expression faded and was replaced with a look of determination. "Look, Tom, this is what I wanted to talk about anyway. We're not working. I don't think you're really my type."

Tom tried hard to look disappointed and then realized that he didn't have to fake an expression because she couldn't see through the face mask anyway. "Is it because I'm in the bath with Stipey?" he asked sorrowfully. "I wanted to call him Librette but he's a boy dinosaur," he added earnestly.

"You never take anything seriously, do you?" Deelylah asked, with a distinctly nasty tone in her voice. "For your information, I was on the rebound when I met you and—well, it's not you, it's the other guy I'm seeing." Before Tom could respond she continued relentlessly. "Don't bother calling me—my life coach Hank told me that it would be against my personal mission statement to retract positive decisions concerning my emotional output, so there's really no point in saying anything further."

Determined to have the last word, she turned and left. Tom listened to her footsteps retreating and then the sound of the front door closing.

Feeling much more cheerful, now that his entanglement with Deelylah had been resolved, Tom put Stipey back into the water and pushed him gently to send him on his way. Filling his cupped hands with water, Tom splashed his face, feeling a cooling sense of freedom as the mask that had covered his face came away.

27.

behaving sensibly

That Lucy often failed to pay attention to what he was saying was not news to Tom, so he was unsurprised when (during a detailed explanation as to why Carlton was the noblest team to ever play football) Lucy sat bolt upright and announced with conviction, "Our relationship has always been ridiculous but this latest situation is the silliest yet."

"What's silly about this?" Tom gestured expansively, taking in the sun-filled grounds of the St. Kilda Botanic Gardens and the green swathe of grass that they were lying on, the weekend newspapers spread out around them. "This is nice. This is being friends."

"This is the most intensive friendship I've ever had. I don't spend this much time with Chloe or Meg. And you can't possibly be spending this much time with Deelylah." Lucy gulped and then, in a small but resolute voice, asked, "Don't you want me anymore?"

Tom prevaricated. He had deliberately not told Lucy about his breakup with Deelylah, wanting the idea of her to act as a safeguard against them falling back into their usual habits. "I wouldn't go that far," he now said wryly. "But why do you always have to push things? If we go back to how we've been in the past it will be over again in another month. I don't want that, Luce. I like having you in my life, and I want to be able to see you and call you whenever I need to. You know that I miss you when you're not around, so being friends seems like the best solution."

Lucy stared at him in disbelief, her heart plummeting as she realized that he genuinely meant what he was saying. This wasn't a game that Tom was playing to get her back. He already had her exactly how he wanted her. She stared at the grass as he continued.

"We've tried so many times, Ginger, and it never lasts more than a few months. Either I want out or you get cold feet and go chasing after some guy that you've decided is your perfect man on the basis of a book he mentioned reading three years ago. We're hopeless."

There was a silence as Lucy digested this undeniable truth. Tom watched her, wondering what she was thinking.

"Flea powder," said Lucy absently.

Amongst the many responses Tom might have anticipated, this wasn't one of them. "Excuse me?"

"Flea powder. Like Jan Brady and Tiger. We just have to work out what our flea powder is and then we can make our relationship work," Lucy said earnestly.

"Lucy? Honey? You're psychotic," Tom said, fondly patting her arm.

"No, Tom, it's true. Every major life problem has already been solved on a Brady Bunch episode. You just have to figure out which episode you're in. Meg thinks we're allergic to something that's stopping us being together."

She mused on this for a moment longer and then, in her typically impulsive manner, she pulled Tom up to a sitting position so that he was facing her.

"Why don't we try again?" She stumbled, as the smile disappeared from Tom's face, to be replaced by something that was akin to anger.

"You can't do this, Luce!" Tom said, and Lucy shrank before the harshness in his voice. "You've just broken up with Byron and now you're telling me that you want us to try again?"

"But . . . but," Lucy stammered, "we always do this."

There was a pause, and when Tom spoke again his tone was softer. "I know we do, Ginger, but it has to stop. I can't do this anymore. It's not good for either of us. Look, maybe we need to have a break. I don't think we should see each other for a while."

"But I don't understand," Lucy said wildly, feeling like she was losing control of the situation. "What are you saying? That we're not going to see each other at all? That I can't even call you?"

"I think it's better if we don't. Just for a while."

There was a silence during which Lucy fought back tears. "But I love you," she whispered.

There was a break in Tom's voice when he finally spoke. "I love you too, Ginger. That's why we have to do this."

Lucy burst into tears and flung herself into his arms. He held her tight for a moment, and then, sobbing uncontrollably, she disengaged herself. Gathering up her things she slipped away. Tom watched her go, fighting the impulse to go after her. Unconsciously he pressed his hand to his chest, feeling the warmth from where Lucy had been, just a moment ago, disappearing.

"Meg, it's Chloe. Have you spoken to Luce lately?"

"I spoke to her last night. Why?"

"Was she okay?"

"She sounded fine."

"That's what's worrying me," Chloe said, chewing her lip. "She and Tom haven't spoken for two weeks."

"That's weird—she didn't mention it at all. But, Clo, you know what those two are like—give them another week and they'll be all over each other again."

"No, Meg, it's different this time," Chloe persisted. "They're really not talking to each other. And Lucy's been crying every night in her bedroom. I can hear her but she won't talk to me, and when I try to bring it up she just brushes me off."

"She won't talk about it at all?"

"No. And she's crying in *private*."

"What breakup song has she chosen?"

"I don't think she has one. By this stage she's usually playing Nick Cave's *Murder Ballads* or Ani DiFranco's *Untouchable Face* nonstop. But all I've heard is that Elliott Smith CD that Tom gave her last Christmas."

Meg started to feel uneasy. "Is she eating properly?"

"I think so. She doesn't seem to be starving herself or taking any of her usual drastic measures, although she does look horribly tired all of the time. But the worst part is she's acting so *normal*. Which, for Lucy, is completely abnormal in itself. I'm really worried about her, Meg."

"Have you spoken to Tom?"

"No. I was kind of hoping you'd call him," Chloe said sheepishly.

"What am I supposed to say?"

"Just tell him how worried we are about her and see what he says. Maybe he'll call her."

Meg sighed. "Am I the only person who's frightened about entering the bizarre world of Tom and Lucy?"

"No. It scares the daylights out of me too. That's why I want *you* to call Tom."

And before Meg could retaliate, Chloe hung up.

"Tom? It's Meg."

"Meg?" Tom sounded surprised. As he would be, Meg thought ruefully, seeing as they hadn't spoken since their argument.

She decided to dispense with formalities. "Tom, I'm calling about Lucy."

When Tom answered he sounded wary. "What about her?"

"She's miserable without you," Meg began, inwardly cursing Chloe for dragging her into this. Not only was it none of her business, it already felt hopeless. She could feel Tom's unresponsiveness down the telephone line.

"She's not behaving like herself at all," Meg continued doggedly.

"Give her a week in bed and let her watch *Eternal Sunshine of the Spotless Mind* as many times as she likes. She'll be fine," Tom diagnosed discouragingly.

"But that's what I mean," Meg said, gratefully latching onto this opening. "She's not staying in bed or listening to sad songs or doing any of her usual drama queen misery routine." Too late, Meg realized her fatal mistake.

"Oh I see," Tom said, and Meg cringed at the icy politeness of his tone. "So you mean Lucy's *not* upset about not seeing me?"

"No, of course not, I mean, she is, it's just she—" Meg floundered, uncharacteristically at a loss.

Tom waited, unyielding.

"Look, I'm only calling because Chloe's really worried about her," Meg said, ruthlessly deciding to sacrifice Chloe to the cause.

"So Lucy didn't ask you to call me?" Tom's voice grew even colder.

"No," Meg admitted reluctantly.

"I should have known this was Chloe's idea. Well you can tell Chloe from me that she doesn't need you to do her dirty work for her. But considering that it's Chloe behind this and *not* Lucy who, according to you is perfectly fine, I'm going to hang up now. Bye, Meg."

And for the second time that day, Meg was left holding a receiver, listening to the sound of a disconnected telephone.

When Chloe arrived at Meg's that night, she was fully expecting to be read the riot act for making Meg call Tom in the first place. She was therefore immensely relieved to be met by a relaxed Meg who greeted her with the words, "It's not hopeless, Clo."

"How do you know?" asked Chloe, collapsing onto Meg's luxurious sofa and fending off Clooney's joyous greeting.

Meg smiled at Clooney's affectionate display and then turned her attention back to Chloe. "I suddenly realized. When I spoke to Tom he didn't make a joke of the situation. Don't you see? He's taking his relationship with Lucy *seriously* for the first time."

"Well, what are we going to do about it?"

"What can we do? They're adults and it's their relationship. We tried but we can't interfere anymore."

"They're our friends," Chloe argued. "And they're both miserable when any idiot could see that they're made for each other."

"Well, what do you suggest we do? Kidnap them and put them on a deserted island?" Meg stopped and drew in her breath as she saw the speculative expression on Chloe's face.

"Oh no you don't, Clo," she said grimly, removing Clooney from Chloe's grasp, as though she was contagious.

"What?" asked Chloe, a seraphic expression instantly sweeping across her countenance.

"I know exactly what you're thinking, and I'm not going to let you do it. This is not an episode of *The Brady Bunch*," Meg said firmly.

"Of course it is," said Chloe, dismissing this objection with the scorn that it deserved. "*Every* major life issue has already been resolved on *The Brady Bunch*."

"Oh is that right? I must have missed the episode where Cindy became a heroin-using hooker and sold Jan's glasses to score a hit."

"You shouldn't talk about Cindy that way," Chloe said reprovingly. "Although she *is* the only one who won't take part in televised reunions which seems to me like *someone* is still just a little too big for their boots," she added pensively. "Anyway, that doesn't matter right now. We just have to figure out which episode this is and then we'll know the solution."

"Chloe, if you have any insane ideas about pretending to be ill to bring Lucy and Tom together at your hospital bedside then you can forget them right now. a) I'm not helping you and b) I won't let you do it."

Chloe was looking uncharacteristically obstinate. "Considering that you were the one who set the drag queen onto Byron and encouraged Percy to hire a shepherd, I really don't see how you can stop me. And if you won't help me, Percy will."

"I don't care how good in bed you are, I'm almost positive that even Percy won't agree to anything so stupid."

Chloe looked at Meg in shock.

"Of course I know," Meg said impatiently. "You're amateurs the pair of you. And why everyone felt they had to hide it from me I have absolutely no idea." She stopped and added in a gentler tone, "I think it's great, Clo."

"Right," Chloe managed, her cheeks very flushed. She looked like Percy, Meg thought with amusement. Recovering her composure to some extent, and anxious to change the subject, Chloe persisted, "Well, what are we going to do then? We can't let them go on like this. Lucy is already so sensible and well-adjusted that if it continues much longer she'll be investing in property soon. We have to *do* something."

"I own property," Meg said, affronted.

"Yes, but you're *you*. In Lucy it's unnatural. And Percy told me that Tom attended an information session on working as a volunteer overseas. We're going to lose all our friends. I don't want to be friends with the new Lucy. She's no fun at all."

"At least Tom has changed for the better." Meg thought for a moment and then added pensively, "In a slightly alarming 'victim of alien abduction and lobotomy' kind of way."

"You can't be serious, Meg," Chloe said in disbelief. "He's become so sensitive and caring it's getting to the point where he won't be able to change a light bulb unless it *wants* to change."

"I know," Meg admitted guiltily. "He's so clean-living and into emoting positive energy these days that after spending five minutes with him I keep getting the desperate urge to snort cocaine and shoot up an ashram."

"See? It's not just about them anymore. It's become our problem too. Which is why we're going to do something about it. What if we wrote a letter to Tom pretending that it's from Lucy?"

"Absolutely not, Chloe," said Meg forbiddingly. "Look, let's just leave it for a week and try to get Lucy out of the house. They'll probably get back together by themselves and then we'll feel like idiots for interfering. Promise me you won't do anything?"

"I promise," said Chloe meekly, hoping that Meg wouldn't notice that she was sitting on her hands so that her crossed fingers were hidden from view.

28.

the wish list

Despite the outward show of sensible, well-adjusted behavior that had Chloe and Meg so worried about her, Lucy was miserable. She had also developed a number of stupid habits, which all served to reinforce just how big a role Tom had played in her life. Constantly checking her cell phone, the thud of disappointment when there was neither a text nor voice message from Tom refused to lessen. Driven increasingly frantic by his absence, she turned from her cell phone to her computer, logging on to her e-mail every hour; always holding her breath and willing the computer to deliver a message from Tom that never came.

Sitting in the bath she gave way to tears, sobbing, while the hot water flowed comfortingly from the tap. She felt as though someone had kicked away a support from underneath her, a support that she had come to lean heavily upon. Tom was the one person who understood exactly her motivations and histrionics, who could be relied upon to see right through her, pull her up when she was out of line, and laughingly indulge her. She thought about the endless times that he had cooked dinner for her (refusing all her offers of help from both a sense of self-preservation and the belief that a princess shouldn't soil her hands with mundane tasks), the way that they always held hands in movies (even when they were officially just friends), and, with a twist of her heart that brought on a fresh bout of tears, she recalled the teasing affection in his voice when he called her Ginger.

When she could cry no more and the hot water was in danger of running out, she dried herself off and went to her room. Stretching out on her bed with a pen and a notepad, she started to write.

An hour later the forlorn figure of Lucy appeared in the doorway of the living room. Clad in her pajamas, she padded over to where Chloe and Percy were snuggled up on the couch watching television.

Seeing the tearstains on Lucy's face, Chloe turned the volume down.

"Would you like me to leave?" Percy asked considerately.

Lucy shook her head and held out several sheets of paper towards Chloe.

"What's that?"

Lucy curled up beside them on the couch. Chloe noticed how drawn she was looking but decided to say nothing. It was time Lucy snapped out of this.

"It's the list that you said I should write," Lucy said. "The list of qualities that I value and admire and that I want in a partner."

Chloe accepted the proffered sheaf of paper and started to read aloud. "Kind, funny, intelligent, good in bed—" She stopped and raised one eyebrow at Lucy.

"Don't think for a second you can tell me that doesn't matter in a life partner, Chloe Clairmont," Lucy threatened, as Percy promptly started to panic as he assessed his sexual repertoire.

"Fair enough. Politically aware and small-*l* liberal. Honest, committed, interested in the arts but sporty, loves reading, passionate, romantic—I can't believe how far down that one is on your list—loving, decent dress sense, likes dogs, compatible star-sign—" Chloe paused, turned the page, took a deep breath, and continued, "large vocabulary, adventurous, independent, gives good massages, stimulating conversationalist, faithful—Lucy, this list had better not be in order of priority—creative, has own toolbox and knows how to change washers and what washers are—"

"I really think I should leave you two alone," Percy reiterated feebly, partly out of thoughtfulness but mostly because of a sense of foreboding that as soon as she looked up from the list Chloe would quite justifiably break up with him.

Chloe tucked one arm through his. "Don't be silly, Percy. We need you to provide the male perspective in case Lucy has missed anything."

"In case she's *missed* anything?" Percy asked faintly.

"Yes. Now where was I—oh here we are—gets along with my friends, supportive, didn't read *The Da Vinci Code*, likes to travel, wears glasses, generous, human male—"

"It's a wish list," Lucy said defensively, as Chloe paused again and demanded elucidation. "You know what fairytales are like—the princess wishes for someone handsome, good, and charming and she ends up with the Brad Pitt of the frog world. It pays to be specific."

Placated on this point, Chloe returned her attention to the list. "Educated, expressive, quirky, intellectual, mouthwatering—Lucy, is that a *c* or an *o*?"

Lucy peered at her handwriting. "It's an *o*."

"Thank heavens for that. Mouthwatering cook, emotionally mature and—" She reached the end and sighed. "And loves me very much. Oh Luce."

"I know," Lucy said miserably, fresh tears starting to form in her eyes. "It's Tom. He has everything I want in a partner. Even the toolbox. So why can't we ever make it work? Why does he always leave me to be with someone else?"

Chloe shot a quick glance at her and decided that this was not the time to pull her punches. "I don't know," she said thoughtfully. "And I could never figure out why you take him so much for granted either."

Lucy stopped sniffing and looked at her in surprise. "What are you talking about? I don't take Tom for granted."

Chloe couldn't help laughing. "You can't be serious. Lucy, the reason that your other relationships never last is because you don't really need those other guys. You already have a boyfriend in Tom. He's always the person you call when you need anything—whether it's a date for an event, an emotional crisis, or your car has broken down."

"Of course I call Tom," Lucy said defensively. "He's my friend. I can depend on him."

"But that's my point. Why didn't you feel like you could depend on Taylor? Or Byron? Why is it always Tom that you call?"

"Because—" Lucy stopped. "I don't know. I just know that no matter how much I drive him crazy I know that he loves me and will never let me down."

"And what exactly," Chloe asked gently, "do you think a relationship is?" She fell silent for a moment to let her point sink in and then decided to drive it home. "I know that Tom has his faults, but he's not entirely to blame. You've kept taking him for granted over and over again. And just when Tom was making an effort to be a good friend to you, you had to go and push it again. You two can't go on as you used to."

"I asked him if we could be together and he said no," Lucy said tearfully. "How can he be in love with me and not want to give us another chance?"

"Lucy, you're a basket case! You'd broken up with Byron approximately forty-five seconds before you asked Tom if he wanted to try again. Any self-respecting person would say no. Besides which, I assume he's still sleeping with that horrible Deelylah woman?"

Percy, who was well aware that Tom had stopped seeing Deelylah, had to summon all of his self-control not to betray Tom's confidence as he saw an expression of hurt misery settle on Lucy's expressive face.

Lucy's whole posture slumped even further. Taking a deep breath, she said wretchedly, "Chloe, I'm so grateful to you for giving me somewhere to stay, but I think I need to go and stay somewhere else for a bit.

I just couldn't bear bumping into Tom and that creature right now. And if I hear them in her bedroom through the wall . . ." She shuddered at the thought.

Chloe hugged her sympathetically. "I understand, Luce. But where are you going to go? I don't think you should start apartment-hunting again right now. You're so depressed already and you know it will only make you feel worse."

Percy, who had considerately kept quiet throughout the conversation, now spoke up unexpectedly. "I have an idea. Why don't you move in with me, Lucy?"

Lucy stared at him openmouthed. "But you don't want a roommate."

"I don't really, but I'm spending so much time here lately," he paused and both he and Chloe blushed, "and I have a spare bedroom that you'd be very welcome to. We could always try it for a little while anyway. If nothing else it would give you time to figure something else out."

"Do you mean it, Percy?" asked Lucy gratefully, the lump in her throat easing slightly.

"Of course. You can move in tomorrow if you like."

Forgetful of Percy's dislike of blatant affection, Lucy clambered on top of him and threw her arms around him. "I'm going to kiss your boyfriend, Chloe," she announced, with proper regard for correct etiquette, before proceeding to plant a heartfelt kiss on the side of Percy's face.

Chloe laughed as Percy flushed tomato red. Lucy scrambled off after hugging Chloe for good measure, and then, displaying tact for once in her life, she demurely announced that she was going to her room to write a letter to Tom and to pack, leaving Chloe and Percy alone.

When she was gone, Chloe looked at Percy, who was slowly returning to his normal complexion. "Do you really think you and Lucy will get along okay? She's like that all the time you know."

Percy laughed and drew Chloe closer to him. "Do you know I'm not quite at the stage where I like it, but I can honestly say I'm almost used to her." He paused and then added shyly, "And if all else fails perhaps I'll just have to spend more time over here."

Chloe sighed contentedly. Closing her eyes and nestling in closer, she made a mental note to encourage Lucy's exaggerated behavior on every conceivable occasion.

29.

love letters

Two days later, having settled into Percy's spare bedroom and mailed her letter to Tom, Lucy had managed to push thoughts of Tom, if not to the back of her mind, at least to a more manageable and appropriate space, somewhere slightly behind breathing and motor skills. She was therefore immensely shocked when she logged on to her e-mail at work to see that her in-box contained one new message. From Tom.

She stared at the header for several minutes, unable to open the message; thoughts and scenarios flashing through her mind at lightning speed. Uppermost was the knowledge that he wouldn't have received her letter yet so he couldn't be responding to that. Faintly aware that thoughts of Tom had once again taken precedence over basic functioning, she clicked open the message with a hand that wasn't completely steady and breathing that had become shallow.

I miss you, Ginger. Have dinner with me?

Lucy stared at the screen, sitting firmly on her hands to stop the old Lucy from immediately typing back YES. Doggedly concentrating on the repulsive thought of Tom and Deelylah together, to stop herself giving in to the joy of hearing from him, she drafted a careful response.

I've sent you a letter. I want you to read it before we see each other again.

She then spent a further ten minutes typing and deleting the words "I miss you too." Finally convincing herself not to include it, a further half hour passed deciding how to sign the e-mail. "Love, Lucy," "Love, Ginger," "I love you," and "Your friend" were all agonized over, until a client entered the gallery and she hastily pressed Send with no farewell salutation at all.

When the client finally left, twenty minutes later, Lucy promptly bolted to the computer. She wasn't disappointed.

I think you should let me take you out for a romantic dinner and I'll explain (in iambic pentameter naturally) why you were right that day in the St. Kilda gardens and I was wrong. And then we'll see if it's necessary for me to open this letter of yours.

Lucy giggled and tried to control the surge of lust that rolled over her, triggered by Tom's contextual usage of iambic pentameter. She was about to type back a cheeky response when her fingers stilled on the keyboard and she read the last line again. *Screw him*, she thought, suddenly furious with its typically cocksure tone. *In spite of everything that's happened, he thinks he can have me whenever he wants me. And for all I know, he's still sleeping with Deelylah.*

Remembering her tears over the past few weeks and how she had tried so hard to be honest and loving towards Tom in her letter she suddenly felt as though she hated him. *First he says we can't see each other anymore and then he changes his mind, clicks his fingers, and expects me to come running,* she thought bitterly.

With a tremendous feeling of loss, she realized that as much as she wanted Tom back in her life, she would rather be without him than have him back in his previous role. She didn't want to be his best friend and substitute girlfriend anymore. It was all or nothing.

Lucy sat there thinking about what to write back, and in the end she simply deleted his message and turned off her computer. For the first time in her life, she found she had nothing to say to Tom.

Two hours later, Tom was still glancing at the lower right corner of his computer screen, willing the envelope icon to appear to inform him that he had an e-mail from Lucy. He knew that she was at the gallery because, like a schoolboy, he had called and then immediately hung up when she answered. So if she was there, why the hell hadn't she answered his e-mail? Sending her a flirtatious e-mail had made it seem just like old times for a moment. He tried to concentrate on his work and then checked the lower right-hand corner of the screen again. Still nothing. Exasperated, he glared at the clock. It was three thirty. The mail would be waiting for him at home. He sat there for another two minutes, and then, startling his assistant who had just entered his office, he bounded out of his seat, grabbed his jacket, and left without a word.

Opening his mail box, Tom was startled when a sheaf of letters fell into his hand. Discarding the junk mail, he was left with three letters. He quickly unlocked the door to his apartment, threw his jacket on a chair, and then loosened his tie. Sprawling on the couch, he nervously opened the first letter.

Half an hour later Tom was on his third beer, and the matter was no clearer than it had been before. He looked at the letters spread out on the table again and picked up one, rereading it carefully to see if he had missed anything. He shook his head, trying to clear his thoughts.

Two of the letters were supposedly written by Lucy. The third was from Stipey. He glanced up at the windowsill, to where the dinosaur was resting. He was on the brink of opening his mouth to demand whether Stipey had really written the letter, before he realized that down that particular road lay Lucy-strength imaginary friend psychosis.

The worst part was that both of the letters purporting to be from Lucy could have been written by her—except for the fact that they expressed completely opposing sentiments. In one letter she was deeply sad and missing him and wanted more than anything to see him. In the other she was angry and hurt and never wanted to be with him again. Unhelpfully, both of the letters were typed, which was typical of Lucy, who was a quick typist and impatient with the amount of time it would take to handwrite a letter.

In contrast to the emotion-filled letters from Lucy, the letter from Stipey was brusque and practical. In no uncertain terms the dinosaur told him to get off his pathetic Homo sapiens butt and do something about the situation while there was still a chance to save it. Feeling as though his head was about to explode, Tom picked up the phone and dialed Percy's number.

Percy read through the letters carefully and then put them back on the table and reached for his beer. Tom watched him anxiously for a reaction.

"Well? What do you think?" Tom prompted anxiously. "What do I do? She's sent me two letters saying completely different things. What do you think she means by doing that?"

"I'd be more worried about the letter from the dinosaur quite frankly," Percy said, casting an uneasy glance at Stipey.

"Forget the dinosaur letter and concentrate on Lucy's letters! I don't know whether she loves me or hates me. Or if she wants to see me or to be left alone forever."

Percy gazed thoughtfully at him. "What do you want?"

"I want to see her of course! I miss her like crazy."

"Of course you miss her. She's your best friend. But do you just want her back because you've broken up with Deelylah? Which, by the way, Lucy still doesn't know."

Tom stared at him. "Deelylah? What does she have to do with it?"

"She *was* your girlfriend or whatever the hell she was up until about three weeks ago," Percy reminded him, somewhat taken aback by Tom's callous forgetfulness.

"Yes but—" Tom floundered. "Deelylah didn't mean anything to me. Luce knows that."

"She probably does," Percy agreed. "But you have to admit it would appear to Lucy like business as usual. You're having casual sex with an unsuitable girl but falling back on Lucy to provide the companionship that you're not getting from your relationship with Deelylah. Lucy breaks up with Byron and wants to get back together with you. You say you need a break from each other and proceed to ignore her for two weeks. Then just when she's thoroughly miserable and has decided that she needs to get on with her life without you, you invite her out for dinner when for all she knows you're still sleeping with Deelylah." Percy paused for breath and was pleased to see that Tom was looking appalled when presented with this comprehensive summary of his and Lucy's erratic behavior.

"But it's different this time," Tom began. He ran one hand wearily through his hair. "Look, Percy, I know it seems like I'm doing what I always do, but I'm not. I've been thinking the last few weeks and I want to try again with Lucy. I just don't know how to go about it and I'm scared that if I do the wrong thing I'll blow what might be my last chance. Assuming that I still have a chance left," he added bitterly, looking at the negative letter from Lucy.

"Well, it's not exactly brain surgery, is it?" said Percy.

Tom looked at him in surprise. "What do you mean?"

"We're talking about *Lucy*. She's the world's sappiest girl." Seeing a mutinous look appear on Tom's face at this unflattering description of his beloved, Percy hastened to add firmly, "Sorry, Tom, but she is. All that carrying on over flowers and puppies and the way that she wears pink all the time. The girl's like Barbara Cartland on ecstasy."

Faced with this incontrovertible evidence Tom swallowed hard, then said stoutly, "I *like* that about her."

"Yes, I know you do," Percy said with fascination. "Remind me to ask you why sometime. Would drive me barmy in about an hour if she were my girlfriend. But that's my point anyway. Do something romantic for her."

Tom groaned. "Oh good grief. She's been going out with Byron the Latin lover for the last few months. I'd have to become an astronaut and name a new planetary system after her to top him."

"Fine. Give up then. Find another Deelylah to waste time with," said Percy, with unaccustomed spirit.

Tom lifted his head from his hands and regarded Percy bleakly. "What do you suggest I do? Serenade her? Write poetry? Enter myself in a Patrick Swayze–style dance-off?"

"You'll think of something I'm sure," Percy said kindly but unhelpfully, finishing his beer and getting up from the couch.

"You're going?" Tom asked pathetically.

"'Fraid so. I have to pick up Chloe in half an hour." Percy leaned down and patted Tom awkwardly on the shoulder. "It will all work out." He closed the door behind him, and Tom was left alone, staring at Stipey, racking his brains for inspiration.

30.

the war of the roses

Lucy opened the door to Percy's apartment with a flourish. "Welcome to the Tom Keats Memorial Gardens."

"Oh my God," breathed Chloe in disbelief. "I've never seen so many flowers."

"They've been arriving every day for the past week," said Lucy, ushering Chloe, Meg, and Clooney into Percy's living room. Every conceivable flat surface—tables, bookshelves, and the closed lid of Percy's baby grand piano—was adorned with bouquets. "I had to buy more vases," Lucy couldn't resist adding, as she practically bubbled over with excitement.

"They're beautiful," said Meg frankly, eyeing the arrangements of tulips, cottage flowers, white roses, and wildflowers. "The whole place smells divine."

"I know. Do you want a coffee?" asked Lucy, heading into the kitchen.

"Tea please. We're following you. I want to hear everything. What has he said? We haven't seen him for ages."

"Neither have I. And he hasn't said a word. I've left messages thanking him for the flowers and asking him to call me but he won't return my calls. Has he left any messages on the answering machine at the apartment, Clo?"

"The machine is broken," Chloe said, spooning sugar into Percy's elegant teacups. "I must remember to get it fixed before the owners return, but I haven't been that bothered about it because most people call me on my cell anyway."

"I have no idea what he's playing at," Lucy said happily, patently thrilled by the romantic intrigue of the situation.

"What do the notes with the flowers say?"

"There aren't any. Every time I get home there's just another bunch lying on the doorstep. I have no idea how long he's going to keep this up. And it's increasing. There were gladioli yesterday when I woke up. I went out for a few hours to do the shopping, and when I got home there were poppies waiting for me."

"Luce?" Chloe hesitated.

"What?"

"How do you know they're from Tom? What if they're from Byron?"

Lucy shook her head. "They're not from Byron. I ran into him and his new girlfriend the other day."

"You did? I can't believe you didn't tell us!" exclaimed Chloe.

Lucy smiled oddly. "How funny. I'd forgotten about it till now."

"Could it be someone else then?" persisted Chloe, once she was settled on the couch with her legs tucked up under her. "A secret admirer?"

Lucy shook her head and took a sip of tea. "I can't think of anyone else who would send me flowers every day—sometimes *twice* a day for a week. I did wonder because it's such an un-Tom thing to do. But we haven't had any contact since the flowers started to arrive. It must be him. Otherwise there'd be no reason for him not to return my messages."

"But what's he trying to *say?*" argued Chloe. "You'd think he'd send a note or something."

"I don't think he would at all. That's the only bit that makes sense.

Tom would rather send me flowers every day for the rest of our natural lives than actually tell me how he feels about me."

Chloe shook her head again. "I don't think it's Tom. He'd send you chrysanthemums or something tasteless. You know what he's like."

Meg, who had been sitting silently throughout this conversation, suddenly spoke up. "It's Tom," she said, with quiet conviction.

Lucy and Chloe looked at her and for the first time Lucy noticed how pale and withdrawn Meg appeared. "How do you know?"

Meg smiled wryly. "Do you remember when I had that argument with Tom? I never told you what it was about. Well, Tom came around to my flat and noticed a bunch of flowers that I'd bought. I pointed out that he'd never notice flowers if it wasn't for you, and we had a terrible fight and he left. But you should have seen his face, Luce, when I told him how horrible he was giving you ugly flowers for so long. He looked like I'd hit him."

"I don't understand," Lucy said in confusion. "You had a fight with Tom over my liking flowers?"

"Partly. And he was being horrible about how I never give my relationships a chance."

Lucy sat bolt upright. "Hold it right there. Are you saying that *Tom* gave *you* a lecture on commitment?"

As Chloe and Lucy watched in horror, Meg's face started to crumple and she set her teacup down on the coffee table with shaking hands. Silent tears started to roll down Meg's cheeks and she turned blindly to search for a tissue in her purse.

"Meg, what's wrong?" Chloe asked in an awed whisper. In ten years of friendship she had never seen Meg cry.

"It's me. Tom was right," Meg said tonelessly, as her tears continued to fall. Sensing her distress, Clooney pawed her anxiously and whimpered softly. "I'm the reason that I'm miserable. I'd rather break up with someone before it has a chance to get serious than put time and energy into something and then have it fail. How stupid is that?"

Lucy got up from her chair and came to sit beside Meg on the couch, forcing her to move along so that she was sandwiched between Lucy and Chloe. She put one arm around Meg, who remained stiff and resisting, even as she continued to sob.

"The good thing, Meg, is that you're not a coward," Lucy said cheerfully. "You can be stubborn and pigheaded, but you're very far from stupid and now that you've realized what's making you miserable, you can do something about it."

"Like what?" asked Meg, lifting her tear-stained face.

Lucy thought hard. "You can practice being in a relationship. You know how they tell recovering alcoholics and drug addicts to start off by looking after a plant and then a pet before progressing to a relationship with a partner? Well you could do that. In fact, it's perfect because you already have Clooney to look after. We just have to get you a plant."

"I'm not a recovering addict!" Meg said indignantly.

Chloe hastened into the breach. "Look at it this way, Meg—you're a very successful girl and you're used to controlling every part of your life and succeeding at anything you put your mind to. But relationships are different. You can't control the other person, and that's where the leap of faith comes in."

"I know that I'm a control freak. And I know that in a relationship I can't control the other person—sit, Clooney! I said SIT!" Meg turned her attention back to her friends and sniffed dolefully. "I just can't believe that I have the same emotional issues as Tom. That in itself is enough to make me want to throw myself under a train."

"You're not exactly the same," Lucy said fairly. "You never give anyone a chance. Tom gives everyone a chance. Anyway, don't forget that there are lots of different types of relationships, Megs. It's possible to be with someone without giving up your independence. Somewhere between Percy-style adoration, Byronic fervor, and Tom—well who knows what Tom's style is—there'll be someone who is perfect for you. And you're extra lucky because in the meantime you have Clooney to worship you."

Meg looked at the puppy, who was sitting obediently at her feet, watching her with devoted eyes. "He's okay," she said grudgingly, "for a smelly, uncontrollable pooch."

"Oh thank goodness you're back," Lucy said with a grin. "I was really worried about you for a moment."

Meg gave her a watery smile and then, as though suddenly realizing that both Chloe and Lucy had their arms around her, she tried to shake them away. "Get off me," she said, trying hard to muster an acidic tone to hide how deeply mortified she was at breaking down in front of them.

Lucy looked at Chloe, a hint of mischief dancing in her eyes. "Sorry, Meg, but we can't," she said cheekily, holding Meg even tighter. "I'm stuck. What about you, Clo?"

"I'm definitely stuck," Chloe nodded, pinning Meg's arms to her sides. "You're just going to have to put up with this touchy-feely moment for a bit longer, Meg."

Meg started to struggle and protest, but they held on for all they were worth, until they collapsed in a screaming and laughing pile on the floor, with a joyful Clooney barking exuberantly and leaping on top of them.

From outside, where he was bending down to lay a bouquet of pink lilies on the doorstep, Lucy's suitor paused and listened to the sound of her laugh. Smiling, he straightened up, and when he was safely out of earshot, he started to whistle, imagining the look of delight on Lucy's face when she discovered the flowers.

31.

behaving recklessly

Meg tied Clooney to a pole as she prepared to go into the delicatessen, trying not to laugh as Clooney, realizing that temporary abandonment was imminent, launched into his Orphan Annie routine and became pathetically despondent. Flopping onto his stomach with a gusty sigh, he raised reproachful eyes to Meg's face.

"Oh stop it, you ridiculous creature," she said, trying to muster a stern tone. "I'm going into the deli for ten minutes at the most, and then we'll go for a walk on the beach. Okay?"

Clooney gave her a look of mute, long-suffering love, as though he was in the last stages of a terminal illness and was bidding her farewell.

"Oh for heaven's sake," Meg muttered, completely undone by this canine form of blackmail. "We'll go to the butcher afterwards and I'll get you one of those disgusting bones that you like. Now stay there and be good."

Clooney refused to lift his head but his tail thumped agreeably.

Hastily pushing open the heavy door to the deli, Meg ran straight into a couple who were on their way out. Their purchases went flying, and Meg promptly dropped to her knees to help pick them up as she started to apologize. Lifting her head, the words dried up on her lips as she recognized the couple.

"*Marlon!*" Taken completely aback, she dazedly handed him his errant tub of hummus and then did another double take as she looked properly at his companion. "*Janice?*"

"Oh hi," Marlon said, in his customary flat tone. "You're that bitchy friend of Lucy's, aren't you?"

Meg threw him a filthy look, but then, remembering that Marlon was completely devoid of social mores, she decided to adopt a bright and perky tone, which would undoubtedly irritate him more than a rude retort. "Well, it looks like Hank's relationship guidance worked for you two!" she simpered.

Janice glared at her suspiciously from beneath her curtain of hair. "You didn't remember Janice immediately, did you?" she asked suddenly. "No one ever remembers poor Janice."

Oh good, thought Meg, noting Janice's self-pitying refrain. *So it's Smeagol's turn today. Wonder where Gollum is?* "Of course I remember you, Janice," she said heartily.

Marlon didn't give Janice the opportunity to respond. "How's Lucy?" he asked, as eagerly as his monotone voice would allow. "Make sure you tell her that Janice and I are engaged. I want her to be jealous. Really jealous," he finished in a satisfied tone of voice.

Janice cast him a malevolent look and started to mutter unintelligibly under her breath.

But Meg wasn't paying her any attention. As soon as Marlon had mentioned Lucy, an idea had flashed into her head, and she was already fighting the impulse to meddle that had arisen within her. Since the disastrous outcome of the shepherd episode, Meg had kept her fervent desire to behave recklessly under wraps. But now her demon of restlessness was prompting her again, and she knew that with this golden opportunity in front of her, it wasn't to be placated by a bottle of hair dye.

"Marlon," Meg said, with a sudden bright smile that unnerved Marlon completely, "I was wondering if you could do something for me?"

Ten minutes later an extremely satisfied Meg bade farewell to Janice and Marlon, who were still staring doubtfully at her. "Oh—and Marlon?" Meg paused, balancing the weight of the open door against her hand, and looked at Janice, "If I were you I'd be very careful choosing a wedding ring." With that, Meg exited the deli. Stooping down, she untied Clooney, who sniffed and licked her wrist, puzzled by the change that he could sense in her mood. Meg wished that she could make Clooney understand that she had set in motion a chain of events whose outcome she couldn't control.

And it felt wonderful.

Finally there was a note.

Lucy unlocked the front door to Percy's apartment and then bent down. With both arms she carefully lifted the potted orchid that sat on the threshold, managing to push open the door with her back. Depositing the orchid in the center of the living room she paused for a moment to soak in the beauty of the pink flowers that were offset by an elegant celadon pot. Unable to resist any longer, she caught up the envelope that was tied to one slender stalk by a silk ribbon. Tearing it open, she sat on the edge of Percy's piano stool to read it.

Have dinner with me tomorrow night? Seven o'clock at Circa.

Hearing the front door open, Lucy looked up, tears of happiness coursing down her cheeks as she clutched the note to her heart.

Percy took one profoundly horrified look at her smiling and

tear-stained countenance and promptly tried to back through the door. But it was too late. Squealing with joy, half sobbing and half laughing, Lucy flung herself across the room at him. For the next ten minutes Percy was hugged, kissed, and almost deafened, in an exceedingly appalling display, for which, try as he might, he could not think of *any* situation in which it might conceivably be deemed appropriate behavior.

32.
towel appeal

As Chloe approached Percy's front door the following evening she saw that it was wide open. "Percy, it's me," she called cheerfully, dropping her bag on the couch. She went in search of him and found him sitting on Lucy's neatly made bed, holding a letter.

"She's gone," Percy said bleakly.

Chloe looked at him in confusion and took the letter that he was holding out to her. She read it through hastily and then collapsed onto the bed next to Percy.

"I don't understand." Chloe's voice was strained with anxiety. "What happened to upset her so badly?"

"God knows." Percy ran a hand through his hair with frustration. "She was absolutely fine yesterday. Over the moon about all her flowers and seeing Tom tonight."

"Have you called her cell?"

"That's the first thing that I did. It's switched off."

Chloe grabbed Percy's wrist and looked at his watch. "It's half past seven," she groaned. "She was meant to be meeting Tom at seven. What the hell has gotten into her? I spoke to her this morning, and she couldn't have been more excited about seeing him."

"Maybe that's where she is?" Percy suggested hopefully.

Chloe scanned Lucy's letter again. "I doubt it, considering she says one of the reasons she's left is because she can't bear looking at all of the flowers anymore. But maybe you should call him to check."

Percy went into the living room to call Tom, and Chloe followed him, still frowning over the letter and trying to make sense of it. A minute later he put down the phone. "She's not with Tom. He sounds furious. Worse than furious, actually."

"Did you ask him what he did to upset her or where she might have gone?"

"I didn't get the chance. He hung up on me."

Seeing that Chloe was looking seriously distressed, Percy put a comforting arm around her. "Chloe, don't get too upset. You know what Lucy is like—she's probably just overreacting as usual. She'll be fine once she's had time to calm down."

"Yes, but until she calms down she's completely volatile! Lucy always lets her heart rule her head and she was overexcited as it was by this dinner tonight. Whatever it is that's upset her has obviously sent her right off. And I know Lucy is a drama queen, but that's exactly why I'm so worried. God only knows where she's gone or what she intends to do."

They were sitting there in anxious silence, trying to work out the best course of action, when Meg walked in. "Hello there—did you know you left the front door unlocked?" she said breezily, adding, "Where's Lucy? She took Clooney for an early walk but she was short of time because she was going out tonight, so I said I'd collect Clooney from here to save her dropping him back." Getting no response, she peered closer at their glum faces. "Goodness, you two don't look very cheery," Meg commented lightly.

"Have you heard from Lucy?" Chloe asked, without preamble.

"Lucy? Not since this morning when we spoke about Clooney," said Meg, suddenly looking wary.

"She's gone," Percy disclosed worriedly. "Something happened to upset her, and the only thing she left behind was this note which doesn't really tell us anything." He held out Lucy's missive to Meg.

Meg read it quickly and then gulped. "She had to know, Clo."

Chloe looked at Meg in confusion. "She had to know what?"

"I ran into Marlon the other day and made him promise to tell Lucy that the flowers were from him, not Tom. He must have called her this afternoon."

The color drained from Chloe's face. "You did *what?* But Meg, all those flowers couldn't possibly be from Marlon!"

"Well they are, and it wasn't fair to Lucy. She has the right to know that they're not from Tom."

"You idiot, Meg!" Percy said furiously. "The bloody flowers aren't from Marlon! Tom told me what he was going to do over a week ago, and he's been sitting in a restaurant waiting for Lucy to show up for the past half hour!" He broke off in confusion as he saw a grin break out on Meg's face.

"What's going on? Why are you looking like that?" asked Chloe, completely thrown by the expression on Meg's face.

"Well, I didn't really think Marlon sent the flowers, Clo," Meg said apologetically. "But I didn't think it would hurt Lucy if she thought that."

"I don't understand," Percy said, with a look of complete bewilderment on his face. "You lied to Lucy *knowing* that Marlon didn't send her the flowers?"

"Pretty much," Meg said cheerfully.

"But *why?*" chorused Chloe and Percy.

"Because my hair is brown. And because I've never set fire to a clock or had someone mistake me for a dog. It just felt like the right thing to do." Meg paused, and chuckled at the shared expression of confusion on Chloe and Percy's faces. "Look, it doesn't really matter why I did it. Just stop and think for a minute. How do you think Lucy is feeling right now?"

"Like crap," Chloe said bluntly. "She was thrilled that Tom was finally doing something romantic for her."

"That, Clo, is *exactly* the reason why I asked Marlon to lie to Lucy. See the problem is, I have absolutely no doubt that Lucy would fall in love with *anyone* who sent her flowers every day for a week."

There was a silence while she watched this sink in.

"She has a point," Percy conceded uncomfortably.

Seeing that Chloe was still looking unconvinced, Meg put on her most persuasive tone. "Don't you see, Clo? As much as Tom needed to develop his romantic side, Lucy needed a heavy dose of reality. What I want to know is if she still loves him, regardless of grand romantic gestures."

"That's a pretty big risk you're taking with Lucy and Tom's relationship, isn't it?" Chloe asked.

Seeing that Chloe was genuinely shocked by her meddling, Meg spoke again in a much softer and more hesitant tone. "Those two are meant to be with each other, Clo—any idiot can tell that. I know it was terrible to lie to Lucy, but I really think she needed a shock to start thinking about what's truly important."

"Meg's right," said Percy unexpectedly. "And apart from anything else, Tom can't keep up this sort of behavior for the rest of his life. It's about time that Lucy realized that having someone love you constantly and unconditionally is the most dramatically exciting thing that can ever happen to a person."

Chloe gazed at him through misty eyes. "Percy, that was beautiful," she sighed. "Can you remember to tell Lucy that?"

"Not exactly sure what I said," Percy said regretfully.

Meg interrupted hastily before Percy and Chloe could start exchanging loving looks.

"You know, I was telling the truth when I said that I hadn't seen Lucy for days. I really don't know where she's gone."

"What *exactly* did you say to her?" asked Chloe, snapping back to Lucy's predicament.

"*I* didn't say anything. But I asked Marlon to call her and tell her that the flowers were from him."

"How did you get him to agree to do it?" Chloe asked suddenly.

"Never you mind," said Meg, looking extremely guilty.

Chloe and Percy cast suspicious looks at her but she refused to meet their gaze.

"Why on earth didn't you tell me what you were up to?" Chloe said, trying not to sound as aggrieved as she felt at being left out of Meg's plan. Considering that it was Meg who had forbidden *her* from interfering with Tom and Lucy's relationship, she couldn't help but feel that her petulance was justified.

"Because you would have taken one look at Lucy when she was upset and admitted everything. You're too soft-hearted."

Chloe had to admit the fairness of this. "Okay, well let's just try to think where Lucy might have gone. I know she's a drama queen, but she's been so miserable lately and acting so out of character that I can't help worrying."

"She has Clooney with her," Percy broke in sensibly, seeing that Chloe was working herself up again. "So she's hardly done anything drastic." The girls shot him a grateful look, and they all started to think hard once more.

Meg gave a wan smile. "The only place I can think of is Tom's. That's who she always runs to when she's in trouble."

"Well, she's obviously not at Tom's," Chloe said. "Come on, Meg, *think*. Where would Lucy go if she was really upset?"

"I don't know! It's Lucy for God's sake. She could be wandering along the cliffs doing her French Lieutenant's Woman impression. She could have signed up as a volunteer worker to Somalia. She could have—"

Chloe's eyes widened in hope. "She could have gone home," she finished.

Lucy turned her key in the lock and let herself into the empty apartment.

"Clo?" she called out uncertainly. There was no answer, so she carried her small case into her former bedroom. Trying very hard not to burst into tears again, she let Clooney off his leash, and he promptly scampered off to sniff with interest in promising corners. Lucy filled a bowl of water for him, left it on the kitchen floor, and decided to run a bath. She needed to think.

"What are you doing?" Meg took her eyes off the road to survey Chloe anxiously. She had never seen Chloe in such a decisive mood before.

"Calling Tom," Chloe said, furiously punching the keypad of her cell phone.

"Clo, I don't know if that's a great idea," Meg began. "Why don't we just wait and see if Lucy's there before we drag Tom into this? He doesn't even know that Lucy's run off. We don't want to upset him for no reason."

"Yes we do," Chloe said, with a mulish expression on her face. "In fact, I want him worried out of his mind about her. Serve him right."

"Now hold on," Percy protested, feeling that he ought to stick up for Tom. "He's been sending her flowers every day for over a week now."

"Well, yes," Chloe conceded. "But that doesn't make up for being celibate to Lucy." Then as she heard Tom's voice, "Tom? It's Clo. Can you meet us at the flat I'm house-sitting as soon as possible? It's urgent. Lucy has had a bad shock and run off, and we think that's where she's gone."

Tom's voice came sharply through the phone. "Stay out of this, Chloe."

"I can't stay out of it, and neither can Meg because it's partly our fault," confessed Chloe heroically.

"Chloe, as I recall, the last time that you and Meg called me about Lucy you were worried because she was acting normally. Now that she's acting melodramatically again you should feel reassured."

"Tom please, you have to listen to me," Chloe begged. "I know you think you've been stood up by Lucy, but you haven't. Lucy thinks the flowers were from Marlon, not you."

There was a pause while Tom digested this information. "Why would Marlon send Lucy all those flowers?"

"Well, exactly," Chloe said, pleased that he had grasped the flaw in this scenario so quickly. "He wouldn't. He's very fond of Lucy of course, but quite frankly I don't think a chicken sexer could afford to send her flowers every day."

"Chloe, will you please stop babbling and explain to me what is going on?" commanded Tom, dangerously close to losing his temper again.

"Meg asked Marlon to tell Lucy that the flowers were from him."

"Why on earth would Meg do something like that?"

"Because her hair's brown. Oh look, Tom, it's too complicated to explain over the phone. Can you just please, please meet us there? *Please?*" Chloe held her breath and crossed her fingers tightly.

There was a long pause and then Tom let out a sigh. "If this ends in disaster I'm going to hire that shepherd to drown you in sheep dip, Clo," he threatened, as Chloe let out a yelp of delight. "Now stop squealing and put Meg on."

"I can't. She's driving."

"Well, hold the phone up to her ear then," he said uncompromisingly.

"He wants a word with you," Chloe said apologetically to Meg. She whispered, "I don't think it's going to be a nice word."

Meg gestured for her to hold the phone up, and as soon as he heard Meg's voice Tom could be heard blasting her at full volume for interfering in his and Lucy's affairs. Chloe and Percy both winced, and Chloe considerately removed the phone half a foot away from Meg's ear. Meg listened to Tom's tirade with apparent unconcern. When he had vented the majority of his spleen she said mildly, "Okay then. We're almost there. We'll see you in twenty."

Lying with her eyes closed and her head resting against the rim of the bathtub, Lucy was startled out of her comfortable state of warm drowsiness by a tremendous commotion at the door that was only equalled in volume by Clooney's vociferous barking. She felt a momentary dart of panic, as what sounded like rampaging hordes crashed through the front door, but as she recognized Chloe and Meg's voices, anxiously calling her name, her panic swiftly transmuted into the mere disinclination to entertain visitors while lying naked in the bath.

Hastily wrapping a towel around her, she emerged from the bathroom, bubbles of bath foam still clinging to her skin. Her frantic search party promptly skidded to a stop in the hallway, their fretful cries fading away as relief flooded their faces, although Percy's relief was tempered with acute embarrassment at Lucy's state of undress.

"Lucy!" Chloe flung her arms around her soapy friend and hugged her exuberantly. "You're okay?"

"I think so," Lucy said cautiously, not quite sure what was going on. She added politely, "How are you?"

Chloe looked at her in confusion. "I'm fine. But we've been worried out of our minds about you."

"Really?" asked Lucy, perking up slightly at being the focus of a drama and leading the way into the living room. "Why?"

Her three friends stared at her in amazement. Meg, who had managed to quiet Clooney, found her voice first. "Didn't Marlon call you and tell you the flowers were from him?"

A shadow crossed Lucy's face. "Yes he did," she said quietly.

"And you were devastated, so you ran away," Percy prompted, when it appeared that Lucy wasn't going to say anything further.

Lucy looked at him curiously. "Ran away? I didn't run away. Didn't you get the note that I left?"

Completely bewildered by Lucy's composure, when, based on all precedents, she ought to have been weeping hysterically or determined to commit suttee, Percy thrust her letter at her. Clutching the top of her towel together with one hand, Lucy read over the letter quickly and then looked up, her brow creased. "I still don't understand. What is there in this to make you all come charging after me screaming your heads off?"

Chloe stared at her, completely flabbergasted. "*Lucy!* You wrote that you needed to be alone, to think somewhere where no one could disturb you . . ." Her voice trailed off as she properly took in Lucy's towelled attire for the first time.

"I wanted a bath," Lucy explained patiently. "You know that I always think better in the bath, and Percy doesn't have one." She surveyed her friends sternly. "What's got into you all?"

For the first time since they had set off on their rescue mission, Percy, Chloe, and Meg started to feel slightly silly.

"How were we to know you wanted a bath?" Chloe asked defensively. "You get a phone call from Marlon, stand Tom up, leave behind cryptic notes . . ." She trailed off, as she realized that none of this sounded very convincing. "Of course we were worried. You know what a drama queen you are, Luce," she added accusingly.

"It seems to me that you're all being the melodramatic ones," Lucy countered, adopting her best schoolma'am tone and clearly enjoying the novelty of being the sensible one for a change. "Meg's the only one who really has a proper excuse for being here," she said fairly. "I forgot that you were picking up Clooney," she added apologetically.

It was a measure of how far Meg had fallen from Percy's pedestal of idolatry that he now, rather unchivalrously, had no hesitation in comprehensively dropping her in it. "Wait just a minute—this was all Meg's bloody fault in the first place!"

"Thanks, Percy," Meg drawled sarcastically. She sighed and decided to get Lucy's wrath out of the way before Tom arrived and gave her another serving. "I ran into Marlon the other day, and I asked him to call you and tell you that the flowers were from him."

Lucy sank limply into a chair, her towel perilously close to coming unwrapped. "I don't understand. *You* asked Marlon to call me?"

"Yep."

Thoughts chased each other across Lucy's face. She looked up at Meg with an inscrutable expression. "So you mean Marlon didn't really send me all those flowers?"

"Of course not," Meg said impatiently. "Tom did."

Lucy shrieked. Jumping up, she flung her arms around Meg, and Percy hurriedly averted his eyes as her towel once again made a dive towards the floor. For a moment Chloe feared that Lucy was trying to strangle Meg, but then she realized that Lucy was squealing with joy.

"Even if I change my citizenship," Percy said with heartfelt sincerity, staring grimly at the ceiling, "I will *never* understand that girl. We try to help her and she calls us drama queens. Meg gets people to lie to her and she can't stop hugging her. Strong medication and therapy, that's what she needs."

"It's okay, Percy, you can look now," Chloe said reassuringly. "She's fastened her towel again."

Lucy, whose first ecstatic throes had subsided, was unable to stop tears of happiness brimming in her eyes. "So you mean the flowers really are from Tom?" she asked for the third time.

"Yes," groaned Meg. Hearing a noise at the front door, she added laconically, "That'll be him now."

Lucy shrieked again, her love-smitten euphoria evaporating, as she belatedly recalled that she had recently stood up her beloved, who was now most probably in search of vengeance. Before she could escape to the safety of her room however, the front door opened and four people trooped into the living room, none of whom were Tom.

The middle-aged man leading the procession was carrying two large suitcases and wearing a rather harassed expression. He was looking down at his feet, which was why he didn't notice the assembled crew in front of him, until his wife, who was bringing up the rear with their two young sons, nudged him so hard that startled, he dropped the suitcases.

"Jeffrey!" his wife hissed loudly, nodding her head towards Lucy, Percy, Chloe, and Meg, just in case he still hadn't glimpsed the four strangers standing directly in front of him.

"Oh," he said in surprise, unable to take his eyes off Lucy's semi-naked figure. "Why hello."

This clearly wasn't the response that his wife had anticipated as she promptly subjected him to another, much harder nudge with her extremely pointy elbow.

Enlightenment came first to Chloe. "Oh my goodness," she beamed sunnily, trying to reassure the two young boys who were hiding shyly behind their mother. "This must be your apartment that I've been looking after."

Chloe's friendly overture made no impression on Mrs. Jeffrey, who was looking completely outraged by this cheerful statement of the obvious and had clearly been expecting either shamefaced excuses or evidence of burglar-like intentions from the four friends.

Before Chloe could commence introductions however, Clooney came trotting happily into the room, thrilled that new people had arrived, upon whom he could bestow his infinite love. Meg saw the horrible sight first and tried vainly to intercept him. "Drop it, Clooney! Drop it!"

But she was too late. Seating himself squarely in the center of the room Clooney cocked his head to one side and looked at them enquiringly, his tail wagging as the remnants of Bertie's tail hung limply from his mouth.

"So *that's* what happened to Bertie," said Chloe, her pleasure at having the mystery solved outweighing its gruesome conclusion.

"I don't know what you mean by saying 'So that's what happened to Bertie' like that," Meg said irritably, getting onto her knees and rolling up her sleeves in preparation for wrestling Clooney's disgusting treasure away from him. "Clooney's only chewing on his skeleton. He hardly helped him escape from his bowl."

"Who's Bertie?" asked Mrs. Jeffrey, looking bewildered.

Chloe looked at her in amazement. "Your fish." In an audible aside to Percy, she whispered indignantly, "Honestly, they've only been gone six months and they've already forgotten him. No wonder Bertie was depressed."

Jeffrey strode over to Chloe and pulled her aside. "Do you mean to tell me that's Donald? Why the hell couldn't you just buy a new fish?" he hissed, nervously eyeing his children for signs of trauma, and obviously a firm advocate of the "Deceive and Placate with New Toys" approach to child-rearing.

"I couldn't remember what he looked like," Chloe said sheepishly.

"What do you mean, you couldn't remember what he looked like?" Meg asked. "He is, I mean was, a *goldfish*. It's not like he had a distinguishing mole on his left buttock. Clooney, if you don't open your mouth in the next ten seconds Mommy is going to smack you very hard."

Lucy opened her mouth to protest at Meg calling herself Clooney's mother but then subsided as she saw Clooney obediently open his jaws. Realizing sorrowfully that Clooney responded more to Meg than he did to her, she couldn't help being secretly rather glad that she wasn't responsible for the disgusting mess that he spat into Meg's capable hands.

Seeing the grim look on Mr. Jeffrey's face Chloe explained hastily, "We couldn't remember what color he was. I knew he was a goldfish, but did you know that you can have red goldfish and even black goldfish? Fish are quite complex creatures you know. They must be or else they wouldn't even think to commit suicide," she added philosophically.

"Are you trying to tell me that Donald committed suicide?" asked Jeffrey, looking outraged at the suggestion that any pet of his could have been emotionally maladjusted.

"Of course not," said Percy, sensing that things were not going well and trying to help Chloe. "He was the most well-adjusted fish that I've ever met. Not that I've met that many. Except for the ones I've eaten with chips and tartar sauce but I don't think they count," he finished reflectively.

The smaller of the two boys promptly burst into tears and, pointing at Percy, started to scream. "He's a bad man! He ate Donald! DADDY, THAT BAD MAN ATE DONALD!"

Looking extremely harassed, Percy strategically retreated behind a couch as though this would offer some protection from the accusations of a hysterical child. It didn't do him much good, however, for Chloe turned to him with a look of tremendous disappointment on her face and said, "How *could* you, Percy? How could you talk about eating Bertie? Did you learn nothing from Hammie's death?"

"I didn't eat the fish! The damn dog ate the fish," Percy protested indignantly, pointing at Clooney, who wagged his tail and barked cheerfully.

"I think I need to lie down, Jeffrey," said Mrs. Jeffrey faintly.

At this inauspicious moment Tom erupted into the room, his fearsome appearance and expression of righteous anger somewhat diminished by the plastic dinosaur that he held in one hand. "Where is she?" he asked, paying no attention whatsoever to Jeffrey and his family, whose demoralization caused by the scant regard paid to their homecoming became complete when Tom's vitriolic entrance promptly commanded the attention of the whole room.

Lucy shrank back against the wall, trying to make herself as small as possible, but Tom's gaze, although it lingered on her for a moment with a curious expression in his eyes, swept on. Spotting his quarry, he pounced.

"Hello, Tom," Meg said resignedly, reentering the living room and wiping her clean hands on her skirt, having disposed of Bertie's remains into the kitchen trashcan.

"Margaret," Tom said icily. "What the fu—" Catching sight of the two young Jeffreys he caught himself and changed it to "Heck, did you think you were doing? Why did you get Marlon to call Lucy?"

Meg waved a hand impatiently at him. "That can wait, Tom. Lucy's over there." She couldn't resist adding irritably, "That's the problem with you two. You're forever getting sidetracked from the main issue by things that don't matter."

A strangled noise from Lucy's corner made them swing towards her.

"Luce? What's the matter?" asked Tom, genuinely concerned by the strange look on her face.

"Flea powder," Lucy said faintly.

"What?" asked Tom disconcerted.

"That's our flea powder!" Lucy's voice grew stronger. "We always get distracted by things—or people—that don't really matter at all."

There was a slight cough, and they turned impatiently towards Jeffrey. "Look, this is all very interesting, but we still don't know who the hell you all are."

"DIDN'T YOU HEAR WHAT I JUST SAID?" Lucy bellowed, casting a furious look at him. "WHAT ARE YOU TRYING TO DO—JINX US? WHY WOULD YOU WANT ME TO DIE ALONE? WHY? WHY?"

Completely intimidated by Lucy's seminaked wrath, Jeffrey temporarily subsided, and Lucy, belatedly realizing that she was the heroine of an unfolding romantic moment, hastily abandoned her screaming harpy persona and tried to look considerably more like a demure damsel about to be wooed.

For the first time in weeks, Tom looked Lucy straight in the eyes. "You know the flowers were from me, don't you, Ginger?" he asked softly.

Overcome by an unfamiliar emotion that Lucy decided must be shyness, she nodded.

"Do you know why the last thing I sent you was an orchid in a pot?"

Lucy shook her head, and then bowed it, unable to withstand the intensity of his gaze any longer.

Partly from a desire to be closer to Lucy and partly from an uncomfortable awareness that a roomful of people was listening in, Tom moved even closer towards her and lowered his voice. "It's a good omen. I wanted to give you something that you could keep for longer than a week. So that maybe we could try again and make it last this time."

Lucy's head sank even lower, and a small sob broke forth.

Tom put his hands on her shoulders. "Lucy, you're a drama queen and you're high maintenance and I can't for the life of me think why I want to spend the rest of my life rescuing you from chicken sexers, killer mosquitoes, scary curtains, and the consequences of setting a clock on fire, but I do."

"No you do-on't," sobbed Lucy, completely undone by this speech and refusing to look up. "You'll be sick of me again in two weeks and wa-ant to be with someone else."

Tom grinned ruefully and put a hand under her chin, forcing her to look him in the eyes. "Lucy, you've got me to the stage where I even brought Stipey along to try to convince you that we're meant to be together."

Lucy raised her head slightly and a small, watery smile crossed her face as she caught sight of the dinosaur that Tom was proffering hopefully.

"I promise I'll take up trout fishing and start ballet classes if that's what it takes to have you," Tom said quietly.

Lucy finally met his gaze, and after a long moment a sob burst from her as she flung herself into Tom's arms.

The others gazed with immense satisfaction at this scene, with only Percy unable to suppress a disbelieving murmur of "She's crying *again*." Taking a leaf from Mrs. Jeffrey's book of partner-management skills, Chloe elbowed him sharply in the ribs and Percy promptly subsided.

"Now look here," said Mrs. Jeffrey, clearly deciding that someone had to take the situation in hand. "Who are you people? I want an explanation right this second."

"Oh sorry," Chloe immediately apologized. "I'm Chloe. I'm your house sitter. And this"—she flushed slightly and pulled Percy towards her—"this is my boyfriend Percy."

Percy blushed fiery red and put a protective arm around Chloe.

"And those two?" asked Mrs. Jeffrey, obviously far from placated and indicating Lucy and Tom who were still passionately kissing.

"That's Lucy and Tom." As Lucy and Tom's liplock threatened to become X-rated, Chloe added defensively, "They're best friends."

"Yes, they look rather fond of each other. Jeffrey dear, perhaps you could detach Lucy and Tom before they reproduce in our living room in front of our children."

Jeffrey looked helplessly at Tom and Lucy as he tried to find an opening through which he could separate them that wouldn't involve touching Lucy's bare flesh, which would undoubtedly earn him another bruised rib. To his immense relief however, this last speech had penetrated through to Lucy.

"Sorry," Lucy said coyly, grabbing Tom's hand. "We'll just go to my room." She pulled Tom in the direction of her bedroom.

"No you damn well will not," said Mrs. Jeffrey, incensed. "That's my son's room."

"Did you stay in my room?" asked the older Jeffrey eagerly. "You don't have to move out you know. Ow!" He rubbed his ear as his mother promptly cuffed him.

"And that's Meg and Clooney," Chloe continued hastily, wanting to forestall any further displays of ire on Mrs. Jeffrey's behalf. Meg waved cheerfully. "Clooney has been staying with Meg," Chloe added prudently. "He's just visiting. So that's everyone."

"No it's not. I still need to know who that is," said Mrs. Jeffrey implacably, gesturing to a figure in the doorway who was eyeing Tom and Lucy with outrage.

Chloe looked up and went white. *"Lucy!"* she hissed.

Lucy lifted her head, and gazing dreamily around, she promptly went into shock as she recognized the figure in the doorway. *"Taylor!"* she gasped in horror.

"I've been trying to contact you for months now, Lucy. I guess this is why you never returned any of my messages," Taylor said icily.

"But Taylor—" Lucy groped for words, "I haven't spoken to you since we broke up!"

"Oh, so we have broken up then? I know that we only went out for a few weeks but it would have been nice if you could have told me," Taylor said sarcastically.

"But I *did* tell you. You never returned my message so I assumed that you were angry with me and didn't want to speak to me again," Lucy said, her brain still trying to process the fact that Taylor was standing in front of her while she was wrapped in both a towel and Tom's arms.

"I had to leave urgently to attend a dig in a remote part of Libya. I left my cell phone at home, and I didn't have access to a telephone or e-mail so I sent you a letter."

Lucy groaned. "I moved, and the letter mustn't have been forwarded. And I changed my cell number after we went camping."

"Sorry to interrupt, but what kind of situation would be urgent in archaeology?" Percy enquired with interest. Everyone turned to glare at him. "It's a legitimate question," he muttered defensively. "I mean, the stuff has been lying there for millions of years and all of a sudden it's urgent? Where's a dinosaur bone going to go?"

Ignoring Percy, Taylor continued his cross-examination. "I know you moved. I tracked down your new home number last week. I must have left ten messages, Lucy."

"But I never got any of your messages," Lucy defended herself vehemently.

At this, Chloe coughed delicately. "Luce? The answering machine is broken, remember?"

"Well that would explain why you obviously had no idea that

we were arriving home today," Mrs. Jeffrey said testily. "But exactly
what kind of house sitter are you, Chloe? Our answering machine is
broken, our pet fish is dead, and our apartment is filled with lunatics
and harlots."

As Chloe collapsed into incoherent guilt-laden excuses, Taylor
continued with the grim implacability of the rejected lover who had
clearly spent an inordinate amount of time rehearsing and perfecting a
speech that balanced wrathful content with a self-righteous tone. "I
finally get back this week, turn on my mobile phone, and hear a message from you from months ago telling me that you're very sorry but
you've been with someone else and can't see me anymore."

Lucy looked at him with genuine remorse. "Oh Taylor, I'm sorry.
You're lovely and I didn't mean to break up with you over the phone,
but I did and then I didn't hear from you so I just assumed you were furious with me and then I started seeing someone else and . . ."

"So this is the guy you've been seeing?" Taylor's tone of voice indicated that he didn't think highly of Lucy's taste.

"I'm not her boyfriend," Tom said, offering his hand. "But I will be
soon. As soon as she's broken up properly with you of course," he added
considerately.

Taylor ignored Tom's outstretched hand. "I don't get it, Lucy. If he's
not your new boyfriend, who's the guy that you left the message about?"

"He is my new boyfriend but he's not the one that I've been seeing
while you were away. But he is the guy that I was with that meant I
needed to break up with you. Oh dear." Lucy pulled her towel tighter
around her for protection and wondered miserably if she would be han-
dling this with more aplomb if she were properly dressed.

"You've been seeing someone else? And kissing him too?" Taylor
looked at Lucy, and she flushed with shame at the condemnation in his
expression.

"It sounds much worse than it is," she said feebly. She sneaked a
look at Tom and was relieved to see that he was completely unsurprised
by her latest fiasco and even appeared to be enjoying it. "Taylor, I

thought we had broken up," Lucy said helplessly. "I never heard from you, so I started seeing a guy called Byron."

Completely incensed, Taylor swung around on Percy. "Are you Byron?"

"Good grief, no. Do I look Italian?" Percy said, visibly offended. "I'm very fond of Lucy, but as I have previously stated you're all welcome to her. No, Lucy and I have just been living together for the past few weeks."

Bridling indignantly, Mrs. Jeffrey snatched up her sons' hands. "Come along, darlings."

"Where are we going, Mommy?" asked the elder Jeffrey.

"To your room. We're going to strip your bed and burn your sheets."

Before she could exit in high dudgeon, Taylor spoke up passionately. "Look, Lucy, I have no idea what's going on. Can you please get dressed and then can we go somewhere and talk about this?"

"Of course," Lucy said, her warm heart hating to cause distress to anyone. "But Taylor—we can't be, that is, Tom and I—"

Seeing her distress, Tom came to her rescue. "Sorry, Taylor, but you can't have her. I won Lucy fair and square in a duel," Tom said cheerfully.

As much as she wanted Tom and Lucy to be together, Chloe, who took her duties as duel referee seriously, couldn't let this pass. "But Byron gave Lucy the puppy," she protested. "How could you beat the puppy?"

"There's been quite a few occasions when I would have liked to beat the puppy but I didn't," said Tom, casting a malevolent look at Clooney, who thumped his tail innocently.

"Tom sent me flowers every day for a week," Lucy interjected, anxious not to be awarded to Byron.

"You never bring me flowers anymore, Jeffrey," Mrs. Jeffrey said, looking quite moved by this tale.

Both Jeffrey and Taylor glowered at Tom, who shot them a smug look.

"Sometimes twice a day," Lucy amended. Jeffrey wearily crossed his arms protectively over his ribcage in a preemptive defensive maneuver.

"The flowers were beautiful," Chloe conceded, "but, Lucy, you love having a dog of your own."

Lucy looked ruefully over to where Clooney was sitting contentedly on Meg's lap. "I do," she said wistfully, "but Clooney belongs to Meg more than to me really."

Meg's head shot up and she looked at Lucy for a long moment.

Lucy, who had been looking rather sad, suddenly grinned. "Oh go on and keep him. You've been taking care of him for ages now, and he listens to you more than me anyway. But I'm godmother, okay?"

Meg smiled and nodded, her gratitude evident in her eyes. Aware that she was horribly close to giving way to a cheerful emotion in public, she promptly started to scold Clooney instead. He listened to her happily and, ignoring her strictures, licked her face in a truly unhygienic manner.

"But the flowers weren't my thing," Tom protested, wanting to settle the question of the duel once and for all.

"What do you mean? You did send the flowers, didn't you?" Lucy panicked.

"Yes, but they were only an extra. Don't you see, Ginger? I fell in love with you. That was my thing."

Eyeing the visibly melting expression on Lucy's face with barely concealed horror, Percy frantically interjected in a tone of powerful revulsion, "For the love of God, man, and in the name of all that's sacred, hold off on the soppy stuff until you get home. You'll set her off again if you're not careful."

Recalled to the present by Percy's distressed plea, Lucy pulled both herself and her towel together and gently disengaged herself from Tom. Making her way over to Taylor she grasped the towel firmly with one hand and placed the other on Taylor's arm. "Taylor, I'm sorry," she said softly, genuine remorse in her eyes as she lifted them to his face.

He held her gaze for a moment. "Don't worry about it, Lucy," he said brusquely. He nodded towards Tom and lowered his voice. "I hope it works out for you."

Lucy was about to fling herself into his arms to express her gratitude for this noble speech when, for perhaps the first time in her life, she stopped and considered whether that type of impulsive response would be appropriate. Deciding that it probably wasn't, she settled for stretching up on tiptoe and kissing him chastely on the cheek. "Thank you, Taylor," she said warmly. "I just know that the girl of your dreams is waiting around the corner."

He gave her a slight grin. "Unless you happen to know any girls who read science fiction and practice martial arts I think I might be waiting for my dream girl for a long time."

Lucy's mouth fell open and she knew from Clooney's sudden indignant yelp at being squeezed too tightly that Meg had caught this last comment too. Before either of them could say anything however, Taylor gave a quick nod to everyone and then left the room.

Clearly giving up on the idea of controlling the circus in her home, Mrs. Jeffrey had collapsed into an armchair and was fanning herself with a magazine, while her husband was still quite obviously trying not to look at Lucy and was making sheepish, throat-clearing noises that were intended to convey some element of authority. It was left to their youngest son to break the brief silence that had fallen.

"Is your dog vicious?" asked the smaller Jeffrey, who had summoned up the courage to advance slightly closer to Clooney.

"Very," Meg said cheerfully. "He's quite likely to lick you to death. I'm sorry about your fish, by the way."

"I'd rather have a dog," said the child, who was evidently a rapid learner and appeared to have leapfrogged to step five, "Acceptance," of the traditional grieving process. "Fish are stupid. All they do is go in circles. Daddy, could we have a dog?"

"I'd rather have a girl like that," said his older brother, ogling Lucy's towel-clad form in a manner that was eerily reminiscent of his father.

Tom surfaced from his latest clinch with Lucy in time to hear this. "Down, boy," he said heartily in a fatherly tone, but couldn't resist

adding, "But good to see the youngster has taste." Mr. Jeffrey concurred
until he caught the gimlet eye of his wife and collapsed once again into
incoherence.

With a great show of fatigue, Mrs. Jeffrey hoisted her slim frame out
of the armchair. "I think, Jeffrey," she began tremulously, "that it would
be best if we retire to our room. Perhaps," and here she paused and
swept a debilitating glance around at the assembled company, "you will
be so good as to have left by the time we have finished unpacking."
Another pause and another glare. "Chloe, you may return tomorrow to
collect your things, at which time we will discuss this situation further."
With this masterly combination of order, reprimand, and threat, Mrs.
Jeffrey swept from the room, flinging a peremptory "Come, Jeffrey.
Boys!" behind her.

With his head hanging even lower and with one last yearning and
surreptitious glance at Lucy, Mr. Jeffrey followed his spouse, trying to
ignore his eldest son, who trailed him out of the room, firing a barrage
of eager questions. "Daddy, why did that man say he'd do trout fishing
and ballet for the girl? Is that what girls like? Can I learn ballet?"

The youngest Jeffrey stopped to pat Clooney tentatively, and then,
completely overcome at finding himself alone with a roomful of
strangers, he darted out of the room followed by a volley of barks from
Clooney, who was sad to see his new acquaintance leave.

Left alone, they all looked at each other in silence for a moment.

"Would you call this a happy ending?" asked Meg wryly.

"Yes," Lucy said instantly, smiling up at Tom, who tightened his
arms around her.

"No," said Chloe glumly. She saw Percy's face fall and gave him
a swift hug. "I'm not talking about you, you idiot. But can you imagine
what those people are going to say to my parents? I'm going to have to
put up with having them 'Disappointed in me' until next Christmas."

"Look on the bright side, Clo," Tom said helpfully. "Imagine if
they'd come home when the shepherd was here."

Chloe shuddered and Percy flushed bright red. Anxious to change the subject, he asked, "Meg, how *did* you get Marlon to agree to tell Lucy that he sent her the flowers?"

Meg suddenly became intensely interested in Clooney's identification tag.

"Meg?" Lucy said, in a tone filled with foreboding. "What did you do?"

"Nothing," Meg said defensively. "That is, I agreed that you'd be bridesmaid at Marlon and Janice's wedding, but personally I think that's a small price to pay for Marlon's help in showing you the love of your life."

"I'm going to *what?*" shrieked Lucy. "Meg, there is no freakin' way I'm walking down any aisle that is remotely connected with Marlon. He'll probably rig it so that *we* end up getting married."

"I don't think he will, Luce. He and Janice are very well suited." She paused and added reflectively, "I'm sure that the three of them will be very happy together."

Lucy groaned. "I just know that Janice will make me wear a puce-colored taffeta dress with a great big bow on my butt and a matching hairband," Lucy said despairingly. "There are some sacrifices that I'm not prepared to make even for Tom."

Tom looked hurt. "I think being bridesmaid at Marlon and Janice's wedding is an extremely small price to pay for realizing that I'm The One," he said haughtily.

"I'm very glad you feel that way, Tom," Meg said briskly. "Because you're best man."

While Lucy promptly burst into gleeful chuckles, Tom looked at Meg with apocalyptic vengeance in his eyes. "That's it. I've had about enough of this urge of yours to break out and be irresponsible. You're a danger to others."

Meg smiled sweetly. "I don't know, Tom," she drawled. "I'm kind of having fun. And everything has worked out for the best, hasn't it?"

"Well, unless you happen to be Bertie I suppose it has," he agreed reluctantly. "Okay, time to go. Come on, Ginger, let's get your things from Randy Junior's room. Although," he stopped and surveyed her lustfully, "perhaps you shouldn't get changed just yet."

Lucy tried, not very successfully, to sound demure. "Tom, I can't wander around in a towel."

"No, you probably can't," Tom assented regretfully. "Shame though. You kind of look like that woman off the Victoria's Secret commercial and I've always had a thing for her."

"I knew you couldn't be that unnaturally sweet to me for the rest of your life," Lucy said bitterly, nevertheless allowing Tom to guide her out of the room.

Meg, Chloe, and Percy watched them leave, and then looked sheepishly at each other as they realized they were all wearing satisfied smiles.

"Do you really think they'll last this time?" asked Meg thoughtfully.

"They'd better bloody last," Percy said, with unexpected spirit. "I'm not going through all of that again. The letter writing, racing after Lucy—it's exhausting." He stopped as Chloe looked at him with wild surmise.

"The *letter writing?*" she asked in a curious tone of voice. "What exactly did you mean by that, Percy?"

Percy flushed bright red and immediately started to stammer. "Nothing. That is—nothing."

"You wrote one of those letters to Tom that was supposed to be from Lucy, didn't you?" Chloe said, her conviction growing stronger. "I remember the card that you wrote to Meg. You write beautifully."

Percy gazed bashfully at his shoelaces. "I just wanted to help. Somehow it didn't seem that odd a thing to do after Meg's shepherd, Byron's puppy, and you signing us all up for that camping trip. Are you mad at me?"

"Not really. I still think it's the height of cheek for Meg to forbid me from interfering and then run around recruiting Marlon, but it's rather sweet that you tried to play Cupid, Percy."

Percy looked at her in horror. "Chloe? Please, please, please don't *ever* repeat that comment in front of anyone. Especially Tom's football buddies." Visions of having beer poured over him in scorn and being publicly dacked took strong possession of his mind.

"Does it bother you that Tom has received a love letter from your boyfriend before you have, Clo?" asked Meg mischievously.

"Not really," Chloe said cheerfully, as she linked arms with Percy and prepared to depart. "As Percy said, it's the sort of thing that seems to make perfect sense after you spend too much time with Lucy and Tom. What I *would* like to know is if we'll ever find out how Bertie got out of his bowl."

"If that's the only mystery that remains, I think we've done pretty well," Percy said comfortingly, leading her towards the door.

Left alone in the living room, Meg whistled for Clooney and dropped to her knees to fasten his leash. He promptly scampered towards her, Tom's plastic dinosaur held proudly in his mouth. With minor difficulty Meg wrested Stipey away from Clooney. Holding the dinosaur up to eye level she looked at him sternly and whispered, "If you *ever* say *anything* to *anyone* about who really wrote that letter from you, I'll put you in the freezer to experience your very own Ice Age. Got it?" Stipey stared back at her seriously, and, satisfied, Meg turned her attention to the puppy.

"Hypothetically speaking, Clooney," she said casually, "if we were going to the bookstore to buy a present for Taylor do you think we should buy A Room of One's Own or Enduring Love?"

Clooney cocked his head to one side as he considered her question, and then gave a short, sharp bark.

Meg took a deep breath. "*Enduring Love* it is then. And while we're at it we may as well buy a potted plant." She stood up and headed for the door.

Clooney sat back on his haunches and whined anxiously, wondering what had happened to the normal tone and mood of his beloved mistress.

"Just don't blame me if it dies," Meg said over her shoulder.

And reassured, Clooney trotted happily after her.

six months later . . .

Lucy looked up from her section of the newspaper and across the breakfast table at Tom. There had been silence for the past forty minutes, broken only by an occasional absentminded comment on an item of news or a request to pass the orange juice. Lucy sighed contentedly and then smiled to herself.

It was really rather romantic.

about the author

Melanie La'Brooy studied at Melbourne University, majoring in Art History and Classics, which finally came in handy with the release of *Troy*. She has a pathological crush on Hugh Jackman and her hobbies include reading and systematically killing potted plants. She believes that there are ten different ways to misspell and mispronounce her surname but would be interested to hear any further suggestions. When Melanie grows up she wants to join Charlie's Angels.